Christopher Isherwood was born in 1904 in Cheshire. He left Cambridge without graduating, tried briefly to study medicine and in 1928 published his first novel, *All the Conspirators*. In 1929 he lived in Berlin for four years, then travelled round Europe writing about his experiences in novels such as *Mr Norris Changes Trains* (1935) and *Goodbye to Berlin* (1939).

With W. H. Auden, Christopher Isherwood wrote three plays and a travel book. During part of the war he worked with the American Friends Service Committee and in 1946 became a naturalized American. He has worked in films, reviewed books and lectured at the University of California. He is a member of the Wider Quaker Fellowship and the American Civil Liberties Union.

Among his other most well-known books are: *Lions and Shadows* (1938), *Kathleen and Frank* (1971) and *Christopher and his Kind* (1977). Christopher Isherwood now lives permanently in California.

CHRISTOPHER ISHERWOOD

Down There On a Visit

METHUEN LONDON LTD

To Don Bachardy

Author's Note

Thirty years ago, John Lehmann was chiefly responsible for the publishing of my second novel, *The Memorial*. This was the beginning of a literary association and a friendship which has lasted to this day. So I am particularly happy that it was John Lehmann who was the first to publish a part of this book of mine, the episode called *Mr Lancaster*, in the October 1959 issue of *The London Magazine*.

A Methuen Paperback

DOWN THERE ON A VISIT
ISBN 0 417 02720 6

First published 1962
by Methuen & Co. Ltd
Magnum edition published 1979

Copyright © 1962 by Christopher Isherwood

This edition published 1982
by Methuen London Ltd
11 New Fetter Lane, London EC4P 4EE

Made and printed in Great Britain
by Hazell Watson & Viney Ltd
Aylesbury, Bucks

Mr. Lancaster

Now, at last, I'm ready to write about Mr. Lancaster. For years I have been meaning to, but only rather halfheartedly; I never felt I could quite do him justice. Now I see what my mistake was; I always used to think of him as an isolated character. Taken alone, he is less than himself. To present him entirely, I realize I must show how our meeting was the start of a new chapter in my life, indeed a whole series of chapters. And I must go on to describe some of the characters in those chapters. They are all, with one exception, strangers to Mr. Lancaster. (If he could have known what was to become of Waldemar, he would have cast him forth from the office in horror.) If he could ever have met Ambrose, or Geoffrey, or Maria, or Paul—but no, my imagination fails! And yet, through me, all these people are involved with each other, however much they might have hated to think so. And so they are all going to have to share the insult of each other's presence in this book.

In the spring of 1928, when I was twenty-three years old, Mr. Lancaster came to London on a business trip and wrote my mother a note suggesting he should call on us. We had neither of us ever met him. All I knew about him was that he managed the office of a British shipping company in a North German harbor city. And that he was the stepson of my maternal grandmother's brother-in-law; there is perhaps a simpler way of saying this. Even my mother, who delighted in kinship, had to admit that he wasn't, strictly speaking, related to us. But she decided it would be nice if we called him "Cousin Alexander," just to make him feel more at home.

I agreed, although I didn't care a damn what we called him or how he felt about it. As far as I was concerned, everyone over forty belonged, with a mere handful of honorable exceptions, to an alien tribe, hostile by definition but in practice ridiculous rather than formidable. The majority of them I saw as utter grotesques, sententious and gaga, to be regarded with indifference. It was only people of my own age who seemed to me better than half-alive. I was accustomed to say that when we started getting old—a situation which I could theoretically foresee but never quite believe in—I just hoped we would die quickly and without pain.

Mr. Lancaster proved to be every bit as grotesque as I had expected. Nevertheless, hard as I tried, I couldn't be indifferent to him; for, from the moment he arrived, he managed to enrage and humiliate me. (It's obvious to me now that this was quite unintentional; he must have been desperately shy.) He treated me as though I were still a schoolboy, with a jocular, patronizing air. His worst offense was to address me as "Christophilos"—giving the name an affected classical pronunciation which made it sound even more mockingly insulting.

"I'm willing to wager, most excellent Christophilos, that you've never seen the inside of a tramp steamer. No? Then let me counsel you, for the salvation of your immortal soul, let go of your Lady Mother's apron strings for once, and come over to visit us on one of the company's boats. Show us you can rough it. Let's see you eat bacon fat in the middle of a nor'easter, and have to run for the rail while the old salts laugh. It might just possibly make a man of you."

"I'll be delighted to come," I said, just as nonchalantly as I knew how.

I said it because, at that moment, I loathed Mr. Lancaster and therefore couldn't possibly refuse his challenge. I said it because, at that time, I would have gone anywhere with anyone; I was wild with longing for the whole unvisited world. I said it also because I suspected Mr. Lancaster of bluffing.

I was wrong. About three weeks later, a letter came for me from the London office of his company. It informed me, as a matter already settled, that I should be sailing on such and such a day, on board the company's freighter *Coriolanus*. An employee would be sent to guide me to the ship, if I would meet him at noon outside the dock gates in the West India Dock Road.

Just for a moment, I was disconcerted. But then my fantasy took the situation over. I started to play the lead in an epic drama, adapted freely from Conrad, Kipling, and Browning's "What's become of Waring?" When a girl phoned and asked me if I could come to a cocktail party a week from Wednesday, I replied tersely, with a hint of grimness, "Afraid not. Shan't be here."

"Oh, really? Where *will* you be?"

"Don't know exactly. Somewhere in the middle of the North Sea. On a tramp steamer."

The girl gasped.

Mr. Lancaster and his shipping company didn't fit into my epic. It was humiliating to have to admit that I was only going as far as the north coast of Germany. When speaking to people who didn't know me well, I contrived to suggest that this would be merely the first port of call on an immense and mysterious voyage.

And now before I slip back into the convention of calling this young man "I," let me consider him as a separate being, a stranger almost, setting out on this adventure in a taxi to the docks. For, of course, he *is* almost a stranger to me. I have revised his opinions, changed his accent and his mannerisms, unlearned or exaggerated his prejudices and his habits. We still share the same skeleton, but its outer covering has altered so much that I doubt if he would recognize me on the street. We have in common the label of our name, and a continuity of consciousness; there has been no break in the sequence of daily statements that I am I. But *what* I am has refashioned itself throughout the days and years, until now almost all that remains constant is the mere awareness of being conscious. And that awareness belongs to everybody; it isn't a particular person.

The Christopher who sat in that taxi is, practically speaking, dead; he only remains reflected in the fading memories of us who knew him. I can't revitalize him now. I can only reconstruct him from his remembered acts and words and from the writings he has left us. He embarrasses me often, and so I'm tempted to sneer at him; but I will try not to. I'll try not to apologize for him, either. After all, I owe him some respect. In a sense he is my father, and in another sense my son.

How alone he seems! Not lonely, for he has many friends and he can be lively with them and make them laugh. He is even a sort of leader amongst them. They are apt to look to him to know what they shall think next, what they are to admire and what hate. They regard him as enterprising and aggressive. And yet, in the midst of their company, he is isolated by his self-mistrust, anxiety and dread of the future. His life has been lived, so far, within narrow limits and he is quite naïve about most kinds of experience; he fears it and yet he is wildly eager for it. To reassure himself, he converts it into epic myth as fast as it happens. He is forever play-acting.

Even more than the future, he dreads the past—its prestige, its traditions and their implied challenge and reproach. Perhaps his strongest negative motivation is ancestor-hatred. He has vowed to disappoint, disgrace and disown his ancestors. If I were sneering at him, I should suggest that this is because he fears he will never be able to live up to them; but that would be less than half true. His fury is sincere. He is genuinely a rebel. He knows instinctively that it is only through rebellion that he will ever learn and grow.

He is taking with him on this journey a secret which is like a talisman; it will give him strength as long as he keeps it to himself. Yesterday, his first novel was published—and, of all the people he is about to meet, not one of them knows this! Certainly, the captain and the crew of the *Coriolanus* don't know it; probably no one in the whole of Germany knows. As for Mr. Lancaster, he has already proved himself utterly unworthy of being told; he doesn't know and he never will. Unless, of course, the novel has such a success that he eventually reads about it in a newspaper. . . . But this thought is censored with superstitious haste. No—no—it is bound to fail. All literary critics are corrupt and in the pay of the enemy. . . . And why, anyhow, put your trust in treacherous hopes of this kind, when the world of the epic myth offers unfailing comfort and safety?

That spring, totally disregarded by the crass and conceited littérateurs of the time, an event took place which, as we can all agree, looking backward on this, its tenth anniversary,

8

marked the beginning of the modern novel as we know it:
All the Conspirators *was published. Next day, it was found
that Isherwood was no longer in London. He had vanished
without a trace or a word. His closest friends were bewildered and dismayed. There were even fears of his suicide.
But then—months later—strange rumors were whispered
around the salons—of how, on that same morning, a muffled
figure had been glimpsed, boarding a tramp steamer from a
dock on the Isle of Dogs—*

No, I will never sneer at him. I will never apologize for
him. I am proud to be his father and his son. I think about
him and I marvel, but I must beware of romanticizing him.
I must remember that much of what looks like courage is
nothing but brute ignorance. I keep forgetting that he is as
blind to his own future as the dullest of the animals. As
blind as I am to mine. His is an extraordinary future in
many ways—far happier, luckier, more interesting than most.
And yet, if I were he and could see it ahead of me, I'm sure
I should exclaim in dismay that it was more than I could
possibly cope with.

As it is, he can barely foresee the next five minutes. Everything that is about to happen is strange to him and therefore
unpredictable. Now, as the taxi ride comes to an end, I shut
down my own foresight and try to look out through his eyes.

The company's employee, a clerk scarcely older than I,
named Hicks, met me at the dock gates as arranged. He was
not a character I would have chosen for my epic, being
spotty-skinned and wan from the sooty glooms and fogs of
Fenchurch Street. Also, he was in a fussy hurry, which epic
characters never are. "Whew," he exclaimed, glancing at his
watch, "we'd better look smart!" He seized hold of the handle of my suitcase and broke into a trot. Since I wouldn't let
go and leave him to carry it alone, I had to trot, too. My entrance upon Act One of the drama was lacking in style.

"There she is," said Hicks. "That's her."

The *Coriolanus* was even smaller and dirtier looking than
I had expected. The parts of her that weren't black were
of a yellowish brown; the same color, I thought—though this
may have been merely association of ideas—as vomit. Two
cranes were still dangling crates over her deck, which was
swarming with dock hands. They were shouting at the top

of their voices, to make themselves heard above the rattle of winches and the squawking of the sea gulls that circled overhead.

"But we needn't have hurried!" I said reproachfully to Hicks. He answered indifferently that Captain Dobson liked passengers to be on board in plenty of time. He had lost interest in me already. With a mumbled goodbye, he left me at the gangplank, like a parcel he had delivered and for which he felt no further responsibility.

I elbowed my way aboard, nearly getting myself pushed into the open hold. Captain Dobson saw me from the bridge and came down to greet me. He was a small, fattish man with a weather-scarlet face and the pouched, bulging eyes of a comedian.

"You're going to be sick, you know," he said. "We've had some good men here, but they all failed." I tried to look suitably anxious.

Below decks, I found a Chinese cook, a Welsh cabin boy and a steward who looked like a jockey. He had been on the Cunard Line for twelve years, he told me, but liked this better. "You're on your own here." He showed me my cabin. It was tiny as a cupboard and quite airless; the porthole wouldn't unscrew. I went into the saloon, but its long table was occupied by half a dozen clerks, scribbling frantically at cargo lists. I climbed back up on deck again and found a place in the bows where, by making myself very small, I stayed out of everybody's way.

An hour later, we sailed. It took a long time getting out of the dock into the river, for we had to pass through lock gates. Lively slum children hung on them, watching us. One of the cargo clerks came and stood beside me at the rail.

"You'll have it choppy," he said. "She's a regular dancing master." And, without another word, he vaulted athletically over the rail onto the already receding wharf, waved briefly to me, and was gone.

Then we had high tea in the saloon. I made the acquaintance of the mate and the two engineers. We ate soused mackerel and drank the tea out of mugs; it was brassily strong. I went back on deck, to find that a quiet, cloudy evening had set in. We were leaving the city behind us. The docks and the warehouses gave way to cold gray fields and marshes. We passed several lightships. The last of them was called Barrow Deep. Captain Dobson passed me and said, "This is the first

10

stage of our daring voyage." In his own way, he was trying to create an epic atmosphere. All right—I awarded him marks for effort.

Back to my cabin, for it was now too dark to see anything. The steward looked in. He had come to propose that I should pay him a pound for my food during the voyage, and eat as much as I liked. I could see he thought this was a stiff bargain, because he was sure I'd be seasick. "There was another gentleman with us a couple of months ago," he told me with relish. "He was taken very bad. You'll knock on the wall if you want anything in the night, won't you, sir?"

I smiled to myself after he had left. For I had a second secret, which I intended to guard as closely as my other. These seafolk were really quite endearingly simple, I thought. They appeared to be absolutely ignorant of the advances of medical science. Naturally, I had taken my precautions. In my pocket was a small cardboard box with capsules in it, wrapped in silver paper. The capsules contained either pink powders or gray powders. You had to take one of each; once before sailing, and thereafter twice a day.

When I woke next morning, the ship was rolling powerfully. Between rolls, she thrust her bows steeply into the air, staggered slightly, fell forward with a crash that shook everything in the cabin. I had just finished swallowing my capsules when the door opened and the steward looked in. I knew from the disappointment in his face what it was he'd been hoping to see.

"I thought you wasn't feeling well, sir," he said reproachfully. "I looked in half an hour ago, and you lay there and didn't say a word."

"I was asleep," I said. "I slept like a log." And I gave this vulture a beaming smile.

At breakfast, the second engineer had his arm in a sling. A pipe had burst in the engines during the night, and he had scalded his hand. Teddy, the Welsh cabin boy, cut up his bacon for him. Teddy was clumsy in doing this, and the second engineer told him sharply to hurry. For this the second engineer was reproved by the first engineer: "You won't half be a bloody old bugger when you're older—my God you will!"

Despite the second engineer's semiheroic injury, I was beginning to lose my sense of the epic quality of this voyage. I had expected to find that the crew of this ship belonged to

11

a race of beings apart—men who lived only for the sea. But, as a matter of fact, none of them quite corresponded to my idea of a seaman. The mate was too handsome, rather like an actor. The engineers might just as well have been working in a factory; they were simply engineers. The steward was like any other kind of professional servant. Captain Dobson wouldn't have looked out of place as the owner of a pub. I had to face the prosaic truth: all kinds of people go to sea.

Actually, their thoughts seemed entirely ashore. They talked about films they had seen. They discussed a recent scandalous divorce case: "She's what you might call a respectable whore." They entertained me by asking riddles: "What is it that a girl of fourteen hasn't got, a girl of sixteen is expecting, and Princess Mary never will get?" Answer: "An insurance card." I told the story about the clergyman, the drunk and the waifs and strays. When I got to the payoff line: "If you wore your trousers the same way round as your collar . . ." I faltered, not sure that it would be good taste to mimic a Cockney accent, since both engineers had one. However, the story went over quite well. They were all very friendly. But the answer to that constantly repeated young man's question, "What do they really think of me?" seemed to be, as usual, "They don't." They weren't even sufficiently interested in me to be surprised when I took a second helping of bacon, although the ship was going up and down like a seesaw.

All day long we lurched and slithered through the rugged sea. On deck the sea glitter was so brilliant that I felt half stupefied by it. Now that everything was battened down and squared away, the ship seemed to have grown to twice its original size. I walked the empty deck like a prize turkey. Now and then Captain Dobson, who stood benevolently on the bridge smoking a brier pipe and wearing an old felt hat, pointed out passing ships to me. Whenever he did this I felt bound to hurry to the rail and scrutinize them with professional intentness. Later he embarrassed me by bringing me a deck chair and setting it up with his own hands. "Now you'll be as happy as the boy who killed his father," he said. And he added: "I'd like your opinion of this," as he gave me a paperbound book with a sexy picture on the cover. It was called *The Bride of the Brute* and contained a lot of scenes like: "He cupped her ripe breasts in his burning hands, then savagely crushed them together till she cried out in pain and desire." If I had been in London among my friends, we should all have felt bound to make sophisticated fun of this book. It was the sort of book you were supposed to dismiss as ridiculous. But here I could admit to myself that, absurd as it was, it excited me hotly. Captain Dobson took it as a compliment that I read right through the book in an hour. Meanwhile, Teddy served me mugs of tea with large jam puffs.

In the middle of the night I woke, just as if somebody had roused me. Kneeling on my bunk, I peered out through the porthole. And there were the first lights of Germany shining across the black water, blue and green and red.

Next morning we steamed up the river. Captain Dobson drank with the German pilot in the chartroom and became very cheerful. He had exchanged his old felt hat for a smart white cap, which made him look more than ever like a comic music-hall sea dog. We passed barges which were as snug as homes, with gay curtained windows and pots of flowers. Captain Dobson showed me various places of interest along the shore. Pointing to one factory building, he said, "They've got hundreds of girls in there, cleaning the wool. It's so hot, they strip to the waist." He winked. I leered politely.

In the harbor, the *Coriolanus* became tiny again, as she made her way humbly to her berth amidst all the great ships. Captain Dobson shouted greetings to them as we passed, and was greeted in return. He appeared to be universally popular.

When we tied up, our deck was so far below the level of the dock that the gangplank had to be nearly vertical. A police officer, who had come to inspect my passport, hesitated to descend it. Captain Dobson mocked him: "Go 'vay, Tirpitz! Go 'vay!" He had called the pilot "Tirpitz," too, and all the captains of the ships he had hailed. The police officer climbed down cautiously backward, laughing but holding on very tight.

After the stamping of my passport, there were no other formalities. I shook hands with the steward (who was sulking a little; a bad loser), tipped Teddy and waved good-by to Captain Dobson. "Give my love to the girls!" he shouted from the bridge. The police officer obligingly came with me to the dock gates and put me on a tram which stopped outside Mr. Lancaster's office.

It was an impressive place, even larger than I'd expected,

13

on the ground floor, with revolving glass doors. Half a dozen girls and about twice that many men were at work there. A youth of sixteen ushered me into Mr. Lancaster's private room.

I had remembered Mr. Lancaster as tall, but I had forgotten how very, very tall he was. How tall and how thin. Obeying the strong subconscious physical reaction which is part of every meeting, I defensively became a fraction of a millimeter shorter, broader, more compact, as I shook his bony hand.

"Well, Cousin Alexander, here I am!"

"Christopher," he said, in his deep, languid voice. It was a statement, not an exclamation. I expanded it to mean: Here you are, and it doesn't astonish me in the least.

His head was so small that it seemed feminine. He had very large ears, a broad, wet mustache, and a peevish mouth. He looked sulky, frigid, dyspeptic. His nose was long and red, with a suggestion of moisture at the end of it. And he wore a high, hard collar and awkward black boots. No—I could find no beauty in him. All my earlier impressions were confirmed. I reminded myself with approval of one of my friend Hugh Weston's dicta: "All ugly people are wicked."

"I shall be ready in exactly—" Mr. Lancaster looked at his watch and seemed to make some rapid but complicated calculation—"eighteen minutes." He walked back to his desk.

I sat down on a hard chair in the corner and felt an indignant gloom fill me from my toes to my head. I was violently disappointed. Why? What had I expected? A warm welcome, questions about the voyage, admiration for my freedom from seasickness? Well—yes. I *had* expected that. And I had been a fool, I told myself. I should have known better. Now, here I was, trapped for a week with this frigid old ass.

Mr. Lancaster had begun to write something. Without looking up, he took a newspaper from the desk and tossed it over to me. It was a London *Times*, three days old.

"Thank you—*sir*," I said, as spitefully as I dared. It was my declaration of war. Mr. Lancaster didn't react in any way.

Then he began to telephone. He telephoned in English, French, German and Spanish. All these languages he spoke in exactly the same tone and with the same inflections. Every now and then he boomed, and I realized that he was listening to his own voice and liking the way it sounded. It was noticeably ecclesiastical and it also had something of the government minister in it; nothing of the businessman. Several times he became commanding. Once he was almost gracious. He couldn't keep his hands still for a moment, and the least problem made him irritable and excited.

He wasn't ready for more than half an hour.

Then, without warning, he rose, said, "That's all," and walked out, leaving me to follow. All of the adult employees had left the outer office, presumably to get their lunch. The youth was on duty. Mr. Lancaster said something to him in German, from which I learned only that his name was Waldemar. As we went out, I grinned at him, trying instinctively to draw him into a conspiracy against Mr. Lancaster. But he remained expressionless and merely made me a small, stiff German bow. It really shocked me to see an adolescent boy bow like that. Mr. Lancaster certainly broke them in young. Or did he—horrible thought!—class me with Mr. Lancaster and therefore treat me with the same mocking-contemptuous respect? I thought not. Waldemar was probably every bit as stuffy as his employer, and tried to imitate his behavior as a model of gentlemanly deportment.

We took a tram back to Mr. Lancaster's home. It was a warm, humid day of spring. Carrying my suitcase and wearing—in order to transport it—my overcoat, made me sweat; but I enjoyed the weather. It disturbed and excited me. I was glad that the tram was crowded—not only because I thus became separated from Mr. Lancaster and didn't have to make conversation with him, but also because I was pressed up close against the bodies of young Germans of my own age, boys and girls; and the nationality barrier between them and me seemed to rub off as the swaying car swung us into a tight-packed huddle. Outside there were more young people, on bicycles. The schoolboys wore caps with shiny peaks and bright-colored shirts with laces instead of buttons, open at the neck. The gaily painted tram sped clanking and tolling its bell down long streets of white houses, where broad creeper leaves shadowed fronts of embossed stucco, in gardens dense with lilac. We passed a fountain—a sculptured group of Laocoön and his sons writhing in the grip of the snakes. In this sunshine you could almost envy them. For the snakes were vomiting cool water over the hot, naked bodies of the men, and their deadly wrestling match appeared lazy and sensual.

15

Mr. Lancaster lived in the ground-floor flat of a large house that faced north. Its rooms were high, ugly and airy. They had big white sliding doors which shot open at a touch, with uncanny momentum, making a bang which resounded through the building. The place was furnished in Germanic *art nouveau* style. The chairs, tables, closets and bookcases were grim, angular shapes which seemed to express a hatred of comfort and an inflexible puritanism. An equally grim stenciled frieze of leafless branches ran around the walls of the living room, and the hanging center lamp was an austere sour-green glass lotus bud. The place must have been dreary beyond words in winter; now at least it had the merit of being cool. Mr. Lancaster's only obvious contribution to the décor were a few school and regimental group photographs.

The most arresting of Mr. Lancaster's photographs was a large one showing a vigorous, bearded old man of perhaps seventy-five. What a beard! It was the real article, no longer obtainable, made of sterling silver; the beard of the genuine Victorian paterfamilias. It roared in torrents from his finely arched nostrils and his big-lobed ears, foamed over his cheeks in two tidal waves that collided below his chin to form boiling rapids in which no boat could have lived. What a beard-conscious old beauty—tilting his head up to be admired, with an air of self-indulged caprice!

"My dear old father," said Mr. Lancaster, making it clear, by his memorial tone of voice, that The Beard was now with God. "Before he was sixteen he had rounded the Horn and been north of the Aleutians, right up to the edge of the ice. By the time he was *your* age, Christopher—" this was a faint reproach—"he was second mate, sailing out of Singapore on the China Seas run. He used to translate Xenophon during the typhoons. Taught me everything I know."

Lunch was cold. It consisted of black bread, hard yellow Dutch cheese and various kinds of sausage—the indecently pink kind, the kind that smells gamy, the kind full of lumps of gristle, the kind that looks in cross-section like a very old stained-glass window in a church.

Before we had eaten anything, Mr. Lancaster informed me that he didn't approve of after-dinner naps. "When I was managing the company's office at Valparaiso, my second in command was always telling me I ought to take a siesta, like the rest of them did. So I said to him, 'That's the time when the white man steals a march on the dagoes.'"

16

This, I was to discover, was a characteristic specimen of Mr. Lancaster's line of bold reactionary talk. No doubt, in my case, he was using it for educational reasons, taking it for granted that I must have romantic, liberal views which needed a counterbalance. There he was both right and wrong. I did have liberal views, in a vague, unthoughtout way; but he was quite wrong in thinking that by expressing opposite opinions he could startle me. I should have been startled only if he had agreed with me; as it was, I accepted his prejudices as a matter of course, without curiosity, finding them entirely in character.

Actually, I think, Mr. Lancaster felt himself to be beyond left or right. He took his stand on the infallibility of his experience and his weary knowledge that he had seen everything worth seeing. He was also beyond literature. He told me that he spent his evenings carpentering in a small workshop at the back of the flat—"to keep myself from reading."

"I've got no use for books as books," he announced. "When I've taken what I need out of them, I throw them away. . . . Whenever anyone comes and tells me about some philosophy that's just been discovered, some new idea that's going to change the world, I turn to the classics and see which of the great Greeks expressed it best. . . . Scribbling, in these latter days, is nothing but a nervous disease. And it's spreading everywhere. I don't doubt, my poor Christophilos, that before long you'll have sunk so low as to commit a novel yourself!"

"I've just published one."

The moment I had spoken, I was horrified and ashamed. Not until the words were in my mouth had I known what I was going to say. Mr. Lancaster couldn't have provoked me more artfully into a confession if he'd been a prosecuting lawyer.

The most humiliating aspect of my confession was that it didn't even seem to surprise or interest him in the least. "Send me a copy sometime," he told me blandly. "I'll let you have it back by return post, with all the split infinitives underlined in red pencil and all the non sequiturs in blue." He patted my shoulder; I winced with dislike. "Oh, by the way," he added, "we have a trifling foolish banquet towards—" he spoke this line in a special, whimsical tone, as if to draw my respectful attention to the fact that here was a quotation from the Divine Swan in playful mood—"All the local worthies from

17

the shipping companies, the consulates and so forth will be there. I've arranged for you to come."

"No," I said. And I meant it. I had had enough. There was a limit to the amount of my valuable life I could afford to waste on this ignorant, offensive, self-satisfied fool. I would simply walk out on him, at once, this very afternoon. I had some money. I'd go to a travel bureau and find out how much it would cost to get back to England third class by the ordinary, civilized means. If I hadn't enough, I would take a room in a hotel and telegraph my mother for more. It was perfectly easy. Mr. Lancaster wasn't dictator of the world, and there was nothing he could do to stop me. He knew this as well as I did. I wasn't a child. And yet—

And yet—for some absurd, irrational, infuriating, humiliating reason—I was afraid of him! Incredible, but true. So afraid that my defiance made me tremble and my voice turned weak. Mr. Lancaster didn't appear to have heard me.

"It'll be an experience for you," he said, munching his hard old cheese.

"I can't." This time, I spoke much too loudly, because of overcompensation.

"Can't what?"

"Can't come."

"Why not?" His manner was quite indulgent; an adult listening to the excuses of a schoolboy.

"I—I haven't got a dinner jacket." Again, I horrified myself. This betrayal was as involuntary as the other; and, up to the moment of speaking, I'd supposed I was going to tell him I was leaving.

"I didn't expect you would have one," said Mr. Lancaster, imperturbably. "I've already asked my second in command to lend you his. He's about your size, and he has to stay at home tonight. His wife's expecting another baby. Her fifth. They breed like vermin. That's the real menace of the future, Christopher. Not war. Not disease. Starvation. They'll spawn themselves to death. I warned them, back in '21. Wrote a long letter to *The Times*, forecasting the curve of the birth rate. I've been proved right already. But they were afraid. The facts were too terrible. They only printed my first paragraph—" He rose abruptly to his feet. "You can go out and look around town. Be back here at six, sharp. No—better say five fifty-five. I have to work now." And with that, he left me alone.

The banquet was held in some private rooms above a big restaurant in the middle of the city.

As soon as we arrived, Mr. Lancaster's manner became preoccupied. He glanced rapidly away from me in all directions and kept leaving me to go over and speak to groups of guests as they arrived. He wore a greenish-black dinner jacket of pre-1914 cut and carried a white silk handkerchief inside his starched cuff. My own borrowed dinner jacket was definitely too large for me; I felt like an amateur conjurer—but one without any rabbits to produce out of his big pockets.

Mr. Lancaster was nervous! He evidently felt a need to explain to me what was worrying him, but he couldn't. He couldn't say anything coherent. He muttered broken sentences, while his eyes wandered around the room.

"You see—this annual meeting. A formality, usually. But this year—certain influences—absolute firmness—make them see clearly what's at stake. Because the alternative is. Same thing everywhere today. Got to be fought. Uncompromisingly. State my position—once and for all. We shall see. I don't quite think they'll dare to—"

Evidently this meeting, whatever it was, would take place at once. For already the guests were moving towards a door at the other end of the room. Without even telling me to wait for him, Mr. Lancaster followed them. I had no alternative but to stay where I was, sitting at the extreme end of one of the settees, facing a large mirror on the wall.

Very very occasionally in the course of your life—goodness knows how or why—a mirror will seem to catch your image and hold it like a camera. Years later, you have only to think of that mirror in order to see yourself just as you appeared in it then. You can even recall the feelings you had as you were looking into it. For example, at the age of nine, I shot a wildly lucky goal in a school football game. When I got back from the field, I looked into a mirror in the changing room, feeling that this improbable athletic success must somehow have altered my appearance. It hadn't; but I still know exactly how I looked and felt. And I know how I looked and felt as I stared into that restaurant mirror.

I see my twenty-three-year-old face regarding me with large, reproachful eyes, from beneath a cowlick of streaky blond hair. A thin, strained face, so touchingly pretty that it might have been photographed and blown up big for a poster appealing on behalf of the world's young: "The old hate us because we're so cute. Won't *you* help?"

And now I experience what that face is experiencing—the sense which the young so constantly have of being deserted. Their god forsakes them many times a day; they are continually crying out in despair from their crosses. It isn't that I feel angry with Mr. Lancaster for having deserted me; I hardly blame him at all. For he seems to me to be an almost impersonal expression, at this moment, of the world's betrayal of the young.

I am in mortal dread of being challenged by the manager of the restaurant or by any one of the various waiters who are hanging around the room, waiting for the banquet to begin. Suppose they ask me what I'm doing here—why, if I'm a bona fide dinner guest, I'm not with the others attending the meeting?

Therefore I concentrate all my will upon the desired condition of not being accosted. Fixing my eyes upon my reflection in the mirror, I try to exclude these men utterly from my consciousness, to eradicate every vestige of a possible telepathic bond between us. It is a tremendous strain. I tremble all over and feel sick to my stomach. Sweat runs down my temples.

The meeting lasted nearly an hour and a half.

The guests returned from it mostly by twos and threes, but Mr. Lancaster was alone. He came straight over to me.

"We've got to eat now," he told me with an air of nervous impatience, just as though I had raised some objection. "I've had them put you next to old Machado. He'll tell you all about Peru. He's their vice-consul here. You speak French, I suppose?"

"Not one word." This was quite untrue. But I wanted to disconcert Mr. Lancaster, and so punish him a little for leaving me alone by making him feel guilty.

But he wasn't even listening. "Good. It'll be an experience for you." And he was off again. I joined the crowd that was now moving into the dining room.

It was a very big place, a real banqueting hall. There were four long tables in it. What was evidently the table of honor was placed along the far wall, under an arrangement of many national flags. At this table I saw Mr. Lancaster already in the act of sitting down. It was equally easy to identify the least important table, right by the door. And, sure enough, one of its place cards had my name on it. On my right I read the name of Emilio Machado; and, a moment later, Sr. Machado himself took his seat at my side. He was a tiny man in his seventies. He had a benevolent mahogany-brown face netted with wrinkles—these were a slightly paler shade of brown—and hung with a drooping white mustache. His lips moved in a rather pathetic, silly smile as he watched the expressions on the faces of some loudly chattering guests across the table, but I didn't have the impression that he wanted to be spoken to.

The dinner, to my surprise, was excellent. (I associated everything in this city so completely with Mr. Lancaster that I was apt to forget he couldn't possibly have had anything to do with the catering.) As soon as the soup course was over, the guests began to toast each other, pair by pair. To do this, a guest would half rise to his feet, glass in hand, and wait until he had succeeded in catching the desired eye. The other guest, when caught, would also rise; glasses would be raised, bows exchanged. It was obvious that this was a serious matter. I felt sure that no toast went unremembered, and that to omit any of them would have led to grave consequences in your subsequent business dealings.

Watching all this toasting made me aware that I myself had nothing to drink. It appeared that the drinks didn't come with the dinner; they had to be ordered separately. In the fuss of changing my clothes, I had forgotten my money; I would have to send the bill over to Mr. Lancaster to be paid. But this didn't bother me. Serve him right, I thought, for his neglect. I made up my mind to speak to Sr. Machado, and ask him to share a bottle of wine with me. He didn't have any, either. I drew a deep breath: *"Si vous voulez, Monsieur, j'aimerais bien boire quelque chose—"*

He didn't hear me. I felt my face getting hot with shame. But now I heard a voice in my other ear: "You are the nephew of Mr. Lancaster, yes?"

I started guiltily. For I had been so absorbed in the problem of communicating with Machado that I'd scarcely noticed my other neighbor. He was a smiling, greedy-faced man, with a gleam in his eye and no chin. His sleek, thin gray hair was brushed immaculately back from his forehead. An unused monocle hung down on a broad silk ribbon against his shirtfront. His mouth pulled down at the corners, giving him a slight resemblance to a shark—but not a very dangerous one; not a man-eater, certainly. Squinting at his place card, I read a Hungarian name which no one but a Hungarian could possibly pronounce.

"I'm not his nephew," I said. "I'm not related to him at all, as a matter of fact."

"You are not?" This delighted the Shark. "You are just friends?"

"I suppose so."

"A frriend?" He rolled the *r* lusciously: "Mr. Lancaster has a young frriend!"

I grinned. Already I felt that I knew the Shark very well indeed.

"But he leaves you alone, no? That is not very friendly."

"Well, now I've got you to look after me."

My reply sent the Shark off into peals of screaming laughter. (On second thoughts, he was also partly a parrot.)

"I look after you, yes?" said Parrot-Shark: "Oh, very good! I shall look after you. Do not be afraid of that, please. I shall do it." He beckoned to a waiter. "You will help me drink one great big bottle of wine, yes? Very bad for me, if I must every time drink up all alone."

"Very bad."

"And now tell me, please—you are the friend of Mr. Lancaster, since how long?"

"Since this morning."

"This morning, only!" This didn't really shock Parrot-Shark, as he pretended; but it did puzzle him sincerely. "And he leaves you alone already?"

"Oh, I'm used to that!"

He was looking at me much more inquisitively now, aware, perhaps, that here was something not quite usual, just a bit uncanny, even. Maybe if he could have seen what a very odd young fish he had at the end of his line, he would have fled screaming from the room. However, at this moment the wine arrived, and soon his curiosity was forgotten.

From then on, dinner became quite painless. It was easy enough to keep Parrot-Shark amused, especially after we had finished the first bottle and he had ordered another. At the end of the meal, the lights were turned out and the waiters brought in ice puddings with colored lamps inside them. Then the speeches began. A fat, bald man rose to his feet with the assurance of a celebrity. Parrot-Shark whispered to me that this was the mayor. The mayor told stories.

22

Someone had once explained to me the technique of story-telling in German; you reserve, if possible, the whole point of the story and pack it into the final verb at the end of the last sentence. When you reach this sentence, you pause dramatically, then you cast forth the heavy, clumsy, polysyllabic verb, like a dice thrower, upon the table.

At the end of each story the audience roared and wiped perspiring faces with their handkerchiefs. But, by the time it was Mr. Lancaster's turn to speak, they were getting tired and not so easy to please. His speech was followed by applause that was no more than barely polite.

"Mr. Lancaster is in bad humor tonight," Parrot-Shark told me, with evident sly satisfaction.

"Why is he in a bad humor?"

"Here we have a club for the foreign people who have work in this city. Mr. Lancaster is the president of our club for three years now. Always before, he is elected with no opposition—because he represents so powerful a shipping firm—"

"And this year you elected someone else?"

"Oh no. We elect him. But only after much discussion. We elect him because we are afraid of him."

"Ha, ha! That's very funny!"

"It is true! We are all afraid of Mr. Lancaster. He is our schoolmaster. No—do not tell him that, please! I joke only."

"I'm not afraid of him," I boasted.

"Ah, for you it is different! You also are English. I think when you are Mr. Lancaster's age, people will be afraid of *you.*" But Parrot-Shark did not mean this; he didn't believe it for one instant. He patted my hand. "I like every time to tease you a little bit, no?" On this understanding we drank each other's healths and finished a third bottle.

The rest of the evening I remember only rather vaguely. After the speeches, the whole company rose. Some, I suppose, went home. The majority got possession of chairs in the outer room, where they ordered more drinks. Little tables appeared from somewhere to put the drinks on. Those who had nowhere to sit wandered about, on the alert to capture an empty place. The lights seemed very bright. The tremendous clatter of conversation tuned itself down in my ears into a deep, drowsy hum. I was sitting at a table in an alcove. Parrot-Shark was still looking after me, and several of his friends had joined him. I don't think they were all

23

Hungarians—indeed, one of them seemed obviously French and another Scandinavian—but they had the air of belonging together. It was as if they were all members of a secret society, and their talk was full of passwords and smilingly acknowledged countersigns. I felt intuitively that they had all been involved in the opposition to Mr. Lancaster's re-election. They didn't seem very formidable; it was no wonder that he had defeated them. But they were more dangerous and more determined than they looked. They were smiling enemies, snipers, heel-biters, quick to scurry away, but sure to return.

Machado had long since disappeared. But I kept getting glimpses of Mr. Lancaster. I was surprised to realize that he was every bit as drunk as I was. I had supposed he would be extremely abstinent, either from conviction or caution, or else that he would have a very strong head. We were drinking liqueur brandy, now; I had begun to loll on the table. "Feeling sleepy?" Parrot-Shark asked. "I fix you up, eh?" He called the waiter and gave a detailed order in German, winking at his friends as he did so. They all laughed. I laughed too. Really and truly, I didn't care what they did with me.

The waiter brought the drink. I sniffed at it. "What is it?" I asked.

"Just a small special medicine, yes?" The faces of Parrot-Shark and his fellow-conspirators had moved in very close, now. They formed a circle within which I felt myself hypnotically enclosed. Their eyes followed my every movement with an intentness which pleased and flattered me. It was certainly a change, being at the burning-point of such focused attention. I sniffed the drink again. It was some kind of a cocktail; I could distinguish only a musky odor which perhaps contained cloves.

But now something made me turn my head. And there was Mr. Lancaster. My sense of distance had become a bit tricky; he appeared to be about twenty-five yards away and at least twelve feet tall. Actually, he must have been standing right behind my chair. He said sharply, "Don't drink that stuff, Christopher. It's a plot—" (or perhaps, "It's a lot"; I can't be sure).

There was a long pause during which, I suppose, I grinned idiotically. Parrot-Shark said, smiling, "You hear what Herr Lancaster says? You are not to drink it."

"No," I said, "I certainly won't. I won't disoblige my dear-

24

est Coz." With these words, I raised the glass to my lips and drained the entire drink. It was like swallowing a skyrocket. The shock made me quite sober for a moment. "That's very interesting," I heard myself saying; "pure reflex action. I mean—you see—if he'd told me *not* to drink it—I mean, I shouldn't—"

My voice trailed off and I just could not be bothered to say any more. Looking up, I was surprised to find that Mr. Lancaster was no longer there. Probably several minutes had gone by.

"He doesn't like you," I abruptly told Parrot-Shark.

Parrot-Shark grinned. "It is because he is afraid that I steal you from him, no?"

"Well, what are you waiting for?" I asked aggressively. "Don't you *want* to steal me?"

"We shall steal you," said Parrot-Shark, but he kept glancing apprehensively toward Mr. Lancaster, who had reappeared in the middle distance. "There is a bar," he whispered to me, "down by the harbor. It is very amusing."

"What do you mean—amusing?"

"You will see."

His words broke the spell. I was suddenly, catastrophically bored. Oh yes, in my own sadistic way, I had been flirting with Parrot-Shark; daring him to overpower my will, to amaze me, to master me, to abduct me. Poor timid creature, he couldn't have abducted a mouse! He had no faith in his own desires. He was fatally lacking in shamelessness. I suppose he thought of himself as a seducer. But his method of seduction had gone out with the nineties. It was like an interminable and very badly written book which I now knew I had never meant to read.

"Amusing?" I said. "*Amusing?*"

With that I rose, in all the dignity of my drunkenness, and walked slowly across to where Mr. Lancaster was sitting. "Take me home," I told him, in a commanding voice. It must have been commanding, because he instantly obeyed!

The next morning, at breakfast, Mr. Lancaster seemed very much under the weather. His poor nose was redder than ever and his face was gray. He sat listlessly at the table and let me get the food from the kitchen. I hummed to myself as I did so. I felt unusually cheerful. I was aware that Mr. Lancaster was watching me.

"I hope you take cold baths, Christopher."

"I took one this morning."

"Good boy! It's one of the habits you can judge a man by."

I wanted to laugh out loud. Because I never took a cold bath unless I had been drunk, and would indeed have thought it shameful and reactionary to take one for any other reason. I agreed with Mr. Lancaster, for once: cold bath taking was a habit you could judge a man by—it marked him as one of the enemy. Nevertheless—I had to confess that part of myself, a spaniel side of me that I deplored, eagerly licked up Mr. Lancaster's misplaced praise!

Altogether, I felt a distinct improvement in our relations; at any rate, on my side. I felt that I had definitely scored over him and could therefore afford to be generous. I had defied him last night about drinking that drink, and had got away with it. I had had a glimpse behind the scenes of his business life and realized that he wasn't quite invulnerable; he was at least subject to petty ambition. Best of all, he had a hang-over this morning and I hadn't—well, not much of one.

"I'm afraid I was a little preoccupied, yesterday evening," he said. "I should have taken you aside and explained things to you quietly. It was a very delicate situation. I had to act quickly—" I became aware that Mr. Lancaster didn't really want to tell me about the club and his fight for re-election; it wouldn't have sounded important enough. So he took refuge in grandiose generalizations: "There are evil things abroad in the world. I've been in Russia, and I know. I know Satanists when I see them. And they're getting bolder every year. They no longer crawl the gutters. They sit in the seats of power. I'm going to make a prophecy—listen, I want you to remember this—ten years from now, this city will be a place you couldn't bring your mother, or your wife, or any pure woman to visit. It will be—I don't say worse, because that would be impossible—but as bad—as bad as Berlin!"

"Is Berlin so bad?" I asked, trying not to sound too interested.

"Christopher—in the whole of *The Thousand and One Nights*, in the most shameless rituals of the Tantras, in the carvings on the Black Pagoda, in the Japanese brothel pictures, in the vilest perversions of the Oriental mind, you couldn't find anything more nauseating than what goes on there, quite openly, every day. That city is doomed, more surely than Sodom ever was. Those people don't even realize how low they have sunk. Evil doesn't know itself there. The most terrible of all devils rules—the devil without a face. You've led a sheltered life, Christopher. Thank God for it. You could never imagine such things."

"No—I'm sure I couldn't," I said meekly. And then and there I made a decision—one that was to have a very important effect on the rest of my life. I decided that, no matter how, I would get to Berlin just as soon as ever I could and that I would stay there a long, long time.

That afternoon Mr. Lancaster arranged that Waldemar should take me to see the sights. We looked at the paintings in the Rathaus and visited the cathedral. Captain Dobson had made me curious to see the Bleikeller, the lead cellar, under it, in which corpses of human beings and animals are preserved. Captain Dobson had described how he had been to see these corpses with his brother: "One of them's a woman, you know. She's wearing a pair of black drawers. So I thought to myself, I'd like to see how things had panned out down there. There was a caretaker on guard, but he'd got his back turned to us. So I said to my brother, just keep an eye on old Tirpitz. And then I lifted them up. And, do you know, there was nothing—nothing at all! The rats must have been at her."

The flesh of the corpses had shriveled on their bones so that they were hardly more than skeletons; it looked like black rubber. There was a caretaker on this occasion, too; but he didn't turn his back and I had no chance of testing Captain Dobson's story. The thought of it made me smile; I wished I could tell it to Waldemar. An American lady who was down in the cellar with us asked me how the corpses had been preserved. When I told her I didn't know, she suggested I should ask Waldemar. I had to explain that I couldn't. Whereupon, she cried to her companion: "Say—isn't this cute? This young man can't speak any German and his friend doesn't speak any English!"

I didn't think it was cute at all. Being with Waldemar embarrassed me. He was probably a nice boy. He was certainly nice looking; in fact he was quite beautiful, in a high-cheek-boned, Gothic style. He looked like one of the carved stone angels in the cathedral. No doubt the twelfth-century sculptor had used just such a boy—maybe a direct ancestor of Waldemar—for his model. But an angel isn't a very thrilling companion, especially if he doesn't speak your language;

27

and Waldemar seemed so passive. He just followed me around without showing any initiative. My guess was that he found me as tiresome as the sights and only consoled himself by reflecting that it would be even more boring back in the office.

The four days which I now spent with Mr. Lancaster seemed like a whole life together. I doubt if I should have gotten to know him any better in four months or four years.

I was bored, of course; but that didn't bother me particularly. (Most of the young are bored most of the time—if they have any spirit at all. That is to say, they are outraged—and quite rightly so—because life isn't as wonderful as they feel it ought to be.)

But I had decided to make the best of Mr. Lancaster. I was ashamed of my adolescent reactions to him that first day. Wasn't I a novelist? At college, my friend Allen Chalmers and I had been fond of exchanging the watchword "All pains!" This was short for Matthew Arnold's line in his sonnet on Shakespeare: "All pains the immortal spirit must endure." We used it to remind each other that, to a writer, everything is potential material and that he has no business quarreling with his bread and butter. Mr. Lancaster, I now reminded myself, was part of "all pains," and I resolved to accept him and study him scientifically.

So the first time I found myself alone in his flat, I searched it carefully for clues. I felt ridiculously guilty doing this. There were no rugs on the floors, and the noise of my footsteps was so loud that I was tempted to take off my shoes. In a corner of the living room stood a pair of skis. They looked somehow so like Mr. Lancaster that they might have been his familiars watching me. I used to make faces at them. I was being watched, anyway, by the photograph of The Beard. How dearly he would have liked to have me aboard his ship, to be ordered aloft in a blizzard off the Horn! When you looked at him and then considered his victim and pupil, Mr. Lancaster, you realized how much the old monster had to answer for.

On the whole, my search was disappointing. I found almost nothing. There was a locked writing desk which might possibly contain secrets; I would watch for a chance to see inside it. Otherwise, all the drawers and cupboards were open. My only discovery of any interest was that Mr. Lancaster kept a British Army captain's uniform in the wardrobe with his other clothes. So he was one of those dreary creatures who made a cult of their war experiences! Well, I might have known it. At least it was something to begin on.

At supper that night—our only eatable meal, since it was cooked by a woman who came in—I got him onto the subject. It certainly wasn't difficult. I barely had to mention the word "war" to start him intoning:

"Loos—Armentières—Ypres—St. Quentin—Compiègne—Abbeville—Épernay—Amiens—Bethune—St. Omer—Arras —" His voice had gone into its ecclesiastical singsong, and I had begun to wonder if he would ever stop. But he did, abruptly. Then, in a much lower voice, he said "Le Cateau," and was silent for several moments. He had pronounced the name in his most specially sacred tone. And now he explained: "It was there that I wrote what I regret to say is one of the very few great lines of poetry on the war." Again, his voice rose into a chant: "Only the monstrous anger of the guns."

"But surely," I involuntarily exclaimed, "that's by—?" Then I quickly checked myself, as I realized the full beauty of this discovery. Mr. Lancaster had genuine delusions of grandeur!

"I could have been a writer," he continued. "I had that power which only the greatest writers have—the power of looking down on all human experience with absolute objectivity." He said this with such conviction that there was something almost spooky about it. I was reminded of the way the dead talk about themselves in Dante.

"Tolstoy had it," Mr. Lancaster mused, "but Tolstoy was dirty. I know, because I've lived in six countries. He couldn't look at a peasant girl without thinking of her breasts under her dress." He paused, to let me recover from the shock of this powerful language. He was in the role of the great novelist now, talking simply and brutally of life as he sees it without fear or desire. "Some day, Christopher, you must go there and see it for yourself. Those steppes stretching thousands of miles beyond the horizon, and all the squalor and the hopelessness. All the terrible rot of sloth. The utter lack of backbone. Then you'll know why Russia is being run today by a pack of atheist Jews. . . . We in England never produced anyone greater than Keats. Keats was a clean-hearted lad, but he couldn't see clearly. He was too sick. You have to have a healthy mind in a healthy body. Oh, I know you young Freudians sneer at such things, but history will prove you wrong. Your generation will pay and pay and pay. The sun's touching the horizon already. It's almost too late. The night of the barbarian is coming on. I could have written all that. I could have warned them. But I'm a man of action, really—

"I'll tell you what, most excellent Christophilos—I'm going to make you a present. I'll give you the idea for a book of short stories that will make your reputation as a writer. It's something that's never been done. No one has dared to do it. Their heads were full of this so-called expressionism. They thought they were being subjective. Pooh! They hadn't the stamina. Their minds were costive. All that they could produce was as dry as sheep droppings—

"You see, these fools imagine that realism is writing *about* emotions. They think they're being very daring because they name things by the catchwords these Freudians have invented. But that's only puritanism turned inside out. The puritans forbid the use of the names; so now the Freudians order the use of the names. That's all. That's the only difference. There's nothing to choose between them. In their dirty little hearts, the Freudians fear the names just as much as the puritans do—because they're still obsessed by this miserable medieval Jewish necromancy—the Rabbi Loew and all that. . . . But the true realism—the kind nobody dares to attempt —has no use for names. The true realism goes behind the names—

"So what I would do is this—"

Here Mr. Lancaster paused impressively, rose, crossed the room, opened a drawer, took out a pipe, filled it, lighted it, shut the drawer, came back to his chair. The process took nearly five minutes. His face remained dead-pan throughout it. But I could sense that he was simply delighted to keep me in suspense—and, in spite of myself, I really was.

"What I would do," he at last continued, "is to write a series of stories which do not describe an emotion, but create it. Think of it, Christopher—a story in which the word 'fear' is never mentioned and the emotion of fear is never described, but which *induces* fear in the reader. Can you imagine how terrible that fear would be?

"There'd be a story inducing hunger and thirst. And a story

arousing anger. And then there'd be another story—the most terrible of all. Perhaps almost too terrible to write—"

(The story inducing sleep? I didn't say this, but I thought it—very loud.)

"The story," said Mr. Lancaster, speaking very slowly now to get the maximum effect, "which arouses the instinct of—reproduction."

My efforts to view Mr. Lancaster scientifically were not merely for art's sake. I realized by now that he was capable of having a truly shocking effect on my character. It was very dangerous for me to stop regarding him as a grotesque and start thinking of him humanly, because then I should hate him for bullying me. And if I went on hating him and letting myself be bullied by him, I should sink into a vicious, degenerate bitchery; the impotent bitchery of the slave. If there was such a thing as reincarnation—and why not?—I might well have been Mr. Lancaster's slave secretary in the days of classical Rome. We had probably lived out in a tumble-down villa on the wrong side of the Appian Way. I would have been the sort of slave who fancies himself as a poet and philosopher, but is condemned to waste his time transcribing the maunderings of his master and endure his earth-shakingly trivial thoughts about the mysteries of nature. My master would have been poor, of course, and stingy, too. I would have had to double my duties, fetching wood and water, and maybe cooking as well. But I would have put on airs with the slaves from the other villas and pretended that I never had to do anything menial. At night I would lie awake planning his murder. But I should never dare go through with it, for fear of being caught and crucified.

No—Mr. Lancaster had to be taken scientifically or not at all. You had to study him like lessons. I actually made notes of his table talk:

"The worst of this work I'm doing now is, it doesn't really use more than a hundredth part of my brain. I get mentally constipated. In the war, my battery major used to set me gunnery problems. I'd solve them in the day. Gave three alternative solutions to each—without mathematics—

"There's one thing, Christopher, that you *must* realize. It is necessary in this world to believe in a positive force of evil. And the joy of life—the *whole* joy of life—is to fight that

31

evil. If we lose sight of that, we lose the meaning of life. We fall into the ghastly despair of Glycon:

> Panta gelōs, kī panta konis, kī panta to māden,
> panta gar ex alogōn esti ta ginomena. . . .

> *All is but laughter, dust and nothingness,*
> *All of unreason born. . . .*

That's where the Pagans came to an end, the edge of the shoreless sea. That was all they knew. But we have no excuse to follow them. For against their negation we can now put Gareth's tremendous affirmation, his reply to his mother when she urged him to stay at home and amuse himself with the distractions of a purposeless life:

> *Man am I grown, a man's work must I do.*
> *Follow the deer? follow the Christ, the King,*
> *Live pure, speak true, right wrong, follow the King—*
> *Else, wherefore born?*

Never forget that, Christopher. Repeat it to yourself every morning, as you wake up. Else, wherefore born? Never ask, Can we win? Fight, fight!

> *Charge once more, then, and be dumb!*
> *Let the victors, when they come,*
> *When the forts of folly fall,*
> *Find thy body by the wall.*

None of your clever modern men has Arnold's voice. Meredith had it. William Watson had it—he was the last. Then the clever-clever moderns swarmed onto the stage, and we lost the message.

"I could have given it back to them. I could have revived it. But I heard another call. It was one morning in early summer —at the edge of the Mer de Glace, just below Mont Blanc. I stood looking out over that vast dazzling sea of ice, and a voice asked me: Which will you be? Choose. And I said: Help me to choose. And the voice asked: Do you want love? And I said: Not at the price of service. And the voice asked: Do you want wealth? And I said: Not at the price of love. And the voice asked: Do you want fame? And I said: Not at the

32

price of truth. And then there was a long silence. And I waited, knowing that it would speak again. And at last the voice said: Good, my son. Now I know what to give you—

"You have everything before you. Christopher. Love hasn't come to you, yet. But it will. It comes to all of us. And it only comes once. Make no mistake about that. It comes and it goes. A man must make himself ready for it; and he must know when it comes. Some are unworthy. They degrade themselves and are unfit to receive it. Some hold back from receiving it —call it pride, call it fear—fear of one's own good fortune— who shall judge? Be ready for the moment, Christopher. Be ready—"

One morning, when Mr. Lancaster had started out for the office, I saw that the writing desk he usually kept locked was standing open. As he had left the key, with his key bunch attached to it, sticking in the keyhold, I guessed he would soon discover his mistake and come back. So my investigations had to be quick.

The first thing I found was an army service revolver, evidently another of Mr. Lancaster's sentimental war souvenirs. This couldn't have interested me less; I felt certain the desk must contain some worthier secrets. I leafed through old paid bills and obsolete railway timetables; handled bits of wire, blackened light bulbs, broken picture frames, rusty parts of some small engine, perished rubber bands. It was as if Mr. Lancaster had sternly bundled up all that was untidy in his character and stowed it away here out of sight.

However, in the top drawer—the most prominent and therefore least likely place, I had thought, which was why I looked there last—I found a thick notebook with a shiny black cover. I was thrilled to see that it was full of poetry in Mr. Lancaster's hand-writing; a long, narrative poem, apparently. I could do no more than hastily skim through it—lots of nature, of course—mountains, seas, stars, boyhood rambles and ruminations in the manner of Wordsworth—and God—lots and lots of God—and travel—and the war—oh dear, yes, the war—and more travel—hm—hm—hm—aha, what was this? Now we were getting somewhere at last!

And there was One—
Long, long, ago—dear God, how very long—
Who, when the lilac breathed in breathless bloom

And later buds their secrets still withheld
Yet promised to reveal, as soon they must,
Since it was so ordained—as evening came
She too was there, her presence felt ere seen
By him who watched for it. She never knew
What meaning filled the twilight with her step,
What emptiness, for him, the twilight brought
When, soon, she came no more—the ways of Life
Leading her elsewhere. And she never knew,
Going her ways about the world, what deed,
Unknowing, she had done; into what heart
She had brought beauty and left bitter pain.

I can't remember how the lines struck me then, because I regarded them simply and solely as a find. My treasure hunt was successful. I was triumphant. Seizing pencil and paper, I scribbled them down, thinking only of how I would read them aloud to my friends when I got back to London.

I had barely finished my copying when I realized that Mr. Lancaster had re-entered the flat. He had made far less noise than usual. There was no time to cover up the traces of my search. All I could do—and I think it showed great presence of mind—was to drop the notebook into the drawer and take out the revolver. It was at least less embarrassing, I thought, to be caught examining a revolver than an autobiographical poem.

"Put that down!" Mr. Lancaster barked hoarsely.

He had never used that tone to me before; it startled and enraged me. "It isn't loaded," I said. "And, anyhow, I'm not a child." I put the revolver back in the drawer and walked straight out of the room.

(Looking back, I now reinterpret Mr. Lancaster's behavior. I see how his conversation was full of attempts to arouse my interest in him. Didn't he expect, for example, that I'd ask him what it was that that voice on the Mont Blanc glacier had finally given him? Hadn't he even hoped that I'd beg him to tell me about his love life? And wasn't the leaving of the key in his desk a deliberate, if subconscious, attempt to make me read his poem? If I'm right—and I think I am—then my cruelty to Mr. Lancaster was in my lack of curiosity. My would-be scientific study of him was altogether unscientific, because I was sure in advance of what I was going to find—which no scientist should be. I was sure he was a bore.

So, when Mr. Lancaster came in and found me looking at the revolver instead of the notebook, he must have been bitterly disappointed; even if he couldn't have explained to himself why. Hence his outburst of temper.

As for the revolver, maybe he had almost forgotten its existence. And maybe it was actually I who reminded him that it was lying there, all the time, in the bottom drawer, a gross metallic fact in the midst of his world of fantasy.)

Two days before I was due to return to England, Mr. Lancaster took me sailing. He didn't ask me if I wanted to do this; he simply announced his plan and I accepted it. I didn't really care what happened, now. Since the incident of the revolver, our relations were chilly. I was merely counting the hours till I could leave.

We left after the office closed that evening, in his car, to drive out to the village on the river where he kept his boat. On the way, we picked up Sr. Machado. I was glad to have him with us, for I didn't want to spend any more time alone with Mr. Lancaster. Much later, it occurred to me that Machado was probably the only one of Mr. Lancaster's acquaintances left who would agree to come with him on a trip of this kind. No doubt many of them had tried it—once.

The three of us were squeezed into the front seat of Mr. Lancaster's little car, with the outboard engine, under its tarpaulin cover, sitting up in the back. Quite soon we lost our way. Mr. Lancaster, who had forgotten to bring the map, became increasingly jittery as we bumped along a narrow sand road in the twilight, skirting a marsh. Old farmhouses stood half awash amidst water meadows. A crane walked stiffly along the wall of the dike and went flapping away over the lush, wet landscape. I felt a dreamy, romantic contentment steal over me. What did it matter where we were? Why be anywhere in particular? But Mr. Lancaster was frantic.

Just as it began to get really dark, two figures appeared out on the marsh in a punt. Mr. Lancaster stopped the car, ran up on to the dike and hailed them. They were very small and towheaded, a boy and a girl. It was almost incredible that they could manage the punt at all, and this made them seem more like very intelligent animals than terribly stupid children. They stood hand in hand in the punt, staring up at Mr. Lancaster with their big, vacant blue eyes, their mouths open, as if they expected he was going to feed them. Mr. Lancaster addressed them—as he told me later—in High and Low German. He spoke as one speaks to idiots, so slowly and with such elaborate pantomime that even I could understand what he said. But not those children. They just stared and stared. Mr. Lancaster began to shout and wave his arms but they didn't flinch. They were too stupid to be afraid of him. At last he gave it up in despair, turned the car around and drove back the way we had come.

Very late at night we finally arrived at our destination. The place was crowded with holiday-makers, and only one room was vacant at the inn. It must have been one of the best rooms, however, for it had an imposing bed on a dais, as well as a studio couch. The chief decoration was a photogravure of an almost nude woman in an "artistic" pose; this stood on an easel with a piece of figured material like tapestry draped around it. Mr. Lancaster decided that he would sleep on the couch and Sr. Machado on the bed. I was to go back to the cabin of Mr. Lancaster's boat. "It'll be an experience for me," I said sarcastically, before he could say it. But Mr. Lancaster was deaf to sarcasm.

I woke in the early but already brilliant morning, and found myself undecided whether to romanticize my situation or sulk. My situation was romantic, I had to admit. Here I was, all alone in this foreign land, in sole occupancy of a sailing boat! No doubt these people were watching me and wondering about me. Although it was barely six o'clock, most of the holiday-makers seemed to be up.

The village was built along the riverbank, with beer gardens running down to the water's edge. The boats were decorated with sprays of poplar at their mastheads; and schoolboys had fastened them to the handle bars of their bikes. On board the boats there were gramophones, and people were playing concertinas and singing. Beer was being drunk and sausages munched, and you could smell the delicious smell of out-of-door coffee. The girls were plump but pretty; the men were cropped blond and piggy-pink. As they sang they shaved or combed their hair, and were temporarily silenced as they brushed their teeth in the river.

All this filled me with joy. But on the debit side of the day there was my stiffness from sleeping curled up on the tiny bunk in the cabin, plus a headache. And there was Mr. Lancaster, who now appeared and was cross because I hadn't tidied the cabin or finished dressing; I was, in fact, sprawling on the deck in the sun. By the time we had had breakfast at the inn and I had become constipated—my usual reaction to having to use strange lavatories and being told to hurry—the sulks were on.

And then the engine was mounted on the boat, but it wouldn't start. A mechanic had to be fetched from the garage; while he was working, quite a large crowd gathered. All that Mr. Lancaster could contribute was his fussing and nagging. Nevertheless, he made the occasion a text for one of his reminiscent sermons: "This reminds me of the war. I remember getting out of a village near Loos just before dawn, because we knew the Hun would start shelling as soon as it got light. I was curious to see how I would stand the strain, because our colonel obviously had the wind up. So I took my pulse. It was *absolutely* normal. I found my brain was functioning so well that, as I was giving orders to my sergeant-major, I visualized a chess problem I'd read in *The Times* a few days before. It was black to play and mate in three moves, and I *saw* the solution, Christopher. I didn't have to think about it at all. I simply looked at it, as you look at the map of a town and say to yourself: 'Well, quite obviously, *that's* the quickest way to the market square.' There couldn't be any question. And I have no doubt whatsoever that I could have played at least half a dozen games simultaneously at that moment, and won all of them. What is it Sophocles says about the greatness of man when his mind rises to its highest in the face of fate—?" And he was off again into a long, straggling string of Greek. How right Hugh Weston was in saying that it is the most hideous of all languages!

At last we were off, heading towards the sea. Mr. Lancaster snapped at me because I dropped some of his fishing gear. I scowled back at him. To snub me and show me my place he then concentrated on Machado, talking to him in Spanish. This was nothing but a relief, as far as I was concerned; but it worried Machado, whose courtly Latin manners demanded that he should communicate with me, now that he was aware of my existence. (I'm sure he simply did not remember we had sat next to each other at that dinner.) So he spoke to me from time to time in French, which I had great difficulty in understanding because of his fearful accent. The worst of Machado's remarks was that they were not only hard to understand but harder still to develop into any kind of conversation. For example, he said: "*Je suppose que le sujet le plus intéressant pour un écrivain, c'est la prostitution." To* which I could only reply enthusiastically: *"Monsieur, vous avez parfaitement raison."* And there we stuck.

We were in the estuary now; the river was already very wide. Mr. Lancaster ordered me to steer the boat while he got the fishing rods ready for action. "You've got to be on the alert from the first moment," he told me. "This river's full of sand bars. Careful. Careful! CAREFUL! Look at the color of that water ahead! Dead slow through here! Steady, now! Steady. Steady. Steady. Steady. *Now*—open her up! OPEN! Quick, man! Port! HARD to port! Do you want to swamp us?" (There was a very mild swell as we left the river mouth; you could hardly even feel the change of motion.) "Away, now. Dead ahead! Hold her two degrees sou'west of the point. Hold her on her course. HOLD HER! Careful, man! Good. *Good!* Oh, good man! *Very* pretty! Well steered, sir! I'm greatly afraid, Christopher, that we're going to make a sailor out of you yet!"

I had done nothing to be praised for, except that I hadn't run us into a buoy as big as a haystack. Mr. Lancaster's enthusiasm was as crazy as his anxiety. Yet once again—as in the case of the cold bath—I was idiotically flattered. Ah, if he had realized how easily manageable I was; how instantly I responded to the crudest compliment! No—even if he had realized it, this would have made no difference in his treatment of me. Flattery was something Mr. Lancaster would never have bestowed upon me; he would have regarded it as bad for my soul.

I suppose he felt no responsibility for Machado's soul. For he began to butter him up in a manner that was absolutely shameless, speaking French, now, for my benefit. He called Machado a "good sport," using the English words and then explaining them in French, until Machado understood and clapped his hands with delight: "Good spot! I—good spot? Oh, yes!"

"Isn't he a dear old man?" said Mr. Lancaster to me, benevolently. "He's three quarters Peruvian Indian, you know. His father probably chewed coca and never wore shoes. That's your real unspoiled dago for you. Doesn't matter what age he is—he always stays a child."

We were now quite far out on the flat shallow sea; the low shore of dunes was already only a pale line between the sparkle of the water and the shine of the sky. White sails were

38

curving all over the seascape. Mr. Lancaster, evidently feeling very pleased with himself, stood in the bows intoning:

Pervixi: neque enim fortuna malignior unquam erepiet nobis quod prior hora dedit.

I knew, with sudden intense force, just how awful the Odyssey and the voyage of the *Pequod* must have been, and that I would have sooner or later jumped overboard rather than listen to either of those ghastly sea bores, Ulysses and Ahab.

Presently Mr. Lancaster announced that it was time for us to fish. Machado and I were given the rods. We trailed our lines inexpertly in the water. This might have been quite restful, if heaven hadn't rebuked my laziness by performing a most tiresome miracle—nothing less than a miraculous draught. We ran into a school of mackerel!

Mr. Lancaster was absolutely beside himself. "Careful! CAREFUL, MAN! Easy—easy—easy! Don't let the line slack! You'll lose him! Play him, man! Keep playing him! Fight him! He's a wily devil! He'll trick you yet! Don't look at *me*, man! Watch him! WATCH HIM! Keep your head! Keep calm! NOW—"

All of this was more superflous than words can tell, for, in fact, there was nothing—absolutely nothing—we could have done to avoid catching those miserable fish—short of throwing the rods away and lying down in the bottom of the boat. Machado wasn't speaking French now, or even Spanish. He emitted what sounded like tribal hunting sounds, maybe in some Indian dialect of the Andes. At first I caught some of their excitement and yanked the fish in as fast as I could. Then I began to get tired. Then rather disgusted. It was so indecently easy. By the time we were through, I think we had at least thirty fish in the boat.

After the catch Mr. Lancaster set himself to clean some of the fish we were to eat, so he didn't pay much attention to Machado. I was steering. Happening to glance over in the old man's direction, I saw that he was leaning right over the side. His back was tense and his legs were stiffly straddled. My first thought was that he was having a stroke. But no—he was pulling desperately at something in the water. He looked as if he were trying to haul up the bottom of the sea. He turned his head toward me, half strangling with the exertion. "*Poisson!*" he gurgled, only it sounded more like "possum!"

Naturally, I jumped to my feet to help him. What was my amazement—and subsequent fury—when I received a violent backhander in the chest from Mr. Lancaster! He knocked me right over backwards, and I sat down very hard. I think if I'd had a knife I'd have whipped it out right then and there, and finished him. As it was, I merely mentally shouted: "Touch me again, you old goat, and I'll throttle you!" Mr. Lancaster, meanwhile, was yelling in my face: "Leave him alone, you silly little fool!" I suppose he saw the blazing hate in my eyes, for he added, somewhat less hysterically, "*Never* help a man when he's landing a fish! NEVER! Don't you even know *that?*"

He turned from me to attend to Machado, who was heaving in his line. Mr. Lancaster knelt beside him, speaking to him in French, soothing him, urging him, entreating him, imploring him to breathe deeply, to relax, to keep up the pressure, gentle and slow. "*Ça va mieux, n'est-ce pas? Ça marche? Mais naturellement—*" He was absurdly like a midwife encouraging a woman in labor. And sure enough, slowly, slowly, with infinite pain, Machado was delivered of an enormous fish—a tuna, Mr. Lancaster said. When he had gaffed it we let it trail in the water behind the boat, to keep it fresh.

Then Mr. Lancaster cooked the mackerel on a spirit stove. I would have liked to be strong-minded and refuse to eat. But I was ragingly hungry. And although Mr. Lancaster, with his usual incompetence, had burned the fish badly, it smelled and tasted delicious. Besides, I was in an awkward position because I couldn't possibly be nasty to Machado, who was in a state of utter triumph and had to be congratulated repeatedly. Quite probably, this would be the last really happy day of his life. I compromised by ignoring Mr. Lancaster. He didn't appear to notice this.

In this mood, we started for home. Mr. Lancaster kept remarking complacently on his own foresight; he had calculated our timetable so that we were going with the tide both ways. But the long, chugging voyage seemed tedious enough, even so. As we got into the river mouth, I was steering again and Mr. Lancaster was nagging at me. We must have been off course, but how was I to know? It was no use trying to follow his pseudonautical directions. I just went ahead by sight. Suddenly he screamed: "SAND! SAND AHEAD! PUT HER ABOUT! HARD! HARD OVER!"

What happened next was quite unplanned. At least, I had no

conscious knowledge of what I was going to do. Nevertheless, I did it. I had the feel of the tiller by this time; I could sense pretty well how much it would stand. All I did was to obey Mr. Lancaster's order just the merest shade too energetically. I swung the tiller hard over—very hard. And with the most exquisitely satisfactory, rending crack, the crosspiece to which the outboard engine was clamped broke off, and the engine fell into the water.

I looked up at Mr. Lancaster and I nearly grinned.

For a moment I thought he would swallow his Adam's apple. "You fool!" he screamed. "You fool! You confounded little idiot!" He stepped over to me, making the boat rock. But I wasn't in the least scared now. I knew he wouldn't—couldn't—hit me. And he didn't.

As a matter of fact, the water was so shallow that we didn't have much trouble in dragging up the engine. But of course there was no question of getting it started again; it needed to be thoroughly cleaned first. So there was nothing for it but to sail back to the village.

The sail lasted all the rest of the day. There was very little wind, and Mr. Lancaster seemed to be making the worst possible use of it, for nearly every boat on the river passed us. He steered, glumly. Machado was peacefully asleep after his exertions. Finally we were taken in tow by a pleasure steamer. Mr. Lancaster had to accept this courtesy because it was beginning to get dark, but I could see how it humiliated him. A man and a woman, neither of them slender or young, were sitting in the stern of the steamer, invisible to the other passengers but right in front of us. Throughout the trip they made love with abandon. And this, too, was a sort of humiliation for Mr. Lancaster, because the lovers evidently felt that his reactions weren't worth bothering about. I felt that I was on the side of the lovers, and smiled at them approvingly; but they weren't bothering about my reactions, either.

As for myself, I was in a wonderful mood. The semideliberate ditching of the outboard engine had discharged all my aggression, like a great orgasm. Now I no longer felt the least resentment against Mr. Lancaster. Indeed, I had stopped thinking about him. My thoughts had gone racing on ahead of my life, of me on this sailing boat; they had left Mr. Lancaster and Germany far behind. They were back in London, in my room, at my desk. But I wasn't even unduly impatient to return there physically, for, meanwhile, I had plenty to think about. After all—despite Mr. Lancaster—this silly day would be memorable to me throughout my life. For, right in the midst of it—maybe at the very instant when that engine had splashed into the water—I had had a visitation. A voice had said: "The two women—the ghosts of the living and the ghosts of the dead—the Memorial." And, in a flash, I had seen it all—the pieces had moved into place—the composition was instantaneously *there*. Dimly, but with intense excitement, I recognized the outline of a new novel.

The day came for my return to England. The *Coriolanus* was sailing in the evening.

That morning Mr. Lancaster informed me, with his usual nonchalance, that Waldemar was to take me to the art gallery. Waldemar and I were to have lunch together—since Mr. Lancaster had a business appointment—and I was to be back at the flat at four fifteen precisely. I made no comment.

But, as soon as Waldemar and I were alone on the gallery steps and Mr. Lancaster had disappeared around the corner, I turned to him and firmly shook my head. "*Nein,*" I said.

Waldemar looked puzzled. Pointing to the gallery entrance, he asked: "*Nein?*"

"*Nein,*" I repeated, smiling. Then I pantomimed a breast stroke.

Waldemar's face brightened instantly. "*Ach—schwimmen! Sie wollen, dass wir schwimmen gehen?*"

"*Ja,*" I nodded. "*Swimmen.*"

Waldemar beamed at me. I had never seen him smile like that before. It changed his whole face. He no longer looked at all angelic.

He took me to a big municipal open-air pool. I had passed this place several times, but with my almost utter lack of German, had never had the nerve to go in there alone. Waldemar didn't seem passive now. He bought our tickets, got me my towel and soap, greeted numerous friends, steered me into the locker room, made me take a shower and showed me how to tie on one of the triangular red bathing slips he had rented. When he undressed, it was as if he took off his entire office personality. It was astonishing how he had managed to disguise his physically mature, animally relaxed brown body in that prim office suit. He no longer behaved to me as if I were forty years old and in league with Mr. Lancaster. We smiled

42

at each other tentatively, then started to wrestle, splashed and ducked each other, swam races. But though we were playing like kids, I was chiefly aware of the fact that he was already a young man.

Presently we were joined by a friend, a boy of his own age named Oskar. Oskar was monkey-faced, impudent, dark and grinning. He spoke fairly fluent English. He was a page, he told me, in one of the large hotels. And I was aware of the page mentality in him; he had been around, he knew the score, and he looked at me speculatively, like one of his hotel guests who might have special requirements he could satisfy in exchange for a tip. He had giggly asides with Waldemar and I knew they were discussing me; but I didn't mind, because Oskar took great trouble to make me feel one of the party.

After swimming, we went to a restaurant for lunch. Both the boys smoked and drank beer. I had the impression that Waldemar was anxious to appear as sophisticated as his friend. By this time, we were calling each other Oskar and Christoph.

Waldemar said something to Oskar and they both roared with laughter.

"What's the joke?" I asked.

"Walli says he thinks his bride will like you," Oskar told me.

"Well—good. Is she coming here?"

"We go to see her. Soon. All right?"

"All right."

"All right!" Waldemar laughed very heartily. He was slightly drunk. He reached across the table and shook my hand hard. Oskar explained: "Walli's bride likes also older gentlemen. Not too old. You—very good! Pretty boy!"

I blushed. A most delicious gradual apprehension began to creep over me.

"You have five marks?"

"Yes." I produced them.

This amused the boys. "No, no—for later."

"But, Oskar—" I felt we were somehow at cross-purposes —"if she's Walli's bride—and, anyhow, isn't he much too young to have a bride?"

"Already at twelve I have a bride. Walli also."

"But—won't he be jealous if I—?"

More laughter. Oskar told me: "We shall not leave you alone with her." I must have looked more and more bewildered, for he patted my hand reassuringly. "You need not be shy, Christoph. First, you watch us. Then you see how easy it is." He translated his joke to Waldemar and they laughed till the tears ran down their faces.

Braut in dictionary German means a bride or fiancée. But boys like Oskar and Waldemar used it to refer to any girl they happened to be going with. This, my first lesson in the language, I learned during that unforgettable, happy, shameless afternoon—an afternoon of closed Venetian blinds, of gramophone music and the slippery sounds of nakedness, of Turkish cigarettes, cushion dust, crude perfume and healthy sweat, of abruptly exploding laughter and wheezing sofa springs.

I didn't return to Mr. Lancaster's flat until nearly six o'clock. I was too dazed with pleasure to have cared if he had scolded me; but he didn't. In fact, he appeared to be back in the mood in which he had received me on the day of my arrival. He just didn't seem particularly interested in my existence. "Give my regards to your mother" was all he said when we parted. I felt hurt by his coldness. However little *I* might care, I was still sincerely surprised when my indifference was returned.

When I got back to London, I found that my novel was indeed a flop. The reviews were even worse than I had expected. My friends loyally closed ranks against the world in its defense, declaring that a masterpiece had been assassinated by the thugs of mediocrity. But I didn't really care. My head was full of my new novel and a crazy new scheme I had of becoming a medical student. And always, in the background, was Berlin. It was calling me every night, and its voice was the harsh sexy voice of the gramophone records I had heard in the bed-sitting room of Waldemar's "bride." Sooner or later, I should get there. I was sure of that. Already I had begun to teach myself German, by one of those learn-it-in-three-months methods. While riding on buses, I recited irregular verbs. To me they were like those incantations in *The Arabian Nights* which will make you master of a paradise of pleasures.

I never sent a copy of *All the Conspirators* to Mr. Lancaster, of course. But I wrote him a thank-you letter—one of those thankless, heartless documents I had been trained since my childhood to compose. He didn't answer it.

44

When I tried to describe him to my friends, I found I could make very little of him as a significant or even a farcical character. I just did not have the key to him, it seemed. And when I read my copy of his poem to Allen Chalmers, we were both rather embarrassed. It simply wasn't bad enough in the right way. Chalmers had to be polite and pretend that it was much more ridiculous than it actually was.

I also touched on the subject of Mr. Lancaster's love life in talking to my mother. She smiled vaguely and murmured, "Oh, I hardly think *that* was the trouble." I then learned from her what she hadn't thought even worth telling me before—that Mr. Lancaster had actually been married for a few months, after the war, but that his wife had left him and they had separated legally. "Because," said my mother dryly, "Cousin Alexander wasn't—so one was given to understand —at all adequate as a husband." This revelation of Mr. Lancaster's impotence quite shocked me. Not on his account—it was pretty much what I would have expected—but on my mother's. I never fail to be shocked by the ability of even the most ladylike ladies to live in cozy matter-of-fact intimacy with the facts of nature. My mother was surprised and rather pleased by my reaction. She was aware that she had managed for once to say something "modern," though she couldn't altogether understand how she had done it.

I suppose I should gradually have forgotten all about Mr. Lancaster if he hadn't regained my interest in the most dramatic way possible. Toward the end of November that same year he shot himself.

The news came in a letter from Mr. Lancaster's assistant manager, the "second in command" who had lent me his dinner jacket for the banquet. I had met him briefly after that at the office and thanked him. I remembered him only as a florid little Yorkshireman with a broad accent and a capable, good-natured manner.

The letter informed us of the bare facts in a tidy, business-like style. Mr. Lancaster had shot himself one evening at his flat, but the body had not been discovered until next day. No suicide note had been found, nor any papers "of a personal nature." (He must have burned the notebook with his poem, I supposed.) He had not been unwell at the time. He was in no financial difficulties, and the affairs of the company

45

were giving him no cause for anxiety. The assistant manager concluded with a line of formal condolence with us on our "great loss." No doubt he mistook us for blood relatives, or felt that we had anyhow to represent the family, since there was nobody else to do it.

Mr. Lancaster's act impressed me a great deal. I strongly approved of suicide on principle, because I thought of it as an act of protest against society. I wanted to make a saga around Mr. Lancaster's protest. I wanted to turn him into a romantic figure. But I couldn't. I didn't know how.

The next year I did at last go to Berlin, having thrown up my medical career before it was properly started. And there, some while later, I ran into Waldemar. He had grown bored with his native city and had come to Berlin to seek his fortune.

Waldemar, naturally, knew very little about Mr. Lancaster's death. But he told me something which amazed me. He told me that Mr. Lancaster had often spoken of me, after I had left, to people in the office. Waldemar had heard him say that I had written a book, that it had been a failure in England because the critics were all fools, but that I should certainly be recognized one day as one of the greatest writers of my time. Also, he had always referred to me as his nephew.

"I believe he was really fond of you," said Waldemar, sentimentally. "He never had any sons of his own, did he? Who knows, Christoph, if you'd been there to look after him, he might have been alive today!"

If only things were as uncomplicated as that!

I think I see now that Mr. Lancaster's invitation to me was his last attempt to re-establish relations with the outside world. But of course it was already much too late. If my visit had any decisive effect on him, it can only have been to show him what it was that prevented him from having any close contact with anybody. He had lived too long inside his sounding box, listening to his own reverberations, his epic song of himself. He didn't need me. He didn't need any kind of human being; only an imaginary nephew-disciple to play a supporting part in his epic. After my visit he created one.

Then suddenly, I suppose, he ceased to believe in the epic any more. Despair is something horribly simple. And though Mr. Lancaster had been so fond of talking about it, he probably found it absolutely unlike anything he had ever imagined. But, in his case, I hope and believe, it was short-lived. Few of us can bear much pain of this kind and remain conscious. Most of the time, thank goodness, we suffer quite stupidly and unreflectingly, like the animals.

Ambrose

Five years have gone by—this is May 1933—and here I am, starting out on another journey. I am on a train going south from Berlin toward the Czechoslovakian frontier. Opposite me sits Waldemar.

What am I doing here? What is he?

I suppose I could answer "escaping from the Nazis." Waldemar would back me up in this, because he loves melodramatic explanations. And I shall probably describe this journey as though it were an escape and dangerous, one day when I am far from here and among people who are ill-informed enough to be impressed. But, this morning, I am well aware that that kind of posing would be heartless and childish. Not only are we perfectly safe, but we are surrounded by those who aren't. For this frontier, which we two shall soon so easily cross, chaperoned by my British passport, has already become a prison wall. On this very train there must be at least a few people in danger of their lives, traveling with false papers and in fear of being caught and sent to a concentration camp or simply killed outright. It is only in the past few weeks that I have fully grasped the fact that such a situation really exists —not in a newspaper or a novel—but here where I have been living. This seems horribly strange, but not unbelievable; it has already become a way of life. The terror may still be a bit amateurish and disorganized, but the authorities will soon have it functioning smoothly and bureaucratically. Official murder, like everything else official in Germany, will involve a lot of red tape.

Oh yes, I could make out a sort of case for saying I'm escaping, all the same. It's true that I would probably have been asked to leave, sooner or later, if I'd stayed on in Berlin. I'm pretty sure my resident's permit wouldn't have been renewed. I've been seen around in the cafés with a British journalist who has made himself particularly unpopular with the Nazis because of the stories about S.A. tortures he has smuggled out of the country to his newspaper. Several of my Jewish friends have either been arrested or escaped abroad; I still don't know which. And the police have actually been around to question my landlady about me. Quite casually—they were just making a routine check-up on all foreigners, they said. Still, you never knew.

But—be all this as it may—my reasons for taking this particular trip, and for taking Waldemar along with me, have nothing directly to do with the Nazis. They are quite unserious. And I suppose they show how little I've changed, in some respects, since the days of my visit to Mr. Lancaster.

Since our meeting again in Berlin, Waldemar and I had developed an intimate but casual relationship which was typical of that period of my life. I knew at least half a dozen young men in much the same way. We would not see each other for weeks or months at a time. Then the telephone would ring. "Christoph, can you lend me ten marks?" "Christoph, can I stay at your place tonight? My landlady is acting funny." ("Acting funny" meant that the landlady had got tired of asking for the rent.) It wasn't that Waldemar and the others were just spongers. They simply thought that friends should help each other; that the arrangement happened to be more or less one-sided was, from their point of view, merely an economic accident. Waldemar was a charming guest—one of the kind who feels it is his duty to entertain his host, not vice versa. And he was generous with whatever he had. When he was earning money, he would invite me out to the movies or to come dancing with a couple of girls at one of the beer gardens by the Spree. He had had a succession of small jobs; he was a good worker, I believe, and honest. Only he didn't care to work for more than a few weeks at a time. Mostly he tended bar, or helped out at bakeries or butcher shops, or set up the pins in a bowling alley. He seemed to have acquired, from his early days in Mr. Lancaster's office, a contempt for desk work. It was a bore, he said, and *spiessig*—a word which he used to mean bourgeois, stuffy, timid, respectable, as opposed to proletarian, forthright, physical, sexy, adventurous. I rather like Waldemar for taking this attitude, absurd as it was.

Waldemar often used to talk to me about a friend of his named Hans Schmidt. Soon after Waldemar's arrival in Berlin, he had found a job in a bar where Hans was head bartender. Before this, Hans had been a physical instructor in the *Reichswehr*. He had taught Waldemar some boxing and wrestling as well as bartending. Waldemar spoke to me with awed admiration of Hans's muscles, and with tolerant amusement of his sexual tastes. It seemed that Hans, in his army days, had given individual after-hours instruction to some of the better-looking soldiers in his gym class. If they were clumsy, he had beaten them with a riding crop—but not very hard, and only after the culprits had admitted they deserved punishment and had even begged for it. According to Waldemar, Hans had no trouble in getting whipping boys; it appeared to be an easily acquired taste. "Can you imagine such a thing, Christoph?" Waldemar would exclaim. "Such perverse swine!" But he couldn't keep a straight face as he said this, and there was a gleam in his eye which made me suspect he had sampled Hans's riding crop for himself, at least once. Altogether, I got the impression that Hans had been, and still was, quite a hero in his eyes.

But Hans had already been away from Germany for some while. He had left Berlin abruptly, perhaps because of some scandal. Waldemar got post cards from him from time to time. First he had written from Italy, then from Morocco, then from Egypt—just an address and a few words, but never any explanation of what he was doing there or how he managed to live. Waldemar had conscientiously answered the post cards with letters. I think they were the only letters he ever wrote, and indeed Hans was about all he had in the way of a family.

However, a couple of weeks ago, an entire long letter had arrived from Hans—the first news of him for many months. Hans wrote from Athens, and he now explained that he had been traveling around all this while with "a crazy Englishman" who was—to translate Hans's slang expression literally —"stone rich." "I am his bodyguard," Hans continued. "Who knows what he did before he met me? He might have had his throat cut a hundred times over. He is a good, sweet fellow, but totally crazy. You should see him drink! And now he wants to buy an island near here. He has the maddest ideas. Suddenly, he must build a house—a regular palace, with marble floors! We shall go to this island very soon, to set up our camp, while the house is being built. I say to him, 'Ambrose, what do you know about this island? Aren't you afraid? Suppose it's full of snakes?' And do you know what he answers? 'If a snake bites you, it's quite simple—you need only drink a bottle of cognac. But a whole bottle, and without stopping.' You see, he is a real curiosity. So, we shall live on this island like the wild Indians, eating octopus, and drinking this wine of theirs, which tastes like disinfectant. In Germany one would use it to clean the water closet. It is good, though, when you're thirsty, and it cures the fever. Well, I shall be glad to get him away from the city, at least. When we are in a city, he is always in trouble."

Finally, Hans came to the point of his letter. "You know something, Walli? It would be no bad idea if you would come to us here. On this crazy island I must be the cook, and I could use a regular German boy like you to help me. These boys Ambrose has around him are good for nothing—not even, well, you know what. They steal like ravens and they are not clean. I have spoken to Ambrose about you already, and he says he will pay you a wage and you can have your bed and food. He is funny about money sometimes, but he keeps his word. So, if you can in any way get yourself down here to Athens, perhaps you would not regret it. To stay at home —that's no life for an adventurous boy like you, a proper wanderbird. And if you stay, who knows, Hitler may make a soldier out of you, and you will have to wear a uniform and drill. Left! Right! Stand up straight! I got my snoutful of that in the army. It's nothing for you. So think this over."

Even before I had read Hans's proposition I knew, from Waldemar's manner as he handed me the letter, that he had some scheme in mind which depended on my help. And he knew that I knew it. He was watching my face closely as I read. As soon as I had finished, he asked eagerly, "Well, Christoph, what do you think?"

"It doesn't sound like a job that's worth going all that way for," I said, putting on, to tease him, a prudent elder-brother tone. "You have to think twice before starting on a journey like that. It'd take three days, at least—"

"Seventy-one hours and twenty minutes," said Waldemar

promptly. "You have to spend the night in Vienna. But you could sleep on a bench in the railway station—so that wouldn't cost you anything."

"What about food?"

"Oh, you could take some bread and cheese along. And what does it matter if you do feel a bit hungry? People fast for weeks sometimes. That's nothing."

"The ticket wouldn't be nothing."

"Only seventy-three marks seventy, third class."

I couldn't help laughing. "You've really got this worked out, haven't you?"

Waldemar grinned. "I stopped by the travel bureau and asked them."

"I see."

"Just out of curiosity. There's never any harm in asking, is there?"

"No, of course not."

There was a pause. We were silent, grinning at each other. It is really very pleasant, dealing with people like Waldemar. I knew in advance that, whatever I did or didn't do, he would never bear me any grudge. Of course it was also true that, if I *were* to give him anything, he wouldn't feel any particular gratitude. As far as he was concerned, this was just a problem which had suddenly appeared, like a large stone, in his path. He stood there, as it were, staring at it. Could it be removed? Would anyone remove it for him? He didn't know. He waited. He was almost fatalistic about the whole thing.

"How much money *have* you got?" I finally asked.

"Eleven marks," he told me, after rapid calculation. The discovery seemed to cheer rather than depress him. "So you see," he added, "I only need sixty-two."

"And seventy pfennigs."

Waldemar smiled, as if he could afford to ignore such a trivial sum and thought me a trifle petty to have even mentioned it. Getting into the spirit of our game, I asked, in the tone of one who seeks advice on an abstract moral issue, "So you really think I should give you this money?"

Waldemar, just as I expected, looked sincerely horrified. "Why—*no*, Christoph! Have I ever asked you to *give* me anything? Have I? Look me in the eyes and tell me. Have I? Don't you know me any better than that? What do you think I am?" He paused, as if to allow me time to become ashamed of myself. Then, his hurt feelings instantaneously forgotten, he added, coaxingly: "Naturally, it'd be just a loan. You saw what Hans says in his letter? This Englishman's going to pay me. I could pay you back out of my wages. Yes—that's right—" he grew excited, seeing the stone already beginning to move—"that's it, Christoph! You make the Englishman pay you my wages, every week! You take everything, until the debt's paid off. Or perhaps he'll even give you the whole lot in advance, as he's so rich—"

"You mean, he should send all that money to a complete stranger—someone he's never set eyes on—in another country?"

"But, Christoph, you wouldn't be a stranger by then, and you wouldn't be in another country—you'd be *there*—with me! Why, you don't suppose I'd go without you, do you? Alone—all that long journey? That'd be no fun at all."

"I'll have to think this over," I told him. "We'll talk about it tomorrow. And listen—don't start packing. I haven't promised anything, understand. I very, very much doubt if I can manage—"

"Christoph!" Waldemar hugged me in his delight; then very solemnly took both my hands in his. "I knew you were my friend. I've always known it. Have I come to you and been refused anything? Never! But now, Christoph, listen —you're to remember this, because I swear it: what you've done for me today, you'll never regret, as long as you live. You remember, Waldemar swore that—"

"But I haven't done anything. I haven't promised anything. Listen, please, don't get any wrong ideas—"

Waldemar merely smiled. He wasn't listening. He didn't have to. He understood me perfectly. A minute later, without any more efforts at persuasion, he left me—entirely satisfied that everything would now be arranged.

And he was right. Although Waldemar's plan had taken me by surprise, it didn't disconcert me at all. Indeed, it suited very well the state of mind I was in at that moment. As I lay in bed that night, I began to say to myself that maybe this was the finger of fate, pointing out to me the next step I should take. The truth—which up to now I hadn't recognized—was that I didn't really want to go back to England and settle down there. Not just yet, at any rate. I was in a nervous, excited mood, in which I wanted more movement, more change of scene. In this respect, Berlin had affected me like a party at the end of which I didn't want to go home. London would be an anticlimax. If I couldn't stay in Germany, I would prefer to get right away into another kind of atmosphere altogether. So why shouldn't I go to Greece? It was said to be cheap there; I could stay all summer and work on my new novel. And why shouldn't I take Waldemar along with me? I was feeling quite rich just then, having lately received a present from my uncle and an advance from my publisher. Naturally, I didn't expect Waldemar to repay the money—even if this job with the mysterious Englishman ever materialized, which I was inclined to doubt. But Waldemar would be well worth the price of his ticket simply as a traveling companion. For I knew I was going to feel lonely when I had left Berlin and all the people I had known there.

So here we are, already en route. Needless to say, we aren't going to live for the next three days on bread and cheese, or even travel third class all the way. I have booked sleepers for us from Vienna, where we shall spend the night comfortably in a hotel, not on a bench in the station. When I told Waldemar about these arrangements, he protested that I had made our trip less adventurous; but he didn't protest very vigorously.

Waldemar sits looking out of the train window. Though the landscape is still German and familiar in outer appearance, I suspect that it already seems exotic to him. His destination lends it magic. All he needs to know is that he is headed for a land *wo die Zitronen bluehen* and the girls have dark eyes. Everything in his German soul responds to the pull of this traditional Nordic wanderlust: to go south—that, for a North German, is the only real adventure. As for the happenings in the city we have left behind us—Hitler in power, the Reichstag burned, the beginning of the Terror—all that he takes for granted. He actually remarked to me this morning, "I'm so glad we're going away, Christoph. There's nothing doing here."

Waldemar is a convinced anti-Nazi—but perhaps chiefly because that is the way the people whose opinions he respects happen to feel. If he had ever been exposed to the influence of a personable big-brother type of Nazi youth leader, I wouldn't care to answer for the consequences. As for himself, he has grown accustomed, like every Berliner, to brown uniforms, mass meetings, police raids, street fights and beatings; to him, they come under the heading of "politics"—the manner in which things get done. He is a good-natured, happy-go-lucky,

54

easygoing boy, and I don't think he is personally capable of serious cruelty; but it is obvious that brutality in others doesn't particularly shock him. Again and again I have noticed in boys like Waldemar this rather sinister instinctive acceptance of sadism; they don't have to have read one page of Krafft-Ebing, or even know what the word means. I'm sure that Waldemar instinctively feels a relation between the "cruel" ladies in boots who used to ply their trade outside the Kaufhaus des Westens and the young thugs in Nazi uniforms who are out there nowadays pushing the Jews around. When one of the booted ladies recognized a promising customer, she used to grab him, haul him into a cab and whisk him off to be whipped. Don't the S.A. boys do exactly the same thing with *their* customers—except that the whipping is in fatal earnest? Wasn't the one a kind of psychological dress rehearsal for the other?

Unlike Waldemar, I am not looking toward the southern city at our journey's end but back toward the northern city we have just left. Until quite recently, I have never expected to have to leave Berlin because I have never seriously believed the Nazis could get into power. Although I've talked glibly enough from time to time about the possibilities of a *Reichswehr putsch* or a Communist revolution, I have never thought anything decisive would happen. I suppose I was prepared to stay on in Berlin for the rest of my life, with only occasional visits to England, where I already feel myself half a foreigner.

During these years in Berlin, I have come to think of myself as being deeply involved in German politics. The letters I sent back to England have often had the terse snooty don't-bother-me-now tone of a war correspondent in the midst of a battle. On my visits to London, I have let myself be regarded and questioned as an authority on the German situation, and I have given out the kind of answers which begin, "Well, of course, the first thing people here have got to understand is—"

But now the Nazis are in power. And now I have to admit to myself that I have never been seriously involved, never been a real partisan; only an excited spectator. When I first came to Berlin, I came quite irresponsibly, for a thrill. I was the naughty boy who had enjoyed himself that afternoon at the flat of Waldemar's *Braut*, and wanted more. However, having thoroughly explored the Berlin night life and begun to get tired of it, I grew puritanical. I severely criticized those depraved foreigners who visited Berlin in search of pleasure.

They were exploiting the starving German working class, I said, and turning them into prostitutes. My indignation was perfectly sincere, and even justified; Berlin night life, when you saw it from behind the scenes, was pitiful enough. But have I really changed underneath? Aren't I as irresponsible as ever, running away from the situation like this? Isn't it somehow a betrayal?

I don't know. I don't know. I don't want to think about all that, just now. I'm bored with feeling guilty. And why should I feel guilty if I don't choose to? Who decides my guilt except myself? Who tells me to be responsible for Germany? Who has the right to? No—I can't discuss this matter. I'm too confused. I feel like a cupboard in which all the clothes are mixed up; everything has got to be thrown out on the floor and sorted. I must stop wondering what I ought to think, how I ought to feel. I must try to discover some basis of genuine feeling and begin with that, no matter how small it is.

What *do* I really care about? I suppose, as of this moment, if I love anything, it is Waldemar. Not Waldemar personally, but what he represents. Just now I am identifying myself with him to such an extent that I'm really only experiencing this journey through his eyes. What I love in Waldemar is the candor and innocence of his experience; his innocent setting forth in search of adventure. And I love his selfishness and his lack of guilt. *He* has no conscience which forces him to take attitudes and hold opinions. He is quite free and unprotected and alone. I love him—but somewhat as you love an animal. I don't want anything from him, except that he shall remain young and fearless and silly. In fact, I want the impossible.

We are traveling along the valley of the Elbe. High above, on the apparently inaccessible face of a cliff overlooking the river, a hammer and sickle have been hugely daubed in red paint.

"Man," says Waldemar, turning to me with a gleeful smile, "the Nazis will have their work cut out scrubbing *that* off!"

This is my last memory of Germany.

Hans Schmidt was at the railway station to meet us when we got to Athens. And his Englishman was with him. I wouldn't have needed Waldemar to identify them. They stood out from the crowd simply by being different; even their gestures had a different rhythm altogether.

Hans hugged Waldemar and gave him a familiar slap on the

bottom. "*Servus*," he said to me, grinning at me in a way which made me wonder just what Waldemar had told him about me in his letter.

"How do you do," said the Englishman. I hate the expression "a limp handshake"; it seems to imply the kind of moral judgments which are made by scoutmasters. So I will put it that Ambrose placed his hand briefly in mine and then drew it away again as though it were an inanimate object he was holding by the wrist.

"I'm so glad you could come," he said, in the tone of a hostess welcoming a guest to a garden party. I felt at ease with him immediately.

Ambrose was about my age, I supposed; he looked both older and younger. His figure was slim and erect and there was a boyishness in his quick movements. But his dark-skinned face was quite shockingly lined, as though life had mauled him with its claws. His hair fell picturesquely about his face in wavy black locks which were already streaked with gray. There was a gentle surprise in the expression of his dark brown eyes. He could become frantically nervous at an instant's notice—I saw that; with his sensitive nostrils and fine-drawn cheekbones, he had the look of a horse which may bolt without warning. And yet there was a kind of inner contemplative repose in the midst of him. It made him touchingly beautiful. He could have posed for a portrait of a saint.

He was wearing a very old but obviously expensive tweed jacket, almost threadbare flannel slacks, stained and misshapen suede shoes. None of his clothes were clean, and I didn't get the impression that he was, either; but this wasn't offensive. I couldn't smell him at all, though my nose was—and still is today—extraordinarily keen.

He and Hans took us over in a taxi to the hotel where they were staying and arranged for us to have a room there. Then we sat outside the café which was in front of it, looking out across a square. Ambrose urged us to try the resinated wine. "You'd better get used to it," he told me. "It's usually all we can get to drink on the island."

I was a little surprised he took it so casually for granted that I was coming to his island, even for a short visit. I had vaguely assumed that I should do so, but I had expected an invitation and a polite discussion—I protesting that I should be a nuisance and he assuring me that I shouldn't. What I found disconcerting was that Ambrose showed so little curiosity about me; that he didn't even ask questions about our journey or what was going on in Berlin. I felt that he was absolutely self-sufficient within his own world. If you cared to enter it—well, good; that was your affair.

As I have said, he seemed both nervous and relaxed. His postures were relaxed, but there was desperate nervousness in his thin fingers and in the way he talked. His hands shook all the time. His gold signet ring was loose and kept nearly slipping off his finger. As he talked, he fished a string of beads out of his pocket—amber beads with a black tassel—and played with them. I didn't think he was at all drunk; but then, as I was to discover later, it was very hard to tell when Ambrose was drunk and when he wasn't.

"I hope you won't mind sleeping in a tent?" he said, in his country hostess voice. "I had meant the house to be built long before this, but they've scarcely started. However, now I shall be on the spot all the time. One has to stand over them and scream. Otherwise it's hopeless. . . . Let me see, we'd better buy your tent this afternoon. And some blankets. We can get those at the Thieves' Market. . . . You've never been in Athens before, have you? Then I suppose you *ought* to see the Acropolis. I always think it's a good thing to get *that* over, as soon as possible—"

"You don't like it?"

"I'm afraid it's *much* too late for me." Ambrose gave a co-quettish little wriggle; it was his way of apologizing for an unfashionable opinion. "I can't really get up any enthusiasm for anything after the Minoans, and the Eighteenth Dynasty." Then, with hardly a pause, he continued meditatively, "I don't know exactly how much your food will cost—I shall have to work that out—but you'll be surprised how cheap it is. And then there'll be your share of the petrol. We shan't be using the car much, though. The drinks will be free—except when we go into Chalkis to shop."

"I certainly don't want to cause you any extra expense," I said, rather stuffily, shocked to see Ambrose turn so abruptly from a hostess into a landlady. I was to get quite used to such transformations, later.

Meanwhile, Waldemar had been talking in German to Hans Schmidt. A few minutes later, when we got up and prepared to start out on our shopping and sight-seeing, Waldemar drew me aside and whispered in a shocked tone, "I'd never have recognized him!"

58

"Hans?"

"Man! He looks terrible! And what's happened to his arm?"

"His arm?"

"His left arm. You mean, you didn't notice anything?"

"No."

"But, Christoph, you must be blind! It's absolutely *kaput*! And he won't tell me how he got it. He says he will later, when we're alone, on the island. You know, Christoph—I'll bet you there's some dirty work going on. Perhaps Ambrose has enemies who keep trying to kill him. Didn't Hans tell me in the letter that he's his bodyguard? Do you think that's how he got wounded?"

"No, I don't."

But Waldemar was romantically determined to believe the worst. He grinned with delighted anticipation. "This island —it's going to be really dangerous, Christoph. We'll be out in the wilderness. It'll be a real adventure. Perhaps we'll wish we were safe back in Berlin."

Hans didn't come with us that afternoon, and it wasn't until supper that I got a good look at his arm. Then I couldn't imagine how I hadn't noticed the injury when we first met. The whole forearm was quite stiff and the hand was puffy-pink and bloated. You could see several deep scars on the back of it. Evidently, Hans had developed a technique for keeping it as inconspicuous as possible, but now he was obliged to let Waldemar cut up his meat for him.

He seemed to be taking his disablement quite cheerfully, I thought. In appearance, he was a real picture-book Prussian; a big, pale, muscular man with fair, almost white, close-cropped hair. You could still glimpse the catfooted, heavy-shouldered, smooth-skinned body of the fighter beneath the belly sag and the unwholesome flesh puffy with drinking. His face was pug-nosed; piggish but good-humored. His blood-shot eyes were a very pale, watery blue. I liked his sleepy smile and the lazy movements with which he heaved his big, fat, powerful body around. Once, becoming aware that I was watching him, he stretched himself and suddenly winked at me: "*Ja, ja,*" he said. "*So ist die Sache*"—a noncommittal, yet somehow appropriate, remark. It means approximately: That's the way things are.

"I've decided to get a pair of peacocks," Ambrose was telling me, meanwhile, "as soon as the house is built. And I rather thought one might have a camel, as well. A camel would give the place an *air*, don't you think?"

Perhaps it was a slight gesture he made with his cigarette; perhaps it was the odd way he smilingly lowered his eyelids and looked away, as if avoiding the glare of a strong light. (I realized, a few moments later, when he looked directly at me, that he had never done so before; never, at least, while I was looking at *him*.) Anyhow, whatever the clue may have been that I subconsciously picked up, the recognition came to me in a flash.

"Why, Ambrose," I exclaimed, "*I know you!*"

Ambrose said nothing. He kept his eyes averted, still smiling.

"What I mean is," I continued, "I've met you before, somewhere. Years ago. Yes—yes, of course! It was while we were both up at Cambridge. We met at a lecture. I think it was in the Hall at King's."

It was then that Ambrose looked straight at me. "Trinity, not King's. The lecture was on the ruins of Machu Picchu. You told me you'd come to it to get some ideas for a story you wanted to write."

"I never did write it, I'm afraid."

"I lent you a book on Inca costumes—mostly guesswork; the illustrations were quite pretty though."

"I hope I returned it?"

"No, you didn't, actually."

"I say, how awful of me! Can't I get you another copy?"

"No, of course not. It couldn't matter less. Actually, I've long since decided that the Incas aren't my sort of thing. So madly ungay."

"Tell me, Ambrose—when did you recognize me?"

"The moment I saw you at the railway station."

"Then why on earth didn't you say so?"

"Oh, I don't know—I wasn't sure you'd want to be reminded—"

"But that's nonsense! Why shouldn't I want to be? It was just that I didn't recognize you. It was terribly stupid of me—"

"Oh, I wouldn't say that—" Ambrose had let his cigarette go out. He fumbled rapidly with the matches—it was really shocking, how violently his hands shook—then looked straight at me again and smiled, with touching sweetness. "After all, lovey, I'm dead and you aren't."

60

All my life I have had a resistance to other people's whimsy remarks. So I should probably have let this one go without comment, even if, at that moment, a newcomer hadn't made his appearance—a young man of about twenty-three, whom Ambrose introduced as Aleko. Aleko had very bright, dark, somewhat protruding eyes, oily black curls and a number of gold-capped teeth. He wore a gaudy striped shirt, mechanic's overalls and long, elegantly pointed shoes. A flower was stuck in behind his left ear. The fingernail on the little finger of his left hand had been allowed to grow nearly half an inch long. "That's the fashion in Athens, just now," Ambrose told me. His eyes followed Aleko's movements with benevolent approval.

Waldemar and I watched him, too. For us he was the first human contact with Greece, and so he fascinated us. He must have been aware of this, because he behaved with a self-conscious swagger, though he pretended to take little notice of us. After greeting us graciously but casually, he sat down and began talking to Ambrose and Hans in Greek. Cheekily yet flatteringly, naughtily rolling his eyes, he addressed them in turn, plucking at Ambrose's sleeve, wagging his finger in Hans's face. Hans obviously understood most if not all of what Aleko said, but he answered with a few words of Greek only, or in German, and his manner toward Aleko was noticeably gruff and surly. I felt that Ambrose was aware of this, and that a certain tension existed between the three of them. Ambrose spoke Greek fluently, but with nervous haste, screwing up his mouth and stammering over the difficult words. He politely kept Waldemar and me within the conversation by frequent asides to us in German and English. This switching from language to language seemed to cause him a great nervous strain. To relieve it, he brought out his conversation beads and began to rattle them. Immediately, Aleko produced an identical string of beads and rattled them in exactly the same way. This imitation was so faithful that it seemed somehow sinister. It made me think of an uncannily clever pet monkey or of a sorcerer's familiar. Aleko looked boldly into Ambrose's face, watching it with an affectionate cunning which was at the same time beastlike and potentially dangerous.

After a while, an argument developed between the three of them. I couldn't understand what it was that Aleko was suggesting, but Hans was against it. "We have to get up in the morning," he protested to Ambrose in German. "We have to start early—you said so yourself."

"Don't be so fussy, lovey," Ambrose told him, in English. Then he explained to me: "Aleko thinks we should show you the town. There are two or three bars you might find rather amusing."

I excused myself, saying that I was tired after the journey. But Waldemar was eager, as always, for fun of any kind, and Hans was overruled. "You don't have to come, ducky, if you don't want to," Ambrose told him, with a slightly mischievous smile. To which Hans replied gruffly, "You know quite well I have to come. What'll happen to you if I don't? Do you think I want to have to hunt around in the gutters for you to-morrow morning?" As we were leaving, he added to me in an undertone, with a jerk of his head toward Aleko, "You can see for yourself who's the boss around here."

Waldemar returned in the small hours of the morning, startling me out of a sleep full of anxiety dreams about Berlin and the Nazis. With his characteristic lack of consideration, he sat down heavily on my bed and slapped my shoulder to waken me. "Man, Christoph, this is really a town! Such perverse old bags! One of them put her hand right on my crotch—I promise you! She said something to Ambrose, and he told me she'd said I was a pretty boy! I wanted to go with her, but Hans wouldn't let me. He said she had clap. I'll bet she was forty at least, but interesting; not like any of them I ever had in Berlin. You know what—she had a mustache! And I'll tell you something you won't believe, Christoph, it was sexy! It made me hot for her! Man—just let these old bags wait till I learn Greek!"

Next morning, in Ambrose's car, we started for the island. It lay about a hundred kilometers north of Athens, in the channel between the big island of Euboea and the mainland of Boeotia. The only way to reach it was by a very rough road, in some places a mere cart track, over the mountains.

Aleko sat next to Ambrose, in front. Hans, Waldemar and I were on the back seat, surrounded by a great rampart of baggage and miscellaneous objects. The old car floundered along at seventy kilometers an hour, with a noise like a hardware shop in an earthquake. Everything was loose, everything rattled, yet nothing had actually broken or would break, probably, for another six months at least. The car was a savage, sickening bumper; its rear wheels landed plump in every hole with a dead, springless crash which shook you from spine to teeth. And after each crash came a landslide of baggage which drove the handle of a spade, the rim of a bucket or the corner of a suitcase brutally into you.

We met very few other cars, which was lucky, for whenever we did so we were smothered in dust. Seen approaching us from the far distance, flashing in the sunlight, over the dusty ghost-pale mountains, the other car would look like the burning tip of a fuse, with a great dust cloud smoldering away behind it, slowly consuming the road. Once we met a herd of goats. Ambrose was going too fast to pull up, so he swung over to avoid them. The car skidded and its wheels churned loose shale for several moments on the edge of a cliff, a hundred-foot drop at the least, with a dried-out water-course at the bottom. But I was too drunk to feel really scared. We were all drunk, because Ambrose had decreed that we should have what he called "a substantial breakfast" before starting, since it was uncertain when we should get our evening meal.

From time to time, Hans and Waldemar sang—those German songs which have a haunting sad-sweetness even when they are most pornographic. Waldemar loved to sing "Anne-marie," and would do so many times a day. He regarded it, so to speak, as his theme song, because of the couplet,

> *Mein Sohn heisst Waldemar*
> *Weil es im Wald geschah. . . .*

which can be translated as, "My son's called Woody, because it happened in a wood."

Ambrose smiled faintly as he drove. His smile apologized for the state of the road and for his own driving, yet seemed to accept both as being in the nature of things. He had an air of being not altogether present, not entirely aware of the vicious bucking of the steering wheel between his hands. It was this air of aloofness which made his driving so alarming; yet it also inspired a certain confidence. You felt that, like a sleepwalker, he would be quite all right as long as he wasn't disturbed.

At last we had crossed the mountains and zigzagged down onto a narrow plain beside the sea. Here the going was much better, except that a strong breeze blew our own dust over us, so that our skins were powdered and gritty. I had relaxed, and even let go my grip on the side of the car, when Ambrose accelerated and deliberately swung us right off the road. I thought for a moment that we were going to turn over. The baggage surged upon us. Hans swore. "Sorry," said Ambrose, "I never *can* remember where to turn off. Nearly missed it again."

The first plunge had got us over the ditch. Now we were rocking across a red, bumpy wasteland, baked into cracks by the sun. In the middle distance a column of dust moved hither and thither, like a stooping ghost. Some scrawny birds with indecently naked necks rose into the air, flapping dust from their great, dirty wings. It was the first time I had ever seen vultures outside a zoo.

"We're nearly there now," said Ambrose, turning to smile at me reassuringly, in the midst of this wilderness.

And, sure enough, after about a quarter of an hour, signs of life began to appear. There were high, flat-topped booths, their legs planted in the shallow waves of the mirage, roofed with pine branches to shelter herdsmen from the sun. A roughly scarred track led downhill into an olive grove. We passed close to a well, where men and boys were grouped around a freshly painted vermilion cart. They evidently recognized Ambrose. They ran along with the car, waving their arms and yelling greetings.

"There's Geoffrey," Ambrose said, without surprise.

Sitting alone at a table under one of the booths, with a glass and a bottle of wine in front of him, was a big young man dressed in the most improbably British fashion; he wore a blazer, flannel slacks and a silk club scarf loosely knotted within an open-necked shirt. Seeing us, he rose and came over to the car as Ambrose stopped it. The others crowded around, excitedly questioning Ambrose and Aleko in Greek.

"Huge local enthusiasm," said Geoffrey, "at return of popular young squire."

He said this in a manner which I think of as peculiarly British; it is a sort of fossilized humor. If, in youth, you cultivate the mannerism of delivering all your comic lines with an absolutely straight face, you will produce, as you grow older, an effect which is no longer at all funny, but woodenly, truculently eccentric.

Although he was certainly my age, he had an air of debauched boyishness. His eyes were inflamed, but very blue.

From time to time, they flashed with a burningly innocent indignation; then he became quite handsome. Under the roughened, pimpled skin, you saw the beefy good looks of an Anglo-Saxon athlete. His blond hair was thinning.

"How long have you been here, lovey?" Ambrose asked him.

"Christ! How should I know? I've long ago lost count of time—since you left me alone with those bloody minions of yours."

"You know perfectly well, ducky, it was you who refused to come with us to Athens, this time. You said you *wanted* to stay here—"

"Your bloody minions," Geoffrey repeated, altogether disregarding this interruption, "jabbered and jabbered until I couldn't stand it another instant. Besides, I'd drunk up all the wine. So I told them to bring me over here."

"Did they take the boat on to Chalkis, do you know? Or did they go back to the island?"

"How the devil should I know? Didn't wait to look. I knew if I didn't get another drink inside me pronto, I should shoot them down like dogs."

"Oh, well," said Ambrose philosophically, "they're somewhere or other." And he added to Geoffrey, "Get into the car, lovey."

Geoffrey got into the front of the car, beside Ambrose and Aleko. Since nobody else seemed about to do it, I said, "This is Waldemar." "Hullo," said Geoffrey, staring at him rudely and briefly, as much as to say: If you don't talk English, I can't be bothered to acknowledge your existence. Waldemar grinned cheerfully and answered, "How *do* you *do?*"—one of his very few English phrases. When Geoffrey didn't grin back or seem to think this charming, I found myself beginning not to like him.

We bumped slowly through the olive grove. The track came out of it suddenly, on the very edge of the shore. Ambrose had to tug at the hand brake with all his might, or we should have slithered down the steep slope and into the water. The car squealed, gave a final lurch and stopped dead. For a moment the world seemed unnaturally quiet. Then little sounds intruded—the hasty lick-licking of small waves on the stone. Ambrose fumbled with shaking fingers in his pocket for matches and a cigarette. "Well," he said to me, "here we are, ducky."

He got out of the car unsteadily and opened the door on my side. A suitcase and a roll of wire netting fell out at his feet, while a bucket clattered down the slope to the edge of the waves. Ambrose didn't attempt to retrieve it; he sat down abruptly on the running board as though his legs had failed him. The rest of us got out; Hans, Waldemar and I extracting ourselves stiffly from the ruins of the luggage.

"There you are," Geoffrey told me, pointing. "There's our charming little Devil's Island."

"It's called St. Gregory," Ambrose said.

The island lay perhaps half a mile from where we stood; it was closer to the mountainside, where the cliffs rose sheer from the sea. Beyond it was the wide blue roadstead, and along the horizon to the northeast rose the peaks of Euboea. It was a compact whaleshaped lump of land, half bald, half wooded, with a humped back.

"I wonder if they've seen us," said Ambrose, looking across at the island. As he spoke, he reached into the car and squeezed the rubber bulb of the horn. There was a hoarse, throaty honk—the kind of sound which might have been uttered by a very old bird. Geoffrey laughed contemptuously.

"My good fool—you don't expect them to hear *that?*" Putting his hand into his pocket, he wrenched something out of it; then, stepping back a couple of paces, brandished what I now saw was a little automatic pistol above his head. "This'll damn well wake them up!" With bloodshot, listening eyes fixed on Ambrose's face, he stood aiming into the air. "Look out for yourselves!" he cried. "One! Two—!"

Aleko was jumping about in excited anticipation. Hans muttered, *"Total verrueckt!"* Ambrose asked mildly, "Lovey, haven't you got the safety catch locked?"

"Curse and bugger it!" Geoffrey wrenched furiously at the pistol. "All right now—stand back, everyone! One . . . two . . . three!" The shot crashed out, startlingly violent in that quiet place, and back volleyed the echo from the sheer cliffs of the shore—against which the waves rose and spread themselves and withdrew, rose and spread and withdrew, like an opening and withdrawing hand. A distant sheep dog began barking frantically from somewhere behind the grove. Other dogs answered him, very faintly, high up on the mountainside.

Nothing happened.

"They're probably taking a nap," said Ambrose.

66

"A *nap?* I never heard anything so bloody bogus! They're your servants, aren't they? My dear man, if you take that attitude, you'll end up bringing them their morning tea in bed. . . . What do you propose to do now, for Christ's sake?"

"Wait for them."

"*Wait* for them? And suppose they don't show up for a couple of days?"

"I don't quite see what else we can do, ducky."

Geoffrey gave a snort of disgust. "I don't know what brought you to this filthy country," he said to me. "But unless you're actually hiding from the police, I advise you to get out of it at once, before you go raving mad like the rest of us. . . . Ambrose, I don't propose to wait for your beastly little minions on this loathsome *plage*. Besides, if I don't have another drink within five minutes, I shall become unmanageable. That's a warning."

"There's not the slightest necessity to warn me, my dear Geoffrey. We'll walk back and have all the drinks you want."

"Why not drive?"

"Because, sooner or later they'll see the car. And then they'll know we're here. . . . Christopher, are you coming?"

"I think I'll stay here," I said. I felt a sudden desire, after the strains of the journey, to take a nap. Ambrose then asked Hans and Waldemar if they wanted to come. Waldemar said, No, he would stay with me. Hans went off with the others.

Waldemar and I stood looking at the island.

"Man!" said Waldemar, squeezing my arm. "We're in *Greece!* Imagine! We're in *Greece!*" Then, evidently repeating the name of some film he had seen, he added wonderingly, as if to himself: "The Mysterious Island." He picked up a pebble and skimmed it. "Do you suppose there are sharks, Christoph?"

"No."

"Then why don't we swim across?"

"It's further than it looks."

"I'm going swimming anyhow. Come on."

"Not now," I said. I felt a kind of superstitious awe, hard to define, which made me unwilling to enter this alien water. But Waldemar had no such qualms. He stripped off his clothes in a moment; his body was white after the city winter and looked startlingly naked. He ran splashing boldly into the water. "It's *warm!*" he shouted, amazed. Then he began swim-

67

ming strongly away into the dazzle of light. He was almost invisible.

I dozed on the stony beach, uncomfortably, with my jacket for a pillow, and was presently awakened by the sound of approaching hoofs. A train of small, delicately stepping donkeys straggled by, ridden by women and girls who wore scarves covering their mouths, like yashmaks. The effect was excitingly oriental. Just as the cavalcade was passing, Waldemar came swimming back to shore. Without hesitation, he waded out of the water stark naked, holding one hand over his genitals, and grabbed up his shirt.

"Man!" He giggled. "Did you see how those girls looked at me? I'll bet they've never seen a blond German boy before!"

Meanwhile, at some unperceived moment, the afternoon had lost its glare. The sun had moved around behind the ridges of the mountain, and the beach now lay in the mountain shadow. Out on the roads, the sea still sparkled, the peaks of Euboea still showed hazy in the heat; but here on the beach it had turned almost chilly. "Come on," I said to Waldemar, who had finished dressing, "let's go and find the others."

Ambrose, Geoffrey, Hans and Aleko were sitting drinking under one of the pine-branch arbors. Besides the resinated wine, they had gobbets of liver and cheese, slices of orange, raw beans dipped in salt, and Turkish delight. Waldemar and I ate the Turkish delight greedily, and Waldemar, instructed by Ambrose, repeated "*loukoumi*" over and over again.

"When did you buy this island?" I asked Ambrose, and was immediately conscious of the strangeness of talking in a tone of social chitchat while sitting in this booth, which looked like something out of the Old Testament.

"Actually, I haven't bought it. I *want* to buy it. But, you see, the trouble is that it's part-owned by every member of the village near here—just over on the other side of the hill. There's three hundred and nineteen of them. They all have to agree, if it's to be sold. And the idea of having to agree about *anything* just throws the poor dears into a tailspin. I mean, *not* agreeing is their whole philosophy of life. We've been negotiating for months already. Unfortunately, to make matters worse, they're all convinced one's a millionaire, so they make the most insane propositions. They say I can have the island if I'll supply the entire village with electric light. Or if I'll build a bridge across from the mainland—which incidentally, would be one of the engineering wonders of the world. And they've split into two parties—one in favor of selling, the other against. The opposition party claims that I'm a spy and that I want the island as a base for the British fleet. I don't think they *really* believe that—but now it hardly matters what they believe and what they only pretend to, because the whole thing has turned into a game. So one just has to be patient. As a matter of fact, I do think I'm slowly beginning to wear them down. . . . Here comes the priest now. He's my most important ally—"

He indicated a heavy dark man who was just seating himself at a table within another of the arbors; he was bearded and long-haired and wore a black serge gown and elastic-sided boots. Several men hurried to provide him with wine and food, which he accepted with a benevolent gesture. "I'd better go over and speak to him," said Ambrose, "or he'll think I'm plotting something against him behind his back. He's too ridiculously touchy." He rose and went over to the priest, who greeted him majestically.

"Bloody heathen popery!" Geoffrey muttered.

He seemed to be speaking to himself rather than to me; but I felt curious about him, and this was a good moment to start a conversation, especially since Hans and Waldemar were giggling together over German jokes.

"You don't seem to like this place much," I said.

"*Like* it? What is there to like about it?" Geoffrey had turned on me indignantly. "Will you tell me one single damned thing?"

"Then why do you stay here?"

"What the devil's that got to do with it? Where do you expect me to stay? Where else do you suggest I should go?"

"Well—there's quite a lot of other places, I would have thought."

"Oh, *you would have thought*, would you?" Geoffrey thrust his face close to mine with an aggressiveness which wasn't unpleasant because it showed a kind of touching desperation. "*Quite a lot of places*, eh? I suppose you'd include England and France and Germany and Russia and the United States of America?"

"I might."

"Then that just proves you don't know what you're talking about. Or rather, what *I'm* talking about. And if you don't

69

know what I'm talking about I suggest we drop this discussion."

"All right."

"Well, thank God you're not the argumentative type, anyhow. I can't stand people who argue with me. Ambrose does it all the time. . . . You'll just have to take my word for it, my dear fellow—there *isn't* any other place."

"But you told me to get out of here as soon as possible."

"I told *you*. That's entirely different. You aren't me. Or *are* you?"

I laughed. "I don't think so."

"And I don't think so, either. In fact, I'm bloody well sure you aren't."

"How long have you been here, Geoffrey?" I asked, to change the subject.

"I forget. A few months. Why?"

"You met Ambrose here?"

"Ran across him in Athens. At least, I didn't *run*. I passed out in some ghastly squalid bar. And then I woke up again, and there he was, sitting opposite me."

"Does he invite strangers to come and live on this island?"

"I didn't say Ambrose and I were strangers. Where did you get that idea?"

"Oh—I see. You'd known each other before?"

"Want to know everything, don't you?" said Geoffrey, with a sudden return to his aggressiveness.

"The funny thing is, I found *I'd* met him before. It was while we were both up at Cambridge."

For the first time, Geoffrey seemed interested in our conversation. He asked abruptly, "What college?"

I told him.

"You remember Halloween of 1923—when someone put a chamber pot on the pinnacle of your chapel?"

"Why, yes—now that you mention it—yes, I do."

"No one ever found out who it was." Geoffrey smiled to himself with quiet satisfaction. "Roddy Calhoun, who'd climbed in the Alps—at least, that's what he claimed—said, 'That bloody chapel is worse than anything on the Matterhorn. There's no way up the blasted thing,' he said, 'unless you use *pitons*.' He was damn well right, too."

"Then how do you suppose this man did it?"

"I don't suppose. I know. Jumped—from the roof of the library. That's a good seven feet, with practically no take-off.

And getting back is worse, because of the parapet. I slipped and had to make a grab for it. Nearly dislocated my arm."

"You mean—it was you?"

"Well, obviously."

"I suppose this is a silly question, but—what makes someone do a thing like that?"

"It *is* . . . a bloody silly question." But Geoffrey didn't seem to be annoyed with me for asking it, and almost at once he continued, "I mean, one's got to do *something*, hasn't one? And all the things people tell you you ought to do—they're so damned bogus. . . . Besides, that blasted pinnacle annoyed me every time I went by your college and looked at it. And so did Calhoun—that mustache of his; I suppose he thought it made him look like a bloody cavalry officer. I couldn't stand his attitude. Thought he knew everything; bloody superior ass. His friends made me sick, too, the way they buttered him up. Like a pack of schoolgirls. Bragging about how they'd wrecked someone's rooms because they didn't like his ties or his pictures. Not one of them would ever do anything alone —only while the others were watching. What's the good of anything you haven't got the guts to do by yourself? So I said to myself, I'll bloody well show them—"

"They must have been pretty impressed when they knew you'd done it?"

"But they never did know! Christ, do you think I'd have *told* them? You think I wanted to impress those swine? I did it for myself, not them. . . . Matter of fact, you're the first person I've ever told. And God knows why I'm telling *you*."

Geoffrey obviously didn't expect me to thank him for the confidence. But, as I had to make some sort of comment, I said, "You must have felt pretty wonderful—knowing you'd done it and no one else knew."

"That's where you're bloody well wrong," Geoffrey told me, with a vehemence which surprised me. "It wasn't wonderful. It wasn't anything. It didn't do any good. It didn't make any difference, at all."

Before I could ask him what he meant by this, Ambrose returned to our table. He told us that the priest had commanded one of the villagers to take us across to the island in his boat. The boat was in a cove on the other side of the village; its owner had already started off to get it.

"Well, how soon will it be here?" Geoffrey asked impatiently.

"No idea, lovey," said Ambrose, placidly smiling. "But I suppose it won't take more than two or three hours."

By the time we got word that the boat had landed at our beach, it was nearly night. We walked slowly and drunkenly down to the shore. As we came out of the olive grove, I became aware that a stiff breeze was blowing; the waves on the shore were much bigger and we all got wet while clambering into the boat, which was laden deep in the water with the baggage we had brought in the car. The old man who owned the boat got the outboard motor started. We began to hit the waves; the water was really rough.

The island grew gradually nearer. As we looked towards it, we saw, in the midst of its blackness, two moving sparks of light.

"Good," said Ambrose. "They've seen us."

"*Good?*" exclaimed Geoffrey. "Is that all you can say— *good?* Do you realize what this means, my dear man? *They were on the island all the time!*"

"It does seem like it, doesn't it?"

"In that case, they ought to be hung up by their thumbs and thrashed."

Ambrose merely smiled.

The waves now began splashing into the boat and we shipped a lot of water, which Aleko and Waldemar bailed out again with cans, thoroughly enjoying themselves. Geoffrey cursed. Ambrose, who was in the bows, got wetter than any of us. Yet his attitude, as he reclined on the angular pile of baggage, was almost languid. In the midst of this confusion, he seemed perfectly relaxed.

"You know," I told him, with drunken admiration, "I can quite imagine you getting out and walking on the water."

Again he smiled.

Now, as we came under the lee of the island, we no longer felt the wind, though the sea still ran high. On the rocks of the shore, the two boys were plainly visible; they swung their lanterns wildly back and forth. Aleko shouted to them. They shouted back. All of them were making as much noise as they knew how. Landing was a tricky business. There was a place where the rocks made a natural harbor pool, but you could only ride into it on the crest of a wave. Our old fisherman miscalculated slightly, and we scraped the rocks as we went

72

over. A few moments later, we were scrambling out of the boat.

We started up a steep trail. Behind us, the folded tent was being carried by the boys, like an enormous dead body. The flickering of their lanterns gave our procession an air of nocturnal melodrama. Being now in the mood for making biblical associations, I thought that it was like a painting of the descent from the cross—except that we were going uphill. Above us towered a small but sheer cliff, so heavy with bushes and the half exposed roots of trees—in addition to the weightless but massive tangle of its shadows—that it seemed about to topple upon us. I had an extraordinary sense of tropical enchantment, which was heightened by what I took to be the cries of jungle birds from the cliff-top, above.

What with the drunkenness and the dark, it's difficult to remember just what I did and did not notice that first night. I was certainly aware of the two huts. They stood on a flat natural clearing, a bald spot, on top of the cliff, and were in fact nothing more than pine-branch shelters of the local type, draped over with rubber ground sheets. As for the jungle birds, they proved to be domestic chickens and ducks which had been roosting in the bushes and were now making indignant noises before settling back to sleep; our arrival had disturbed them. In front of the huts stood a kitchen table and several wooden packing cases to be used as stools. Ambrose, Geoffrey, and I sat down and started drinking at once; we had brought wine with us in the boat.

Geoffrey seemed to have a genius for sustained indignation; he was still furious with the two boys and demanded that Ambrose should cross-examine them immediately, to find out why they hadn't come over to fetch us. The boys were about the same age as Aleko—though one of them, Theo, looked a little older because he wore a mustache. He was the best-looking of the three. Petro was plump, cheerful and spotty. It was clear that they both regarded Aleko as their leader.

The inquiry at once turned into a game and a huge joke, although Ambrose was obviously doing his best to get to the bottom of the affair. He concentrated all his energy upon Theo and Petro, pressing them with questions in his stammering-fluent Greek and smiling with good-humored exasperation at their obviously absurd excuses. Aleko got into the act, interrupting Ambrose with grotesquely exaggerated gestures. The other boys screamed with laughter at this. Geoffrey, beside himself with impatience, kept asking, "What are the little beasts saying, for Christ's sake? For God's sake, man, stop that jabbering and tell me!"

Finally, Ambrose turned to us and announced: "The boat's sunk, apparently. In shallow water. Somewhere on the other side of the island. It doesn't sound very serious. We'll take a look in the morning."

"*Not serious?*" Geoffrey roared. "They sunk the boat, and it's not serious? If it's not serious, tell them to bloody well go and mend it, this instant, or you'll make them swim ashore."

"They can't very well mend it in the dark, can they?"

"Well, how did they sink it, in Christ's name? Or don't you want to hurt their feelings by asking them?"

"Well, that's what I can't quite understand. There seems to be some extraordinarily complicated story about a corkscrew. At least, I *think* they're saying corkscrew. I'm not absolutely certain what this particular word means. But I'm pretty sure it means corkscrew, and that's what's so puzzling—"

"Nonsense! They mean they were *screwing*. They were screwing somebody or something. Each other, most likely. Loathsome little sodomites—"

"My dear Geoffrey, you *must* learn that on the island of St. Gregory that kind of talk simply cannot be tolerated—"

"Sodomites. That's the name for them and that's what I intend to call them—"

"Lovey, do I ever insult those raddled, noisomely perfumed females you produce whenever we go to Athens?"

"I don't give a damn who you insult. A sodomite's a sodomite—"

At this point, Hans and Waldemar appeared with a ham they had just unpacked. It had got wet and was saltier than hams usually are. I didn't care. We cut slices off it and stuffed them into our mouths, suddenly and fiercely hungry. I don't remember anything more about the evening.

[*From my diary: the entries have no dates.*]

Christ, I have a hang-over! Not that that's new. I always have a hang-over in the mornings here. I am writing this on one of the packing cases in front of the huts and the sun is shining down with an appalling vertical intensity. I can feel the whole island throbbing with my head. By night it is huge and mysterious. By day it is very small, a tiny, dry crumb of land in the midst of the unthirstquenching sea. At this time of day, the mountains around the gulf have paled and paled to the point where they fade right out; all you see is the ghostly shine of snow streaks on the sides of Mount Dherfis. Ambrose says they will melt very soon.

This island is covered with a wiry kind of grass which gets into your clothes, working its way through the cloth and suddenly pricking you like a needle. The grasses are so dry that they rustle metallically in the breeze. Chickens and ducks poke around everywhere; they make messes on our beds. And there is a goat which eats the thatch of the huts. It stands watching me now, motionless in a narrow strip of shadow; a lean, black, shaggy-legged devil with goblin teeth and slanting Levantine eyes.

Waldemar and I spent our first morning putting up the tent and digging a latrine hole amongst the bushes. I wanted to get this finished while Waldemar was still in his strip-to-the-waist, young pioneer mood. I know how long his enthusiasms last.

Waldemar says: "I'm going to learn to speak Greek like a nigger" (meaning native), and "You and I are going to explore every bit of this island, Christoph. Who knows if we won't find an oil well or a diamond mine? If we do, we won't be selfish, will we? We'll let Ambrose have half of it—well, no—a third."

On the ridge of the island, a gang of workmen from the village are building Ambrose his house. It is to have a reservoir for rainwater; and this has to be dug within the foundations, to check evaporation. The day after our arrival, Ambrose went up to inspect the progress of the work during his absence. He found that they'd already started building the walls of the house without having dug out a pit for the reservoir. The workmen and Ambrose had a big scene about this, part serious, part clowning, with much shouting and hand-flapping. According to Ambrose, the gist of it was as follows:

"How can you dig the pit now? The walls will be in your way. You can't move the earth out."

"Doesn't matter. Quite simple. Just a little dynamite."

"But the dynamite will blow the walls down."

"Never mind. We build them up again."

Ambrose tells this with pride—possessive pride. He feels

75

that he owns these people—their charm, their unreliability, their madness; everything about them. And, in a sense, he does, since it is he who is interpreting them to us. In a sense, this place is merely the projection of his will.

Despite all his talk about peacocks and other amenities, he wouldn't seriously care if this house never got built at all. What he enjoys is the situation, exactly as it is at this moment.

He has assigned roles to all of us. Hans is supposed to cook, with Waldemar to help him. The boys are supposed to fetch and carry, under Aleko's direction. Geoffrey is supposed to make as much fuss as possible. (I already realize how necessary this is to Ambrose's way of life.) I am supposed to write my novel. (Rather as the hens are supposed to lay eggs; not so much for consumption as to create a general atmosphere of productiveness.)

And what is Ambrose's role? He presides over, but he doesn't exactly run this community. In a way, it runs itself. Or it is run, as you might say, by the spirit of the island. But, since Ambrose is the only person who knows what the spirit of the island wants at any given moment—he is, as it were, its priest—you have to receive and obey the orders which are issued through his mouth.

The water from our one well is brackish. The earthenware cups stink of it. It has given me a stomach ache.

When we have eaten supper, we sit out in front of the huts, at the kitchen table, around the lamp, unhurriedly getting drunk. As soon as the lamp has been placed on the table, this becomes the center of the world. There is no one else, you feel, anywhere. Overhead, right across the sky, the Milky Way is like a cloud of firelit steam. After the short, furious sunset breeze, it gets so still that the night doesn't seem external; it's more like being in a huge room without a ceiling.

Another thing that gives you a feeling of indoors is the rats. They infest the huts and are constantly scuttling about, just outside the circle of lamplight. Sometimes, we throw things at them.

Ambrose, Geoffrey, Hans and I sit drinking on the packing cases. Aleko and Petro hover around. Waldemar is going through a craze for fishing. He and Theo spend their evenings in a boat offshore, with an acetylene flare to lure the fish to the surface; then the boys try to spear them. Neither Theo nor Waldemar is good at this, both of them being city boys.

They often fall into the water. But they have a lot of fun.

Aleko is always interrupting our talk. His voice is certainly maddening, but I feel excused from minding it because Geoffrey hates it so intensely. Aleko is well aware of this. Whenever he has emitted a particularly nerve-scraping shriek of glee, he rolls his eyes at Geoffrey, who never fails to react. "Shut up, you loathsome little beast!"

"Sher-ter lose-um litt beeze!" Aleko mimics, delighted.

"It's all your fault," exclaims Geoffrey, turning on Ambrose. "Why do you talk to them in that foul pidgin dago? It only encourages them. Why don't you teach them to speak a white man's language?"

"My dear Geoffrey, must you always be so shatteringly British?"

"I'll be as British as I bloody well want to be."

"I Britiss!" Aleko interrupts, either partly understanding or —which is much more likely—reading some altogether incorrect and dirty meaning into Geoffrey's words. "Aleko Britiss! Ah, na na!" He wags his finger at Geoffrey, who makes a drunken, poorly timed attempt to hit him. Aleko jumps easily out of range. Geoffrey overbalances from his packing case and falls on his back.

"Ambrose," he gasps, scrambling furiously to his feet, "will you at least order your obscene little paramour to keep his voice down? My nerves are about to snap. I warn you. I'm quite apt to tear his throat out with my bare hands."

"Really, lovey—this is not a medieval castle! These are not my serfs. Everybody on this island has equal rights, which I insist on respecting. And, as I've told you a thousand times, I must decline *all* responsibility for anybody else's behavior— including yours."

"Do you know what you are? A bleeding bolshevik! Why don't you sing the 'Internationale'? Get out that hammer and sickle, *tovarisch!* Come on, now—show us that bogus sickle!"

"Ducky, how often must I explain to you that I am not a bolshevik? I never was a bolshevik. I am an anarchist. In point of fact, I am diametrically opposed to the bolsheviks. In Russia—"

"Not listening!" cries Geoffrey, stopping up his ears. "Go on spouting tripe all night, if you want to. Can't hear a word you say!"

"In Russia, all anarchists have long since been liquidated, as deadly enemies of the regime—"

"Can't hear a word!" Geoffrey bawls, shutting his eyes tight and drumming on the packing case with his heels.

"Lovey, one does rather wish that you'd at least read your Kropotkin—"

"Tripe! Tripe!"

"Take what's happening in Germany—"

"All right!" Geoffrey instantly removes his fingers from his ears. "Take Germany!" He leans across the table toward Ambrose until their faces almost touch. At moments like this, you see how dependent Geoffrey is on Ambrose for his continued vitality. almost for his very ability to go on living. Their seriocomic conflict, which can never end and in which neither can ever be the loser, recharges him and gives him strength. "Take Hitler! I suppose a bloody bogus bolshevik like you thoroughly disapproves of Hitler! Now come on—do you or don't you? Of course you do! Well, allow me to tell you, Hitler's a bloody sound man! At least he's cleared out all these damned bolsheviks—"

"Even if that were true, which I—"

"Tripe! Tripe! Tripe! Tripe!" Geoffrey stops up his ears again. "Tripe! Tripe! Tripe! Tripe! Tripe!"

Throughout all of this, Hans hasn't said a word. He never speaks unless he has to while Geoffrey is present. He sits smiling into his glass, in a way that makes him appear enigmatic and meditative; more likely he is just dazed.

That Hans should dislike Geoffrey isn't at all surprising, for Geoffrey behaves to him like a rude child. Geoffrey refers to Hans as "von Bloggenheimer" when talking to Ambrose. He keeps up an incredibly babyish pretense that Hans's name, Schmidt, is too difficult and foreign for him to remember! But even if Geoffrey were nice to Hans, I still believe that Hans would dislike him. I am sure that he's jealous—of the influence he thinks Geoffrey has on Ambrose. How can he be so stupid? Even after these few weeks on the island, I already know that nobody could influence Ambrose—that butterfly with wings of steel.

I imagine that Hans, with the traditions of the Prussian drill sergeant in his blood, looks on Ambrose as his commander-in-chief, a privileged being whose function it is to be eccentric, like Frederick the Great. Waldemar is Hans's corporal. Theo and Petro are privates in his platoon, awkward and insubordinate and incurably unmilitary. Hans roars at them, whacks them with his big cooking spoon, throws pots at them, chases them around the island and, I presume, goes to bed with them. They understand each other perfectly; their relationship seems uncomplicated, animal and innocent.

Hans's relations with Aleko are much more mysterious. I keep noticing signs of this tension between them. They would never clown or play around together. They are cautious of each other and sometimes almost polite.

Consciously or unconsciously, Ambrose encourages jealousy. He has the coquetry of the benevolent despot. His coquetry consists in a display of impartiality when ever a quarrel arises. Since one person in the quarrel is usually in the wrong and the other in the right, his impartiality amounts to favoring the one who's in the wrong. I experienced this myself yesterday, when I got furious with Theo in the boat—

No—that story's too childish. I'm ashamed to write it down.

Nearly every morning, very early, I get up and go swimming. If possible I do this without waking Waldemar, because I treasure this first hour when, for the only time in the day, I am quite alone. (Ambrose may well be awake, but he never shows himself. He stays in his hut and, I suppose, reads, smokes and takes a few first drinks. I have never yet seen him go in the water.) I also enjoy this swim because it is the only one I can take naked. Ambrose, who is surprisingly—but, no doubt, wisely—sensitive to local prejudices, despite his declarations of our individual freedom on this island, tells me that the builders were greatly shocked when they heard how Waldemar stripped on the beach and swam, our first afternoon. (Like everything else we do, this has doubtless been circulated through all the villages of the district and discussed by several hundred people.) Nakedness is one of the features of classical culture which the present-day Greeks appear to have rejected. When any of the builders swim, they keep on their long cotton underpants.

I climb cautiously down the rocks—they are lava-sharp and cut you deeply if you slip—and ease myself into the water. At this hour it is almost unrippled and has a luminous, bluish milk-skin. I don't duck my head under. Because I have a feeling that, as long as I don't break the skin of the water, the morning spell will remain unbroken; the world will remain magically unreal—the mountains and shore just coming into being, forming themselves out of empty light; the fishing boats floating on air. The water is very salt and buoyant, and I can swim far out. Then I lie on my back and look at the sky.

These seas and this shore can't have changed very much in the past two thousand years. A classical Greek, looking out from the olive groves and seeing me in the middle distance, couldn't possibly suspect that I wasn't his time-fellow. This is a thought which ought to be thrilling, but which actually isn't, in the least. I couldn't care less, here, about classical Greece; I feel far more remote from it than I ever do in Northern Europe.

But Northern Europe is becoming remote, too; quite shockingly so. The first time we went into Chalkis on a shopping excursion, not long after our arrival, I kept pestering Ambrose to translate the news bulletin which was coming over the wireless in the café where we had drinks. He was patient and good-humored about doing this, although, obviously, he wasn't really interested. The news was terrible; and, by this time, it's probably much worse. There may easily be war with Hitler this year, or next. I say this and believe it, but somehow I can no longer quite care. When we go into Chalkis, I no longer worry about the wireless or ask Ambrose to translate the newspaper headlines. We never take a newspaper on this island. Ambrose goes on talking about anarchism, fascism, communism, etc., but he uses the words only in reference to his world, not to the one outside. And now I am beginning to live, more and more, in Ambrose's world. When I admit this to myself, I feel I ought to feel guilty. But I don't.

Spread-eagled on my back on the surface of the water, looking up into the sky, I know almost nothing but now and here. Even this body I'm floating in might as well be that of a teen-age boy or a healthy old man—myself at seventeen or seventy; I would scarcely be aware of the difference. Normally, I'm very much aware of my age, because my mind is busy with anxiety about the future and regrets about the past. But not now, not here. In Berlin, I wrote a novel about England. Here, I want to get on with my novel about Berlin; but already I know that I shan't. All I can possibly write nowadays is this diary, because, here, one can only write about this place.

Swimming back to the shore, I keep a lookout for jellyfish. They are very much a part of now and here; and if they sting you, Hans says, you will be sick for a week. The other morning the surface of the sea was covered with them, however, and Theo and Petro went swimming—despite the warnings of the rest of us—and took no harm. I thought this proved that Hans was wrong. But Geoffrey had a different theory: "I always suspected those two weren't human. Now I'm sure of it! Did you see how those obscene jellyfish positively fawned on them? *They* knew! You don't believe me? All right, I'll bloody well prove it to you. . . . I suppose you'll admit that this place is unmitigated and utter hell, as far as normal human beings are concerned? Well—what sort of creatures are at home in hell? Devils, obviously! Devils don't mind the heat—they fairly revel in it. And they can't be stung by jellyfish. Very well then, what else can those two be?"

Soon after I get back to the tent, Petro, sometimes accompanied by Aleko and Theo, brings in coffee. This must be drunk at once while it's hot, otherwise it becomes impossibly bitter and nasty. The coffee is to wake Waldemar, so he can go to the kitchen and help Hans. Waldemar is bone-lazy in the mornings and never wants to get up; but the three boys accept this and don't seem to mind waiting on him. The four of them are already great friends. "Walli!" shrieks Petro. "*Cusina! Vasaria!*" (I don't have any idea how I should write this, but some such words mean "Kitchen" and "trouble," or maybe "anger"; the joke being that Hans is supposed to be angry because Waldemar is late for work.) And then Waldemar is coaxed and finally dragged out of bed, yelling and fighting. It's a relief when at last he grabs his trousers and shirt and stumbles out of the tent, dressing as he goes.

If you keep the tent closed during the day, you can't stay inside it long because of the heat. If you open it, you let in the flies. There are big hopping beetles which keep thudding on the tent roof like raindrops. The sound is so realistic that it sometimes fools me into believing that for some miraculous reason it is raining in the midst of the blazing sunshine. But when I stick my head out, there is the prickly, tinder-dry island and the hard gem sea. The very thoughts in your head seem almost annihilated by the blazing intrusion of the sky. You're not aware of the sun itself; it's too directly above you.

Over in the ruined cottage without a roof, Hans and Waldemar are cooking. Hans wears a greasy old hat belonging to Ambrose. He stirs a broth of goat's meat with a stick. When he approaches the rough wooden shelf on which the other food stands, the flies rise up in clouds, buzzing furiously. But the only constant sound is the shrilling of the cicadas. If you let yourself listen to it for long, it becomes extraordinarily disturbing, like millions of tiny telephones which nobody answers.

Suddenly there will be wild shouts from the hilltop. The workmen are warning us of a dynamite blast. (But since they never do this until the very last moment, they might save themselves the trouble; there's no time to take cover.) They have finished blasting out the foundations for the reservoir; now they are quarrying for stone to use in the building. Despite all their experience, they seem to have no idea how much dynamite they should use. It is always far too little or too much. We become completely indifferent to their yells of warning, followed by an absurd little firecracker pop. And then, just when you're least expecting it, there will be a stunning explosion which shakes the whole island and sends big rocks spinning through the air, bombarding our huts and tents and even splashing into the sea. A couple of times things have been smashed, but no one has been hurt, so far.

The workmen take a great interest in all our activities. Two of them came into the tent the other day and stood there a long time watching me type and laughing and making comments, exactly like tourists in a native quarter watching a craftsman engaged in his quaint craft. When they came in, I had been trying to write a letter to my mother and had just decided to give it up, because it is actually impossible to write about this island to anybody who has never been here. Once you have described it, there is no way of making your correspondent understand why you didn't leave it again instantly, five minutes after your arrival. I couldn't stop typing as long as the workmen were watching me; it would have spoiled their fun. So I went on banging out quotations, nonsense and dirty words, never taking my eyes from the machine or giving any sign I knew they were there, until they got bored and left.

The better I get to know Ambrose, the more he amazes me. He is never idle from morning till night. Even when he is drinking, he manages to make an occupation of it. He always has this simple, modest air of being occupied.

Frequently he suggests to Hans that we shall eat some incredibly nasty kind of food because it is so cheap. Hans puts this down to stinginess, but I think it is sheer indifference.

Ambrose has the sort of indifference to discomfort and hardship which you would expect to find in a great hero or saint. And as he is quite unaware of this, he keeps expecting us to have it, too. If he were commanding soldiers and they refused to follow him on some absolutely hopeless campaign, he would never dream of accusing them of cowardice; he wouldn't think of them as cowards, even. He would merely say that they were "fussy."

Again and again he reminds me of one of Shakespeare's exiled kings; exiled, but by no means without hope. This is how he talks about his kingdom:

"Of course, when we do get into power, we shall have to begin by reassuring everybody. We must make it clear that there'll be absolutely no reprisals. Actually, they'll be amazed to find how tolerant we are. . . . I'm afraid we shan't be able to make heterosexuality actually legal, at first—there'd be too much of an outcry. One'll have to let at least twenty years go by, until all the resentment has died down. But meanwhile it'll be winked at, of course, as long as it's practiced in decent privacy. I think we shall even allow a few bars to be opened for people with those unfortunate tendencies, in certain quarters of the larger cities. They'll have to be clearly marked, with police at the doors to warn foreigners what kind of places these are—just so that no one shall find himself there by mistake and see something which might upset him. Naturally, from time to time, some tourist with weak nerves may have to be rushed to hospital, suffering from shock. We'll have a psychologist on hand to explain to him that people like that do exist, through no fault of their own, and that we must feel sympathy for them and try to find scientific ways of reconditioning them. . . . What most people don't realize is that, when we take over, women will be much better off, actually, than they are now. They'll be beautifully looked after on the breeding farms, as wards of the State. And, surely, most of them would greatly prefer artificial insemination, anyway? It's quite obvious that they have no real interest in men—beyond wanting to order them about—that's why they have no taste whatsoever when it comes to picking attractive ones. They just don't know men's points; they've no eye for them. Women are all Lesbians, really—they take naturally to all that ineffectual feminine messing about—cuddling and petting —the kind of thing Ingres shows so brilliantly in that Turkish bath painting of his—though, I must say, I never could look

83

at it without a shudder of cold horror."

Ambrose only talks like this when Geoffrey is present. As he speaks, he smiles teasingly at Geoffrey; and yet I feel that he is partly serious. For him, these statements have at least a sort of poetic truth. Geoffrey is the ideal audience for him. There is something childlike in Geoffrey which makes him able to believe in and enter into Ambrose's imaginary kingdom, as a child enters into the world of a fairy story. Nevertheless, he heckles Ambrose constantly, exclaiming "Old sodomist!" "Catamite keeper!" "Bugger man!"

As a matter of fact, Geoffrey loathes women in a way which only some heterosexuals can; Ambrose's mild distaste for them seems quite benevolent in comparison. Geoffrey betrays this loathing from time to time. Quite spontaneously, and without seeming to realize what he is admitting, he will mutter approvingly, "That's the spirit—that's the way to treat those bitches!"

No wonder Geoffrey loves to imagine himself in Ambrose's kingdom! To begin with, he would have unchallenged pick of all the women. Then, having enjoyed them in the privacy of the heterosexual ghetto, he could vent all his aggression on them in public as members of the slave sex. Indeed, it seems as if it were chiefly for Geoffrey's benefit that Ambrose's kingdom exists.

Waldemar has finally coaxed out of Hans the whole story of how he got his wounded hand and arm. I wish I could have been present to hear Hans tell it; we just don't know each other well enough. Anyhow, Hans probably meant Waldemar to pass it on to me. He never told him not to.

Hans began by describing his life with Ambrose since their first meeting. He said that Waldemar and I couldn't possibly imagine how wild, unmanageable and obstinate Ambrose becomes when he is in a large city, instead of being more or less out of temptation's reach, as he is on this island. Hans is wrong there; I can imagine it quite easily.

(As far as I can make out, Ambrose's obstinacy is chiefly expressed by his absolute demand for politeness. He demands it heroically, without the least fear of the consequences. He refuses to be threatened or bullied in any way. If you want him to give you money, you must either ask for it nicely or else beat him into unconsciousness and then pick his pocket. One would think it could never be too much trouble to say please. But unfortunately, Ambrose is trying to impose his demand on the sort of men and boys who frequent the toughest bars in the roughest parts of town. Such simplicity is too subtle for them; they suspect a trick. Instead of taking any chances, it must often seem to them much safer and more practical to beat Ambrose up.)

Hans says they've had this problem in every city they've been in. Whenever Ambrose was wandering around alone, he was in danger of getting into trouble; and it was impossible for Hans to keep track of him all the time. Ambrose had a trick of returning with Hans to their hotel and then leaving it again in the small hours of the morning, after Hans had gone to sleep. Or else Ambrose would keep Hans up so late that he would fall asleep at last over his drink and Ambrose would leave him; it must have been most humiliating for Hans to wake up in some outlandish bar, surrounded by the mocking faces of people who knew what had happened to him but couldn't or wouldn't tell him where Ambrose had gone. Hans doesn't think that Ambrose was consciously trying to give him the slip; he just couldn't stay put anywhere for very long.

Ambrose quite agreed with Hans—on general principles and when sober—that their way of life was unnecessarily hectic. And so, after they had arrived in Athens, they evolved between them a really bright idea. Ambrose would give up roaming from bar to bar running all these risks; he would have a bar of his own, where he could drink all night with Hans or a substitute to protect him and throw out undesirables. It was quite easy to arrange this, and not even very expensive. There were plenty of small bars to be had in the poorer districts of the city, at reasonable prices. There was only one problem. Ambrose's lawyer told them that it would be much simpler to deal with the police and the other municipal authorities if the legal owner of the bar were a Greek.

That was how Aleko came into the picture. Although Ambrose had only just met him, he was convinced that Aleko was an entirely suitable person to be cast in the role of bar proprietor. This sounds crazy, certainly; but one must remember that Ambrose is a Shakespearean king. Shakespearean kings—the kind that get themselves exiled—always have favorites. And it is a peculiarity of the king-favorite relationship that, in it, the king vents a sly aggression against his subjects by choosing the most unworthy favorite he can find and then egging him on to behave as badly as possible.

No sooner had the bar been found, the money paid down and the papers signed, than Aleko began to take full advantage of his official position. He put on the airs of a real proprietor. He took every opportunity of bossing Hans in public. (Hans says that Aleko was jealous of him from the first moment they met.) It was easy for Aleko to boss Hans, because Hans was the bartender in this new establishment and Aleko was therefore—on paper and in the eyes of the world—his employer.

One evening, not long after the opening of the bar, Hans, Ambrose and Aleko were drinking there alone. It was very late at night and the customers had all gone home. Hans had thought that the three of them were on the best of terms—or, at any rate, the best terms possible. Hans had got onto the subject of his mother, now dead, to whom he had been greatly attached. He doesn't remember exactly how the conversation went. It was complicated by being partly in German and partly in Greek. Hans says that he was doing his best to be nice to Aleko and include him as much as possible in their talk, so he spoke Greek whenever he could and only used German when he couldn't express himself otherwise. Then Ambrose would translate what had been said to Aleko. Aleko hadn't seemed much interested, anyway.

Hans remembers that he was talking, in mixed Greek and German, about his mother's fondness for honey; she lived in the country, near the Spreewald, and always kept bees. At this point, Aleko, who had been drinking and staring into space, apparently bored and not listening to Hans at all, had suddenly jumped to his feet. His face, says Hans, was like a wild animal's. Both Hans and Ambrose were too surprised to move. Aleko didn't say a word; he grabbed a bottle from the table and hit Hans over the head with it. The bottle broke, giving it a deadly jagged edge. Hans was half stunned, and the blood began to pour down his face. Aleko hit him again. Ambrose picked up a chair and drove Aleko back out of range. Aleko threw away the bottle and ran out of the bar.

Hans had been terribly cut. He fainted, and when he came to himself he was in hospital. The tendons of his left arm, which he had raised to guard his head, had been severed and his hand would be permanently crippled.

Ambrose came to visit him every day; and immediately they started an argument. Hans had begun it by vowing that he was going to find Aleko and kill him. "I'm going to strangle him to death," he said. "I'll show him I can do it one-handed." Ambrose objected—I can just hear the patient, good-humored obstinacy in his tone!—that this would only get Hans into very serious trouble. After a few more days of threats, Hans saw that Ambrose was right; so now he demanded that Ambrose should help him to prosecute Aleko for assault. Ambrose replied, gently but very firmly, that he couldn't possibly do this. As an anarchist, he couldn't recognize the authority of the police and the law under any circumstances. Hans then returned to his threats of violence. Ambrose told him he was being most unreasonable and inhumane; for obviously Aleko had been insane, and therefore not responsible for his action. Thereupon, Hans demanded that Aleko should at least be hunted down, certified and put under restraint as a dangerous madman. Ambrose replied that Aleko had now completely recovered. It was thus that Hans learned Aleko had shown up again and that Ambrose was seeing him regularly. Hans was furious. Ambrose was soothing. Hans demanded that Ambrose should at least give up seeing Aleko. Ambrose refused, saying that Aleko needed someone to keep an eye on him and that he, Ambrose, felt that this was his responsibility, especially after what had happened to Hans. Besides, he added, now that they had all had time to calm down, Hans really must try to look at the whole affair objectively and admit that he himself had been, at least a little bit, to blame. Hans was outraged. How could Ambrose have the nerve to suggest such a thing? "Well," said Ambrose—I can see that teasing little smile of his—"you know what Aleko says? He says you said his mother was a whore." "But I never said any such thing!" Hans gasped. "I was talking about *my* mother and her bees—you know I was!" "Yes," said Ambrose, "I know that, of course. But you mustn't be so hard on Aleko. You must make allowances. After all, lovey, you know you *do* make a lot of mistakes when you talk Greek. You might easily be misunderstood. And you can't say *that's* Aleko's fault—now, can you?"

At this point, it seems, Hans simply gave up. The whole affair was just too difficult. And, characteristically enough, as soon as Hans stopped protesting, Ambrose began tacitly admitting that he too had been to blame. Without saying anything to Hans in advance, he one day produced a legal document drawn up in German in which he promised to employ or otherwise support Hans for the rest of his life. Also, in the event of Ambrose's death, Hans was to have half of his estate. Hans was quite shrewd enough to realize that there were all sorts of legal holes in this agreement; but it impressed and touched him, nevertheless. He keeps it, he told Waldemar, in a bank in Athens.

Toward the end of Hans's convalescence, Ambrose brought Aleko round to see him. Aleko didn't make any kind of an apology; but Hans found this sincere and therefore preferable. They ended up by behaving as if nothing whatsoever had happened.

"But," Waldemar told me gravely, as he finished this story, "do you know what Hans says, Christoph? He says: 'I don't bear the boy any ill will. But one of these days I'm going to kill him or he's going to kill me. And Ambrose knows that. That's the way he wants it.'"

The boys are swinishly dirty, inhumanly destructive and altogether on the side of the forces of disorder. Waldemar is fascinated by them. His North German soul recoils from some of their dirtier habits, and their cruelty shocks him, up to a point. But they always end by making him laugh.

Theo and Petro caught an owl and started pulling out its feathers. Luckily, Hans saw them, and drove them away with kicks. They put a rabbit in a box without airholes and forgot about it; this I happened to find before it was too late. The three boys steal dynamite from the builders and make bombs which they explode in the sea, blowing fish to bits. Then they run around brandishing fish heads and tails and screaming with joy. When they washed up the dishes, they used to wipe them with the rag which Petro wears knotted round his greasy hair. Geoffrey saw them doing this and was so "fussy" that Ambrose gave orders that the dishes were not to be wiped at all, in future, but left in the sun to dry.

The boys delight in any kind of confusion or untidiness. If there is a sudden high wind, they furtively assist its actions. For example, a roll of toilet paper once got blown out of our tent and partially unrolled. Pretending to catch it for me, they kicked it hither and thither until the paper was festooned over all the nearby bushes. Last week there was a fire, undoubtedly caused by Aleko, who throws matches everywhere when he smokes. The fire broke out in the morning; and so, in the brilliant sunshine, the flames were nearly invisible. You kept treading on them or grabbing them in your hands. It took us nearly an hour to beat the fire out, and no wonder—several times I saw the boys grinningly fan the flames with their hats.

Only once have I known them to assist actively in any project; and that was a destructive one. It was when Ambrose and Hans decided to kill at least some of the rats.

(The rats swarm all over the inhabited part of the island. They seem to have increased about ten times since we arrived. They are as bold as dogs, and nothing is safe from them. Once they somehow managed to climb *upside down* along the horizontal beam at the top of our tent and get at a basket of melons which was hanging there. We are all accustomed to their running over our beds at night. Hans says that one night he dreamt he could move his fingers again. He woke to find that a rat was nibbling at his paralyzed hand!)

So, one evening, Ambrose had the traps set and arranged in a semicircle around the huts. Then he and Geoffrey and Hans sat down to drink and wait. I didn't much like the prospect of this pogrom, so I persuaded Waldemar to come out with me in the boat. But after a while neither of us could resist our curiosity to see what was going on. We found Ambrose and Hans sitting silent with dazed smiles, staring, as they so often do, at the lamp like clairvoyants probing a crystal ball. Geoffrey, however, was hugely excited; he kept shouting the score and encouraging the boys to raise it. "Eleven! Eleven! Come on, chaps! Got to do better than that! Do I hear twelve? Come on, let's make it twelve! What's wrong with these bloody vermin? Where are they hiding? Do they think they're going to keep us waiting all night? *Twelve!* Oh, good show! Twelve it is! Now then for the thirteenth! The unlucky rodent! Thirteen! Thirteen! Do I hear thirteen?"

In the darkness there was a continual snapping of the traps. Sometimes the rats escaped; sometimes they didn't, and the boys gleefully dropped them, inside the traps, into a bucket of water. They took a horribly long time drowning. Geoffrey enjoyed himself so much that he became quite friendly toward the boys—but only for that evening; next day he was himself again. They caught nineteen rats altogether. I'm sure these have long since been replaced by fresh recruits from other parts of the island.

Yesterday Geoffrey nearly left the island because of a row about a chicken. It was actually Hans who started the row—by hinting coyly to Geoffrey that the chicken we had just eaten for lunch had been raped by Petro before he killed it. I'm sure Hans wasn't prepared for the violence of Geoffrey's reaction; for a while I really thought he had gone out of his mind. He began roaring incoherently; and at the same time he pulled his pistol out and fired several shots at Petro, who happened to be passing, in the middle distance. The bullets went wide, and Petro never dreamt that Geoffrey was trying to hit him and that his life was in extreme danger. Taking it for granted that this was a game, he was delighted and flattered; for Geoffrey seldom condescends to take any notice of him at all. Roaring with laughter, he ran down to the rocks and dived into the sea with all his clothes on. Geoffrey got in a couple more shots at him in the water; then Hans intervened.

After this Ambrose was fetched, and the case explained to him; and Petro was cross-examined. He absolutely denied any part in the crime; though, obviously, he still thought it nothing to get so excited about. "And, after all, lovey," said Ambrose to Geoffrey, "the chicken *was* thoroughly cooked afterwards—"

Geoffrey answered that he was getting out of "this bloody obscene filthy Sodom" just as soon as he had packed his bags. But instead of doing this he got helplessly drunk; and today nothing more is said about his leaving.

I assumed that the chicken story had been invented by Hans, who takes a delight in teasing Geoffrey and would love to see him go. But no—Waldemar has now discovered the truth: Petro *is* innocent; Theo did it. Having told me this, Waldemar laughed aloud and said, "Man, what you learn abroad! Just imagine anybody doing such swinishness in Berlin!"

As for me, I am disgusted, of course. Not so much for reasons of prudery as because it was cruel to the chicken; and, yes, to be frank, because I ate some of it and the thought of this kind of indirect contact with Theo makes me want to throw up. Yet—it *had*, as Ambrose says, been thoroughly cooked. And—I can't help it—I'm grinning as I write this. . . .

What is this island doing to me?

This morning, I had a long conversation with Ambrose, alone. This is much more unusual and harder to accomplish than one would think. Of course, you can talk to Ambrose alone if you're prepared to sit up half the night—until Geoffrey and Hans have gone to bed—but by that time he has become vague with drink and doesn't make much sense. During the day he wants to be in the midst of everything; and so he tacitly encourages all of us to accost him whenever we feel like it, and tell him anything which happens to be on our minds, no matter how trivial it is. Therefore, though you can always speak to Ambrose, you must be prepared to be interrupted every few moments. And when an interruption is over, Ambrose has forgotten what you were saying to him—or pretends to have forgotten; so the conversation has to start again from the beginning.

But this morning, while I was strolling around—something I very seldom do now, what with the heat and my hang-overs, and an increasing lack of curiosity about the rest of the island—I came upon Ambrose, all by himself, among the rocks along the further shore. He told me he had discovered a rock pool which, he thought, might be enclosed by a wall and used as an aquarium.

"I thought it might be rather fun to have steps leading down here from the house. And then one might plant some trees and have a gazebo, where one could sit and drink wine, when one gets tired of the view from the other side. . . . What are you smiling at, lovey?"

"It's only—well, you always talk as if you were planning to spend the rest of your life here."

"Why shouldn't I?" Ambrose looked at me rather sharply.

"You told me yourself the village people can't agree if they should sell you the island or not. Perhaps they'll suddenly make up their minds to refuse. What'll you do then?"

"I do wish you wouldn't say things like that!" Ambrose exclaimed, quite angrily. "Why do you have to depress me and make me thoroughly miserable?"

"I'm dreadfully sorry, Ambrose. I'd no idea you minded. I'd rather got the impression from Hans that you enjoy moving around—"

"But I *hate* moving! It's *never* because I want to! I never want to move. I even feel depressed when I have to leave a hotel room, or a cabin on a boat. But they won't *let* one stay —*anywhere*—" I've never seen Ambrose upset like this before; there were actually tears in his eyes. "That's what makes most places utterly impossible—the people. They're so completely hateful. They want everybody to conform to their beastly narrow little way of looking at things. And if one happens not to, one's treated as something unspeakable. And then

91

there's nothing for it but to leave at once—"

Ambrose broke off abruptly, no doubt stricken by unpleasant memories of loud scenes with hotel managers, grim interviews with the police of various cities. Wishing to lead him tactfully back to a happier part of his past, I asked: "Were you sorry to leave Cambridge?"

But this question evidently *wasn't* tactful. Ambrose's face became suddenly suspicious. "What's Geoffrey been telling you?"

"Why, nothing. Nothing about *you*—I mean, about you at Cambridge. As a matter of fact, he never even told me if you knew each other there—" I made the last sentence into a half question; but Ambrose ignored it. He seemed reassured, however. His expression softened.

"I could have stayed at Cambridge forever. I even think I'd have liked being a don. I *could* have been one, you know. I came up with a very good scholarship. And my tutor said I was the most promising man of my year."

"Then why—?" I began, and checked myself as I realized that this probably meant he'd been sent down.

"England's impossible," Ambrose snapped—at first rather confirming my suspicions. "I'm never going back there. Never. Whatever happens." He gave me a challenging, hostile look, as if he expected me to protest, patriotically or otherwise. When I didn't, he continued: "I had such heavenly rooms. That part of the college is eighteenth century, and the old ceiling was still in, with the original moldings. And my windows looked out on the Backs. I did the sitting room over in emerald green—I don't know how it would look to one nowadays, but then it was madly fashionable—and I had nothing but green china; and I always kept green apples in a bowl on the table. Then I had a pair of Pamela Bianco engravings. And a really *good* marquetry bureau. And a lot of Venetian glass, which I loved because it had belonged to my grandmother, whom I adored. She left it to me when she died. . . . I was very proud of my fireplace; I got someone to come in and copy a design onto it—it was one of Vanessa Bell's book jackets for the Hogarth Press—all crisscrosses and curlicues. Oh, and there was a lovely old carpet which came from the Turkish Embassy in Paris. . . . The whole place was just my idea of heaven. *So* utterly perfect. Every morning, when I got out of bed and came in there for breakfast, I said to myself, this is *too* beautiful—

"And, you know, that was exactly what it was? Too beautiful. Too beautiful to be true. Because, you see, it *wasn't* true. I'd been living in a fool's paradise. I hadn't realized how horrible everything is—how really obscene people are—below the surface. They pretend to be so nice and friendly. And all the time, they're *swine—swine*—and how they *hate, hate, hate* everything they don't understand—

"This was in the Michaelmas term of 1923—when it happened. . . . I'd been to a dinner party—it was at the Master's Lodge. A dreadfully dull party, actually. Of course, one couldn't refuse; but I'd have much rather stayed in my rooms and read. I remember, I'd just discovered Ronald Firbank, and I couldn't put him down—

"Well, I got back—it was about eleven, I suppose—and I opened the door, and I just couldn't believe my eyes. That's what everybody says, I know. But what I mean is, I just couldn't explain to myself what I was seeing. It was so utterly improbable. Like a very elaborate surrealist joke. I might have been looking at some sort of insane collage in an art gallery —it wasn't like anything that actually happens to oneself. . . . Of course, after the first shock, I realized that it *had* happened. It had happened to *me*—

"The entire place was wrecked—literally everything. They'd broken all the china, all the glass. They'd smeared some filth on the walls, and over the pictures. They'd even found my little eggcup that I loved so. It was a present on my fourth birthday; and I kept it hidden away in a cupboard, because it didn't go with the color scheme. But I loved it all the more, because nobody but me ever saw it. Well, they'd taken it out—this little bit of my childhood—and they'd smashed it. How could they have *known* that I'd mind that most of all?

"For a long while, I just stood there, staring at it all. I was quite numb. I didn't feel anything. But then I began to be furious—*really* furious. I'd never known what it was to hate like that before. I felt as if everything—all my past life—had been smeared with their dirt. They'd put their filthy hands on it. And now I never, never wanted to have anything to do with it again. I suppose it was childish and hysterical of me, but I picked up a plate which they hadn't properly smashed, and I threw it on the floor and stamped on it.

"Of course, the next day I felt the whole thing much more, even. What I couldn't stop being amazed at was that these people—whom one had imagined never thought about one, or were even aware of one's existence—that they'd actually loathed one, without one's dreaming of it. That was so uncanny. It made me realize that I didn't understand Cambridge or England at all. I might as well have been living among a lot of Eskimos. We just didn't make sense together."

"So what did you do?"

"What *was* there to do?"

"You might at least have found out who'd done it."

"Oh, I knew *that*. There was a club in our college—hearties from the rugger fifteen and the college boat and so forth. They'd done this to several other people already. Wasn't it dreadful of me—I'd known that and I hadn't cared particularly? I'd just vaguely supposed the others had brought it on themselves. Made themselves obnoxious, somehow."

"Couldn't you have all got together and done something to these swine?"

"I suppose so, if one had all been Joans of Arc and William Tells, instead of me and a handful of terrified little men with the wrong accent, from the wrong schools. . . . But even if one *could* have wrecked the hearties' rooms, it wouldn't have been the same thing. They had nothing in them but photographs of themselves in teams, and brass toasting forks engraved with the college crest."

"So you never even said anything to them?"

"Only to one. One of them did come round the next day and offer me a check for the damage. He'd signed it already, and he told me to fill in the amount—any amount I liked. I know I was horrid to him, but I just couldn't control myself. I'm afraid I screamed at him. I told him that he and his friends thought they could buy their way out of anything. And that they probably could, most of the time. But that there'd always be a few people, like me, who knew they were *scum*; and nothing they could ever do would change that. And that in the end they'd get to know it themselves; and then all the things they'd bought with their filthy money would be no good to them. They'd know they were scum and they'd die knowing it. . . . And then I tore the check to bits, and told him to get out."

"Oh—*marvelous!*"

"Except that he was quite sweet, actually. I found out later he'd been prepared to pay the whole lot himself. He hadn't told the others he was coming to see me. I think he was really sorry. But of course, that couldn't have interested me less at the time. I loathed him so much I hardly even noticed what he looked like. In fact, I couldn't see anything around me any more; not even the college buildings and the places I used to love so. They'd all disappeared into a kind of fog of hate. . . . That was when I made up my mind to die—" Ambrose uttered his apologetic little laugh. Several tears had run down his face while he was telling this story; he wiped them away now, quite unashamedly, with his very dirty silk handkerchief. "The day you arrived, I told you I was dead. You didn't understand what I meant, did you? I meant, I'm dead as far as England and everybody in it is concerned. I got my guardian to let me leave Cambridge at once. And, as soon as I was twenty-one and had my own money, I cleared out of England. I've never been back. I never write. I never read their filthy newspapers. I have nothing more to do with them. I'm dead—"

I've hurried straight back to the tent to write all this down. I feel something has been revealed to me, not only about Ambrose but about myself. Of course I don't for a moment believe that he left England simply because his rooms were wrecked; that's just the kind of incident you dramatize and dwell on because it expresses a general attitude of mind. I'm sure he would have left England anyway before long; I can't possibly picture him living there. As for his daydream of becoming a Cambridge don, it presupposes a Cambridge as fantastic as his imaginary kingdom.

But what astonishes me is how violently I was affected by his story. While he was telling it, all my undergraduate hostilities came back to me; I was grinding my teeth in fury against those hearties, and the smashing of the eggcup nearly made *me* shed tears, too. In fact, Ambrose has made me aware of feelings I'd forgotten I was capable of. That's because I've been living outside England myself, and in the presence of public enemies, the Nazis, against whom you feel a different sort of hostility—public and proper and respectable.

The other sort of hostility—which isn't respectable or proper, but which sometimes goes much deeper—you can perhaps only feel for your own class and kind. And this is what, in their different ways, Ambrose and Geoffrey feel. I may disagree entirely with their opinions. I may laugh at them for being half-crazy. Nevertheless, they and I—whether we like it or not—are on the same side.

The day before yesterday we had a sudden change in the weather. That afternoon the wind began to blow hard through the channel, and the sea rose and slapped the rocks. Then there was a thunderstorm, followed by a great drumming downpour of rain. When the rain was over, the sky was still starless and black as a hole. Another terrific storm broke around midnight. The tent leaked. Pools of water collected in every hollow.

Yesterday morning was lowering and the temperature had dropped sharply. The mountains were grainy and clear. A strong wind was blowing.

"About eleven o'clock, Waldemar burst into the tent, wildly excited. "Christoph! Christoph! Quick—come out and look: we've got a visitor!"

"What kind of a visitor?"

"You'll never guess! It's a *woman!*"

I came out of the tent and saw one of the fishermen's boats standing offshore, waiting to land. We're all used to the fishermen by this time. They regard this island as part of their territory; that we happen to be living here is quite incidental. They'll come ashore at any hour—in the middle of the night, sometimes—light a fire and cook their fish, which they invite us to share in exchange for drinking up our wine. The boys love these visits. Hans approves of them, because they sometimes lead to orgies. Ambrose accepts them philosophically. Geoffrey grumbles at the noise.

Our visitor was sitting in the bows. She had blond hair and a pretty little face, and she was wrapped in one of the fleece jackets which herdsmen wear. Her head was tied in a kerchief. She would have looked quite rustic, if she hadn't been wearing a double string of pearls. She was a tiny figure; everything about her gave you the impression of a miniature. As the boat rode high on the backwash from the shore, she waved her hand gaily. I turned and saw Geoffrey and Ambrose watching the boat from the rocks. Only Geoffrey returned the wave, and in a halfhearted, unwilling manner. I walked down to join them. As I approached, I heard Geoffrey say: "How could I have known she'd come *here?*"

"Well, the obvious explanation would be that you invited her."

"I've told you already I didn't—damn you! The last time we met, in Athens, I told her it was all off. I can't stand that

96

bloody man-eating octopus. I told her to bloody well leave me alone."

"All the same, lovey, you'll admit that *somebody* must have told her how to find this place."

"My good man, thanks to your filthy amours, you and your doings are known in every bar in Athens. All kinds of people could have told her."

"Well, she can't stay here," said Ambrose. "You must make that clear to her right from the start."

"Have you ever tried making anything clear to *her?*"

"Very well then, ducky—since you refuse to face what is undoubtedly your own responsibility—I suppose I shall have to do it myself."

"Good luck. But I advise you to start right away. Don't let her land. Once she sets foot on shore, you're done for. Want to borrow my pistol? If you fire a couple of shots over her head, it may just possibly dawn on her that she isn't welcome."

"Don't be ridiculous. I shall be polite, of course—polite but firm. That's a combination, lovey, which you never seem to understand."

Meanwhile, Waldemar, no doubt wishing to impress our exotic visitor, had put on his swimming trunks. He now jumped into the sea with the end of a line from the shore and swam out to the boat. As he trod water beside it, we could see him laughing and talking to the lady.

"Who is she?" I asked.

"You don't know her, ducky? I thought everyone knew Maria. You might easily have met her in Berlin. She goes there quite a lot. In fact, she goes everywhere—worse luck. . . . But she's Geoffrey's friend, really. They have repeatedly committed a certain act, too revolting to mention. Now she's pursued him here, driven by her nameless lust—"

"Her nameless lust gets satisfied, wherever she is," said Geoffrey. But he couldn't conceal a slightly self-satisfied smirk: "I don't know why she needs *me.*"

The boat had been half rowed, half dragged into our little harbor, amidst a babel of yelling by the fishermen and the boys. And now they helped Maria ashore. She was even tinier than I had thought. And older; though maybe not more than forty. Her blond hair had black roots, her eyelids were made up as if for the theater, with touches of vivid blue; this made her appearance ridiculous but also somehow put it beyond criticism. She was slim and sparkling with vitality. "*Mais, c'est ravissant!*" she cried, looking around her. "Oh, I *like* your island, Ambrose! One could be *très content* here."

"Charming of you to say so," said Ambrose, becoming a slightly different kind of hostess than usual; languid, with a touch of frost. "Of course, one hasn't had time to do anything with it, yet. But I think, when a house is built, *and one's able to invite guests to stay here—*" he turned to me. "May I introduce Mr. Isherwood? Madame Constantinescu."

"Oh, I know Mr. Isherwood," cried Maria, shaking hands with me. "Only lately, I read your delightful novel. It is the *only* novel written in a long time, I find. Most of the new ones are so stupid. But yours—truly delightful! This young man who is a schoolmaster and becomes imprisoned for the traffic in the white slaves—*quel esprit!*"

"I'm afraid that's by Evelyn Waugh," I said, not charmed. But Maria took this in her stride—if, indeed, she heard me.

"Oh, I love all young British writers. Only one thing—they cannot write about the passion, I find. They do not understand it. Unless, perhaps, it is the passion for the young boys. *Mais, cher Ambrose, je t'assure*, I adore the pederasts. They are so sensitive. So *fine*. . . . Geoffrey, you make such a face! You are not pleased to see me?"

"You might at least have told us you were coming," said Geoffrey sulkily.

But Maria was no longer listening to him. She was giving directions in rapid Greek to the fishermen, who now began unloading various suitcases and large bundles from the boat. As they did this, Waldemar climbed out of the water and came up to her, dripping. Maria looked him over, with one eyebrow slightly raised; Waldemar instinctively began to flex his muscles. "*Huebscher Junge*," she remarked nonchalantly, to no one in particular. Waldemar didn't appear to find her tone patronizing; in fact, he was delighted. He grinned boldly at her and continued to stand around—although the chilly wind was giving him goose pimples—waiting to be admired further. But now she had started counting the pieces of her luggage. "I always say, how silly to travel light," she remarked to me. "*I* travel heavy. They say it's a man's world. Well, that suits me—as long as there are plenty of men to carry things for me!" She laughed gaily.

"I don't think you quite understand, Maria," said Ambrose —languid no longer, but frankly alarmed—"that we can't pos-

sibly put you up here. There are only our tents and these exceedingly uncomfortable huts. You'd better tell them to take
your things back on board. There's quite a passable hotel in
Chalkis—"

"Nonsense," cried Maria, beaming at him, "do not be so
galant! I shall not be of any trouble to you. I am not one of
your helpless females. I have my own tent, of course. I
always travel with it when I go into the country. So much
more comfortable than these hotels with their fleas!" So
there was nothing more to be said.

Maria has brought a portable gramophone with her. I admired the skill with which she used it to get the boys on her
side, just as a trader in an unfamiliar part of the jungle uses
some toy to make friends with the native children. She put on
a record at once, disregarding Geoffrey's still scowling face
and Ambrose's subtler, more disguised hostility. The record
began, with a screech like a devil escaped from a box:

> *Es muss 'was wunderbares sein,*
> *Von dir geliebt zu werden—*

Now that I come to think of it, Maria's choice of a German
record as her opening number seems too clever to have been
unintentional. It is as if she deliberately appealed to Hans and
Waldemar over the heads of us English. Hans started beating
time to the syrupy music with a dreamy smile; Geoffrey
muttered something disgustedly about "von Bloggenheimer's
national anthem." As for Aleko, Theo and Petro, they loved
the record anyway—and would have loved it every bit as
much in Chinese or Urdu; their native language is just Noise.

"Oh!" Maria exclaimed, clapping her hands with childlike
delight, "how I adore *la vie de* gipsy!" She seized one of the
fishermen around the waist, danced a few steps with him,
then transferred herself to Hans, with whom she began to
waltz in the old German style. He coyly liked this and
blushed as she twirled him around. By now, several of the
fishermen had started dancing with the boys and with each
other. Having thus opened the ball, Maria suddenly aban-
doned Hans and went back to teasing Geoffrey, telling him he
looked sullen. "I think you all bore yourselves here!" she
cried. Then, to Ambrose: "I shall make *stimmung* for you;
you will see! Only, please forget I am a woman! Will you accept me as an honorary pederast? How does one become an

initiate? By liking pretty boys? I do that already!" And she flashed a coquettish smile at Waldemar.

In these past four days Maria has established herself as absolute ruler of the island.

I'm sure she didn't deliberately set out to do this. It is probably something which just happens wherever she goes. Her power consists in this: that she knows what she wants, at any given moment, much more definitely than we know what we want. So we let her take over.

All that Maria demands—but she demands it quite ruthlessly—is that she shall be amused, every hour of every day. She is very easily amused. She's prepared to get her amusement wherever and however it offers itself. She is the sort of monster who is often miscalled a good sport. The most monstrous thing about her is her good humor. She never pouts or sulks. She is always cheerful; and as tactless as an elephant. It isn't just that she's thick-skinned; she knows perfectly well that she stirs up resentment. She's used to it. It even amuses her.

I picture her as always arriving with gifts—subversive gifts which set the members of a household against each other. In addition to the gramophone—which is screaming its head off and driving me crazy as I try to write this—she has brought us whisky, a whole case of it. No civilized person, she declares, can drink the resinated wine. This has put Ambrose's back up, of course. He refuses to touch the whisky, saying that "it reeks of England," and he watches us reproachfully as we gulp it down. Maria herself doesn't seem to care much for any kind of drink. In the evenings she rolls herself cigarettes in which the tobacco is mixed with hashish. Much to Ambrose's annoyance, she gave some to the boys the first day she was here. They ran around laughing wildly until they were exhausted and fell asleep.

Maria has Hans, Waldemar, Aleko, Theo and Petro completely under her control. They are her assistants and audience in her search for amusement. She makes them work like beavers, but this they scarcely notice, because she takes such an energetic part in every project that they are hypnotized by her vitality. She will decide to go fishing, or to cook a meal, or to take over the blasting operations, or to cut a path through the woods, or to tear something down and rebuild it elsewhere. Whatever she does turns into a kind of circus—a circus from which Ambrose, Geoffrey and I are excluded.

Ambrose and Geoffrey exclude themselves by sulking. I exclude myself because I feel a certain loyalty to them and because I am too lazy to join in Maria's activities. And yet I can't help being inquisitive. Yesterday I heard the boys yelling with excitement from somewhere in the woods. But when, much scratched by the undergrowth, I finally located them, they all fell silent. I was like a grownup surprising children at a game. "We're going to dig a hole," Maria told me. "You have come to help us, perhaps?" She looked at me with challenging mischievousness; she knew quite well I wouldn't help. Something even prevented me from asking what the hole was for; it would have been playing into her hands. As I walked away, feeling foolish, I heard them all beginning to laugh.

In fact, Ambrose, Geoffrey and I are in a state of siege. Maria has got us immobilized; there is nothing whatever for us to do. Ambrose is the only one of us who really resents this, but he is just as helpless as we are. Maria behaves to us like a kind of mocking housekeeper. When our meals are ready, she announces, "The gentlemen are served!" After supper she plays cards with Hans and Waldemar. True, she always invites us to join in, but she knows we shall refuse. For the card playing, Maria commandeers the kitchen table and thus symbolically ousts Ambrose from his throne room and inner sanctum.

She no longer teases Geoffrey. Indeed, she pays less attention to him than she does to Ambrose or to me. And they aren't going to bed together. These last two nights Waldemar has been in her tent. He giggles to me about it: "Honestly, Christoph, you can't imagine the things she does! I wonder she isn't ashamed! I can tell you—I was glad it was dark in there. If we'd had the light on, I'd have been embarrassed!" But he is hugely flattered by her sophisticated attentions, nevertheless.

As for Ambrose, that now doubly deposed monarch, he says very little about the situation. I imagine he comforts himself by reflecting that Maria is sure to leave soon. It's obvious that she must get bored here in another week, at most. I doubt if she ever stays anywhere long.

This morning we had quite a scene. After spending the night with Waldemar, Maria went swimming with him, naked. This was early—not long after I had been in, myself—

but not quite early enough. Ambrose emerged storming from his tent. He shouted for Aleko and Theo; when they appeared, he sent them for blankets. Then the three of them came down to the water's edge, the boys giggling. Maria was perfectly calm. "Good morning, Ambrose!" she cried gaily. But Waldemar looked rather scared—fearing that this time he had gone too far.

Ambrose was in a gibbering fury. He shrieked at Waldemar in German, "Tell that woman to come out at once!" It was about the worst move he could have made; Maria promptly came out of the water. She took her time doing this, and I have to admit that her figure is surprisingly well preserved. She accepted Aleko's blanket, after smilingly pinching his ear. She was obviously delighted to have provoked Ambrose at last. And Ambrose wasn't the only one. In the background I now saw Geoffrey lurking among the trees. I don't know exactly what he was feeling, but he certainly minded. Now I feel sure of what I always suspected: Maria's behavior with Waldemar has an ulterior motive.

Finally, Maria looked around at me—expecting no doubt to complete her triumph by detecting signs of jealousy. (For of course, being Maria, she takes it for granted that I am Waldemar's lover.) She laughed teasingly. "I shock you all very much, no? You are afraid to look at a woman in the nature?"

"Not me, Maria," I said, smiling very sweetly. "You see, I used to be a medical student."

This afternoon, while I was alone in the tent, Maria appeared—suddenly and quite casually, as though she were in the habit of dropping in. I hadn't heard her approach and was startled, which inclined me to be peevish. I was lying on my bed. Maria sat down on Waldemar's, apparently taking it for granted that I'd be in the mood for a long chat.

"Tell me, Christopher—what are you doing here?"

"I was in the middle of thinking out a story." My tone implied that she'd interrupted me. Actually, I'd been simply lying in a state of mindless torpor, as I so often do nowadays.

"No—I mean, what is it that you do on this island? Why are you hear?"

"Well—I'm on holiday," I said, annoyed with her because this question somehow put me on the defensive.

Maria smiled and shook her head vigorously: "No!"

"What do you mean, 'No'?"

"It is not that."

"Then what is it?" I asked, weakly. I wanted her to go away so I could return to my torpor. But she had no intention of going away yet. Before she would go, she had to extract some kind of amusement from me. I might be an unsociable old lemon, but I had to be squeezed.

"You do not belong here. That is why I ask."

"Well," I said, rousing myself to deal with her, "if it comes to that—what are *you* doing here?"

"Oh, I! I go everywhere!"

"But why do you go everywhere?"

"Because I am curious. That is my life—curiosity. No, I am serious! I think of someone I know and I say to myself, what is he doing now, at this moment? So then I go to see."

I stared at her, wondering if she seriously expected me to believe this. And the amazing thing was, she made me believe it. As far as I could judge, she wasn't showing off or even exaggerating. She was telling the literal truth. "And that's how you spend your life?" I asked.

Maria smiled teasingly. "That shocks you? You think I should make myself active in some profession? Or become passionate for the politics?"

"No, but—does this kind of thing really interest you?"

"Unfortunately, no—not often! For the most time, it is quite *ennuyant*, because, you see, people are doing still what they did before. They do not change."

"So then you leave them again?"

"Then I leave them. Yes."

"I suppose you'll be leaving *us*, soon?"

"Oh, here I am not bored! Here there is much to interest me. . . . But I think perhaps I must leave soon, all the same. Because I make so much trouble, no?" Maria gave me a glance of truly vintage coquetry—not a day younger than 1914—from under her sky-blue eyelids.

"That's too bad."

"Ah, Christopher—how you say that! You think I am just an idle woman who makes trouble where she goes?"

"Well, aren't you?"

She clapped her hands and laughed wildly. "Now you speak frankly! This I like very much! Tell me now—do you detest me?"

"Of course I don't! I'm rather fascinated by you. You're a kind of monster I've never met before."

"Oh, wonderful! Then we can be like brother and sister. Because, my dear, you too are a monster, I find! Do not pretend! Admit now!"

"All right," I said. "I'm a monster." I felt rather flattered.

"Yes! Now I see it more plain than ever! *Tu es vraiment gentil, mon petit.* You look so young. You have such nice clear eyes. But you are an old, old monster, like me. . . . You know when first I recognize this? It was this morning, after the great *scandale* of the swimming! You look at me, and I recognize. Till then, I did not understand you. But always I am interested—in you more than anyone on this island."

"More than in Geoffrey? Really now, Maria! You came here to see him, didn't you?"

"Ah—*mon pauvre petit Geoffrey!* Yes, I come always back to see him. I have known him so long—so many years! When first we met, he was beautiful, you cannot imagine! And already he was in trouble. He had become expelled from the university because always he drank so much and did stupid things. But he was so sweet, so *gentil.* He asked me, I shall take care of him that he does not drink. But I told him, No—I will be your mistress, not your wife. Else I am bored in one week. . . . So then Geoffrey's father puts him into the business of the family, which is to make some paper that one cannot mention politely in England. And Geoffrey becomes always worse—more and more *méchant.* At last it is discovered he has stolen much, much money from the company. There is a great terrible *scandale.* Geoffrey's father has to repay all. Even so, his partners wish to prosecute, but it is arranged—Geoffrey must leave England and not ever return."

"But that's dreadful—"

"Oh, but do not make that hypocritical *grimace, mon cher!* You are not sorry for Geoffrey. We monsters, we feel only curiosity."

"Perhaps I'm a different sort of monster."

"*Un monstre sentimentale?* Do not say that! That kind I detest!"

"Now, wait a moment, Maria—you can't pretend *you* don't feel anything for Geoffrey?"

"*Au fond,* I feel only curiosity, nothing more. You know, he puzzles me enormously? I say to myself: Here was a boy, handsome, athletic, of good family, money—why does he destroy himself? You know what I think? There is some secret here! Perhaps something he did, of which he is very ashamed. Something very, very childish. All the secrets of the Englishmen are childish. That is why they will rather die in tortures than confess them."

"He won't tell you what it is?"

"Never! Always he denies that there is any secret—but he blushes *red*, and I know! One day, I shall find it out."

"And then—what'll you do?"

"Ah, then! I fear I shall be interested in our little Geoffrey no longer."

"That's very heartless, Maria."

"But monsters are heartless, *mon vieux!* You know this—do not be so hypocrite! You cannot hold a monster by his emotion, only by puzzling him. As long as the monster is puzzled, he is yours."

Geoffrey and Maria have gone!

They left the island very early this morning with the party of fishermen who landed last night and staged one of our drunken feasts. This time all of us passed out—except, of course, Maria. I think I was the first to go, and that's probably why I was the first to come to my senses. I was lying on the ground, outside the huts, and it was just beginning to get light. Hans lay snoring a few feet away from me. Waldemar, as I discovered later, was lying naked on the site of Maria's tent.

What startled me out of my stupor was seeing this tent being carried past me, rolled into a bundle, by two of the fishermen. Painfully, I turned my head. Ambrose and Geoffrey were slumped unconscious on their packing cases at the kitchen table, their faces buried in their folded arms. Some of the fishermen still lay where they had collapsed, but these were being roused by their mates, or by dainty prods of Maria's foot. She was in command of the evacuation, giving orders in stage whispers, her eyes sparkling with delight and mischief. The men carried her baggage down to the boat. Then I saw them go into Geoffrey's tent and come out with his suitcases—Maria must have packed them. Finally, when the boat was loaded, Maria signed to the men to pick up Geoffrey himself. They carried him on board with his arms hanging down, his hands trailing the ground, his mouth open, lifeless as a sack.

Technically, I said to myself, this is kidnaping. Better stay out of it.

I turned over and went back to sleep. . . .

"Imagine!" says Waldemar. "Going off like that, without a word to anybody! The sly old bitch!" Naturally, he feels slighted—especially since his last conscious moments yesterday evening were spent in Maria's bed—and that was literally pulled out from under him. I don't doubt he would have gone off with Maria himself, if she had asked him, without an instant's hesitation. He would find that kind of adventure irresistible.

Hans is happy, simply because Geoffrey has gone. The boys are restless and suddenly bored. They actually miss being bossed around by Maria, though they don't realize this. They have begun to talk longingly about Athens and its pleasures.

If Ambrose is happy that Maria has gone, he doesn't show it. He must miss Geoffrey. But he refuses to show that, either. When I said something about the abruptness of their leaving, he answered, with that curious quiet obstinacy of his: "Everyone on this island is free to come and go exactly as he likes."

I can hardly be bothered to write all this down but—

Hans and Aleko got into a terrific quarrel. I still don't know what about. Hans hit him, hard. Aleko's mouth started to bleed. He ran off into the woods. The other boys looked for him, but he wouldn't show himself. Even Ambrose went and shouted for him to come out. He didn't.

That night, Hans woke up to find Aleko in his hut, with a knife. Hans fought him off, managed to throw a blanket over him, grabbed the knife. Again, Aleko ran off into the woods and disappeared.

Next morning Hans was up at the house, looking over the newly built living room and veranda. Happening to turn his head, he caught a glimpse of Aleko running headlong down the hill and into the woods; he must have been hidden somewhere in the building. Hans didn't pause to puzzle over this; with the promptness of an old soldier, he threw himself down flat on his face. The next moment, there was a shattering explosion. If Hans had been standing up, he would certainly have been killed. As it was, his eyebrows were burned, his clothes were singed black and he was hurled against a wall and bruised severely. The island was showered with fragments of rock. A lantern which hangs outside our tent was

106

smashed. The house was almost totally wrecked and will have to be rebuilt from the ground up.

Hans went immediately to Ambrose and demanded that the police should be fetched from Chalkis; Aleko must be discovered and captured without delay. Ambrose told Hans he was being "silly." So then Hans said that he had no choice; he must leave the island, since Ambrose refused to give him protection and his life was in danger. And he did leave, that same day, taking Waldemar with him.

Waldemar made a big sentimental scene with me before he left. He begged me to come with them. I refused. Tears came into his eyes. "We Aryans have to stand together," he said.

I am sure he said this without thinking. That's the disgusting power of propaganda: the Nazis have scattered such millions of these poisonous words around that you are apt to find one of them unexpectedly inside your own mouth. But I wasn't going to let Waldemar get away with it.

"Since when did you join the Brownshirts?"

"Christoph—don't you say that, even in joke! If anyone else said such a thing to me, I'd kill him. But you're my friend. I know you don't mean it. We understand each other."

"Do we?" I said, nastily. To be honest, my feelings were hurt that Waldemar could walk out on me so lightly. But, much more than this, I was irritated by the hypocrisy of this farewell scene. I knew he wasn't leaving out of loyalty to Hans; he was simply bored on the island and eager for the excitement of being in Athens. No doubt he was going to look up the woman with the mustache. "What about Ambrose?" I asked. "Don't you have to stand by *him?* Remember—he's an Aryan, too."

"Ambrose has gone native," said Waldemar, quite seriously. (What he actually said in German was "become nigger.") "You can't stay here with him, Christoph. This island isn't fit for you. It's nothing but a pigsty."

"Well," I said, "maybe I've decided to go native, myself."

So they both left.

No sooner was the boat which was taking them well away from the shore than Aleko came out of the woods—grinning, cheeky and unconcerned as ever. Theo and Petro greeted him with yells of approval. Ambrose behaved as if Aleko had never been away. And so did I.

All this happened four, five, six days ago? I've lost track already. It might as well be six months.

Cigarettes gone from tent. The first time. I suppose the boys feel they know me well enough, now.

Sun. Island. Gramophone. Sea. World without adjectives. Except—hot, hot, hot.

Saw today what this island is. Words no good.

If one could only—
What *am* I doing here?

Oh, Jesus, my head.

Last night, perfect calm. Sitting on benzine can in moonlight, watching sea. Ambrose understands.

That is the end of my diary. The handwriting of all these last short entries is big and straggly and, at the end of the lines, it tends to collapse, like playing cards fallen on top of each other. Obviously, it was done when I was very drunk.

I don't know exactly what most of these entries mean; and yet I can recall the feelings they describe. Our life on St. Gregory was like a play which had to be performed day after day in its original version but with a cast which was no longer big enough. Ambrose was still Ambrose. The boys were still the boys. (Not the same boys, however; for Aleko, Theo and Petro had long since left for Athens, and these others—every bit as noisy, dirty and impudent—had taken their places.) But I had to double the roles of Christopher, Geoffrey, Hans and Waldemar. And thus I almost ceased being myself, or anybody else in particular.

But why did the play have to be performed at all? Why did I work so hard at this clowning? Certainly, it wasn't just to amuse Ambrose. No. Crazy as it sounds, I believe I needed to reassure myself *that I wasn't alone!*

Every night Ambrose and I sat down to our drinking—two lamplit faces opposite each other, in the tremendous presence of the dark, the sea and the stars. We must have looked as if we were about to open a dialogue on the ultimate truths. Had our conversation been worthy of its setting, we should have spoken with the tongues of Plato and Shakespeare—or at least Bernard Shaw. Actually, we never exchanged more than a few words at a time. The gramophone blared. The boys crowded round us, plucked at our sleeves, peered into our faces. Sometimes I yelled and hit out at them, as Geoffrey had done. Sometimes, like Hans, I chased them. Sometimes I fooled and danced drunkenly with them and they accepted me as their buffoon companion, just as Waldemar had been accepted.

And yet, to all intents and purposes, I was alone. The partners of the sex fantasies in which I indulged compulsively, to the point of exhaustion, as I lay naked and sweating in my tent were much more physically real to me than these noisy shadows.

During this period, I seldom thought of Ambrose as a person. Most of the time he was simply a consciousness that was aware of me, a mirror in which I saw my reflection—but dimly, and only if I made big, easily recognizable gestures. Seated at the kitchen table, with our drinks and the lamp, we seemed frankly and completely exposed to each other; and yet there were no revelations, no confidences. I have told perfect strangers on boats or trains far more about myself than I ever told Ambrose.

Only once I committed an indiscretion. It must have been soon after Waldemar and Hans left the island. I don't remember what made me ask the question exactly when I did; it had been in my mind a long time already.

"Ambrose—at Cambridge, when they wrecked your rooms . . . I mean—that one who came to see you next day, with the check—I've often wondered if—"

By now I had realized that Ambrose wasn't going to answer what I should never have asked, and my voice died slowly away. But he didn't remain silent. After a few moments, staring at the lamp, he said softly and thoughtfully:

"I suppose being a writer, lovey, you naturally want to tidy everything up and make it make sense?"

"Yes," I said, "I suppose I do. . . . I'm sorry."

"There's nothing to be sorry about. . . . Only, you know, lovey, things never do quite make sense. Not really." Ambrose looked away from me with a faint, secret smile.

And that was all.

One day right at the end of August we went over to Chalkis on a shopping expedition. And there, in the hotel where we stopped for drinks, I saw a copy of an English magazine, one of the illustrated weeklies. Some tourist must have left it behind him. Although it was already dirty and battered, it was barely a month old.

I started idly leafing through it as we sat at an outdoor table in the hot sun sipping iced drinks, very potent, of a strange, deadly green. There were the usual pictures of tweedy women at race meetings, of blank-faced engaged couples, of sitters-out at dances—collar-awkward boys and leg-conscious girls. And then, amidst all these improbable strangers, I came upon Timmy.

There was a small oval photograph of him, disgustingly flattering, halfway down the central column of the book review page. And to one side of it was a review of his novel— the first and most favorable review of the bunch. Yes, our Timmy had written a novel! A sparkling novel. A novel you couldn't put down. A novel of delightfully impudent wit. A carefree, hilarious, altogether uproarious novel of London stage and society life. Nothing pretentious, nothing abnormal, nothing morbidly modern, nothing turgid, tense, abstruse, mannered, introverted, twisted. Nothing like the unhealthy maunderings of those darlings of the highbrow set—who shall be nameless. No—just simple, wholesome, delicious; and the reviewer went down on his knees and thanked God for it.

And there was Timmy himself, looking at me wide-eyed, as much as to say: I know I'm not in *your* class. Don't think I'm trying to butt in. Don't dream of reading my little bit of nonsense. It hasn't any message; doesn't pretend to. I just dashed if off at odd moments, in between my office hours and cocktail parties. Oh yes, it's *selling* all right. Happened to catch on. All a matter of luck. How many copies? Twenty thousand—and still going strong, they tell me. That's five times what your last novel did? Well—doesn't that only go to show: the public likes this kind of rubbish? Prefers it to serious stuff. Of course, I never *could* be serious like you. Wouldn't even try. I know my limits.

You little whore, I told him. I might have known you'd do this. You haven't changed since Cambridge, have you? And now you think you can call yourself a novelist—just as you called yourself an actor, a painter, a composer. This is what England has come to. This is the kind of thing they want. You're the kind of creature they want. And that's why I'm here, why I've vanished from them without a trace. You think you can make me jealous? You think I'm coming back to compete with you at your own nasty little game? You think I want any part of your world? This only shows how right I am to stay out of it.

And yet that photograph and that reveiw haunted me all day. I hadn't said anything to Ambrose about them, and I wasn't going to. But I did want to assure him, in some direct way, that I was loyal to him and to the island. I wanted him to know how gladly I was accepting his way of life and exiling myself from the world in which Timmy could sell twenty thousand copies.

That evening, when we were already well into our drinks, I began:

"You know, Ambrose, when I first came to this island, I never expected to stay more than two or three weeks. That's funny, isn't it?"

Ambrose smiled into his glass. He didn't answer.

"I mean," I went on, "I thought this wouldn't be my kind of life at all. That's because I never knew what I really did want, until I came here. I imagined I wanted to be in the middle of things—*in the swim*, as they call it. Jesus Christ! I was such an utter idiot. I used to work myself into a state of screaming anxiety—when, actually, down underneath, I didn't care, I didn't give a damn. I realize that now. . . . You know, I've learned so many things, just by being here with you. I think you're the first person I've ever met who really understands what it's all about."

I had never talked to Ambrose like this before. I began to sound as if I was making a declaration of love. And the worst of it was, it didn't ring true. I wanted to force it to be true, and I couldn't. . . . Drunk as I was, I felt suddenly embarrassed—especially since Ambrose didn't respond. I could see that he was embarrassed, too. And yet I had to continue.

"You've made me see how ghastly England is. No wonder you loathe it so."

"It's quite a bit different, lovey." Ambrose coughed apologetically. "My loathing it and your loathing it, you know."

"Why is it different?" I asked, not liking something in his tone.

"Well—in my case— I just don't belong there."

"And you think *I* belong?"

"Well—"

"You think there's something in me that *needs* any of that?"

"That wasn't what I meant—"

"You think I'm not perfectly happy here?" My voice

111

sounded slightly desperate. "Why, I could live like this for years—easily. For the rest of my life. . . . What's the joke? Don't you believe me?"

"I'm sure you *think* you mean it, ducky."

"But you don't believe I could?"

"You couldn't, lovey. Not for much longer. You wouldn't be able to stand it."

"Why wouldn't I?"

Ambrose merely smiled.

I felt rejected, dismayed, sobered. For, of course, he was absolutely right. But I wasn't going to let him see how much I minded.

"Well, we won't argue about it," I said, as lightly as I could. "We shall never be able to find out which of us was wrong. Because, in actual fact, I've *got* to leave. I have to be getting back to London—quite soon. I've been thinking about going, for some time."

Ambrose said nothing.

"Once you've made up your mind to do something," I continued, "it's better to do it at once, don't you think?"

There was a pause.

"Actually," I said, speaking slowly and deliberately, "I suppose there's really nothing to stop me leaving tomorrow."

I had felt sure that this would rouse Ambrose to make at least some kind of protest. But he merely shrugged his shoulders slightly. "Just as you like, lovey."

His indifference shocked me out of my self-control for a moment. "But Ambrose," I began in my dismay, "don't you—?" I stopped myself in time. I'd been about to say, "Don't you *care* if I stay or not?" Now I changed it to, "Don't you mind being alone here—with nobody but the boys?"

Ambrose looked at me gently as if reproaching me for the stupidity of the question. "But one's always alone, ducky. Surely you know that."

So then there was no backing down. Next day I had to pack. Ambrose was quietly helpful and efficient. He took my departure in the most matter-of-fact manner. When I said that I didn't need my tent and that he was welcome to it, he insisted on deducting its price—minus wear and tear—from my bill.

The fishing boat that was to take me to Chalkis was late; I

didn't leave until just after sunset. Ambrose came down to the rocks to see me off.

"I shouldn't be surprised if Geoffrey showed up again soon," I said, feeling that I should somehow try to console him —though he certainly didn't show the faintest sign of needing it.

"He probably will," Ambrose agreed, casually.

"Hans, too."

"I shouldn't wonder."

He shook hands with me, very much the country hostess. "Have a nice trip," he said. You might have thought that we had met for the first time that afternoon; that I was a neighbor who had called and been given tea.

As the boat chugged away I sat in the stern, looking back. The island lay, more beautiful than I had ever seen it, black in the midst of a molten silver sea, with the afterglow fading behind it. There was no breeze that evening. A thin spiral of smoke went up high, into the calm air. Supper was cooking. The lamp was alight on the kitchen table, and Ambrose had already taken his place there. My eyes filled with tears. Not only was I sad to be leaving, but the effect of it all was of something so poignantly innocent and primitive; the encampment of a pioneer, in an old painting. You looked at it and you said to yourself: Imagine—someone actually lives there— alone, in the midst of the wilderness!

When I got a good look at myself in a mirror at the hotel in Chalkis, I was quite startled to see what these last few months had done to me. My hair was long and matted, my beard had started to grow, I was sunburned nearly black, my face was puffy with drinking and my eyes were red. All that, of course, could soon be tidied up. But there was also a look in my eyes which hadn't been there before. By the time I got back to England, no one could have had any difficulty in recognizing me as my familiar self. Only I caught glimpses of that look now and then while shaving.

And every so often, at a loud party or while listening to bad news on the wireless or on waking up to find myself in bed with someone I scarcely knew, I would think of Ambrose out there alone. He was right, I would say to myself; I didn't belong on his island.

But now I knew that I didn't belong here, either.

Or anywhere.

Waldemar

On a boat this time.

Late in August 1938; a cross-channel steamer, just coming into Dover harbor.

How tiny it always seems! No more than a cranny in the old cheese cliffs; a drab doll town with the stubborn little castle standing guard above it, in a light summer drizzle. Oh, the staring, unblinking, uncompromising familiarity of it all! The loud, rude squawking of the gulls! How compactly the English sit, confronting their visitors: here we are, take us or leave us—this is where you'll do things *our* way, not yours. Byron saw the last of them here. So did Wilde. You say goodbye to them forever and go away to fame and death among the dagoes, and they couldn't care less. Oh, yes, when your name has been a household word everywhere else for the past two generations, they'll concede that they used to know you —slightly. But they'll never really admit that they were wrong about you or about anything. They are indomitable, incorrigible, and so utterly self-satisfied that they no longer have to raise their voices or wave their arms when they address the lesser breeds. If you have any criticisms, they have one unanswerable answer: you can stay off our island.

Well, it may come to that, I think to myself, as I stand at the steamer's rail, looking at them. One day. But why did I come back here last month from China, instead of stopping on in New York—as I could have, as I so badly wanted to? I can't explain. I was just passively spinning back on the return arc, like a boomerang. Who throws me? I don't know, and I'm not really interested in finding out. Or am I afraid to? I refuse to answer that question. All I'll tell you is, I'm spinning.

That sounds like the statement of a madman, or at least of someone in the depths of despair? Not a bit of it! Take a good look at me standing there. Do I seem defeated, downcast, dismal? Anxious—yes. Those crows's feet at the corners of my eyes, I got them from constant, anxious squinting ahead, like a sea captain in a fog. The two deeply grooved brackets in my cheeks have been dug by nervous grimaces, pursings of the lips. But my eyes are bright, my face is still youthfully lean, and a stranger would be surprised to hear that I shall be thirty-four at the end of this month.

How do I appear to my friends and acquaintances?

To judge from the jokes they make about me, they see a rather complex creature, part despot, part diplomat. I'm told that I hold myself like a drill sergeant or a strict little land-lady; I am supposed to have an overpowering will. Hugh Weston compared it once to a fire hose before which everybody has to retreat. Then again they say I'm so sly; I pretend to be nobody in particular, just one of the gang, when all the time I have the arrogance of Lawrence of Arabia and the subtlety of Talleyrand. Oh, yes—and I'm utterly ruthless and completely cynical. But I do make them laugh.

Anyone would have to admit that I'm a good mixer. I listen to other people talking about themselves with genuine interest. I'm capable of enthusiasm, especially for those I have only just met. I make special efforts with the ones who would ordinarily dislike me, and I usually win them over. And why not? Let's have no false modesty about this. I have lots of charm and I'm a quite considerable celebrity. Just now my writing is fashionable to exactly the right degree—chic, not vulgarly famous. The young like me for being a little bit older; the elder brother who has a romantic, slightly world-weary air of having been places and seen things. (You should hear me when I give lantern lectures on our Chinese trip saying nonchalantly, "Weston took that picture while we were in the Chinese front-line trenches at Han Chwang—the Japanese are in that big building opposite, just across the canal.") The elderly like me because I have beautiful manners; with them I am youthful, enthusiastic, respectful, diffident. I flatter them in a different way. Sometimes I lay on the flattery too crudely; then I'm seen through and distrusted. But I learn from these failures and become increasingly careful.

As for my "real" friends, I value their company too much to risk going beyond a certain point with them. I prefer to keep hold of what I have. I know how dangerous it is to make any serious demand on anyone—there's nobody I trust that much. If that's cynicism, I admit to being cynical.

My carefulness has its limits, however. Sometimes I meet people who intimidate me, because I feel that they see through me. With them I'll nearly knock myself out at first, trying to prove I'm sincere. But—if they're still not impressed —then all of a sudden I'll get bored and just brutally snub them. I don't give a damn any more.

Then there's this celebrated will of mine—where would they all be without it? Sometimes it seems to me that I'm keeping the younger generation going, practically singlehanded. Why, I'm a one-man registry office combined with a lonely hearts' bureau! I get them jobs, patch up their love affairs, read their manuscripts, speak to publishers for them, encourage them, console them, feed them lunch and supper. And they *dare* complain of my will!

But the question remains, why do I do it? Why do I take all this trouble?

I suppose the answer is, *I do it to prove I can play their game*. Whose game? The Others' game. The game for which the rules have been made by The Others. And The Others are all the headmasters of the schools I went to, all the clergymen I have ever known, all reactionary politicians, newspaper editors, journalists, and most women over forty. Ever since I've been able to talk and read they have been telling me the rules of their game. And they've been insinuating, until lately, with sneering smiles, "But, of course *you* could never play it." And, until lately, I've been mentally answering them, "I could if I wanted to, but I don't; I wouldn't be caught dead playing it." That wasn't quite convincing, even to me. But now I've changed my defense into an attack. I've accepted their challenge, I've played their game and I've won, even according to their own rules. I'm a success—which is all they really long to be, and mostly aren't.

All right, I've proved it. But now—what next?

While Hugh Weston and I were in China on those immense stop-and-start journeys which seemed like whole lifetimes, we used to amuse ourselves by getting into arguments on every subject we could think of. Nearly all of these arguments were just a friendly game. But whenever we started on God

116

and the soul, I would find myself getting passionately angry —as always in recent years. "I don't give a shit," I'd tell Hugh, "what anybody else says: I know *I* haven't got a soul. And I'm willing to bet that no one else has, either. All that talk makes me sick. I can't just be neutral about it. I think it's obscene and evil. When I hear the word 'God' I want to vomit; it's the dirtiest word in the language. It describes everything that's filthy—Franco, Hitler, the Fascists—everything!" And Hugh would laugh good-humoredly and say, "Careful! Careful! If you keep going on like that, my dear, you'll have *such* a conversion, one of these days! Oh dear, I can just *picture* you being received into the bosom of Mother Church, with all those masses and candles!" So then I'd have to laugh, too. But I still repeated obstinately to myself that I was *certain* I hadn't got a soul.

If I'm right—if I have no soul—if I'm not really even a person at all—if it's not I who chose to challenge The Others at their game—if I'm merely the boomerang—then what's going to happen when I stop spinning? What about the future?

The future—with that word I always feel nowadays a faint chill of fear. And I keep remembering that phrase—it's from Balzac—*un jour sans lendemain*, a day without a morrow. This time we're living through now, this doom-heavy summer, is *un jour sans lendemain*, or my fear whispers that it may be; and everything one does seems to have a tomorrowless quality about it. For example, I'm on my way back today from a weekend in Paris, where I got tomorrowlessly drunk, had tomorrowless sex, and made several people a lot of tomorrowless promises. In London, a couple of equally tomorrowless affairs are waiting to be resumed. Nevertheless, I shall have to talk and act as if I thought tomorrow *would* come, after all.

It must have been just about the moment when the steamer started to make its circle in order to back into the harbor that I came up out of my self-thoughts and was suddenly aware of the girl who was standing near me at the rail. Maybe she had just crossed over from the other side of the ship. I realized that I knew her. She obviously hadn't noticed me yet, or else she didn't recognize me. A second later I remembered her name.

Dorothy and I had seen quite a lot of each other during that last pre-Hitler Berlin winter of 1932-33. At that time

117

Dorothy was teaching at a Marxist school for workers; giving English lessons, with special attention to Communist jargon. She was one of those upper-middle-class English girls who had caught communism like flu. I think she really felt she wasn't worthy of her precious workers; they were purer, nobler, far more spiritually *dans le vrai* than she could ever hope to be. Also, of course, she was using her new faith as an instrument of aggression against her family, her own class and England in general. This I found quite sympathetic. But whenever I had started to warm toward her, she had spoiled everything by making some grimly doctrinaire remark which implied also a criticism of myself as a noninvolved sentimental bohemian. So then I would get impatient with her, deciding she was tiresome, and possibly a Lesbian of the strict kind with whom a man can't even be friends.

Her looks hadn't changed much. She was a short girl, slight, red-headed, with a pale, bony, freckled face. Not pretty; her chin stuck out too far.

"Hullo, Dorothy," I said. "Remember me?"

As she turned and recognized me, I got two impressions: first, that she was startled at being spoken to, as though she had been expecting some unpleasant meeting; second, that she was relieved and even truly pleased to see *me*. Yes, she was *very* pleased. Much more so than I could have expected. And of course I reacted to this and began to feel glad we'd met.

"I'm just back from China, you know." I had thought this would interest her and start an eager political conversation. But she merely asked politely, "Did you have a good journey?"

For a moment I felt severely rebuffed and annoyed. It just showed, I thought, that Dorothy still regarded me as a mere butterfly and my travels as irresponsible tourism. So I continued, in my war-correspondent voice, "It's amazing how nobody in Europe seems to realize what's happening out there. I must say, it's an example to all of us—*their* united front isn't going to crack up. Not that there aren't just the same tensions, but they all know they must beat the Japanese first. Everyone we talked to told us the same thing. We saw Chiang, Madame, Chou En-lai—in fact, most of the top people. And then, of course, we met hundreds of others—everyone from school-teachers and doctors to front-line soldiers and ricksha boys—"

(I shouldn't have talked like this if I hadn't been trying to impress Dorothy and feeling that I wasn't succeeding. It was the kind of thing I said in my worst moments of showing off at lectures. Not knowing Chinese, I had never talked to any front-line soldier or other proletarian without the aid of a highly unreliable official interpreter, sent with us to see that we didn't get the wrong impressions. As for the ricksha boys, one wouldn't anyhow have wasted time discussing politics with *them*. You let them know where you wanted to go and what you wanted to find when you got there, in brutally unambiguous sign language.)

The trouble was, Dorothy wasn't quite attending. She was attending to me as a person, but not to what I was saying. Also, she seemed worried about something. Twice she glanced quickly over her shoulder.

"Well, what about *you?*" I asked, rather bitchily. "You've been in Spain, I suppose?"

But again Dorothy surprised me; her eyes didn't light up and become holy. "Oh, yes," she said, "I was there in 1936. And again last year. Not for long, though." Her manner began to intrigue me. She really did seem to have changed. She wasn't militant any more. And, of course, this made her nicer. After a slight pause, she added almost apologetically, "You see, Christopher, I'm not alone, now."

"You mean, you've got married?"

Dorothy blushed and smiled, "Well, no—not yet. But it may come to that."

"Congratulations!"

"He's a proletarian boy. A German. I met him in Paris."

"So he's a refugee?"

"Well—in a way. He isn't Jewish."

"A Communist?"

"No. Not a party member. But he sympathizes. . . . Christopher—I'm in love. It's the first time I ever was. I've never met anyone like him before. He's so absolutely honest. He makes other people seem—not quite real, somehow—"

"What does he do for a living?" I asked, beginning to suspect this absolutely honest proletarian. Long before meeting Dorothy in Berlin, I had myself gone through a short attack of worker worship; and I had been acutely impatient of it ever since my cure.

"Well, he doesn't actually have a trade. He never learned one. But he can do all sorts of things. Almost anything, in fact. And he's intelligent. I'm sure you'll have to admit that. I don't mean in the highbrow way, of course. But he *feels* things. He

119

has a wonderful way of understanding people. You won't be able to fool him."

"What makes you think I should want to?" I asked, quite cross with her for a moment. But then I saw that she hadn't meant anything personal; it was merely the kind of tactless remark people throw off when they are deep in the reverie of their infatuation.

"He's five years younger than I am."

"That's not so much."

"Except that he seems younger than that, even—Oh, Christopher—you don't know how glad I am I met you today! I really need some moral support. I've been simply dreading this trip for months!"

"Why have you been dreading it?"

"Oh, my family. And England. And—" Suddenly, Dorothy's eyes fixed on someone; by this time the passengers were beginning to form a big crowd all around us, ready to disembark. She looked relieved. "*There* he is!" she murmured. I turned. *And there* was *Waldemar!* Yes, indeed, it was Waldemar! And looking, or so it seemed at first glance, exactly the same as when I'd seen him last, on the island of St. Gregory. Already he'd recognized me. He started elbowing through the crowd to reach us.

"Christoph!" He threw his arm around my neck. I smelled beer. He must have been down in the saloon drinking until they closed the bar. "It isn't true! I can't believe it! What a surprise! Where have you been all this time?"

"In China."

"In *China!*" Waldemar roared with laughter. "That's our Christoph—the crazy old wanderbird! Man, you must have gone crazy! What were you doing with those Chinese? Did they make you eat dogs? I read about that, once."

"No. Only birds' nests."

"*Birds' nests?* You hear him, Dorothy? Isn't he crazy? The same old Christoph!"

Needless to say, Dorothy was listening to all this with bewilderment. "Waldemar and I used to know each other in Berlin," I told her.

"What's that you call him—Waldemar?"

"I changed my name, Christoph," said Waldemar quickly. "Since I've been abroad, I changed it to Eugen . . . *for political reasons,* you understand—" He looked at me very hard, as if to signal some kind of discretion.

"But I think I like Waldemar better," said Dorothy brightly. "I think I'll call you Waldemar from now on."

Waldemar scowled slightly at her. Only slightly—but I saw enough to know that something in him *had* changed. He looked at that moment like an animal unwillingly submitting to a trainer; unfree but not yet tamed. This submission, this half-tameness, had coarsened him, perhaps because it had made him, for the first time in his life, capable of hurting another person. There was a shade of ugliness over his face; and yet, just because of this, he was more sexually attractive than before. I had a strong sense of the sex involvement between him and Dorothy; also of the fact that he was taking this involvement for granted. It didn't flatter him, as he had been flattered by the affair with Maria Constantinescu. In this respect he had matured. I watched Dorothy watching his sullen-captive face, watching it anxiously and with just a hint of timidity—and I thought, as I had so often thought before: really, in spite of all their bluffs and double bluffs, how utterly defenseless women are; and how badly most of us treat them, most of the time!

"All right," said Waldemar, ungraciously and with, perhaps, an underlying intention of cruelty, "you can call me Waldemar—when we're alone with Christoph."

I found myself suddenly laughing at this, very hard, as though it had been a joke. Partly because I wanted to smooth over the slight ugliness of the moment. Partly because the full farce of Waldemar's new incarnation, as the Eugen seen by Dorothy, had now presented itself to me and made me rather hysterical.

By now the boat was being tied up alongside the dock, where porters stood waiting blank-faced in rows, before a train of shunted trucks. There were a few friends of passengers, too, standing there glumly, having tired already of waving to us on board. Our arrival had an air of drab, businesslike ritual, like an unimportant funeral.

"We've been living in Paris," Dorothy explained to me, "but it's so expensive nowadays. I wrote to my family for money—that's something I haven't done for years. And my elder sister wrote back that Mother wanted me to come home for a while. In other words, if I didn't come, I wouldn't get the money."

"Do they know about—him?" I asked, slightly lowering my voice and carefully not looking at Waldemar, who was anyhow absorbed in watching the preparations for landing. Actually, I felt sure—and later I found I was right—that he wouldn't understand English when it was talked in the quick, casual native manner.

"No. They don't. Viola—that's my sister—she's going to get the shock of her life." Dorothy said this with a certain relish; yet she was desperately worried, I could see. "It serves them right," she muttered to herself. "That's a lesson they've had coming to them for a long time. They're all fascists at heart."

"What'll you do if they don't give you any money?"

"Oh, for God's sake!" she exclaimed, as if the strain she was under had almost reached breaking point. "We don't have to bother about *that* yet. The first question is, will they let him off this boat at all?"

There was no time to ask her what she meant by this. For now the gangplank was lowered and we all began to converge towards it. Dorothy was talking to Waldemar urgently in German; she still spoke it very fluently, I noticed, with a strong Berlin accent. "Now listen, you go through that entrance where it says 'Aliens.' We'll be waiting for you at the exit."

"You mean, I have to go alone?"

"Eugen—I've explained to you a hundred times already— it's much better this way. It'll save you so many explanations. Besides, they'll insist on interviewing you by yourself."

"But what'll I tell them?"

"Just answer all their questions quite truthfully. The readier you are to answer, the less they'll ask you."

"But I may not understand what they say."

"Don't be an idiot!" Dorothy's voice trembled—she was obviously making a frantic effort to get him through this ordeal by the sheer force of her will. "They speak German."

"They do?" This only seemed to dismay Waldemar all the more. He looked with resentful appeal at both of us. Then, forlornly, he turned and went toward the aliens' door and entered. Seeing him do this made me quite sick with that vague apprehension which was a part of the feel of the day without a morrow.

I glanced down at Dorothy, by my side. She said quietly, "If anyone ever really hurt him, I think I'd kill them." Her eyes were full of tears. Then suddenly her hand tightened on my arm, and I squeezed it reassuringly—not that I felt reassuring.

"The beastly thing is, he just hasn't the faintest understanding how *rotten* people are. He's like a five-year-old child in that way. Everywhere he goes, he expects people will like him—as if it were all one big children's party. He's so bloody innocent. My God!"

"How do you mean, innocent?" I asked, because I knew she needed to talk about Waldemar anyway, and because I was curious to find out how much he had told her.

"When we first made love, he treated me—" Dorothy giggled— "as if I was an old whore." The mere memory of this seemed to have cheered her up instantaneously. (The rest of our conversation took place in snatches, as the crowd pushed us momentarily apart and we had to pause while the official examined our passports. Now and again, a fellow-traveler would overhear a bit of it and glance at us curiously; but Dorothy was too deeply preoccupied by her problem to notice, much less feel embarrassed.)

"And you liked that?"

"Well, it fascinated me. I suppose he'd only been with whores before. He was so anxious to show me he knew everything—all the tricks! My young men before I met him had always been, well, so damned respectful. But, with him—oh, I can't describe it: it certainly wasn't respectful; in a way it wasn't even serious. It was such—such *fun!* And yet it was beautiful, too—the most beautiful thing I'd ever known in my life. I *cried* with joy—literally!"

"What about him? Did he cry too?"

"Not a hope! He was just puzzled, I think. He couldn't imagine what was the matter. He even asked me if I was ashamed of what we'd done! *Ashamed!* That's the one thing in my life I'll *never* be ashamed of. . . ." At this moment Dorothy seemed to return from the past as abruptly as she had gone back into it. She looked around her, seeming self-conscious and dismayed. "God knows why I'm telling you all this. . . . Well, yes, I *do* know—it's because I'm so bloody nervous today. Oh, Christopher, isn't life hell nowadays? You worry yourself sick all the time. It stops you from doing any kind of work or concentrating. . . . And now things look so ghastly in Spain, don't they?"

"They certainly do. I don't see how the Government can win, any more. Unless there's a miracle."

Dorothy was staring desperately at the aliens' exit door. "Oh my God, what's *keeping* him so long?"

"There were lots of passengers on this boat."

"But not so many foreigners. I noticed. Perhaps they're getting afraid to travel."

"This business always takes a long time."

"I suppose it does. I hadn't had much experience of this kind of thing before I met Eugen. Then I began to notice what was happening to lots of others. One takes one's British passport so for granted, doesn't one? I was ashamed, how smug I'd been about it—even though I've been among refugees ever since Hitler came and we all left Germany—those of us that could. Oh, in Paris it's heartbreaking! You see all these people who know they can't hope to get a permit to stay on in France for more than a few weeks longer wandering backwards and forwards outside the foreign consulates and gazing longingly at them, as if they were shop windows full of things they couldn't possibly afford. . . . You know, there *are* some South American republics you can even become a citizen of before you actually go there? Only that's terribly expensive—a thousand pounds, I heard. And even to get a visa you have to bribe them and show them a lot of money, not to mention your ticket."

"Would you be ready to go to a place like that with Waldemar—I mean Eugen?"

"No, call him Waldemar. I will, when I'm with you. . . . Yes, of course I would. I'd go anywhere with him. I mean—what's the alternative?"

"There isn't one, I suppose."

Dorothy looked at me quickly. "You knew him in Berlin, you said?"

"Oh, yes." I didn't want to risk sounding too casual about this. I didn't want to touch on the subject at all until I knew exactly what Waldemar had and hadn't told her. Because I was perfectly well aware that there was a tiny worm of jealousy coiled up inside her question. Poor old Dorothy! She certainly had enough to contend with, without being made jealous—and of *me!*

"Miss, would you step this way, please?"

This was one of the officials from the aliens' passport room. He stood in its doorway, from which we'd both turned our eyes for a moment. Evidently, Waldemar had pointed Dorothy out to him. We could see Waldemar himself in the room, behind the official.

"Yes." Dorothy turned noticeably pale as she pulled herself together for the encounter. "Come with me," she added in a low voice, gripping my sleeve. We went in together.

Waldemar was sitting on a hard office chair. He looked browbeaten, and suddenly much younger; a sullen peasant youth driven into a corner. His glance at us as we came in was angry and reproachful.

The official who had called us in was only the subordinate. His superior was the one who did the questioning; a neat little man whose dark eyes never stopped smiling and whose tight mouth never began.

"I understand, miss, that this young man is coming to visit your family."

"Certainly he is." Dorothy made the mistake of becoming defiant at once, which was obviously just what he wanted.

"May I ask if this visit is—social?"

"What do you mean, social? Of course it's social!"

"And does your family know him already?"

"What business is that of yours?"

"Dorothy," I said, "they have to ask these questions, you know."

"Are *you* a member of the family, sir?"

"Leave him out of this," said Dorothy. "He's just a friend I happened to meet on the boat."

"Just a friend . . . I see." The official looked at me with his prim mouth and his smiling eyes, as if he intended to use this against me later. Then he turned back to Dorothy and said, "I'll tell you what business it is of mine, miss. I'm an officer of His Majesty's Immigration Service, and it's my duty to see that no undesirable aliens enter this country under false pretenses."

"Who said anything about false pretenses?"

"I'm asking you if your family knows this young man?"

"No, they don't. Why should they?"

"And you still say this is a social visit?"

"Of course I say it! What other kind of visit could it be?"

"Well, miss—if you insist on my putting it frankly—this young man—well, there seems to be some discrepancy between you with regard to class."

Dorothy was about to make a violent retort. Before she could do so, I touched her arm warningly. She gulped, and asked in a controlled, aggressive voice, "And is that a crime?"

"That remains to be seen," said the official, not in the least abashed. "Are you aware that his profession is given in his passport as *Hausdiener*, and do you know what *Hausdiener* means?"

"Of course I do—it means domestic servant."

"And you're quite sure that this young man isn't coming to England as a domestic servant, and not as a friend on a social visit? You refuse to admit that he's coming to work for your family, without a labor permit, in defiance of the immigration laws?"

"That's ridiculous."

"Then perhaps you wouldn't mind telling us what he *is* going to do?" The official leaned right back in his chair, as though he had checkmated us and could now relax. "You see, this young man has already admitted to us that he is not a domestic servant, that his passport in fact contains a misstatement and is therefore an attempt to deceive His Majesty's Immigration Service. . . . Well, we're willing to overlook that, provided you'll be quite frank with us."

"I *am* being frank!"

"I don't think so, miss."

"I think you're being insolent!"

"You can always make a complaint in writing to the Home Secretary, miss. But, of course, while that was pending, we should have to deport this young man to his country of origin on the next boat."

"But you can't do that!"

"I think you'll find we can do most things, miss. In these matters we're given pretty wide powers. Subject to the Home Secretary, of course. But he leaves a great deal to our discretion, you'll find. I'm sure he'd endorse any decision we might make regarding this young man."

"He can't go back to Germany!"

"Do you mean by that that he's a political refugee? That he would be in actual danger if he returned there?"

"I—no, I didn't say that."

"Well then, don't you think you'd better answer my questions a little more fully? You're not helping much, you know. . . . Exactly how long have you known this young man?"

"Six months," said Dorothy. I guessed from her manner that she was exaggerating as much as she dared.

"Where did you meet him?"

126

"In Paris.

"Would you tell us, please, just *how* you met him?"

"I—it was in a restaurant."

"This young man used another word for it. He called it a night club."

"Is that so important?"

"If this young man isn't a domestic servant, what kind of work *does* he do? It wouldn't be connected with a night club, would it? He wouldn't be someone who frequents such places, dances with the female customers, strikes up an acquaintance with them—?" At this point, I was certain Dorothy was going to explode; but the official seemed to realize it, too, for he smoothly changed his line of attack. "While he's in England, does he expect to be entirely dependent on your family's, er, *generosity?*"

"Certainly not! He has twenty pounds of his own."

"*Of his own,* miss? That isn't the way he told it to us. He says the money is yours."

"Well—I gave it to him."

"We rather got the impression that you merely *lent* it to him—just so that he could show it to us and claim it was his. If you *did* do that, you know, miss, you'd be conspiring to deceive the Immigration Service. And that *could* be punishable by law—"

"I *gave* him the money, I tell you!"

"You did? Ah! Very generous, such a gift—in addition to the *generosity* of your invitation. . . . Well, miss, I can't say I find this a very satisfactory state of affairs. You assure us that this young man isn't going to work for your family, but we only have your word for it, you know. And since the nature of his profession seems so doubtful, he might well end up drifting about London—perhaps even becoming involved with criminal elements. . . . All things considered, I don't see my way to giving him a permit for more than one month. You *might* get an extension if you apply to the proper authorities in London, but frankly I doubt it. So this young man had better make the most of your *hospitality,* while it lasts." He stamped the passport and handed it to Waldemar. The interview had ended so suddenly that we all left the office in a daze, as meekly as sheep.

It wasn't till we were on the boat train—which we'd had to run for because of this delay—that Dorothy burst out, "Oh, the *swine!*"

"What was I to do?" exclaimed Waldemar in German, turning on her angrily. "You told me to tell them the truth, didn't you? How could I know what to say? I sat there like a fool. Why did you leave me alone with them?"

"But I had to, Eugen—can't you understand?"

"You left me alone with them. They treated me like a common crook." Waldemar turned his face to the window and sulked. Dorothy and I both felt acutely embarrassed by this, just because the other was present. But when we had ordered tea, Waldemar consented ungraciously to drink some and to eat a slice of sandy yellow railway cake. Then I went out into the corridor and lit a cigarette, wanting to give them a chance to make peace.

However, almost at once Waldemar followed me out—carefully shutting the compartment door after him, as if to make sure Dorothy shouldn't hear our conversation. Yes, he *did* want to hurt her. The old Waldemar wouldn't have behaved like that. Dorothy, I noticed, was careful not to glance at us, even, through the glass. She picked up a magazine and began to study it, rather too carefully.

Waldemar took one of my ciagarettes. As he lighted it, he looked at me with an experimental grin, not sure how I was reacting to his behavior. "It was really all *your* fault, you know, Christoph."

"*My* fault?"

"When you and I left Germany, wasn't it you who suggested I should have them put *Hausdiener* in my passport?"

"Well, yes, it was—but then you were supposed to be going to Greece to be one. Only there wasn't any house. And you were too damned lazy to work, anyway."

Waldemar laughed at this, heartily, throwing his head back, as he would have laughed five years ago. Then he asked, "You didn't tell her anything about me?"

"What should I tell her?"

"Oh, about the island, and Ambrose, and Hans, and that crazy Maria."

"I didn't tell her anything about anything."

"You swear you didn't?"

"I don't have to swear. If I tell you so, it's so."

"All right," said Waldemar meekly. "I didn't mean to offend you, Christoph."

"Is she really so jealous?"

"It's just that she wouldn't understand."

128

"Are you in love with her, Waldemar?"

"Of course I am."

"No—seriously. Because, you know, she is with you. You can't just fool around with a girl like her."

"But, Christoph, what do you mean? Who says anything about fooling? She's my *Braut!*"

"You had a *Braut* before, I seem to remember."

Waldemar grinned and dug me hard in the ribs. "You dirty dog, Christoph! Not *that* kind of *Braut!* This is different."

"How is it different?"

"I'm going to marry her."

"Oh, yes?"

"She asked me to. I swear she did, Christoph! If you don't believe me, ask *her*."

"All right! All right! I'll believe you. . . . And what did *you* say?"

"I told her I have to get a job first and be able to support her. . . . What are you laughing at?"

"At you."

"But, Christoph, how can I get a job when they won't let me work anywhere?"

"Of course you can't. Isn't that convenient?"

"Now listen! If you weren't my friend, I wouldn't let you say such things."

"But I *am* your friend. . . . What's all this nonsense about calling yourself Eugen?"

"Oh, that. . . . Well, you see, Christoph—since I saw you last—I've been around quite a bit. . . . You promise you won't tell Dorothy?"

"For heaven's sake—"

"No—Christoph, I'm sorry. I shouldn't have asked. I trust you. . . . Well, I was in all kinds of elegant places. And the people I met! I'll tell you all about it someday soon. You'll be astonished. . . . So, after a while, I said to myself: that name Waldemar—it doesn't suit you any more. As a matter of fact, several people told me the same thing."

"What was wrong with it?"

"Oh, there's nothing wrong with it. It's common, that's all. Waldemar—that's a name for a working-class boy."

Waldemar said this in such a matter-of-fact tone that I fairly gaped at him. But he wasn't interested in my reactions now. A new thought had struck him. "Has Dorothy talked to you about her parents?"

"No—why?"

"I just wondered. . . . Of course, she's a Communist. She doesn't believe in money. . . . I don't think she likes them, anyhow."

Light began to dawn on me. "You think they may be rich?"

"Well, I suppose they must have *some* money. . . . You know, I was wondering—do you think they might adopt me?"

"*Adopt* you! Are you crazy?"

"Some strange things happen, Christoph." Waldemar smiled a dreamy, fatuous smile of self-confidence. "Suppose, when we meet, they take a fancy to me? Dorothy says they haven't got a son. You never can tell, you know."

"But, Waldemar, if they did adopt you, you'd be Dorothy's brother. You could never marry her then. You couldn't even go to bed with her. You'd be committing incest."

His face fell. "You mean, they could put us in prison?"

"I don't see why not."

"Christoph—you're fooling again! I can see you are!"

At this moment I saw Dorothy abruptly put down her magazine, as if she couldn't stand being left alone one minute longer, and rise to her feet. Sure enough, she came over and opened the door into the corridor. She smiled as nicely as she could. "You two seem to be having a wonderful time out here!"

"I was just talking to Christoph about the Nazis," said Waldemar quickly. He couldn't possibly have been less convincing. All I could do to cover the awkwardness was to suggest we should go back into the compartment. For a while Dorothy and I tried small talk; then we fell silent until we reached London. By the time we had to say goodbye, Dorothy was visibly under the shadow of the approaching meeting with her family. And Waldemar, trailing behind her, seemed infected by her forebodings, even though he couldn't have understood them fully. He was following her passively into a world which was no doubt going to be far more hostile than he dreamed. I saw him, for a moment, with the eyes of Dorothy's family—a far from desirable alien.

As we parted, Dorothy forced a bright smile. "Well—thank you for your moral support, Christopher. I'll call you when we come back to town."

I stood by, watching, while they got into their taxi. Its

130

driver was more than usually friendly. He took charge of them as if they were a pair of children, helped them with the bags, smiled and nodded reassuringly when Dorothy told him they wanted to get to Liverpool Street in time to catch a certain train. As he drove them away it seemed to me that I had caught a momentary glimpse of the mechanism that was moving them, smoothly and relentlessly, into the future. What on earth was going to become of them, I wondered.

And, for that matter, what, at the end of this *jour sans lendemain*, was going to become of us all?

(*From my diary.*)

August 23. At one of the parties I went to last night someone said that the Air Ministry regarded war as inevitable. They think it will last about fifteen years. At the other party a bald man from the Foreign Office said, "If I had a thousand pounds—which I haven't," he added hastily, "I would still bet on peace."

You can hear both kinds of opinions wherever you go. But one has to accept *some* oracle, if only to avoid going into a state of permanent jitters—so I cling to Dr. Fisch. He doesn't think there'll be war; at least, not this autumn.

Dr. Fisch isn't his old assured, dogmatic self, however. Paris suited him marvelously—even better than pre-Nazi Berlin. Here in London he seems for the first time an exile; lonely and seedy and poor Jewish. Even his beloved dialectic appears to bore him. He started off to answer my questions in his usual style. "No, excuse me, Christopher—this again is an incorrect formulation. The question, will there or will there not be war, is relatively superficial. That is to say, it can only properly be considered within the framework of the whole social-economic picture. So we must first analyze this picture, and in fact under seven headings." But, after talking for a few minutes in his Rhineland German (which he makes all the harder for me to understand by keeping his pipe in his mouth) he seemed suddenly to lose interest. He broke off, leaving the first heading only half analyzed, looked vague and sad, coughed, and then spoke of something else.

All the same, I had better admit to myself that the situation is worse than ever before. It is so serious that I must force myself to be interested in it, to observe it step by step, instead of just staring at it in horror. If the ship really *is* sinking, one ought to be sending out wireless signals. But to whom? To V., in New York? No—that's on another wave length; they could never hear our S.O.S. Well then, just bulletins, addressed to no one in particular, sent without any hope of help, for the sake of one's own sanity.

August 29. Just back from a weekend in the country with G. A great mistake. Trailing all the way down to Kent just to make love in an inn gave the love-making an altogether false importance. We had to play up to it; pretend it was romantic, or at least fun. And it wasn't. It was depressing, like the cold bedroom and the lumpy bed. Right in the midst of the act, I found myself grunting and groaning extra loud, out of sheer politeness. I dare say G., who is really very sweet, was doing the same thing. But I couldn't discuss this. We don't know each other well enough.

The other reason why the weekend was a mistake is the crisis, which has suddenly become much worse. Germany has asked the Soviets how they'd react to an "intervention" in Czechoslovakia. A crisis always seems more tolerable in London; you get the latest news more quickly, and there are lots of people you can ring up and discuss it with. In the country, you are thrown upon yourself and your fear. And nature becomes hateful, just because it doesn't worry. Oh, the indifference of the cows and those great, stupid vegetables, the trees! And Sunday—a crisis Sunday in the country! What stodgy, stolid-faced horror! The church bells clanging to each other across the estates of some fascist bastard of a retired colonel, where the gamekeepers still fire at trespassers with shotguns loaded with salt. Sunday lunch at the pub: roast beef and stewed plums and pink soap-cheese—served with that weary English air of "Well, I suppose we've got to eat"—in the rapidly chilling parlor before a smoky fire. The Sunday papers seem even more ominous than in town. There was an article by Garvin called "The Way." (It should have been called "*I* am the Way.") The crowd in the bar on Saturday night—to whom Hutton's record test-match score of 364 is still the most important event of the month. And yet these people are quite ready to fight if Czechoslovakia is attacked. You feel how united they are—not by any leadership or political belief, but by a common absorption in cricket, football pools, the pictorial press.

In some future age a Chinese historian will study us and say, "But I don't understand—how *could* such people have

132

cared what the Nazis did?" But somehow they do care. They care with their own kind of passion, which neither the Nazis nor any other foreigners will believe in until it's too late.

We rode back on the bus, past the hideous little roadside teashops, the cinemas, the shoddy villas—San Leonardo, Ivanhoe, Rookery Nook. This scenery is too tame for tragedy. But that won't stop tragedy from being performed here and pathetic little supporting actors from being pushed onto the stage to play tragic roles. Sophocles for the suburbs. How it makes me loathe those Great Greeks and all that cult of heroic death-glamour!

August 31. Today I feel optimistic, for no reason whatsoever except that the German press attacks on Britain and Czechoslovakia are slightly less violent. But one has to have these days of optimism, anyhow, in order to gather strength for the next fit of despair.

Nearly every day I force myself to get on with the writing of my part of our book about the trip to China. It seems a meaningless, compulsive project just now, and I keep at it chiefly for the sake of being busy. If war breaks out in Europe, this will become the stalest of stale news. Besides, the "line" I have to take—united front, resistance to the Japanese, etc., etc.—has lost whatever meaning it ever had for me. These are only slogans now.

Whenever I think of China, all that seems vivid and poignant is the tragedy of minor actors; the early teen-age conscripts in the trenches, the civilian corpses after an air raid pitted with gravel and sand from the blasts. They make the slogans seem heartless and vile. And yet I still slip into the slogan language when I write, and I talk it quite shamelessly on the lecture platform, where I strut mock-modestly, playing the hero—for the benefit of anyone attractive who may happen to be in the audience.

I certainly couldn't have chosen a worse time to lose my political faith, even such as it was. Any kind of belief would help nowadays. How I envy Mary, who seems still able to belong to the Communist Party in the spirit of a catacomb Christian! How, at the other end of the scale, I envy those carefree ex-public-school cub reporters who run around London fairly reveling in the crisis. I met half a dozen of them in the Café Royale this evening. They were giggling and whispering as they watched a very drunk German at the next

133

table. "We can't make him talk," one of them told me, "but we've picked his pocket and found this visiting card. What does it mean?" The card was printed in German and it said that its owner was on something called *The Spanish Non-Intervention Committee*. "Our only clue so far," the reporter continued, "is that when we mentioned Beaverbrook he gave a terrific start." They were still watching the German when I left and were quite prepared to follow him all over town for the rest of the night.

Underneath all my various feelings about the crisis is a cold rock-bottom resentment. I resent being forced by the crisis to read the newspapers: they are always trash, no matter what they have to report. I resent being forced to take an interest in politicians of any kind. Fundamentally, I find Chamberlain and the other leaders of our side just as tiresome as Hitler; such people—their friends, their enthusiasms, their opinions, their hobbies, everything about them—are an obscene bore. If only they could all destroy each other in single combat!

Of course, this attitude is deplorable, disgraceful, indefensible. I couldn't admit to it, even to my friends. (Though I suspect several of them of sharing it.) Yes, yes, I know—I am a writer, that is to say, a self-advertiser; so how can I criticize the politicians? Furthermore, I am an avowed liberal; so I'm bound to believe in the justice of our cause, aren't I? Well, then? I have no answer—except that I'm weary, weary, weary. This whole business bores me even more than it frightens me. I suppose just now I am in a state of mind which must have been very common during the Middle Ages, when the little men hated, silently and impartially, all of the great ones, and their loudness and their chivalry and their battles.

When the newspapers compare Chamberlain to Abe Lincoln and Jesus Christ, they aren't being in the least sacrilegious, because *their* Lincoln and *their* Christ are utter phonies, anyhow. The newspapers are moved to tears by the spectacle of a gentleman standing his ground against a non-gentleman. So they call him "England."

Well, *my* "England" is E.M.; the antiheroic hero, with his straggly straw mustache, his light, gay, blue baby eyes and his elderly stoop. Instead of a folded umbrella or a brown uniform, his emblems are his tweed cap (which is too small for him) and the odd-shaped brown paper parcels in which he carries his belongings from country to town and back again. While the others tell their followers to be ready to die, he advises us to live as if we were immortal. And he really does this himself, although he is as anxious and afraid as any of us, and never for an instant pretends not to be. He and his books and what they stand for are all that is truly worth saving from Hitler; and the vast majority of people on this island aren't even aware that he exists.

Am reading Clausewitz on war, because Dr. Fisch told me to and because it is so horribly seasonable. After a couple of dozen pages he brings the reader, with relentless logic, to the point where he is forced to accept Clausewitz's thesis: that the purpose of war is to defeat the enemy.

In my diary there is only the briefest mention of my next meeting with Dorothy and Waldemar. Looking back, this doesn't surprise me. My diary writing was, at that time, exclusively about the crisis—which meant the crisis in relation to me. Dorothy and Waldemar just didn't fit into it; their crisis was their own. In the state I was in then, I would never have had the energy to write down was was happening to them; my jitters were accompanied, as they so often are, by a strange, apathetic sloth. But all the same, I *was* interested in them, deeply—I must have been, or I shouldn't be able to remember these details now.

On September 4, quite late in the evening, Dorothy rang me up. She asked if they could come over and spend the night. I was alone in the house, so I said "yes."

When they arrived I was aware at once of their refugee air. They were like a couple who had just been saved from a shipwreck, I thought; you felt they should have been wrapped in blankets. Dorothy had the desperate, birdlike brightness of an English girl on the verge of hysteria. Waldemar was red-eyed and clumsy in his movements. He avoided looking at me as he said, in a thick, indistinct voice, that he was going straight up to bed.

"He's falling-down drunk, poor lamb," Dorothy told me, when she and I were alone together in the kitchen later, drinking cocoa. "That's the only way he knows of dealing with situations like this. You can't blame him, can you? I only wish I could do the same thing."

"Want to try? I've got nearly a whole bottle of gin here. I'll keep you company."

"No thanks, Christopher. That's sweet of you, but it doesn't work for me. I only feel worse and worse. . . . I say, I do hope we aren't being a ghastly nuisance, coming here."

"Of course you aren't."

"I simply couldn't face going to a hotel—especially this late at night. They always think one's a whore. Not that that matters. Only one's infuriated, simply because one isn't. . . . . I'm afraid I'm not making very much sense, am I?" Dorothy paused. Then, her voice rising rather wildly, she exclaimed, "All I know is, if I have to tell one single lie more—about *anything*—I shall start screaming."

There was a long silence. I half expected that she would break down and cry; but her statement seemed to have released a lot of the tension inside her. For, when she spoke again, it was quite calmly:

"You know, at first, I actually thought that perhaps it was going to be all right, after all? I mean, after we'd got through the arrival and the introductions—because *that* went off much more smoothly than I'd expected. Let's face it, I *was* springing Waldemar on them out of a clear blue sky. I suddenly realized that—I mean, I realized how it would seem to *them*—just as the front door was about to open. I was in utter panic—but I needn't have been. They took it so calmly, you'd have thought they'd actually been expecting him. It was one of those occasions when you see the upper-class technique in action. And it really works. It can get people like my family through *anything*. That's what's so loathsome about it—filthy bourgeois hypocrisy! A working-class family might have thrown us out into the street, then and there. But at least they'd have been open and honest—

"Well, anyhow, the next day, they began showing their hand. Not so much Father. If he'd been alone in the house, we could have stayed there indefinitely, I'm sure. That wouldn't have meant that he'd accepted the situation, though. He doesn't have to accept anything. He has ways of getting around it. He has phrases—they protect him from everything that's going on in the outside world. He'll say something like, 'one of Dorothy's lame dogs'—yes, *literally*; that's how he described Waldemar to a friend of his in the village! I heard him with my own ears—over the telephone. As though I were a vet, or something!

"But my sister Viola—she's married and just about to have a baby. So of course she thinks of herself as *the* authority on Marriage and Real Love. Her husband's in Somerset House —deals with death duties, wills, that sort of thing. Looks like it, too. . . . So Viola takes me aside and starts asking, 'But, Dorothy—surely you don't *love* him? Surely it can't be *really serious?*' What outraged her wasn't that Waldemar and I were having an illicit relationship, but that we might get married! Because *that* would be an insult to *England* and *Marriage*. She kept wailing, 'Oh, Dorothy, you *can't*—you'll be *cutting yourself off* from all of us!'

"And then Mother—I'd never realized how much appearances mean to her. That sounds stupid of me, I know, but I hadn't. I found out, after we'd been there a couple of days, that she'd actually started explaining Waldemar away to the people in the village—saying he was a refugee, and that *she and Father* had *persuaded me* to bring him to stay with them for a while, *until he could look around and find his own feet!*

"And then there was the doctor's wife. She's one of these damned wishy-washy liberals—you know, Left Book Club sort of thing. She came to tea—just pop-eyed with curiosity, needless to say. That bitch of a woman—she baited Waldemar from the moment she arrived. Not only did she accept him as a refugee—though I don't believe Mother *had* convinced her—she *knew* there was something fishy—but she also pretended to take it for granted that he was a real active political fighter, practically a member of the anti-Nazi underground. She kept asking him about the organization of the K.P.D. since Hitler came into power, and how far the Gestapo had succeeded in liquidating it, and which cities it was still strong in, and what prospects there were of a strike in the arms factories. Half the time he didn't even know what she was talking about. And then finally he showed it. And she raised her eyebrows and looked at my mother—only just for an instant, but she made her point. . . . Oh God, I wish I could have strangled her!

"What really made my blood boil was that Waldemar couldn't have behaved more sweetly to all of them, poor lamb. He made the most heart-rending efforts to be friendly. And Mother simply would not yield one inch! As long as she lives, I'l hate her for that. She was never rude to him—oh, no!—she just treated him quite pleasantly but as if he was a servant. Of course, from her point of view, that's exactly what he *is*. She realized instantly he was working-class. She has a sixth sense for those things—even if he'd spoken nothing but German—which she doesn't understand a word of—she'd have known. He's working-class, so he's the same as a servant, and she never forgets it for one instant. Even though she happens to be forced to entertain him as a guest, he's still a servant and he can't ever become anything else as far as she's concerned, and that's that—

"At first Waldemar didn't realize what they were doing to him. He was just puzzled. But then after a few days, when it was getting glaringly obvious, he came to me and he said so sadly and sweetly, 'You know, I believe your mother doesn't like me.' I felt horribly guilty—just because I couldn't deny it, and because I'd known it all this time and hadn't told him. . . . Oh, Christopher, he seems so *alone* now! I begin to think there's a barrier building up, even between *us*—

"Do you know what finally brought the whole thing to a climax? Well, Mother had put Waldemar and me in separate rooms. It seems ridiculous now, but for some reason I'd never expected that. I'd taken it for granted we'd be together. And yet, Mother being what she is, what else could you possibly expect? There were the servants to consider. Still, she needn't have put Waldemar into the old schoolroom, as we used to call it; that meant our rooms were as far apart as they could possibly be. You have to walk the whole length of the house *and* go up a flight of stairs. . . . Anyhow, Waldemar didn't seem to mind that; I mean, he accepted it as a kind of game. He enjoyed having to sneak upstairs when the others were in bed; and we made a joke about having to be quiet about it, and so of course we made more noise than usual and laughed a lot. I think Mother *must* have known. Anyhow, we kept on managing somehow—my great problem was not to fall asleep after we'd made love, because he always did; and if I hadn't woken him up again in the early hours he'd have been snoring away in my bed when the tea was brought in—

"Well then, the night before last—no, it was last night, wasn't it?—it's just that it *seems* so long ago, because so much has happened since—the cook happened to come back very late—she'd been over to Ipswich to visit her sister, who's very ill. And just as she's reached the first-floor landing, on her way up to her room on the second, out comes Waldemar from my room! Cook's rather a dear, and I'm pretty sure she wouldn't ever have said anything about it. But Waldemar *has* to say good night to her—I suppose it never occurred to him not to, being the kind of person he is! And that's what Mother evidently heard—she'd be incapable of sleeping properly anyway, as long as one of the servants hadn't got in—

138

because she immediately came out of *her* room. And she said to him, in a really hateful but quiet and not scene-making tone, since Cook was present: 'Don't you think it's time you went down to bed and got some *sleep?*'

"So, this morning Mother didn't appear at breakfast. But Viola did, and she told me Mother was so upset she was staying in her room. Viola behaved just as if it was I who'd deliberately insulted all of them. 'You have to admit,' she said, 'Mother made all possible allowances. It was pretty wonderful of her, having you in the house at all. I don't mind telling you, I advised her not to let you stay—I knew you'd make trouble sooner or later. You sneer at everything we believe in. You always have. You're our enemy—' So then I got furious and started shouting—don't even remember what I said —and that brought Mother downstairs. She sent Viola out of the room and started crying; but the more she cried, the more I hated her. It sounds callous of me, Christopher—but all I could see was a miserable little bourgeois housewife crying because she'd been humiliated in front of her own cook, and because she was terrified the neighbors would get to hear about it. . . . It came to me, as it never had before, even when I was most involved in politics in Berlin, that the Communists are absolutely right: these people *are* the class enemy —they've got to be liquidated at all costs, because their way of life is nothing but death. And, God, when I thought that I have their blood in me—and that the way I think and feel has probably permanently been warped by what they call their educational system—then I could almost willingly say, 'Liquidate me, too'!

"Well, Mother ended by saying that, in view of what had happened, it would be better for everyone if we left at once. Although, of course, I was welcome to come back any time, *alone.* And then she begged me to break it off with Waldemar. She said—you won't believe this, Christopher—*she actually said,* 'Why doesn't he go back to Germany? After all, that's his home and that's where he belongs, isn't it? And, I mean, he isn't a Jew or anything. He'd probably be much happier there.'

"That left me speechless for a minute, as you can imagine. I was more amazed then disgusted. Finally, I managed to ask, 'Don't you know *anything* about the Nazis, Mother?' And do you know what she answered? 'Of course, I know they've

139

done some bad things. But I dare say Hitler's done very well for his own people.'

"After that, what was there to say? All I wanted was to get out of that atmosphere and be somewhere where I could breathe. If we hadn't missed the through train and had to change twice, we'd have been here hours ago."

Next morning, Waldemar came into my room while I was shaving. He seemed very depressed. "I believe everyone in England's crazy," he said, "I really do—except you, Christoph." (He added this politely, without much conviction.) "You know, Dorothy's quite changed, now she's here. She isn't the same girl. She does nothing but worry. She isn't fun any more. She worries so much, she makes *me* miserable. Nothing's worth getting so miserable over. If there's a war, there's a war."

That afternoon he and Dorothy moved to the flat of a girl I knew slightly; she was living with a Negro poet from the States. They were Communists, and this gave them an attitude to the crisis which was majestically aloof. To them, nothing mattered ultimately but Spain and the Soviet Union; the plight of England was secondary. However, if England and France went to war, they would be forced to intervene in Spain on the side of the Government. So going to war would be a good thing. But these two were absolutely certain that there would not be war—simply because they couldn't imagine Chamberlain doing anything good under any conceivable circumstances.

There was a craziness about their conviction which I found stimulating and infectious. As long as I was with them, I could almost see the situation through their eyes. We all drank beer, and I felt more cheerful than I had felt for weeks and as irresponsible as a character in *Alice in Wonderland*. Then I said goodbye to Dorothy and Waldemar and left them with their hosts. By the time I got home again, I was gloomier than ever.

September 8. Yesterday *The Times* published a leader suggesting that the Sudeten areas ought to be handed over to Germany. I rang up F.P. about this, because I was curious to hear the Conservative Party line. "Just tactics," he told me blandly. "We know damn well the Germans don't really want the Sudetenland; it'd only be another political liability. This article'll embarrass them."

Hitler, at Nuremberg, hasn't spoken yet. He probably will on Monday, unless he prefers simply to stage a *putsch* over the weekend. Meanwhile, people here seem to be suffering from anxiety-exhaustion. They're beginning to say, "For Christ's sake, let's have the war and get it over."

Stephen Savage came to tea yesterday. His total preoccupation with himself and his emotional affairs, far from being unsympathetic, is a tiny rock to which I cling in the midst of this raging ocean of headlines. I want to be with people who think about themselves, not me. I don't want to be loved or understood. I don't want anybody's sympathy. And Stephen doesn't, either. He just unfolds this fascinating saga of himself, and you can listen if you like. His problems couldn't be more complicated; the usual triangle has turned into a pentagon. One moment, he will tell you, "I only really feel what my friends tell me I feel"; the next, he will describe how, last night, he felt so guilty that he shed tears for an hour. One doesn't disbelieve him—only, one can't help roaring with laughter. And then he laughs, too. He's naughty-boyish, and so sly. A sly Shelley. But then, I'm sure Shelley was slyer than any of us.

Later, two friends of Stephen's came by. One of them started calmly describing her plans to go to Tunis next month. I stared at her as if she were raving mad. How *dare* she, I felt. And I was superstitiously afraid that the demons of the air would hear her. And yet, why *shouldn't* one plan for pleasure and happiness, even in the blackest shadow of disaster? Isn't this exactly what E.M. means by saying we should behave as if we were immortal? No. Not in this girl's case. Because she hasn't even enough imagination to be aware of the shadow. Just plain stupid.

September 10. All the leader writers suddenly admit that we're on the brink. The Sudetens and the Czechs continue to negotiate, but Hitler is absolutely intransigent. When I rang up Dr. Fisch, he said, "The chances of peace were fifty-fifty; now they're thirty-seventy."

September 13. The menace of Hitler's speech was like a chill throughout yesterday, although the weather has turned very hot. In the morning I went round with Stephen to see John and discuss an article for the magazine. Now that John's hair is prematurely gray, he looks distinguished enough for the Cabinet—especially in that great calm eighteenth-century room overlooking the square. We all three laughed like maniacs. Crisis laughter. Stephen said, "Herr Issyvoo called at Number Ten and remained for half an hour with the Prime Minister. Their conversation was described as useful."

To make the time pass, I got my hair cut. At the barber's, a hateful jaundiced-looking customer was talking confidently about the certainty of war; trying to make the manicure girl's flesh creep. He didn't succeed. She was another of the insensitive ones. But another customer agreed with relish, "Why read the papers? They'll tell us soon enough when it comes. Then we'll be under orders." (This last remark struck a clear note of satisfaction. *Orders*—that's what they deeply want.)

Then I went into a cinema. Nearly always this kills my time-and-place sense; yesterday it wasn't even dulled. I felt absolutely toxic with crisis. The newsreel contained no scenes whatsoever of Hitler or the Nazis. Was this deliberate policy? Anyhow, it seemed fatally ostrich-like. I prefer to be reminded of them, every instant. The film itself bored me, except for a few moments when you were shown somebody being happy—a little girl laughing for no reason, a fat man enjoying his beer. This was almost unbearable, because their happiness seemed so poignantly insecure. My eyes filled with tears. Once I found myself actually beginning to sob. I turned it into a cough.

And then an old man just behind me started muttering to himself. He was either drunk or half out of his mind. "Oh, I do want to die! Oh, I'm so ill! My wife hates me. She says: Why don't you poison yourself? Go on out to the cinema. I'm sick of you. . . . Oh, I do want to die—" The old man kept repeating this, until I couldn't stand it and had to leave. No one else seemed to hear him.

I had to have supper with Aunt Edith, so there was no question of being able to listen to the speech itself. (Even if Aunt E. had stooped to the vulgarity of owning a wireless set, she'd probably still have refused to listen. She'd feel that it was somehow encouraging and abetting "that odious man," as she calls him.) So we talked family gossip, and I kept glancing in misery at the grandfather clock and thinking, "Now he's begun . . . now he's got to the middle . . . by this time he must have said the word—*if* he's going to say it."

I excused myself as early as I could, and rushed over to Dr. Fisch in a taxi. He says the speech has altered nothing. It was very violent but carefully vague. "You see, Christopher, violence is never alarming—what is alarming is lack of violence. The situation now becomes perfectly clear. The neutrality of Czechoslovakia will be guaranteed on condition her French and Russian alliances are dropped. Oh, yes, naturally, the crisis will continue. And one must never discount the possibility of incidents. But that is really irrelevant. One has to learn to analyze these things from an objective, dialectical viewpoint; and not—excuse me that I say this—with the emotionalism of the popular press." This last was a playful little dig at me, of course, because I had admitted to him how worried I've been. But I didn't care; I was much too relieved. Besides, I am fondest of Fisch when he is in this fatherly superior, scientifically oracular mood, puffing away benignly at his pipe. I drank a lot of Fisch's whisky, which made me feel like having sex. So I rang up B., and then G. Both of them were out.

September 14. My relief didn't last long. Yesterday's lunch editions had news of the rioting in the Sudeten areas. Then came the Czech Government's declaration of emergency measures. I had supper with G. As we came out of the restaurant, there were the headlines of the Sudeten ultimatum. I felt at once: this is *really* it. My immediate reaction was that I couldn't bear to be alone with G., who is so sweet but so utterly passive, and who'd insisted, throughout supper, on discussing our "relationship." As though we were characters in a Henry James novel of the nineteen hundreds. G., needless to say, expected that we'd go straight home and make love. But I said firmly, No; we were going to the Café Royale. And there, as I'd hoped, we ran into Stephen and some boys and girls from the ballet. We talked about the ultimatum, of course; but soon we were laughing and joking. Someone had a car and we all drove down Whitehall, "just to see if anything's going on." Downing Street was quite empty, except for a few policemen, and this seemed reassuring.

This morning Fisch refuses to admit that he was wrong or that the situation is worse. One of his stock exchange colleagues knows a man who is just back from Germany. He says the General Staff is absolutely opposed to war.

Some pathetic little man—who didn't have the benefit of sharing Fisch's dialectical viewpoint—killed himself after listening to Hitler's speech. He left a note: "I've never been a hero. Selfish to the last."

He minded, certainly—far more than I do, but in a different way. I sometimes think that nobody minds the crisis in quite my way; at least, no one I personally know.

For instance, when I'm with my friends, I'm ashamed to indulge in my compulsive newspaper-buying. I buy as many as twelve papers a day, barely glance at the stop-press bulletins and then throw them away. And this isn't just because I'm anxious to have the latest news. This is really an absurd act of superstition; I have a superstitious feeling that, if I buy *all* the editions, if I keep my eye on the crisis every moment, then it won't get worse. Actually, if it goes on much longer, I may end up sitting all day over a ticker tape! And then the van from the asylum will arrive.

When I imagine wartime in England, what fills me with panic is not the prospect of being bombed or even of a Nazi invasion; it's the image of *authority*. The state of being under orders, as that man at the barber's put it. I realize that I have a terror of uniform and all that it implies. In China I was scared several times during air raids or when we were at the front, but I was never panic-stricken; and—however ridiculous this may sound—I know it was largely because we were wearing our own civilian clothes! I've only been under authority, in the sense I mean, during one period of my life; my schooldays. So it is *English* authority that I dread. If the Nazis got over here, I should be terrified of them, of course; but I could never, at the deepest level of my consciousness, take them quite seriously. Not as seriously as I took my first headmaster.

September 15. Chamberlain has flown to see Hitler at Berchtesgaden. A bad move, says Dr. Fisch. We shall lose prestige. The whole allied front is cracking. What do I care? At least the showdown is postponed.

This evening the posters and headlines of the Berchtesgaden talks sound like a Victorian love affair. "They Meet." And Chamberlain saying, "Herr Hitler has encouraged me to hope."

September 19. Left early the day before yesterday for Manchester with Dr. Fisch in his car. I didn't want to, but I couldn't put it off any longer; he's been urging me for weeks to show him some of the "real" England. The country as far as Derby isn't country at all, but a suburban building estate as yet undeveloped; petrol pumps, Tudor cafés, cattle which seem as out of place as animals in a zoo. Then the North begins; the sodden fields, the walls of piled stones, the bare, sad, feminine hills. We took the road through Chapel Bridge because I wanted to show Fisch the Hall. Whatever possessed me to do it? I should have known better than to go near the place. It is very nearly a ruin now, though the roof is still on: the wallpaper in tatters, the plaster cracked or already fallen, and great patches of damp everywhere. The air smelled of chilly decay. And the smiling, sly-faced caretakers were camping out in the kitchen, until the tourist season ends, serving dainty teas. Oh, the squalor of the horrible, diseased old house! How can anyone dare to pretend that it's romantic? The past seemed to take me by the throat with its disgusting claw and choke me; I shudder to feel its power, even now. In spite of all my struggling, have I ever really broken its grip? As we drove away, I made an almost hysterical speech to Fisch, saying that the cult of antiquity is obscene; that I wanted to go to America and change my family name and forget that I had any ancestors. Fisch, who comes of a very poor family in Frankfurt, was amazed but also rather intrigued. It's part of *his* romanticism to think of me as a decadent aristocrat at heart.

Meanwhile, the incipient cold I've been suffering from got suddenly worse, and my tonsils became inflamed. We spent the night in Manchester, in a tomblike hotel which was caked with soot like drifted snow. Yesterday we drove home. Poor Fisch—his outing was spoiled! He was very attentive, but I was sulky and feverish and he got on my nerves till I could have screamed.

The Cabinet met with Daladier to persuade the French to sell out Czechoslovakia.

September 22. The Franco-British sellout is like old history; things happen so fast these days that yesterday's newspaper might as well be an Egyptian papyrus. Everybody is horrified, or pretends to be, and much more belligerent. They all curse Chamberlain. Already, since his meeting with Hitler at Bad Godesberg, there's a joke: "Things have gone from bad to Bad Godesberg." And Ribentrop is supposed to have said to Hitler before the Godesberg talks started, "Don't be

145

vague—ask for Prague." Now people are claiming that there was a *Reichswehr* plot to arrest Hitler if he had tried to declare war. As for Dr. Fisch, his new slogan is, "Back to the private life." Europe is lost, he says; and there'll be fascism in this country within two years. He himself is planning to leave for South America.

But, now that there's a new cabinet in Prague, anything may happen. The Nazis are demanding the whole earth; and they've suddenly got lots of allies—Poles, Hungarians, Italians. They're so reckless that there may very well be a war, after all. Chamberlain is with Hitler today, to be told where he gets off.

September 24. Yesterday the Godesberg talks broke down because Hitler wouldn't give a satisfactory answer to Chamberlain's demand that he should promise to withhold from violence during the talks. Later we heard that the Czechs had mobilized. Fisch said on the telephone, "War is inevitable. London will be bombed within two or three days." I went to bed and took a sleeping tablet.

What a tonic for me it was, having lunch with E.M. today! He says he's afraid of going mad, of suddenly turning and running away from people in the street. But, actually, he's the last person who'd ever go mad; he's far saner than anyone else I know. And immensely, superhumanly strong. He's strong because he doesn't try to be a stiff-lipped stoic like the rest of us, and so he'll never crack. He's absolutely flexible. He lives by love, not by will.

That last statement smells unpleasantly of the Christian jargon. But E.M., of course, has no religion. If he did, he wouldn't be E.M. I must admit, he doesn't seem to loathe it as I do; in fact, when he talks about it, he's very moderate and open-minded. But, all the same, he's one more living proof that nobody who is really great can have any truck with that filth.

While we were eating, the manager of the restaurant came over to tell us he'd just heard on the wireless that Hitler has allowed six days for the evacuation of the Sudeten areas. *Six days!*" I exclaimed. "Why, that's marvelous!" At once I felt idiotically gay. It was as if we had all had an almost indefinite reprieve from the crisis. Time has slowed down nowadays to such an extent that six days are about equal to six ordinary months.

This crisis is like a newly discovered dimension. Hitherto we've been taking it for granted that the zone between peace and war is narrow and always quickly crossed. But now it is evident that the neutral zone *can* be enormous. We might conceivably live in this one for the rest of our lives.

To celebrate our reprieve I ordered champagne, just for the pleasure of being extravagant, and we both got rather drunk. E.M. became very gay and made silly jokes. His silliness is beautiful because it expresses love and is the reverse side of his passionate minding about things. The other kind of silliness—ugly, unfunny bar stories, joyless swishing and clowning—expresses aggression and malice and is the reverse side of insensitive not-caring. We need E.M.'s silliness more than ever now. It gives courage. The other kind depresses and weakens me more than the worst prophecies of disaster.

E.M. went back to the country by a late afternoon train. Keeping up my mood of celebration, I had supper with B. at the flat. Since I was there last, B. has bought a big mirror and hung it in the bedroom. We drank whisky and then had sex in front of it. "Like actors in a blue movie," B. said, "except that we're both much more attractive."

But there was something cruel and tragic and desperate about the way we made love; as though we were fighting naked to the death. There was a sort of rage in both of us— perhaps simply rage that we are trapped here in September 1938—which we vented on each other. It wasn't innocent fun, like the old times in Germany—and yet, just because it wasn't, it was fiercely exciting. We satisfied each other absolutely, without the smallest sentiment, like a pair of animals. And that's what I want now. Not poor, dear, tiresome, helpless G.

At the moment I feel splendid. E.M. and B. between them have pulled me together again. Whatever happens, I mean to work a lot on the China book. And I'll start doing my exercises again. For the first time this year.

September 26. The Czechs have refused Hitler's terms. Roosevelt has cabled Berlin urging moderation; but will Hitler take any notice? He is to speak again tonight. Then, people say, we shall know definitely what he's going to do. Shall we? We've been saying that for the past five years.

It seems almost incredible now that one ever thought one was unhappy in the old days. Unhappiness arising only out of one's personal life seems merely neurotic now, or a pose. Why wasn't the state of unthreatened peace enough in itself for me? Why wasn't I simply content to enjoy each moment of my newsless paradise?

I suppose there are quite a number of places in the world where you could still do this; places that won't be seriously affected even if there is a war. But one couldn't go to them now. The idea of running away is meaningless. Because, in a sense, we are all mad here—the crisis is our madness—and, if you ran away to some land where there is sanity and joy, you couldn't help bringing your madness with you. No, I shall stay here, of course. I'd stay even if I were given permission and money to leave. But I hereby make a bargain with fate—if, by some miracle, we do get through this without war, then I am going back to America. For a long time. Perhaps for always. I am going to live with V. and try to unlearn my madness and forget my ancestors and become sane again. When I think of being with V. in New York, I find myself murmuring "the New World. . . ." That's what I caught a glimpse of last summer. And what I mean to create, for both of us.

If—

Despite the latest worsening of the situation, my morale is still very good. Wrote eight pages today, and did all my exercises twice over! Dorothy came by to see me, greatly depressed about W. I think I made her feel better, though I didn't deliberately try to. It was just that she reacted to my new mood. Long may it last!

Dorothy certainly *was* depressed. She told me that she and Waldemar had moved to a wretched little hotel near Paddington Station. They had moved because Dorothy had found out that Waldemar had been going to bed with Pearl, their hostess. "It wasn't anything serious between them, of course," Dorothy added. "Only we couldn't possibly stay on there. That kind of thing creates such an impossible situation —especially in a small flat."

"Has this happened before?"

"Oh, dear, yes—several times in Paris. We even had jokes about it. You know, he really is terribly vain, poor darling. He'd go to bed with almost anyone who flattered him enough."

"Then you can't really mind, can you?"

148

"You'd think I couldn't. But I *do,* damn it! I hate and despise myself for minding, but I do. It's all part of this ghastly way I was brought up—this awful bourgeois thing they teach you, about *owning* people. . . . Oh, I really try, Christopher! But you don't know how hard it is for someone like me. And then, the other women are usually such bitches about it. Pearl was. All she really wanted was to sleep with Waldemar, just like any woman might; but when I told her I knew, she first of all tried to lie her way out of it, and then got noble and made it into a question of principle. As though she'd done something fine and free and revolutionary—liberating Waldemar from a reactionary fascist! It was so ridiculous, really—*her* having the nerve to say that to *me!* I wanted to kill her. And yet, in some sneaking way, I felt guilty and that she was right. . . . I suppose it might be different in the Soviet Union, among people who were *really* comrades and did it without bitchiness—not like this fake Communist thing they play at, over here."

"Have you ever thought of going to Russia?"

"Oh, yes. . . . Waldemar doesn't seem keen on the idea, though. . . . You know, I've wondered—isn't it *wrong* to have personal relationships nowadays? Shouldn't you keep yourself unattached—in case, suddenly, you're needed? I mean, if it wasn't for Waldemar, if I were on my own, I'd almost certainly be in Spain at this moment—teaching, or helping out in a hospital."

"How does he feel about that?"

"Oh, I couldn't take him with me. You can't make a decision like that for another person. Why, he might have to fight! Poor lamb—I can't imagine him doing *that,* can *you?*"

"You couldn't leave him behind in Paris?"

"Never! He'd be lost without me—utterly. He's always telling me so. The truth is, I'm afraid I've let him depend on me too much. . . . You know, Christopher, I envy you! You do travel light, don't you? You don't ever get yourself involved with anyone."

"That doesn't mean I don't want to. And, as a matter of fact, this summer I met someone in New York—"

"Don't do it! Don't get involved! I warn you!"

"Does that mean you're sorry you got involved with Waldemar?"

"Yes—no—oh, how can one say that? It's happened, and that's all there is to it. Perhaps I'm talking nonsense. Perhaps

149

this guilt thing only applies to me. It might be quite different for you. Only—I can't help it—I keep feeling: with all that's going on in the world, isn't it selfish to be happy?"

"*Are* you happy, Dorothy?"

"Good God, no! Of course not! Neither is he. How could we be—as long as we're in this mess. . . . At night I lie awake for hours thinking the most fantastic things. Like—if only it was the other way round—if he was a girl and I was a man—then I could marry him and he'd be a British subject automatically. So many women refugees are doing that now—*paying* some Englishman to marry them, just for the passport. And *we* can't—it seems so *unfair*. . . . Shall I make a confession to you? This just shows you what being involved can do to you—how low it can make you sink! Quite often lately I've caught myself hoping there *will* be a war! So Waldemar will be interned. They couldn't throw him out of the country then. And they wouldn't trust him in the British Army. He might be locked up, but he wouldn't have to fight. He'd be safe, at least. . . . Isn't that shameful?"

"I'm sure I'd feel exactly the same. . . . But what are you going to do if there isn't a war?"

"Well, we shall have to get out of England soon, that's certain. He's overstayed his time already; they probably won't ever let him come back in again. Not that either of us cares about that."

"Where will you go?"

"I don't know. I simply can't make myself make any plans until we know what's going to happen in Europe. . . . Oh, Christopher, isn't it *misery*, just being alive nowadays? I really don't think I could bear it, if I didn't know things are going to get better."

"How do you mean?"

"Why, under Communism, of course. When it's all over the world."

"*Will* they be better then?"

"They must be!"

"Not in our lifetimes, probably."

"All right—not in our lifetimes. As long as one knows they *will*. One day. Otherwise, nothing has any meaning at all."

"Is that really how you feel, Dorothy?"

"Of course it is! Communism's *got* to come. Everything has to have been leading up to that. Or else history doesn't mean anything, does it? Life doesn't mean anything. We might as well never have been born. . . . Surely you feel that too, Christopher? You must! I mean—you don't see any *other* meaning in life, do you?"

"Well . . . no. No, I don't. . . . No meaning at all."

"I'm so glad I came and talked to you today," Dorothy said later, when I had persuaded her to have a drink. "There's something about you—you always cheer me up."

September 27. How simple it would be to live through this time if only one could altogether stop hoping! Well, that's certainly getting easier every day. Poor Dr. Fisch tortures himself; he is glued to the wireless. I try not to listen to it, but I keep hearing it in snatches wherever I am, from some nearby room or house. My ears have become as sharp as a fox's. . . . And I can't break myself of my paper-buying.

The papers talk as if we were at war already. They weigh up our chances—our side has so and so many planes; theirs, so and so many. Conscription is to be decreed tomorrow.

This afternoon I got fitted for a gas mask. You can hardly breathe through them at all. The smiles of the officials at the fitting stations are almost medical in their sweetness, as much as to say that this is a painless and even pleasant operation and that panic is unthinkable. But the children were screaming their heads off as the masks were put on them. Some people have been testing their masks in ovens or over the exhausts of cars, and getting themselves gassed—we are warned.

A.R.P. notices are now up all over town, on the railings of the squares and in windows. Trenches are being dug in Hyde Park. The slogan is, "Keep calm—and dig." Tinned food is being hoarded. There is a shortage of petrol. Lots of people are leaving London; lots are enlisting. I have written to the Foreign Office, volunteering for propaganda work. John has done the same, and he invites me to move in and share his flat. I am trying hard to create a cheerful picture of myself living a snug underground wartime life, right in the midst of things, working and joking with my friends; rather like the animals of Beatrix Potter.

The funny thing is, I am one of the relatively few people in this city who have been in a modern air raid. Of course, I know perfectly well that even the worst of the raids on Hankow would be like a wet firecracker compared to a full-scale bombardment of London. But I don't dwell on this. I just remind myself that I wasn't too frightened then, and I keep

151

assuring my friends (and myself) that we would probably have lots of excitement and even fun—including shelter parties and sex pickups in the blackout.

September 28. Well now, surely, the case is closed? No more reprieves. Pardon refused. Nothing remains but the execution. Wilson has come back from Berlin, snubbed. The German Army mobilizes this afternoon. Chamberlain spoke last night, moaning, "How dreadful!"

I'm just back from lunch with Mary. All her lodgers will be leaving her to go into the army or the navy, and she doesn't know how she'll be able to keep the house on, or where she'll go if she can't. Yet she was marvelously placid, as usual; *her* communism really does seem to give her complete reassurance and moral support. Or is that simply her temperament? Could she have been just as placid, under other circumstances, as a Seventh Day Adventist? Faith always makes me uneasy—any faith. I cling to E.M.'s doubt.

Mary says that no evacuation arrangements have been made for children under school age. There is a rumor that the Government will destroy all dogs when war breaks out, and a lady Mary knows has already had hers "put to sleep" by the vet. A lady went to the A.R.P. center in Mary's street and asked them if one couldn't have some pattern or design stenciled on one's gas mask "to make it more individual." Mary tells you these stories with a slightly gleeful air of apocalyptic prophecy—rather as though you had asked her what would be the signs of the Second Coming.

Exercises this morning. No work on the China book, but that's only common sense. I'll have to wait and see if our publishers are even going to be prepared to publish it, under the circumstances. I don't think I feel any more anxiety; that's over and done with. As far as I can tell, I'm perfectly calm, with just a flicker of exhilaration underneath. What's exhilarating is one's sense of *speed*—rapidly increasing. How quickly and smoothly we're all being swept toward the brink!

Later. After writing the above, I went to Victoria to meet Hugh Weston, returning from his holiday in Belgium. The station was crowded with sailors on their way to rejoin the mobilized fleet. A few women were crying.

The boat train arrived very late, with Hugh on it in a loud, becoming check suit. He was sunburned and in the highest spirits. "Well, my dear," he greeted me, "there isn't going to be a war, you know!" For a moment I really thought he must have some stop-press information, but no; he had merely met a lady at the British Embassy who could read cards, and she had told him there would be no war this year!

As we got into a taxi, he began to tell me about an alleged miracle which had taken place at a village near where he had been staying. The three bad boys of the village claimed one day that they had met the Virgin Mary walking along the railway lines. They managed to convince a lot of people. The spot became a center of pilgrimage. Speculators bought land around it. Peddlers chipped bits off the sleepers and sold them as relics.

Then suddenly through the taxi window I caught a glimpse of the placards: Dramatic Peace Move. I yelled to the driver to stop—Hugh found this excitement slightly exaggerated—and we read how Hitler, Mussolini, Daladier and Chamberlain are to meet in Munich tomorrow.

Later came news of the super-scene in the Commons. Chamberlain's voice breaking. Queen Mary in tears. Only ill-bred Communist Gallagher shouting that it was a sellout.

This evening the newsboys cry, "No war! No war!" rather sadly; no doubt, their papers are harder to sell. No one in the streets looks particularly excited. I suppose we're all feeling the letdown. I'm ready to flop into bed and sleep twelve hours. I realize now that I *was* anxious this morning. And that I *hadn't* stopped hoping. I find this discovery humiliating and even alarming. Does it mean that I can't stop hoping under any circumstances? They talk as if hope was always something noble. Surely it might become merely idiotic, as well as prolonging one's agony for no good reason?

I have made another discovery about myself, and I don't care if that's humiliating or not. I am quite certain of this now: as far as I am concerned, nothing, nothing, nothing is worth a war.

We all slid down from the crisis more quickly than I would have thought possible. Children played battles among the trenches in the park; some of them even wore their gas masks. Chamberlain was "England" no longer; his "nettle danger" was forgotten until the next politician came quotation-picking through poor old Shakespeare's bones. "Hitler has made an enormous concession," Dr. Fisch had said with a bitter smile the morning after Munich; "his troops will

153

march into Czechoslovakia in forage caps instead of steel helmets, to show that the occupation is peaceful." Now Fisch was getting his visa and tickets for Brazil and the private life. And already I was corresponding with New York.

My friends, and thousands of people like us, said that a great betrayal had taken place. I said so myself. And I wasn't being exactly insincere. Only every time I said this, it was as if I mentally added: Yes, but a war has been postponed—and a war postponed is a war which may never happen.

Then early in October I had a visit from Waldemar.

He startled me violently one morning by appearing in the bathroom doorway while I was taking a bath. I hadn't closed the door because I'd supposed I was alone in the house. Evidently I hadn't closed the front door properly, either. For me this post-Munich period was a time of loud, late parties and unsteady, fumbling comings-home in the small hours.

Waldemar hadn't reached the hang-over stage as I had; he was still fairly drunk. Throughout most of what followed, he had that characteristic hostile drunk air of addressing not me but a crowd—maybe Dorothy's family, or the entire English nation.

"Well, that's how it is," he said, lapsing into his harsh, Berlin tough streetboy tone; "the joke's over."

"What do you mean?"

"I mean, the joke's over. Got to get out of here, before they throw me out. My permit's up. More than two weeks."

"I know. That's too bad. Where'll you and Dorothy go now?"

"She wants me to go with her to Niggerland." Waldemar smiled a silly, ugly little smile.

"*Where?*"

"How the shit do *I* know? Ecuador. Where's that?"

"In South America."

"South America! She's crazy! What would I do there, among all those niggers? *You* go there, I told her. Go wherever you want to. Just leave me out of it."

"And what did she say?"

"How should *I* know what she said? Haven't seen her for three days. The joke's over."

"You've had a quarrel?"

"Quarrel? Why should we quarrel? Let her go to the nig-

154

gers—as long as she leaves *me* alone. . . . Why don't you ask me where *I'm* going, Christoph?"

This, I realized at once from his smiling, half-hostile, half-teasing manner, was what he had really come to tell me. He had to tell me—or somebody. That was what he had got drunk for. "Where are you going?" I asked.

"Back to Germany."

Waldemar looked quickly away from me as he said this. But only for a moment. When he spoke again, he was obviously repeating a speech which he had made up in his head and rehearsed until it sounded compulsive, like something said under hypnosis: "Home is home. I'm not a Nazi. I'll never be a Nazi. You know that. But I'm German, and home is home. I can't help what the Nazis do."

I still didn't know what to say.

"You remember Oskar? *He's* still in Germany. He's been there all the time." Waldemar sounded defensive, now, and more human. "I got a card from him."

"And did he advise you to come back?"

"He didn't say anything much. Just that it was nice weather."

"Oh . . . I see."

Waldemar fixed his eyes on mine. And now I felt that he was appealing to me directly. "Where do *you* think I should go, Christoph?"

"Well, I . . . What did Dorothy say when you told her you were going to Germany?"

"Never mind Dorothy. I told you—she and I are finished."

"Finished? Just like that?"

"You were right all along, Christoph. I knew what you were thinking that day we landed off the boat. Dorothy—that's nothing for a boy like me. I'm no family father."

"Aren't you at least going to ring her up and say good-by?"

"Oh, I'll send her a card from Berlin. . . . Let's forget Dorothy. I asked you a question, Christoph."

"What's the use of asking *me* where you should go? You've made up your mind, haven't you?"

"You think I'm doing something bad, don't you?"

"How can I know if it's bad—for you?"

"*You* think it's bad. You do. Admit it!"

"Look, Waldemar—I can't. I can't tell you to go or stay anywhere. I haven't the right to. I'm going away myself, before long."

"*You're* going away?" He became instantly more alert. He seemed almost sober now.

"Yes. To America."

"*Amerika!*" Only a German boy of Waldemar's generation could have uttered the name in quite that tone. No wonder even the Nazis feared its magic—and tried to disenchant their young by calling it the Home of the Jews! Waldemar hesitated for a moment. Then he laid a hand on my bare shoulder—I was out of the tub by now and drying myself—as he asked, very softly and persuasively, "Will you take me with you, Christoph?"

I smiled weakly, pretending I thought he wasn't serious.

"Christoph—do you remember those old days? Perhaps *you've* forgotten, but *I* haven't. I remember everything. We were just boys then. We were so happy, weren't we? Didn't we have some marvelous times together, you and I? Remember how we used to laugh and fool around? If we hadn't any money, what did that matter? We enjoyed ourselves just the same. And then—all the way to Greece! That was a *real* adventure! That's the way to travel—two friends, roughing it. Who wants to have women along? They're no fun. They only think of themselves. Those were the best times, weren't they, with just the two of us?"

He seemed actually to become younger as he spoke; younger and softer. His voice was coaxingly gentle as he conjured up this—largely imaginary—vision of our past; wove this spell which was powerful only by virtue of its utter absurdity.

"Christoph—take me with you! I promise you one thing, on my word of honor; if you do, you'll never regret it!"

"But I can't, Waldemar! It's absolutely impossible. You must *know* I can't!"

And, after all, how weak the poor little spell was—how easily broken! I felt relieved and yet guilty as I saw his face change, become older again and harder.

"*Ja, ja*—that's the way things are! I ought to have got it through my thick head by now. . . . You're like the others. You tell me not to go back to Germany. But you won't really help. Do you think I belong *here?* Or in Paris? They all hate us Germans. Some of them think, at first, I must be a Jew; when they find out I'm not, then I'm a Nazi, as far as they're concerned. Maybe if I understood about politics, it'd be different. But I don't. And I don't want to. I don't give a shit about anything any more. I just want to be some place where they'll leave me in peace."

"Waldemar—believe me—I'm sorry."

"Good-by, Christoph."

"But you don't have to rush off like this? Wait a minute—I'll get dressed. Have you had breakfast?"

"The train's leaving in twenty minutes."

"Good God, is it really? I'll call you a taxi."

"I've got one waiting outside."

This seemed so crazy—since Waldemar had carried on the conversation as though he had hours of time to spare—that I couldn't help smiling.

"Good luck, then, Waldemar. Have a good journey. And—let's hope we meet soon—somewhere—" My voice lost its confidence on this last remark. It rang false—heartlessly insincere. I had only made it out of nervousness. And, of course, it was exactly what Waldemar expected—and wanted. It was his cue to punish me for my unhelpfulness.

"No, Christoph."

"What do you mean, no?"

"We shan't meet again. Ever."

"What nonsense!"

"It's no good. I just know it, that's all. Good-by. Enjoy yourself in Amerika."

He gave my hand a manly squeeze, turned and went downstairs without meeting my eyes. When he was already out in the street, I got a sudden, violent feeling that it was my duty to stop him—to persuade him, at least, to think this over, to wait until he was quite sober, to ring up Dorothy.

But if I ran downstairs and shouted after him, naked except for a small bath towel, what would the taxi driver think? To hell with the taxi driver. . . . My hesitation had been only momentary, but it had been sufficient. For now I heard the taxi driving away.

And then, as I stood there listening to it, I realized something strange; Waldemar's decision had somehow related itself to mine. And now my own departure had become just that much more of an accomplished fact.

Paul

Another look into a mirror—my own face dimly reflected through the fashionable twilight of a Beverly Hills restaurant, confronting three people on a banquette with their backs to the glass. This is the autumn of 1940. We are just getting ready to start lunch. Six thousand miles away is the war. One step outside is the flawless blue sky and the California sun, which will hardly lose its warmth till Christmas. Here inside is richly dark leather with gleams of brasswork; an ambiance of movie agents, mulled contracts and unhungry midday greed.

I don't look happy, and indeed I am not. I am dully wretched because of the war, about which I can seldom stop thinking for more than five minutes at a time. Also, I am sulking because I don't want to have lunch with any of these people; I have been pressured into it by Ronny.

Not that I have anything against any of them so far. In fact, I like Ronny—the only one of them I already know. His impudent, attractively comic face keeps breaking into grins, and his round blue eyes sparkle with a lit-up gaiety which is in its own way courageous, because he isn't as carefree as he tries to appear. He's pretty sure to be drafted soon, and he's worried about this, of course. (I'm over age, unless they raise the age limit.)

As for the other two, they are potentially interesting, at least. I am only hostile to them because I feel that, as far as they're concerned, I'm nothing but a tourist convenience. I'm to buy them their lunch and then show them around the studio. Ruthie has just divorced some tycoon she was married to, most profitably; Ronny told me on the phone that she has "more alimony than she can possibly drink." And then there's Paul—the notorious, the "fabulous" Paul.

I watch my guests sourly as they face the tremendous, the nearly but never quite insoluble daily problem of deciding what to eat. They purse their lips in distaste, they scowl over the menu as though it were a personal insult; and the waiter stands watching them, smiling. He is in no more of a hurry than they are. The place isn't full today, and he expects a big tip.

Ruthie's face is chalky white, with huge vermilion lips daubed upon it. She is a big girl altogether; big hips, big bottom, big legs. I've seldom seen anyone look so placid, so wide open to visitors, so sleepy-slow. Her great, beautiful gentle cow eyes have sculptured lids which make me think of an Asian bas-relief—the carving of some giant goddess. She wears a black silk dress with black lace which would do just as well for the evening; maybe she hasn't taken it off since last night. It is cut low—very low; it could almost be a nightgown. My God, I believe it is! Anyhow, she has a fur coat to go over it if necessary. It is somewhat smeared with cigarette ash.

"Ruthie's still plastered, aren't you, Ruthie?" says Paul, in his peculiar drawling tone, which is probably the result of mixing a Southern accent with the kind of pseudo-Oxford English spoken by cultured Europeans—the people he has been running around with during the past few years.

"Maybe Doctor Paul had better prescribe something," he continues, coaxingly and cozily, to Ruthie. "Shall he do that? Shall he take that nasty sick feeling away?" Then, turning to the waiter, he asks reproachfully, "I suppose you've never heard of a Peeping Tom?"

"I'll ask the bartender, sir," says the waiter, who obviously hasn't.

"And tell him for Christ's sake not to use that filthy anisette."

"Very well, sir."

"My friend just means a perfectly ordinary sazerac, made with absinthe," says Ronny, with his different kind of Anglo-American drawl (Maryland, Harvard and a postgraduate year at Cambridge plus English country house parties): "I'll have the same." Then he adds, "Really, my dear, you must drop these outlandish expressions! Perhaps it was just as well the war made you come back here. You seem to be forgetting your native language."

"That's exactly what I was trying to do," says Paul loftily, but with a gleam of fun at me. Yes—although he's playing it so grand, he's continually aware of my presence. He is even taking trouble with me, in his own way. From his point of view, I suppose, I'm still somebody; even if he hasn't much use for writers, he must be impressed by the amount of money I'm earning right now. (Ronny asked me about this immediately, on the phone, and no doubt he passed the information on.) Also, I think Paul is curious about me. He scents a mystery. I don't altogether fit my role of movie hack. Well, good, I think; let him be curious.

(At this point, I'm trying to remember, as I reshuffle the impressions of all those years, just how Paul struck me that day of our first meeting. I had heard in advance, from at least three people, of his "beauty," and so I was predisposed to be disappointed in it. As a matter of fact, I think he became much more interesting looking later on. At that time, he still had some of his boyish prettiness, and this didn't relate to the very odd things which were developing beneath the surface of his face. But, from the first, I did get a basic impression which never really changed—of the lean, hungry-looking tanned face, the eyes which seemed to be set on different levels, as in a Picasso painting; the bitter, well-formed mouth. His handsome profile was bitterly sharp, like a knife edge. And goodness, underneath the looks and the charm and the drawl, how sour he was! This sourness of Paul's could sometimes be wonderfully stimulating and bracing, especially as an antidote to sweetness and light. But I learned by experience to take it in cautious doses. Too much of it at one time could make you feel as if you were suffering from quinine poisoning.

When I first set eyes on Paul, as he entered the restaurant, I remember I noticed his strangely erect walk; he seemed almost paralytic with tension. He was always slim, but then he looked boyishly skinny; and he was dressed like a boy in his teens, with an exaggerated air of innocence which he seemed to be daring us to challenge. His drab black suit, narrow-chested and without shoulder padding, clean white shirt and plain black tie made him look as if he had just arrived in town from a strictly religious boarding school. His dressing so young didn't strike me as ridiculous, because it went with his appearance. Yet, since I knew he was in his late twenties, this youthfulness itself had a slightly sinister effect, like something uncannily preserved.)

I am watching him, now, across the table. So this, I say to myself, is the "fabulous"—how I loathe the way Americans use that word!—Paul, who has been described to me, more than once, as "the last of the professional tapettes" and "the most expensive male prostitute in the world"; the notorious companion of the Peruvian millionairess celebrating her seventieth birthday on Cap Ferrat, of the Hungarian baron with a yacht on the Baltic, of the Princess somebody or other who actually tried to bring Paul with her to stay at the home of one of the stuffiest English dukes and got spectacularly snubbed. This is the Paul who was expelled from Switzerland for ostentatiously sniffing, or pretending to sniff, cocaine in the lounge of a hotel at St. Moritz; who was arrested in Portugal—but at once released by the intervention of a cabinet minister—for some flagrantly public sexual act. I have also heard that a Balkan royal personage, exiled but hugely wealthy, is giving him an allowance. No doubt at least half of all this is true—perhaps three quarters. The question is: Do I care? Part of me already disapproves of Paul; part of me is bored by the tedious naughtiness of his legend. But, so far, I haven't reached my verdict. I'm waiting to see if he'll do anything to interest me; and I almost believe he knows this. I feel, at any rate, that he's capable of knowing it. That's what intrigues me about him.

The drinks and the food have been ordered at last, and we can relax. Ruthie looks at me with a beaming smile. This smile is partly natural sweetness; partly, no doubt, an attempt to cover up her drunkenness and placate me in case I dislike it. Also, she's probably smiling at me rather than the others simply because she's sitting between them and can't be bothered to turn her head and look at them. Never mind—I do like *her*. I am quite sure of this, already. She is an animal person; she has that cozy quality of a subhuman and therefore guiltless creature; she might just have emerged from a warm burrow under a hill. I feel a throb of warmth toward her as I smile back, and even a certain sex attraction. When the drinks arrive, it's to her that I raise my glass. She goes right on smiling at me, though she doesn't respond.

"Come on, Ruthie," Paul prompts, "bottoms up!"

At this, she raises her glass and drinks. "Hi!" she says shyly. Her voice is hoarse, almost phantasmal, like an echo in a haunted building; what she actually says is "Hay-yee!"— it lasts with you for a moment and then dies away creepily. Having drunk, she slumps on the banquette and sags a little sideways. One of her big pale melon breasts pushes itself out of her low-cut dress. Paul promptly pushes it back again. "Sit up, Ruthie!" he tells her impatiently. And then, as Ruthie does sit up, he pats her hand. "That's my girl!"

Obviously, Paul did that for my benefit. He is showing off in the most uninteresting way; letting me see who's boss with the wealthy Ruthie, and incidentally trying to shock me— *me!* How very boring of him! And how unflattering it is to realize what his opinion of me must be, if he imagines he can impress me like this! He really is a most usual kind of underdog climber. It's a wonder all those European lovers haven't taught him more style.

To show him that I am definitely *not* impressed, not shocked, I smile my "We are amused" smile. I have started using this only recently; it is still in the experimental stage. Properly smiled, it should indicate that the smiler finds life great fun—not on the low human plane of sazeracs, breasts and show-off jokes, but *sub specie aeternitatis* as the eternal dance, maya, mother's play. I also make as if to sip my drink, letting the glass just touch my lips. Pretending to drink is part of the disguise my puritanism is wearing at this lunch. I have already noticed that there is an Olde Worlde brass spitoon in the corner by my chair. (Since the war began, all things English are the rage out here; the bar of this restaurant has lately been renamed Ye Mermaid Tavern Taproom, and redecorated accordingly.) It's so dark that I'll be able to pour my drink into the spitoon presently, without anybody seeing me do it.

Meanwhile, Ronny, feeling he has to make the party go, turns to me with a teasing smile: "After all we've heard about your activities, Christopher, we were expecting to see you in a loincloth and a turban at least, if not eating nails and levitating."

I look severely blank, although I understand instantly what Ronny is referring to. I might have known he would bring it up, sooner or later.

"I mean, Christopher dear, we've been given to understand —that is, the word's gone all round New York—that you've been studying the mysteries of yogi."

"Yoga," I correct him, involuntarily and rather crossly. Such mistakes always seem malicious when one is still in the early stages of enthusiasm for any subject and feels it to be blockaded by the aggressive ignorance of nonenthusiasts.

"*Yoga*, then." Ronny acts as though he were good-humoredly making a concession to my pedantry. "We hear you've been studying with this fabulous man who's lived in Tibet."

"He's never spent one instant in Tibet, as it happens." I smile at Ronny in the acuteness of my exasperation and speak with careful patience. "And I'm *not* studying yoga with him—or levitation or nail-eating—in fact, I'm not *studying* anything with him. We just happen to be friends, that's all."

"Oh, I see." Ronny is mock-meek, delighted that he's been able to get under my skin. "In that case, I must say, these extraordinary stories one's heard about you both *do seem* to have been rather exaggerated."

At this, I'm just about to forget all my resolutions and say something really heated, when Paul interrupts, in a tone of mild boredom, "I suppose you must be talking about Augustus Parr."

"You *know* him?" I'm so surprised and intrigued that I lose interest in hitting back at Ronny.

But Paul doesn't play up to this. "I read a book of his once," he says, with the same weary offhandedness. "It was at the hospital in Tunis," he adds, to the others, not to me, "while I was convalescing from that frightful dose of clap I got from Babs—*she* got it from one of the Arab guides—it's a specially bad kind they have in the Sahara where they're all used to it of course and just ignore it—but if a foreigner gets it, it can kill him. . . . As a matter of fact, I think it was Babs who lent me the book."

Ronny laughs delightedly. "Babs? But of course—it's just the kind of thing she *would* read!" Then realizing that this time he has been seriously and truly offensive, he adds hastily, "I mean, she only likes books she can't understand a single word of."

"I don't know what there was not to understand," says Paul. "Personally, I'd have thought a ten-year-old child could have understood it."

"Well, my dear, we have to bow to your judgment—because I'm sure you know much more about ten-year-old children—of either sex—than anyone else at this table."

"What did you think of the book?" I ask Paul quickly, being now his ally against Ronny's bitchery.

"I've got no business talking to *you* about books." Paul says this most demurely, with just a hint of mockery but not enough to be offensive. Indeed, I suspect a double bluff; he is pretending to sneer at my claims to be a literary authority, but only to amuse the stupidity of Ronny and Ruthie; and I am supposed to understand this. It is as though he were signaling to me: if you and I were alone, we could cut out this play-acting.

Ronny, who isn't stupid at all, evidently gets the same overtone, because he puts in, "False modesty will get you *nowhere*, my dear!"

"No—but tell me," I insist, determined now to stay on Paul's side even if he doesn't want me.

"All right—if you really want to know; I thought the whole thing was so unconvincing. He keeps comparing everything to something else; and then he takes it for granted that that proves something."

"Hardly very lucid, my dear," says Ronny cuttingly.

"No—I think I know exactly what you mean." (Indeed, I'm genuinely taken aback by Paul's perceptiveness.) "And I must admit, it's a valid criticism, as far as it goes. Parr *does* have a tendency to do that. He'll use a metaphor to describe one of his hypotheses; and then, because the metaphor itself embodies some proven scientific truth, he's a little apt to assume that his hypothesis is automatically proved." I am pleased by the neatness of this summary; it makes me feel superior and benevolent. I feel I've shown Paul that I'm a formidable ally.

"I'm afraid you're talking way above our poor little heads," says Ronny, with an uneasy smile; I can see he doesn't like the way the conversation is developing. Ruthie grins at me glassily. She at least makes not the faintest attempt to understand anything; and this gives her, absurdly enough, an air of being intuitively *dans le vrai*. Augustus Parr's table talk, with its wealth of allusions, has made me Bible-conscious, so that now I'm reminded of "Mary hath chosen the better part," and I look at Ruthie and start to laugh. At this, Ruthie begins to laugh too, quite violently, as though she knows what I'm thinking. Our laughter reassures Ronny, who takes it for a sign that I'm getting back into the proper party mood; so he joins in.

But Paul isn't laughing; he seems left out of this. I want to get back to him and our topic. I ask, "How long have you been interested—I mean in the kind of thing Parr writes about?"

Maybe my manner is patronizing. Paul instantly and visibly closes up. "I never said I was *interested*. As a matter of fact, I think all that stuff's a lot of crap. I *know* it is."

Ordinarily, this kind of violence would intrigue me. As it is, I'm angry and disappointed. The little fool, I think—saying he knows! And here was I, climbing over my own prejudices, coming forward to meet him halfway—only to get myself rudely snubbed! I instinctively shrug my shoulders and turn my friendliest face to Ronny, who is asking, "*Do* tell me, Christopher, because I *long* to know—I think she just couldn't be more marvelous—what's Garbo really *like?*"

So off we go into the Hollywood game, and I tell anecdotes—a lot funnier and more authentic than most people's, but they still make me sick with boredom at myself. And Ronny keeps exclaiming, "oh, *no*—how too *utterly* marvelous!" I glance at Paul from time to time. He sits there coldly dead-pan.

When lunch is over, I take it for granted that the guided tour of the studio is about to start. Is Ruthie too drunk for it, I wonder; had we better park her in my office? But Paul, as though no such arrangement existed, says peremptorily, "Come along, Ruthie, honey—time for your beauty sleep! We've got all those people coming up for cocktails at five, remember."

Ronny is dismayed. "Oh, but Paul, I thought it was all fixed."

"You can go some other time," Paul tells him, disregarding me altogether. "Right now you've got to buy the liquor, while I put Ruthie to bed."

"I'm *terribly* sorry, Christopher." Ronny looks at me helplessly, in pleading apology. "Another day perhaps?"

"Perhaps," I say coldly. I'm now unreasonably furious that they're not coming and that I've been spared what I was dreading; the tiresomeness of having them on my hands all afternoon. I add nastily, "I don't imagine Paul would have been interested, anyway. He's probably seen it all before."

"Since you mention it," says Paul with his thin smile, "I have. I saw all I ever want to see when I came over here with the Condesa, six years ago."

Well, to hell with you, I mentally tell him. And I decide, as so often before, that first impressions should always be trusted and that most likely I'll never see any of them again, and certainly not Paul. They leave, and I pay. The bill is astronomical. But that doesn't matter, because the money I earn here somehow doesn't belong to me. I feel I have to keep spending it before it vanishes away.

But what am I to spend it on? For nothing that I buy seems to belong to me, either. My nice big blue convertible certainly doesn't belong to me; how could the sort of person I imagine I am conceivably own such a car? Such pretentiousness isn't even shameful, it's merely absurd. I get into it now, as I always do, with a sense of being an impostor: if this *is* my car, then I must be somebody else. But there's my name on the registration slip, and I have a key in my pocket which fits the ignition.

I drive through a residential district, down a pleasant street lined with jacaranda trees. It is the street on which I live. I drive past the house where my apartment is. My apartment has been rented to me furnished, and, since it doesn't belong to me, I haven't rearranged the furniture in any way or changed the pictures—which are anyhow quite good reproductions of French Impressionists; chiefly of Renoir, who is top artist in the movie colony at present. You'd find so little trace of me in the apartment that you'd have to look for my fingerprints in order to prove I lived there; and even they, I'm sure, would be very faint. I have no time to stop there now; I have to be getting back to the studio. I merely slow a little in passing and note the Japanese gardener watering the lawn, the acacia before my window like a cloud of golden dust, a hummingbird poised at a flower's mouth. I have switched on the car radio. Commercials and music. Bulova Watch Time. Buy a Ford. I Married an Angel. News. Another big raid over London last night. And already in London it must be night again, with people hurrying to their destinations through the blackout, listening for the first sirens and the guns. In that unimaginably remote world, maybe, Stephen or Allen or E.M. or John or Mary is thinking about me at this very moment, saying Christopher used to do this or that, as one talks about the dead. And in another world, far, far more remote, even—light-years of psychological distance away—there is Waldemar. And he may be thinking about me, too.

166

Suppose I have in my power an army of five million men. I can destroy it instantly by pressing an electric button. The five-millionth man is Waldemar. Will I press that button? No, of course not—even if the four million, nine hundred and ninety-nine thousand, nine hundred and ninety-nine others are world-destroying fiends. This, beneath all my acquired convictions and Augustus Parr's arguments, is my own private bedrock reason for being a pacifist. And I'd be embarrassed to tell it to Augustus, even.

How very surprised Waldemar himself would be to hear it!

And what if Waldemar is lying dead already, in Hitler's uniform, killed invading France? My reason is still my reason. It still stands. Once I have refused to press the button because of Waldemar, I can never press it. Because Waldemar could be absolutely anybody.

At the studio, the Writers' Building is white and massive as a bank, with the Americans' flag flying over it. There is a cinematically cute girl at the reception desk, and a messenger boy in the blue studio uniform. The girl doesn't even glance up as I pass; this is part of her act. But she has recognized me and pressed *her* electric button, and the door to the interior opens for me—a plain, smallish, hardwood door, if you can get by it; a magic door to unsuccessful actors, minor agents without pull, tourists. There are always some of these people sitting in the entrance lounge and staring at it, hoping to get let in, or at least to see a star or a producer come out.

Beyond the door is a passage like the corridor on a liner. No daylight is visible except at its far end; it is lighted all day long by streamlined lamp panels set in the ceiling. I meet a couple of my colleagues and we exchange, without stopping, the ritual greeting. "Hi, Chris," "Hi, Bernie," "Hi, Chris," "Hi, Mort," "How's the boy?" "Fine, how's everything?" "Fine—just fine!" And here, strangest of all strangenesses, is my very own name, printed on a neat label on one of the office doors.

I enter, sit down at the desk, pick up the script in its blue cover. TEMPORARY is typed on it—what an ideal title for the film itself!—and PLEASE RETURN TO THE STENOGRAPHIC DEPARTMENT. My producer likes it; but somebody in the front office thinks the scene in the British Museum should be rewritten. "You did a swell job, Chris. All we need now is just a little bit more warmth. See what I mean?" I see what he means exactly.

I put a sheet of paper in the typewriter—registering, with austere satisfaction, the pang of conditioned desire for a pre-work cigarette; very faint now, after six months of abstinence. Then I start to type steadily, almost without hesitation, putting in the warmth as a drafstman puts in the shading. I know precisely what the front office and my producer want, and how to give it to them. The job is too boring for cynicism, too humble for contempt. No doubt one day it will be done by machinery. Meanwhile, it is a job to be done, as expertly as possible. Augustus keeps reminding me how the Bhagavad-Gita teaches that all action is symbolic. You do it in that spirit and then just offer it up.

How glad I am that I didn't let them pump me at lunch, or provoke me into giving away anything about the kind of life I'm trying to live now and its rules! Now, at last—I tell myself—I'm playing *my* game, not the game of The Others. . . . Careful, now! Stop that! Remember what Augustus says about spiritual pride. . . . I take refuge, hastily, in the British Museum scene.

It must have been about two weeks after the Beverly Hills lunch that I heard from Paul again. He called me one morning at the studio.

"Is this Christopher?"

"Yes."

"Are you *sure?*"

"What do you mean, am I sure?"

"*Well—at last!* Do they have orders not to give you messages?"

"Of course not."

"Who are you afraid's going to call you? You're not being blackmailed, by any chance?"

"No. I'm not being blackmailed." It was extraordinary how that sour drawl of his annoyed me, disturbed me, and somehow put me on the defensive.

"Are you still making thousands of dollars?"

"This is my last month. As a matter of fact, I'd already given the studio notice when I met you. But I had to finish this script." Yes, I *was* defending myself! Against the charge that a disciple of Augustus Parr had no business dallying with the fleshpots of the movies. (Augustus himself sometimes used to tease me about this: "Be careful, my dear Christopher! I do beseech you to be careful! Of course, I don't doubt that a man of your remarkable moral stamina can venture to do things which are quite beyond the danger line for most of us. *I* could never venture to stick that old red nose of mine so far out into maya. I should know that, after a *very* short exposure, I should be unable to withdraw it again. And even *you* may be in danger of overestimating . . ." etc., etc.) But what business was all that of Paul's? How could he have the nerve to expect me to answer for my doings to *him?* Especially after what he'd said about Augustus's book!

"Don't think I'm *blaming* you, honey. If I'd made all that money, I wouldn't do one lick of work until I'd spent every cent of it."

I didn't deign to answer this. The uncanny thing was, it was just as if Paul had read my thoughts and was making fun of them.

After a pause, he said: "Ruthie misses you."

"Does she?" I tried to make this sound like, "Cut the crap and tell me what you want."

"She thinks you're cute."

This, too, was beneath answering. I waited. At length, Paul said, "I want to see you, too."

Well, thanks a million, I said to myself; and aloud, "I'm terrifically busy right now. Why don't you—"

"Why don't you call me around the first of the week—that's what all you tycoons say, isn't it?"

"It's not what *I* say," I said—stung, because it often was.

"Oh?" Paul sounded amused. "Listen—you may as well tell me: is this a brush-off?"

Yes—I nearly said. But, as I still hesitated, he added, in the same tone, "You don't have to be scared—I don't want to borrow any of your precious money."

That did it. Now I'd simply hang up on him—

"You're the only one who can help me, Christopher." Paul said this without the least air of melodrama; without inflection, almost. But he had done the trick. He had got me interested.

"How do you mean? How can I help you?"

"I can't talk about it on the phone. I've got to see you."

"Well—all right. Over the weekend?"

"Can't you manage tomorrow?"

"No. Not possibly. Oh—well, yes—I suppose so."

"Don't if you don't want to, now."

"Around eleven?"

"Nobody's twisting your arm, mind."

"Where'll we meet? The Beverly Hills Hotel?"

"Afraid not, honey. You'll have to come up here. We can't leave Ruthie alone for a second—she's apt to drink up the cleaning fluid or get herself married to a Marine—the house is full of them right now. . . . Ever heard of the Rambla de la Cumbrera?"

"No."

"Neither has anyone else," said Paul, and began a series of complicated directions which at once made me repent of my curiosity.

The Rambla de la Cumbrera was up in the hills, which in those days had few houses and formed a wild, romantic no man's land between Los Angeles and the Valley; maybe there were still canyons untrodden since the Indians had hunted in them. At night the hills rose dark and mysterious above the drifting sea fog and the constellated lights of the plain; and teen-agers drove up there to neck in their parents' cars.

The Rambla must have been planned as a grand scenic drive; there were lamp standards and a sidewalk. But now the glass of the lamps was broken, the sidewalk was overgrown with mesquite bushes and dodder, and there were cracks across the road, probably caused by the small earthquake jolts we had been having during the past year. Higher up, the paved road ended and turned into a dirt track, quite dry at this season but with deep ruts in it; during the winter rains it would be nearly impassable. Although it was November, the midday sun was still very hot.

The house Paul had directed me to stood alone, on top of the ridge. It was California Spanish, with white stucco walls and heavy red tiles on its roof. I had expected luxury; but this place had an air of abandonment. Weeds were growing out of the driveway. The front door had most of its paint rubbed off. The bell handle was rusted and obviously broken. I called, "Paul! Ronny! Ruthie!" No answer. So, as the door was standing wide open, I went in. The floor was brick-tiled and the roof was beamed like a Gothic chapel; this was a big living room, full of that curiously theatrical furniture one found in many old Hollywood houses. Those high-backed velvet chairs—you couldn't imagine ordinary people of *any* century sitting in them, only actors in period costume. On one of the chairs hung a complete Marine uniform, with the shoes and socks arranged neatly under it. I wandered across the room and along a passage which brought me out of doors again at the back of the building. The hillside below it was laid out in terraces, Roman villa style; there were stairs inset with mosaic leading down from one level to the next. Some yellowish cypresses still grew there. The flowers must all have died for lack of water; now there were only the brown twisting skeletons of geraniums and some of those juicy-leaved succulents which can live on dew and mist.

Below the terraces was a swimming pool. It was staringly empty, with a hugh crack zigzagging across it. Beside the pool's edge, on mattresses, lay Ruthie and Paul, stark naked. Three youths sprawled on the hard tiles beside them, drinking beer out of cans. Two of them wore jockey shorts; the third, swimming trunks. On his arm was a tattoo of roses wreathed around the word "Mother."

Nakedness suited Ruthie. Her great body was soft and pliant, not in the least flabby. She grinned her slap-happy grin at me, without the smallest embarrassment. As for Paul, he lay there with his eyes closed, seemingly unaware of my presence. At length he drawled, "What are you doing, all dressed up like that?"

"Where's Ronny?" I asked.

"Gone down to get some more liquor. Take your clothes off, why don't you?"

"Not right now," I said. I wasn't wearing undershorts.

"If you don't, Ruthie'll think you're ashamed of your small pecker."

"Ruthie will have to take it on trust." I was starting to get annoyed with him.

"We're bored," said Paul reproachfully, as though this were my fault. "Tell us something. Tell us what's new in dirt."

"I don't know."

"You don't know?" Paul mimicked my voice. One of the three youths grinned. All of them kept shooting brief involuntary glances at Ruthie's body. I was aware I was doing it myself. I couldn't help glancing at that big black curly triangle.

171

"So you won't tell us anything? You absolutely refuse to amuse us?"

"How shall I amuse you?" For Ruthie's sake I kept on smiling, but my smile was getting forced.

"Let's see you screw Ruthie. The boys had a gang-bang with her last night. *Such* a bang—she wore them all out. Go ahead—let's see you do it."

"Maybe Ruthie doesn't want me to."

"Sure she does! Ruthie's game for anything. Ruthie's a good sport. There's only one thing in the world Ruthie's scared of—that someone'll tell her she isn't a good sport. You tell her that, and she'll go the limit. Just to prove you're a liar. People think she'll chicken out—they say no girl would go *that* far—but they don't know our Ruthie. She's a *real* sport. Not one of those show-offs but a real *great* sport. The best that ever was—aren't you, Ruthie?"

Ruthie beamed dreamily. The three youths grinned; half puzzled, half fascinated by Paul's fantasy talk. As for me, despite the absurdity of this situation, I was quite embarrassingly excited. If this were twilight instead of midday, if I had had a few stiff drinks, how hotly exciting to break my own rules, to forget Augustus, to stop thinking altogether about anything, and for an hour let loose the naked panting animal! Provided everybody else joined in. No—not everybody; not Paul. I wouldn't want him either joining in or watching. He didn't belong among the animals. If he tried to join in their play, it would be ugly, sinister, perverse. I was surprised to find how strongly I felt this; and I was at a loss to explain my feeling. All I could say was: he had the wrong kind of body.

What was wrong with it? You couldn't say it wasn't good-looking, lying there in the sunshine, very dark brown and gleaming with oil. And yet it repelled me slightly; it was slender in the wrong way, and somehow too elegant, too wearily sophisticated in its movements—though not to the point of seeming effeminate. Perhaps it had lain too long in the expensive Riviera or Bahamian sun, on the terraces of overweening hotels and villas perched like eagles above the sea; had belonged and yet not belonged to too many people; had been too often valued only for the envy it caused in the hearts of nonpossessors. Perhaps it had lost its unselfconscious animal grace in the process of acquiring the negligent-arrogant art of being looked at.

So there I stood looking at them, feeling overclothed, frus-

172

trated and foolish. And it was all Paul's doing. I said to him, with barely controlled indignation, "I thought you wanted to talk to me about something?"

This pleased him, of course; he had got me rattled. "You're terribly tense, aren't you, Christopher? I thought all this oriental philosophy was supposed to make you calm? You aren't much of an advertisement for it, I *must* say!" Then, turning reproachfully on the three youths, he asked, "Aren't you going to offer our guest a drink?"

"I don't want one, thanks."

"This is Nelson," said Paul, as though I hadn't spoken, "and this is Rex, and this is Red." He put all the names in quotes, as it were, contriving to make each one sound ridiculous. "And this is Mr. Isherwood, who's a famous author." The three of them regarded me, not exactly with contempt, but as if I were hopelessly sick. Underneath they were savages; but Paul and Ruthie had evidently intimidated them—at least for the moment.

"What do you want to drink?" Paul asked.

"I told you—nothing."

"There's some marijuana upstairs. I can't guarantee it, though. Got it at an after-hours Nigra place downtown. It's all you can get in this damned uncivilized city."

"No thanks."

"You won't have sex, and you won't drink, and you won't smoke tea. What *do* you want to do?"

"I've got to be going."

"Oh, all right." Paul rolled his eyes, as if he were humoring a difficult invalid or dotard. He sighed deeply and got up from the mattress, wrapping a towel around his waist as he did so.

"Goodbye, Ruthie," I said. Ruthie smiled at me, as though we had a big private joke between us. It occurred to me that she was probably high on marijuana herself. As for the youths, I tried to propitiate them with a genial hand wave. It did no good. Only one of them very slightly raised his hand from the pavement; and this was probably just coincidence.

Paul followed me up the steps and into the house. It seemed unnatural, after his various kinds of rudeness to me, that he should be playing the conventional host. I found myself making guest conversation. "How did you find this place?"

"It belongs to an aunt of Ruthie's. We'll have to get out before long. It's being sold for taxes."

"And then you'll be going back East?"

Paul didn't answer. But, as we were walking through the living room and had nearly reached the front door, he said abruptly, "Were you just talking the other day at lunch? Or do you believe any of it?"

So that was it, I said to myself; that was why he'd asked me to come up here! I had suspected as much. And no doubt all this bitchery was his way of testing me. Well, I had passed the test and forced him to come out into the open. I was so delighted that I didn't even want to punish him a little by pretending not to understand his question. I answered it as though we were already in the middle of a serious conversation.

"Yes," I said, "I believe it. That is, I believe it as far as I can test it by my own experience. That's not very far, I admit. But then, of course, I believe in Parr's belief, too."

Even as I spoke, a certain falseness in my own tone jarred on me; it was a shade too "direct," too "sincere." And I knew Paul was aware of this.

"Parr has a beard, doesn't he?" Paul asked this in his demurest, least ironical manner. "I saw a picture of him somewhere."

But I wasn't going to let myself be provoked. "Yes, he has a beard, and he's a bit Christlike, and altogether there's quite a bit about him which a lot of people might think was—well, studied, theatrical. But that's exactly *why* he impresses me. I mean, I don't trust these sweet childlike little wide-eyed saints. Augustus is absolutely sophisticated and absolutely aware of the impression he makes. And that reassures me. He's humanly vain, and he's no fool, and at the same time he really believes—"

"Just what *does* he believe?"

"Well, you said you read a book of his. And—" I couldn't resist this—"that a child could understand it."

Paul smiled, as if acknowledging the point I'd scored. "But I want to hear *you* explain."

"He believes in—" I suddenly found I couldn't say "God," not to Paul—so I changed it to, "this thing that's inside us and yet isn't *us*—isn't our individual personality. He believes it's there and that we can get in touch with it."

"If you *want* to get in touch with it." I was surprised at the quickness of Paul's response. He's been thinking about all

174

this a lot, I said to myself.

"Everybody wants to."

"They most certainly don't."

"They do really—even when they won't admit it." (I knew I sounded superior-benevolent here.)

"That's just crap." Paul spoke quite curtly and angrily.

"You mean, you won't admit that *you* want to?"

"I wasn't talking about myself. It doesn't matter what *I* want. The point is, why should any ordinary, sensible person want to get in touch with this thing—as you call it?"

"Because it's—that's what life's for."

"Who says so?"

"Well, I mean—what else *can* it be for—except to find who you really are?"

"What makes you think it's *for* anything? Why can't it just be a filthy mess of meaningless shit?"

"I suppose it *could*. But I'm pretty certain it isn't."

"Because Augustus Parr thinks it isn't?"

"Partly that. And then there's the experience that all kinds of saints and mystics have had, quite independently, all over the world—"

"Which can't really be proved. They just *say* they had it. It isn't something you can take out and show to other people, is it?"

"No—but other people notice the change it makes in *you*."

"Has it changed Parr?"

"Yes. Definitely."

"How can you tell?"

"I used to know him before this—several years ago, in England."

"You're not answering my question. How can you *tell* he's changed?"

"Oh—intuition. I mean—after all, I *am* a writer, and—"

"Pardon *me!*" Paul rolled his eyes mockingly. "I should have known better than to ask! *You* can tell he's changed —that ought to be *quite* good enough for the rest of us! And, of course, *you've* changed, too?"

"No. I wouldn't say that."

"Why haven't you?"

"Because, well, I've only just started—" I stopped guiltily. I hadn't meant to tell him this much.

"Only just started *what?*"

"Well—meditating." If only they'd invent another term

for it, I thought! It always sounds so ineffectual and chin-on-hand.

"*How* do you meditate?" One minute, I'd feel that Paul was really interested; the next, that he merely enjoyed heckling me.

"I—it's rather hard to explain in a few words. Well, briefly, you sit there and let yourself calm down, and then you try to open yourself—" Here I stuck. "Open yourself" was one of Augustus's phrases. When I used it to Paul, it instantly suggested a bowel movement. I forced myself to go on, "I mean —open yourself—to this thing—"

"Why do you keep saying 'this thing'? What's the objection to saying 'God'? That's what you mean, isn't it?"

"Yes."

"Then say *God*, for Christ's sake!"

"*God*," I said. In Paul's presence, it was as exciting as using a new dirty word at my first school.

"And you see God inside you when you meditate?"

"Of course not!"

"Then why do it?"

"You have to keep at it. You can't expect any results for a long time. Maybe years."

"So you just sit there? I know I'd start thinking about all the people I'd had in my entire life. I'd end by jacking myself off."

"I feel like that sometimes. I want to."

"But you don't?"

"No."

"Why don't you? Have you given up sex?"

"I'm trying to."

"Because Parr told you to? I suppose he thinks it's wicked?"

"No, he doesn't, at all. Not for most people. He says sex is fine until you make up your mind to look for—"

"For this thing?" Paul grinned teasingly.

"God."

"And then?"

"Then you have to give it up—and smoking and drinking and—all those things. Not because they're wrong, but—well, it's like being in training for a race."

"Personally, I never was in training for anything in my born days. So I wouldn't know."

"Well, damn you, neither was I! But I have to explain it somehow, don't I?"

176

"I must say, you make the whole thing sound crashingly dull." But, as Paul said this, he smiled at me in quite a new way, with such charm and intimacy that I began to feel something between us—a kind of ease—which might even lead to friendship. Obviously, I must have subconsciously wanted to be friends with him, right from the beginning, or I wouldn't have responded as quickly as I did now.

"No, Paul—you're wrong. It isn't. That's the funny thing. It's terrifically exciting. I mean, there are moments when it is. I wish I could describe—you sit there, and, all of a sudden, you know you're face to face with something. You can't see it, but it's right there."

Just for a few seconds, I was aware that Paul was listening to me with genuine curiosity. He didn't even seem skeptical. But then the look went out of his eyes. He said rather coldly, "Well, personally, I've always stuck to what I can see and touch and smell and grope and screw. That's all you can really trust. The rest's just playing around with words until you talk yourself into something. I don't say these mystics of yours are deliberate fakes. But they can't prove to me that they're not kidding themselves. And neither can your friend Parr."

I heard, or fancied I heard, the hint of a question in his tone. I knew, at any rate, that he wanted me to keep on answering back and defending my position. But now, suddenly, I wasn't in the mood. Paul had chilled me off. After all, I said to myself, he evidently *wasn't* interested. Even if he had read Augustus's book and thought about it for a little while, what did that prove? He had been bored in that hospital, and deprived of his usual kicks—sex, drink, dope. Damn all these playboys and playgirls! They never really care about anything. Never, never, never.

Just the same, I'd give him one more opportunity—

"You said on the phone I was the only one who could help you. Help you about what?"

"I never said 'help,' " Paul said, very quickly.

I was certain he *had* said it, but I let this pass. "All right, what was it you wanted to talk to me about?"

"Nothing."

"Nothing—just like that?"

"Nothing important."

"Then why not tell me what it was?"

"I changed my mind. You wouldn't understand."

177

"That's too bad—after you dragged me all the way up here."

"I told you not to come if you didn't want to."

Yet we were still smiling at each other. Our hostility was oddly intimate and like a game.

"Well, good-by then," I said.

"Goodbye." We shook hands, most politely. Paul opened the front door for me. He had closed it again before I had even reached my car.

A few nights later, I was woken out of my deepest sleep by the phone. It was still thick dark, and dead with the deadness of the small hours. "Hello," I said crossly.

"Christopher—" It was Paul's voice. He didn't sound at all desperate or even tense; and yet I knew this must be an emergency. His voice was very quiet and filtered of his mannerisms, with nothing left in it but the dregs of the Southern accent. "I'm coming over."

"*Now?*"

"In about fifteen minutes. As soon as I can drive over."

"Is it important?"

"Probably not—to you."

"Where are you now? At home?"

"I haven't been home in two days."

"Oh. . . . All right—come on over."

"Christopher—"

"Yes?"

"Are you alone?"

"Yes, of course."

"You haven't got anybody in bed with you?"

"No—" I put some sarcasm into this— "as it happens."

"All right."

I was shocked by Paul's appearance when I let him into the apartment. He had a hideous blood-blistered bruise which nearly closed one of his eyes. He was unshaven, and his clothes were crumpled and dirty. He walked right through the apartment ahead of me and sat down on my bed. "I suppose you haven't anything to drink," he said. "You teetotalers never keep anything for your guests."

"There's some rum."

"*Rum!* Jesus—you *would* have rum! All right—if that's all you've got."

I went out to the kitchen and returned with the bottle. It

was less than a quarter full. "Do you want a Coke with it?"

"A *Coke?*" Paul shuddered. "*Please!*" He uncorked the bottle and drank it in a couple of long swallows. Then he wiped his hand across his mouth. "I'll probably throw up in a little while," he said. "Well, at least it's stopped my hands from shaking," he added, examining them as if with interest.

"How did you hurt your eye?"

"Oh, that?" Paul stood up, walked over to the glass and looked at himself. "That was four or five days ago. Yes, it was the day you came up. That night. I got in a fight with one of the Marines. The one called Nelson. He beat me up."

"Why did he do that?"

"Oh, he was plastered. I just happened to call him a sonof-abitch, not meaning anything special, quite friendly. And he took it personally. Or pretended he did. He said I'd insulted his mother. He wanted for us to have a real corny Old World fight. He even took his shirt off. Told me to stand up and fight like a man. I said, 'Mary, your aunt is *not* a man and would never stoop to act like one, and *you* are just a little male impersonator who's starting to be a great big bore.' So then he lit into me."

"I'm not surprised," I said, laughing. "But I certainly admire your courage, talking to him like that. Those boys all looked pretty tough to me."

Paul smirked. My compliment had pleased him. "If you start taking shit from a Marine, or any kind of serviceman, it's the *end*. It makes them feel so insecure, they'll tear the house apart and massacre everybody in it."

"What were Ruthie and Ronny and the others doing while you were getting beaten up?"

"I guess they'd all passed out. Except for Ruthie—she hardly ever does; she just moons around in a daze, like one of the undead. I didn't notice her, come to think of it. If she had been there, it wouldn't have made any difference, anyway. When she's in that state, you could murder someone in front of her and she'd think you were just kidding."

"You said you hadn't been home in two days. Do they know where you are?"

Paul's expression changed. He walked over to the window. It was starting to get light outside. "They don't know," he said. "And they couldn't care less."

"Why do you say that?"

"We had a big fuss. Oh, I can't be bothered to tell you all

179

the dreary bogus details. It started about something completely unimportant, the way those things do. And then we all three said a lot of home truths we'd been saving up for a long time. I realized that, underneath, they simply hate my guts. So I told them I was getting out. And I got out."

"You mean, you've really broken up?"

"If there was ever anything there to break."

"I'm sorry."

"Oh, Jesus—don't give me that crap! You're not sorry. Why should you be sorry? For Christ's sake, say something you mean."

"All right—why in hell did you have to come busting in here in the middle of the night, just to tell me you quarreled with those two? And, while we're on the subject of that, why did you tell me on the phone you'd be over in fifteen minutes and then you didn't show up for more than an hour? Do you realize you kept me awake all that time, waiting for you? And you haven't even apologized."

"I ran out of gas. I had to walk about twenty blocks before I found a station open."

"You might have told me that."

"I didn't think I had to apologize to you." I saw Paul was keeping his face dead-pan with difficulty. "I thought you were my friend."

"Oh, my Christ! And you dare tell *me* to say what I mean!"

He smiled at this, but it was a smile I couldn't interpret at all. He was certainly in a very strange mood. When I realized that he wasn't going to answer, and was, indeed, waiting for me to say something, I asked, "And exactly what do you expect me to do now?"

"Tell me to get the hell out of here."

"And then what'll you do?"

"Get out."

"And then?"

"Ronny has some special sleeping pills he gets from a drugstore in New York, where the man knows him. They're extra strong. He's always bragging about them, claiming that seven would be enough to kill you. Just before I left I stole the bottle. I thought I was just doing it out of bitchery, because Ronny believes he can't sleep without them and it'd take him at least three days to get more. But now I know what I really wanted them for."

"If you mean suicide, be sure to eat some bread, first. I've heard that if you take them on an empty stomach, you're quite apt to throw up and then recover."

"You don't believe I'd do it, do you?"

"I haven't said that."

"Of course you don't! You won't *let* yourself believe it. Because, if you did, you'd have to talk me out of doing it—maybe not let me out of your sight for days—and that'd be a bore. Whatever I say, I know you won't believe it, so I am going to tell you the exact truth. Then afterwards you can tell Ruthie and Ronny—not that I give a damn if you tell them or not. I'm just telling you for kicks—because this'll be the first as well as the last time I talked like this to anybody. . . . I suppose you think I'm one of those hysterical girls who are always threatening suicide. That only shows you don't know me at all. I've never ever made up my mind to kill myself before; I've scarcely even considered it. Because I think it's a madly tiresome thing to do, and the only possible excuse for making such a nuisance of yourself is to wait until you're quite certain you want to. Then you're pretty sure to do it properly. Until yesterday evening, there was always something left to stop me from being certain—some tiny little thing, like feeling curious about a movie we were going to see, or about what I'd eat for dinner, or just what was going to happen next. Well, yesterday I suddenly found I'd come to the end of all that."

"How do you mean?"

"I just knew I'd come to the end. It happened in a bar on Sunset Boulevard, way downtown, in the middle of the evening. I caught my own eye in the mirror and I looked at myself—not the way you usually do—*really* looked. The bar was crowded, but I might just as well have been alone on a desert island; that was how I felt. I knew this must be the end, because I saw that now I'm not good for anything—anything at all."

"Everyone thinks that sometimes. I do."

"No, you don't. Not seriously. Almost nobody ever seriously thinks that. Because nearly everyone's good for something. I used to be. Now I'm not—so I've come to the end. It's as simple as that."

"And that's why you want to take those pills?"

"Any other suggestions?"

"No. But there's something I don't understand. Why have you come to me? I mean—assuming that you *aren't* good for anything and that you do mean to commit suicide, why didn't you walk out of that bar and do it, right away?"

"I should have thought that was obvious. I'm scared."

"Scared of killing yourself?"

"Hell, no! Not that. Scared of what's going to happen afterwards."

"But, Paul, I thought you said you didn't believe—"

"I don't believe the stuff the Christians give out. I don't *believe* there's anything afterwards. But just not believing isn't good enough. Not when you're right up face to face with it. You've got to be absolutely certain, one way or the other. I'm scared of doing it, unless I'm sure. You've never taken any kind of dope, have you, Christopher? If you had, maybe you'd know what I'm talking about. Or maybe you wouldn't. Some people seem to be able to go on kidding themselves indefinitely. I can't. I've been right down into the inside of myself with dope two or three times—and I know one thing for sure: if, by some wildly unlikely chance, there *is* any afterwards, and I swallow those pills in the state I'm in now, then I'm going to find myself in a mess which'll be a million times ghastlier than anything that could possibly happen to me here. Because there I'll be really *stuck* with myself. *That* much I *know*."

"Then don't risk it. Stay alive."

"You just don't understand one word I've been saying, do you? You think this is all talk. It doesn't mean anything to you, except that I've interfered with your precious sleep. Well, you can go back to bed in a few minutes, because I'm nearly through. I don't care if this is boring you or if you think it's corny, you're going to hear the rest of it. Maybe it'll make sense to you one day. . . . I used to be good for something—for sex. I was *really* good for that. All kinds of people used to get hot pants for me, and that excited me— even when I found them totally unattractive, which I usually did. I got a terrific kick out of giving them pleasure, and I was proud that I nearly always could. But then, by degrees, the whole thing got more and more frantic. I began to feel I'd got to go on and on and on having sex, even when I was exhausted. And then I realized that I loathed sex. I was trying to screw it right out of my system. Several times, when I was going at it like a maniac, I broke a blood vessel and bled. And then, finally, not so long ago, I succeeded. For the past three months I've been impotent. I mean absolutely impotent.

182

I can't even get it hard. . . . It's amazing how long you can cover something like that up. I kept bluffing—talking dirty, and lying about all the ass I was getting; and three or four times, when I got cornered and had to jump into bed with someone, I pretended I was too drunk to be able to do it. But Ruthie found out. That was part of what our fuss was about. *She* told Ronny—and of course he couldn't resist bitching me. Even if he hadn't, I'd have hated his knowing. I can't stand people knowing things about me. When they do, I hate them."

"Is that why you're telling me? So you can hate me?"

"Hell, no—I don't give a damn about you. Why should I want to hate you? I shouldn't think anybody ever *has* hated you; and you probably couldn't hate anyone if you tried. All you know about is books and words. You're a typical cultured limey. They always give me the creeps."

"You don't exactly charm me either, you know. Ever since we met, you've been trying every which way to impress me. And every new stunt you try is more idiotic than the last. We're all supposed to fall down on our asses with amazement because you're such a devilishly wicked Dorian Gray. Actually, you're a rather vulgar little not-so-young boy from the most unpleasant state in the Union, whose chief claim to sophistication is having been thrown out of a few European hotels. Sophistication! Christ! Your idea of *paradise* is probably tea with the Duchess of Windsor! As for me, you haven't the dimmest idea what I'm really like or how I feel or what I think about. And you'll never find out—about me or anyone else—because you're too damned taken up with yourself and your wretched antics. If you ever do commit suicide—which I sincerely doubt, because I don't think you have the guts—it'll be out of sheer conceit. Personally, I'm ready to bet you're just bluffing—"

While I was still in the middle of this outburst, I was shocked at myself, and even more surprised than shocked. Because this wasn't altogether me speaking—the tone, the words were slightly unnatural; and yet I couldn't stop until it was all out of my mouth. Was Paul's kind of hysteria really so infectious? Or was he actually *willing* me to talk to him like this? Was that the real reason he'd come here—to force me to reject him?

Meanwhile, Paul had turned, without meeting my eyes, and was walking out of the apartment. I made no move to stop him. The front door clicked quietly behind him. I stood still for a moment, listening to some early street sounds outside the building.

No, I couldn't do it. If he *had* been bluffing, then so had I. I daren't let him walk out like that, with the sleeping pills in his pocket. I ran after him, fumbled with clumsy haste at the door, pulled it open. Paul was halfway down the staircase. He must have heard me behind him, but he didn't look back and he had almost reached the bottom before I caught up with him. I grabbed his arm roughly, sadistically—again, this wasn't altogether me—turned him around and practically dragged him upstairs again and back into the apartment. He didn't make the least resistance. He kept his face away from me, but I caught a glimpse in the mirror of a smile on it. It was a smile of such sick masochistic bitchery that I was violently repelled for a moment, and said to myself: You damned idiot—why didn't you let him do it?

I let go of his arm and stepped back from him. I was panting. He wasn't the slightest bit out of breath. I was shaken. He was calm. All I knew was that I couldn't bear the tension of standing there with him another minute; we had to do something to break it.

"Listen," I said to him, "go and take a shower. You can use my razor. I'll be fixing us some breakfast."

Paul went into the bathroom at once, without a word or a glance at me. Did he murmur to himself, "If that's the way you want it," or was that my imagination? In any case, I realized with a sinking heart that I had shown him how to use a new kind of aggression on me; from now on, he was going to do absolutely anything I asked.

When Paul came out of the bathroom half an hour later, he was quite transformed. Even his clothes looked neat. He was like an invalid who has been freshened up to receive visitors. His bruise, standing out in contrast to the rest of his handsome, freshly shaved face, now had the distinction of an honorable wound.

Meanwhile, I had dressed, started the coffee, squeezed the oranges, and taken the eggs out of the icebox. I was just about to begin frying some of them when Paul came into the kitchen. "Want me to do that?" he asked. And, because it rattled me to have him standing there and watching, I said, "Yes, please."

"You want an omelet?"

"That'd be fine."

It was uncanny, what had happened; how the situation had changed. We were being polite and soft-voiced with each other now. I was deathly embarrassed; what Paul was feeling, I had no idea. He made the omelet rapidly, with perfect assurance, taking an onion and herbs from the closet and a piece of ham from the icebox as though he had known exactly where to put his hand on them. As he brought it into the dining alcove on a dish, I thought to myself: How easily he turns himself into a servant! And then: Perhaps that's the role he really feels most at home in.

"Why, Paul," I said, eating the omelet, "this is delicious!" And indeed it was. Paul ignored my compliment, except for a slight, demure flicker of the eyelids. No doubt he took it for granted that his omelets would be marvelous; and maybe in his servant role it wasn't his place to thank me. We ate for some minutes in silence; and I felt the burden of his utterly relentless new passivity. At last, when breakfast was over, I said with an effort, "Well, now what are we going to do?"

"I don't think it's a question of what *I'm* going to do," Paul said, with his most provoking smile. "What are *you* going to do?"

But that was where I surprised him. I said briskly, "I'm going to do what I believe you've been wanting me to do all along. Take you to see Augustus Parr."

Paul was silent, poker-faced. Maybe he wasn't as surprised as I'd anticipated.

"That's what you really want, isn't it?" I continued, in a playful-bullying tone. "That was what you wanted to ask me to do when you called me that day at the studio?"

"If you knew that, honey, why didn't you suggest it *then?*"

He had caught me out. Was this sheer mind reading, or just a lucky hit? Unwisely I answered, "When we talked up at the house, I didn't think you seemed really interested. Augustus has to see dozens of people every week, you know. I never bother him with anyone who isn't serious to start with."

"And you think I'm serious now?"

"Yes. I do. I mean after all that's happened—"

"I've told you I don't believe any of that."

"Well, perhaps you don't exactly, but—"

"You're sure you aren't taking me to Parr because now you're stuck with me and I'm a nuisance and you don't know what else to do?" Paul looked straight at me, smiling. And I

185

couldn't answer; I could only smile weakly back and start to blush. This seemed to satisfy him. He wasn't shocked by the truth; it had merely amused him to dig it out of me. "Well, promise me you won't forget one thing—that's all."

"What's that?"

"When I was about to walk out of here, it was you who pulled me back, honey. Don't you go blaming *me* for that later."

"I won't."

"People nearly always do, after something like that."

"Let me tell you something, Paul—*I* am not *people*. The sooner you realize that, the sooner you'll understand me."

Paul laughed aloud. He seemed genuinely amused and pleased. And again, as up at Ruthie's, I felt the possibility of ease and friendship between us. "Well—good for *you*, honey chile!"

I looked at my watch. "I can call him now."

"You mean, he'll be awake?"

"Augustus," I said, rather severely, "gets up before dawn every morning and meditates for two hours. He does two more hours at midday. And two more in the evening. I never can understand how he finds time for all the letters he writes and the people he sees."

"I stopped you from meditating this morning, didn't I?"

"Oh, well—I'm afraid I'm not that regular. I don't do it for as long, either."

"How long do you do it for?"

"Oh, about half an hour. Sometimes only twenty minutes." Paul's questions sounded innocent enough, but they were embarrassing me. To cut them short, I got up and went into the bedroom. I had the impulse to shut the door behind me; but this would have given Paul the moral advantage of having been excluded. So I left it ajar.

"Hello," said Augustus's cautious voice at the other end of the line. It was the voice of a man who is accustomed to get calls from the lunatic half-world: hysterical confessions of guilt or religious doubt, rambling descriptions of occult experiences, mad meaningless jokes, even threats of violence. Such were the occupational hazards of his vocation.

"Hello, Augustus, this is Christopher."

"Ah, Christopher—how nice to hear your voice! Good morning to you."

"Augustus—there's someone I very much want you to see,

if you can possibly spare the time." Partly because Paul was next door, partly because my tone instinctively matched itself to Augustus's, I was speaking in the near whisper of the confessional. "I know how busy you are."

"What a curious thing it is, isn't it, when one says one is busy! So often it only means that one's afraid of having time taken away from one—like a dog growling over a bone it doesn't really want. One begins to growl before one even knows what the intentions of the person who is approaching are, save that he *is* approaching—getting within the zone of one's possessiveness."

"You know, I'd never suggest bringing anyone to you at short notice, unless it was really urgent—"

"Thank you, Christopher. You always show such consideration for one's miserable disorderliness—for that's all it is. If one were properly ordered, there'd be, of course, no haste, no pressure. . . . This is very urgent, you say?"

"Well, yes—as a matter of fact—there's even some possibility—" my voice dropped even lower—"of suicide."

"Oh, I see . . . yes, that *is* urgent. . . . My uncle, who was that curious anomaly, a Church of England clergyman, but nevertheless a man of very considerable spiritual insight, used to say that while a deathbed could be approached always with Christian resignation (once you've done all that's medically and humanly possible, you have to recognize that His will isn't necessarily ours), with a suicide, one's justified in intervening quite radically, because a suicide can *never* be God's will. . . . What does the doctor say? Is the person in question out of danger?"

"Oh, now, Augustus—" I had to laugh, because Augustus was always assuming the worst—to such an extent that he frequently misheard what you told him, just in order to make the situation more dramatic. "I didn't say he'd *done* it! He hasn't even attempted anything yet, though he's got some pills with him. But he seems to be at the end of his rope—" I giggled at the unintended aptness of my metaphor. "I mean, I really don't know if he'll get through the next twenty-four hours, even. And you're the only person I can think of who might be able to help him."

"Thank you. But, of course, in these cases, it isn't really a question of one's being the right person, is it? All that's needed is for someone to get down as near to the site of the disaster as possible—right up against the other side of that

187

terrible ego block—like a huge cave-in in a mine tunnel—behind which a human being is trapped. And then somehow one has to get some signal through to him, persuade him that the rescue party *is* on the way, and that he can help himself by remaining calm. That's the most one can do, as long as the emergency lasts."

"Well, as far as this person's concerned, it'd be a lot."

"Then you'll be coming over at once?"

"Yes, please, if we may. Say in twenty minutes?" Now, I thought, we sounded like doctors arranging for the admission of a patient to the surgery ward.

"I shall be waiting for you. Thank you, Christopher."

"Thank you, Augustus." I hung up the phone and came back into the living room. "He wants us to go over there right away."

"*Well*—" Paul said, "I certainly hope you know what you're doing!"

"I don't, but I'll risk it," I told him with a grin. Suddenly I was enjoying myself. I felt energetic and enterprising, and at the same time gaily irresponsible. This was like my old Mr. Fix-it days in London. It was ages since I had created a situation. Now I was simply curious to see what would come out of it.

At that time, Augustus was living at the home of two elderly ladies, sisters, who had invited him to stay with them after reading his books. They lived in a large, dark, old house on the outskirts of Hollywood, on what was still a country road winding up into the hills. Opposite them was an orange grove, in which Augustus had permission to walk. It was there that I had seen my first rattlesnake; enjoying the warmth of the ground just before sunset. It had seemed fat and sleepy, and didn't even rattle. As we stood looking at it from a respectful distance—and I tried dutifully to practice nonaversion—Augustus had explained how the poor creatures have taken the wrong turning, away from the line of creative evolution; how they have yielded to their anxiety and developed poison glands, and how they now live in misery, unable to control the temperature of their blood—if they lie in the noon sun for more than twenty minutes, it will boil. In winter, Augustus told me, deer came right down into the grove; and every night he could hear the coyotes howling in the surrounding hills. These Hollywood hills were geologically quite new, Augustus said, and they weren't going to last long because they were made of soft decomposed granite and the annual rains washed tons of it down into the valley. Like all evidences of mutability, this apparently gave him the greatest satisfaction. He would even speed up the process, by jabbing at the eroded hillsides with his walking stick when we were out for a stroll. As he did this, he would giggle and seem almost fiendish.

The old ladies and Augustus showed the most extreme consideration for each other's privacy. They never used the kitchen at the same time, except during the meals they occasionally ate together. Augustus had his own telephone, and the ladies never answered it. He meditated in a hut at the high end of the garden, surrounded by a subtropical jungle of giant ferns, palms and banana plants. Here he could under no circumstances be reached; I'm sure the ladies wouldn't have called him even if the house was on fire. They would have thought such a mishap unworthy of his enlightened attention.

Both Paul and I had to take our cars, because I should be going on to the studio later. As we stopped and got out at Augustus's gate, Paul asked me, "How old is he?"

"Oh, around fifty."

"Then he's probably impotent. That's why he's against sex, like me."

"That's the kind of idiotic remark people make when they want to explain away something they're scared of believing in."

"Yes, that's one of them," said Paul good-humoredly. "The other is, where does his money come from?"

"I never asked him. I think he has a small independent income. He gives most of it away. He lives on very little."

"If you'd been an old whore like me, you'd know that a very little is a lot, if it comes in every first of the month."

Augustus was waiting for us, as he had promised, at the side door which always had to be used by his visitors. It was at the far end of a deep redwood porch with cobblestone pillars, under a curving roof which darkened all the rooms and had a Japanese look. We saw him peering out at us through the colored mosaic glass panel; then the door opened and he waved us ceremoniously in, murmuring, "Keep right down the passage to the end door." After the brightness of outdoors,

189

we could see almost nothing and had to grope our way. Paul whispered gleefully in my ear, "It's *exactly* like a speak-easy!" Meanwhile, Augustus was locking the outer door, a precaution apparently required by the apprehensions of the old ladies—though I could never be sure of this, because he had a way of making other people seem abnormally cautious and afraid for their skins and possessions.

When we had got ourselves into Augustus's room and the door had been carefully closed to shut out any disturbing sound, I made the introductions. I saw at once that Augustus liked Paul; a warmth showed around his eyes as they shook hands and the Parr charm began to project itself. "Can I offer you some tea? I was just about to make some. It'll be no trouble. Do say you'll have some tea! I shall have some, whether you do or not. Of course, I keep reassuring myself that it *is* the only permissible stimulant. But the truth is, for an old British tea drinker like myself, it's an addiction, none the less."

How truly lovable he is, I thought. What was most lovable in Augustus was his fearless eagerness. Other people hung back, waited to be convinced. Augustus came to meet you. He was so eager to be interested in you, in absolutely anybody or anything. His intelligence was a function of this boundless curiosity—and how few have it! While Augustus was out of the room getting the tea, Paul and I sat silent, like spectators at the theater who don't want to break the spell because they know that this is only a quick scene change, not the end of an act. But how was Paul taking the performance? I didn't look at him; I was so afraid I'd see a sneering smile on his face and get furious with him for it. If he can't appreciate Augustus, I said to myself, that's *his* loss.

Augustus's room looked out on the sloping garden. In a colder climate, it might have been depressing; here, it seemed pleasantly shadowed and cool. It was quite large and comfortable, and only looked bare because Augustus had taken down all the pictures, explaining that he found them distracting. ("I found myself spending too much time *inside* them, just idling around picking up details. Saying, 'My word, that's clever!' or, 'I don't care for the way he did *that*.' If one were an artist, of course, one could see them quite differently, as wholes. What a very rum thing beauty is, isn't it? It's obviously put there to tell us something, but not the thing it *seems* to be telling.")

Augustus reappeared in the doorway with the tea things, suddenly and silently, like an apparition. The sneakers he nearly always wore made him supernaturally silent on his feet. He was dressed, as usual, in a costume which suggested both the artist and the odd-job man; a blue smock with frayed cuffs, a Navy work shirt, blue jean pants which were patched at the knees and had turned pale from many washings. Despite my partisanship, I couldn't help trying to look at him with Paul's eyes. Of course, there *was* that Christbeard—so neat and pointed, he obviously trimmed it—well, why shouldn't he, for goodness sake! It seemed to tilt the thin, beautiful face upward in a heaven-seeking thrust. Augustus was worldly enough while he fussed over the tea pouring. But when Paul revealed one of *his* addictions by taking out a pack of cigarettes, Augustus made an altogether unnecessary amount of disturbance as he hunted for an ash tray. There was a delicate hint of reproach in this, as much as to say, "What bondage you smokers live in; unable to spend five minutes anywhere without your apparatus!"—and I saw that Paul got the point.

After this, a silence fell. As far as Paul was concerned, it might have been due to embarrassment or growing hostility; but it didn't bother me. I had become quite used to being silent for a while at the beginning of any visit to Augustus. Indeed, he had told me that it was part of the technique of recollection he practiced; you "let the sediment settle and waited for the water to clear" before you started talking.

"I read that essay on the Gita you lent me," I said to Augustus, after an adequate pause. I knew enough about both the others not to bring Paul into the conversation directly.

"Thank you," Augustus said gravely. During the silence, he had sat forward on the edge of his chair, motionless but intensely alert, with his long, sensitive hands folded in his lap. In this pose, he had often reminded me of a radio operator with headphones over his ears, receiving a message which the people around him can't hear. And meanwhile, his pale, brilliant blue eyes would appear to lose focus and go blind—at least to the outer world.

"There was one statement I can't help questioning," I continued, in order to get Augustus started, "and that's the way he takes it for granted that so few people ever get seriously interested in—" (to hell with Paul, I said to myself)—"in this thing."

"Ah, my dear Christopher, how often I envy you your optimism about human nature! It's a form of modesty, really. Because you have found your way to this, you take it for granted that it's quite easy and natural for everybody." (Again I was conscious of Paul's presence. So what if Augustus did flatter me from time to time? I had to admit that he did—and that I loved it. Only I wished he wouldn't, right now.) "I'm afraid that you and I have got to face the fact—and it's an especially painful fact for those of us who care strongly for someone who *isn't* involved in searching for this thing—that very, very few *can* come to it in any one lifetime. Because it's only when the sheer *beastliness* of the world begins to hurt you—*really* hurt—like crushing your finger in a door—" Augustus's face contracted with pain as he spoke; he had a trick of unconsciously miming his remarks—"that you'll make up your mind to do something about it. And, by that time, it's usually too late. . . . This is the Middle World—we must never forget that. The world between what my uncle used to call hell—which perhaps isn't after all such an inapt name for a state which is probably very much more acutely unpleasant, even if temporary, than we moderns are willing to admit—and what my uncle used to call heaven, imagining a kind of Gustave Doré paradise which would no doubt seem like an absurd picture post card you bought on Brighton Pier beside that appalling instantaneity of awareness which the Vedas speak of. *Every* moment *is* eternity. And at *any* given moment we can break through the web of time. Or we could, if we weren't strapped down hand and foot—" Augustus writhed a little, as if straining against the bonds—"so that we can't move a muscle."

"How do you mean, strapped down?" Paul interrupted—to me, most unexpectedly. I hadn't supposed he was even taking the trouble to follow all this. But Augustus took the question in his stride and started to answer it without so much as a glance at Paul or a change in the tone of his voice.

"There are three kinds of bondage, aren't there—" Augustus ticked them off on his long fingers—"addiction, pretention, aversion—what I crave, what I pretend to the world that I am, and what I fear. You remember St. Francis and the leper? Fear is nohing but crystallized greed. And pretention's the worst of them all. That's the very dickens." Augustus winced, as if from a familiar pang of rheumatism. "One's *never* safe. One's got to be on one's guard every instant.

Unwavering recollectedness, unwavering awareness—*nothing* less is enough. Ramakrishna's parable of the monk and the piece of cloth. And, for goodness sake, stop asking the world for its approval! I have to make this resolve; I won't ask the approval of anyone in this matter who hasn't tried it out for himself. The old sneer of the cynic—you can't change human nature. There is no such thing as human nature! We can rise to anything because we can sink to anything. You see, Paul—" now that Augustus addressed Paul directly, he did so with a special, secret-imparting intimacy—"we *must* overcome this terrible desire to luxuriate in our guilt and our scruples. As long as we're going to indulge in that sort of vanity, well, it's just hopeless. You know your Francis de Sales, of course? *Even our repentance must be peaceful.*"

I smiled to myself. Augustus was warming up nicely. Although I had heard the whole thing, with variations, several times, I would gladly have stayed there all morning. What mattered was simply being with Augustus and not having to talk. (Our talks together fascinated me, but that was a different and more usual kind of experience.) If I kept my mouth shut and sat still, listening and yet not listening to that melodious voice, something would begin to communicate itself to me on a nonverbal level. My fears and doubts would slink back into their holes. I would feel calm and sustained; and *almost* absolutely certain that "this thing" was true.

But now I stood up. "Augustus, dear, you know my shame —I have to rejoin the worldlings. I have to go where the noisy and the eager and the arrogant and the forward and the vain fret and chafe and make their usual uproar."

Augustus chuckled at this. One of the things we had in common was that we nearly always recognized each other's quotations from Victorian literature.

"Paul, will you give me a ring at the studio when you leave here? I'll be there till five."

Paul nodded abstractedly, without taking his eyes from Augustus. He was obviously intrigued. Well, so far so good, I thought.

But as I got into my car I reminded myself that it was most unlikely anything could come of their meeting. Augustus, the old spellbinder, might keep Paul bewitched and bewildered for an hour or two, but how could he really help him? Paul couldn't be helped until he had confidence in Augustus, and where was he to find it at such short notice? It was all very well for me to have confidence; I had seen Augustus change from what he was four years ago to what he was now. How could Paul be expected to understand what that meant, meeting him for the first time this morning?

The Augustus I had known in London had been beardless and not nearly so Christlike. He was fastidiously clean-shaven, barbered and tailored, but just as charming and just as talkative. He frequented the literary parties of Bloomsbury, the high tables of Oxford and Cambridge colleges and the reading room of the British Museum. He lectured and he broadcast. He had a great variety of interests: evolution, biology, astrophysics, prehistory, philology, philosophy—and psychical research. His friends made fun of him because he went to seances and made a study of mediums, some of whom were later exposed as frauds. Because he was so lively, so unabashed in his curiosity, we were apt to think of him as irresponsible. We all loved listening to his fantastic theories, usually forgetting that to him they were only theories, on which he reserved judgment.

In 1936 he left for India, because a college in Bengal had offered him a professorship. This disappointed us a little; but we were reassured when a rumor drifted back to England about a year later that he had given up his job to become a yoga adept. That sounded more like the kind of Augustus we wanted to believe in. Hugh Weston and I laughed as we pictured him taking a nasty spill while learning to levitate, getting stuck in some impossibly complicated posture and having to be untwisted by half a dozen instructors, and finally emerging to receive his diploma, a little out of breath after having been buried for twenty-four hours.

I heard nothing directly from Augustus until December 1938, when I was still in London but nearly ready to sail for the States. Augustus wrote from Los Angeles, where he was now living permanently, he said. He had heard I was coming to America myself in the near future. Wouldn't I visit him? He ended with a sentence which struck me, even at the time, as strange: "I don't want to seem intrusive or presumptuous, but lately—not once, but on three separate occasions—I have felt a very strong concern about you."

However, when I did land in the States at the end of January 1939, I had no intention of going on to California. Everything I thought I wanted was there in New York. That

194

was where the new life was to begin.

What happened next was as unfunny as somebody else's practical joke. The true lifetime love I'd thought was waiting for me turned out to be just another quick looking-glass affair, and in two months it was all over. My new life had been built on the foundations of the supposed love, and automatically collapsed with it. One morning I woke up and realized, quite simply and calmly, that I had no idea why I should remain in this city another instant, or what I should do or where I should go if I left it.

I spent the next few weeks almost always alone; wandering around Central Park in the icy pre-spring wind; sitting in my hotel room staring out of the window at a water tower on the roof opposite. When the telephone rang, I turned around and stared at it until it stopped. This satisfied some kind of aggression inside me and made me feel better for about five minutes.

Again and again, I found myself thinking of that last talk I'd had with Dorothy, at the time of the Munich crisis. Dorothy had asked me if I saw any other meaning in life than the one you get through belief in communism. When I told her, No, she hadn't understood what I meant—that I saw no meaning in life at all.

What amazed me was that I could have made such a confession so casually. Why hadn't my own answer filled me with dismay and horror then, as it did now? I supposed it was because, in those days, I could tell the most brutal truth about myself without really feeling or thinking what I was saying. I was protected from thinking and feeling as long as I played the game of The Others.

But now I was forced to think and feel. The game could be played here, of course, but not by me. The American Others existed for Americans; but they had no relation to me. They weren't even my enemies.

In my desperation, I suddenly remembered that last sentence in Augustus's letter It seemed extraordinarily significant now, even promising some supernatural kind of support. If Augustus really did feel a concern about me, he was certainly the only person in America who did. So I wrote to him, telling him all my problems.

He replied by return mail and thereafter sent me two or three letters a week—pages and pages about pacifism, marginal activity, right livelihood, and the group considered as an unlimited liability company. I didn't try to understand much of this; what impressed and attracted me was Augustus's tone of authority. He seemed ready to give me absolutely specific instructions, if I asked for them. And that was just what I wanted now. I longed for discipline.

Was it I who decided to go to California, or was it Augustus who decided for me? His letters implied from the start that he expected me to come out there; and at length he even suggested sending me the bus fare. This touched me all the more because I now had at my disposal a free first-class ticket on the train, if I cared to use it. A few days before, my agent in New York had got me the offer of a screen-writing job at one of the Hollywood movie studios. This seemed like a signal from fate. So I went.

Augustus had certainly *not* spent any of his time in India doing yoga exercises; that much I learned right away. At our first meeting I made some silly joke about crystal balls and beds of nails. Augustus looked politely vague and smiled sadly. Next day, with seeming carelessness, he remarked that all the great mystical teachers agree in condemning such exercises as an obstacle to enlightenment; at best they can only lead to physical vanity and sex-obsession, at worst they may produce certain psychic powers with the inevitable accompaniment of spiritual pride, megalomania and madness. . . . Just the same, the psychic powers sounded rather thrilling. I longed to ask more about them, but thought it best, after my tactlessness, to keep my mouth shut.

Then what *had* Augustus done after he left the college? This I only found out by slow degrees. No doubt he delayed telling me until my interest was serious enough to be worth answering. Also, I had a great deal to learn before I could even partly understand what he was talking about. He began by lending me books. Vivekananda, Brother Lawrence, William James, the Bhagavad-Gita, Thomas Kelly, Evelyn Underhill. Some of these appealed to me at once. The rest I had to struggle through in a spirit of aesthetic self-mortification, enduring a sick-making vocabulary, a slatternly style, or just plain brute dullness, as I tried to dig down to what Augustus assured me was there and valuable underneath.

Then, quite suddenly one day, he began to talk about the monastery. It was up in the foothills of the Himalayas, with forests of pine and deodar all around. The valleys below would be choked with cloud for weeks on end; then the weather would clear and you would see the whole range of giant snow peaks standing along the frontier of Tibet.

"Tourists who go up to Darjeeling to look at them say, "How beautiful!" and of course they *are*—though it's impossible to imagine anything further removed from conventional pretty-pretty picturesqueness. One's in the presence of something *infinitely* remote and forbidding. One could imagine them saying to one, Yes, this *is* a world—but it isn't for wretched little creatures like you. In *your* lack of condition, you couldn't exist up here among us even for one instant. All *you* need do at present is just remember we're there. We shall keep reminding you of it, from time to time."

The monastery was dedicated to the contemplation of Brahman, the Godhead without form or attributes. Therefore it had no shrine, nor even any images or pictures of gods or holy men. No rituals of worship were performed; there was no communal prayer or chanting. In fact, there was no fixed timetable. You meditated whenever you wished, alone, in your room. Augustus said that at first he had found the quietness of the place almost unbearable. "Until one realized that it was one's own tempo that was wrong. Because, up to then, one had been taking one's life *prestissimo*, one tried to do the same thing there—like some hopeless amateur conductor who's missing the composer's whole intention."

Augustus had gone to live at the monastery during the summer; even so, the life there must have been quite hard enough for him, considering that he was still, more or less, the Augustus of the London days. And then the months had passed and the winter had come, with deep snow. There was no heating in the monks' little cubicles. Augustus had to wear a couple of blankets and a woolen cap with ear flaps, even indoors. This was when he had first let his beard grow. ("One began by simply wanting to keep one's face warm, then one got used to it, then one admitted to oneself that it hid one's weak chin.") The monks were charming and friendly, but only one of them spoke English, haltingly and with great effort. Their library had no books except in Bengali and Sanskrit. Their winter diet was restricted to rice and vegetables, mostly dried pumpkins. Often the weather stopped them from going out for days at a time. . . . I couldn't help laughing when Augustus told me all this, but it was with a shudder. The prospect of such boredom was as overwhelming as the mountains—and the only way out of it was to meditate!

It was during the year he spent at the monastery that Augustus had become convinced of the reality of "this thing." That wasn't in itself so impressive; no doubt you could think yourself into believeing almost anything in such surroundings. But he had been able to carry his conviction with him out of India and settle down with it here in California; *that* was what impressed me.

There was no word from Paul all day. This didn't altogether surprise me. No doubt Augustus had been more than he could take, and now he was blaming me, and sulking.

But why no word from Augustus himself? Was he maybe annoyed with me for wasting his time on someone so obstinately unresponsive? No, that wouldn't be like Augustus at all. And besides, I'd felt sure Paul interested him.

By the time I'd returned home and eaten an early supper, I was starting to feel really curious. Augustus's evening meditation period—"the third watch," as he called it—would be over by now; so I called him. No answer. Half an hour later, I tried again. Still no answer. I wondered if I should drive around to his house. Better try once more first.

"Ah, Christopher! How very extraordinary! This really is one more proof—if any further are needed—of that curious thing, E.S.P. . . . I had just laid my hand on the telephone to call you—"

"I called *you*, several times. Have you been out?"

"No, I was here. But I wasn't alone. And I had the feeling that the contact one had made with our friend was so precarious that it mustn't be broken even for a moment. I do hope you'll forgive me."

"You mean—you've been with Paul—all *day?*"

"I do indeed, my dear Christopher. . . . How odd that he should have that name! Although, at present, perhaps *Saul* would be more appropriate. . . . He left here only a few minutes ago, and of course my first impulse was to share this experience with you. It's certainly one of the oddest one's ever met with. And, since one became absorbed in this thing, one *has* met some very rum cases. . . . If I'm not asking you to betray a confidence, may I ask how much you know about our friend?"

"Quite a bit. He's a person who gets himself talked about, you know."

"That was what one gathered. Not that I was referring to

198

the sort of details which are conventionally described as 'spicy'—such an odd application of the word; it makes one ask, what exactly is it that's being spiced? No, I meant the total impression that he creates. You, of course, with your great talent for language, could define it much more precisely. . . . One sees, don't you agree, a figure *with something standing behind it?* The individual himself is quiet, well-mannered, by no means ill-favored. But in the background—if one takes that frighteningly matter-of-fact book, the Bardo Thodol, not as a piece of Asiatic fantasy but as a very exact psychological manual describing certain states which our own western psychology hasn't even begun to recognize—there's something one must assume that he has created for himself, however unwillingly—"

"Augustus, what *do* you mean?"

"I think we must take it as proven that certain acts don't just produce the usual direct first-degree consequences—I choose to drive on the wrong side of the road so I get my citation from the police—no, they set in motion a whole process. And I'm pretty sure, from certain indications, that that's what's happened in this particular case. A sort of vortex forms at a very deep level; and, as it swirls around, something takes shape inside it—something rather terrible—which isn't answerable to the individual's will. It has a life of its own. It *may* for a time remain merely mischievous; sooner or later, it's bound to become quite openly hostile and malign. You remember the great scene in Lear—"beware my follower"? That was what I saw behind our friend. He knows it's there —one's fairly certain of that—or at least there are moments when he knows; and then he knows also that he can't retreat any farther. He *must* advance, in one way or another. Have you looked into his face, Christopher? There's a very curious expression in the eyes—you see it sometimes in photographs of wild animals at bay. But one also saw something else— which no animal has or can have—despair. Not helpless, negative despair. Dynamic despair. The kind that makes dangerous criminals, and, very occasionally, saints."

"Honestly—you think that could happen to Paul?"

"Oh, one never ventures, unless one's excessively unwise, to make any predictions on *that* subject! Nevertheless, something took place this morning which moved one very much. It *might* have been the first sign of a true mutation, and not just a temporary emotional reaction. One always hesitates to hope, when so much is at stake. One *must* keep reminding oneself that, though this thing is only one step away, there may have to be a journey of many lifetimes to reach it. Oh, supreme and unapproachable light—how far art thou from me who am so near to thee! Like that extraordinarily poignant moment when the chick tries to peck its way out of the egg. It's been calculated, you know, that the chick has only a limited number of pecks by which to break the shell. The moment that number has been passed, if the chick has still failed to break through, it'll begin to weaken and presently suffocate. And I believe that's something more than an analogy; perhaps one may venture to call it an homology. We're all frantically working to escape, to make our breakthrough, and we're working against a time limit—"

"Augustus—please!" I cried in desperation, feeling like one of the chicks that suffocate. "Just tell me—*what did happen this morning?*"

I could almost see Augustus's faint smile of satisfaction at my impatience. For of course these enormous digressions were not due to a wandering mind; they heightened his climaxes, and well he knew it! But now, having reduced me to just the right state of frustration, he changed his tone, speaking with ostentatious care and simplicity, like a witness under oath. "When it was time to begin the second watch, I suggested he might care to share some part of it with one. He agreed, so we went up together to the hut. I had no idea, at that time, if he had agreed to accompany me out of curiosity, or mere politeness. He seemed perfectly calm; rather thoughtful, perhaps. We neither of us spoke as we walked through the garden. When we reached the hut, I showed him where to sit, and gave him a cushion. I had left the door open, so that he could see everything and get accustomed to his surroundings; as you know, when the door's closed, there's a deep twilight because of the shades on the windows. When he had settled himself, I closed the door and took my own place. I suppose about ten minutes passed. I don't know what your own experience is, Christopher; I find that that's about the minimum period which has to elapse before one can get one's wretched distractions under some semblance of control. Well, one had just managed to center down, to some degree at least, when our friend began to sob. At first, one thought he was coughing; then the sounds became like the panting of a runner who's gone to the very limit of his

200

strength, and whose whole body's protesting against the effort. Indeed, the spasms were so very violent that one felt sure they must end quite soon. But they went on and on. Then he actually started to roll about on the mat, jerking his knees up to his chest and relaxing them again; until one realized that this literally was a kind of accouchement. Something was being violently expelled and perhaps brought to birth. And the suffering was desperate."

"So what did you do?"

"Oh, one simply waited. One tried to maintain a state of readiness, as soon as one should be needed. There was nothing to be done until the crisis itself was over. Because, of course, it's entirely possible that in these cases pain is actually necessary. It's the thing of childbirth. You remember the experiments Bloch did in Zurich. . . . So one waited. And by very slow degrees, this tormented young animal calmed down; the human individual reasserted itself and got up off the floor. And then he said a very strange thing. He said, 'Why did you do that to me?' "

"What did he mean?"

"One knew what he meant, I think. He was only wrong in supposing that it was oneself who had intervened in any way. All that another person can do at best is to create a field. Within that field, all kinds of insights may occur. What was so enormously impressive was the completeness with which he gave himself to the experience. Self-knowledge is impossible for most of us because we can't push aside this thing that stands in the way of it; but here one felt that the entire ego-sheath had been sloughed off. Do you know, Christopher, his face—it was suddenly the face of a pre-adolescent boy? One was in the presence of true innocence."

"So then what happened?"

"We walked together in the hills; and he told one with the most total frankness about this life he's been leading. Greed and fear, greed and fear! There were moments when one was almost reminded of the Inferno. And one had somehow to listen without betraying how terribly one was shaken. When he had finished, one said what seemed appropriate. One hoped it was the right thing."

"And where is he now?"

"He left saying that he wished to be by himself and think. One didn't dream of trying to detain him, of course. . . . I believe we can be sure of one thing, Christopher; he's going to need you a great deal in the immediate future."

"Need *me?*"

"It was to you he first came for help."

"But you were the one he really wanted to see."

"There are certain ways in which one can be of use to him, yes. But it was to you he instinctively came, knowing that your own experience had been such that you could receive him with understanding as well as charity. His instinct was right. You didn't reject him. And I believe the day may come, and soon, when you can say to yourself: Through God's grace, I have rescued a human soul. . . . You know, Christopher, I don't make such statements lightly. But I venture to say that, save for you, our friend might have found himself in a very dark place indeed. . . . It's significant that he did *not* tell me one thing he told you—that he was about to take his own life."

"Well, yes, but—"

"I am absolutely convinced he would have done so. Now I think that corner has been rounded, at least for the present. But you'll have some anxious days ahead of you. And, believe me, I shall watch you with great admiration and affection. Good night, my dear."

"Good night, Augustus."

"And God bless you—both."

I had been through various moods during this conversation. To begin with, I had simply felt astonished that Augustus and Paul had taken each other so seriously. Then I had been frantic with curiosity, while Augustus would not come to the point. Then I had strongly suspected Paul of just trying to make himself interesting with this weeping act. Then, however, I had reflected that Augustus was a shrewd old thing and that it was very unlikely he could have been so easily fooled. So then I had had to admit to myself that, if Paul *was* on the level, he had manifestly established himself as Augustus's number one disciple and my spiritual superior; and this made me meanly jealous of him. But then, at the end, Augustus had made everything all right again by appointing me Paul's savior, which left me feeling wonderfully benevolent toward Paul and quite a bit of a saint myself.

At first I planned to sit up with a book and wait for Paul, who would almost certainly show up before long, I thought. But my early rising had made me sleepy. So I put sheets on the couch-bed in the living room, with a note pinned to the pillow saying, "It's all yours." I left a table lamp alight beside the bed and the door of the apartment ajar. Then I went into the bedroom and slept.

When the telephone rang, it was already broad daylight. "I hope I didn't wake you?" said Ronny's voice.

"It's time for me to get up, anyway."

"I suppose you've heard the news about your friend?"

"My friend?" I was still a bit stupid with sleep.

"Let's face it, Christopher—from now on, he's either *your* friend or he's nobody's."

"Oh, you mean Paul. I think he's probably asleep in the next room. Wait a minute and I'll see."

"You needn't trouble yourself, my dear. I happen to be able to tell you *exactly* where Paul is, right at this moment. Downtown, in jail."

"My God! What for?"

"Drunk driving."

"How do you know all this?"

"The bail bond people called us. They wanted *two hundred and fifty dollars!*"

"And you refused?"

I must have said this somewhat blankly, because it was dawning on me that I was now committed to dealing with this huge nuisance myself. But Ronny took my tone for disapproval and was on the defensive at once.

"We most certainly did! And I must say, I think it was perfectly outrageous of Paul, giving them our address. You probably don't realize, Christopher, the *things* he said to Ruthie—*and* to me! And now, after making it only *too* clear that he never wanted to see either of us again, he calmly demands that we shall get him out of this mess—"

"Don't worry," I said—coldly now, since I had been maneuvered into behaving nobly and wanted at least to make the most of it. "I'll look after everything."

"Oh, my dear, I *knew* you would!" Ronny let out a huge sigh of relief.

The jail was crammed with people. A whole line of visitors —Negroes and Mexicans mostly—stood packed elbow to elbow in front of a wire netting; on the other side were the prisoners. You had to yell to be heard above the din. In one way it was like a hospital; almost everybody was talking about the same thing—when the "patient" would be "well" enough to get discharged.

Amidst all the noise and dirt and stink, Paul seemed relaxed and somehow quite at home. "You didn't have to come," he told me, but not aggressively and with a slight grin.

"What did you expect? That I'd leave you to rot down here? I must say, though, I think you might have asked me instead of Ronny and Ruthie."

"I *never* asked Ronny and Ruthie! What do you think I am? It was that sonofabitch, the bail bondsman. When I told him I didn't *want* to be bailed out, he called them."

"How did he get their names?"

"I saw him talking to the cops who booked me. They must have gone through the papers in my pockets and told him. I bet I could sue them for that, the bastards. They'd screw their grandmothers if it was worth a couple of bucks. . . . Honestly, Chris, you don't think I'd be seen dead crawling to Ronny and Ruthie, do you?"

"No—I guess not."

"You *guess* not!"

"I'm sure not."

"That's better."

"Now listen—Ronny says the bail's two hundred and fifty."

"He had his nerve, calling you. I'll never forgive him for that, the bastard."

"But I'm glad he did. And I'll go and take care of it now, right away."

"You will do no such thing. I told you once already—*I don't want* to be bailed out."

"Oh, for Christ's sake, Paul! Sure, I can understand your not wanting to ask Ronny and Ruthie; but I can lend it you, easily. In fact, I'm going to, whether you want me to or not."

"You don't understand, Christopher. I can't borrow this money. Because I haven't got *any* money, *anywhere*."

"But, Paul, you—well, you're right—I *don't* understand. . . . You had some yesterday, though, didn't you?"

"A hundred and some dollars. That's all gone, now."

"How about your car?"

"It's a total wreck."

"And the insurance?"

"I'm not insured. There'll be trouble about that too, probably."

"I see. . . . Well, all that's beside the point for the present. The first thing is to get you out of here."

"Why should I let you?"

"You seriously expect me to believe you're going to stay shut up in this dump because of your *honor?* Really, honey chile, how *dare* you be so pretentious!"

Paul grinned at this, and for a moment I felt quite delighted with myself. Hadn't I handled this situation like a worthy disciple of Augustus?

Four hours later, I didn't feel so sure.

The formalities with the bail bondsman and the police took much longer than I'd expected; and, when Paul had finally been extracted from the jail, we had to go down to a police car lot to which his wrecked car had been towed and get permission to take his suitcases out of it. There was an added delay because the lid of the trunk had been bent in the accident and had to be wrenched open with a crowbar.

And, in the middle of all this fuss, Paul had casually informed me that this wasn't his first drunk driving offense in California. He had been arrested and fined during his last visit. This time he might quite possibly get a three months' prison sentence, without the option of a fine!

So, as we drove westward along Wilshire Boulevard, I asked myself with misgivings, what was I going to do with him now? Certainly I couldn't dump the problem on Augustus again. We were back at position A, but with a big difference: yesterday Paul could at least claim the glamour of a male Magdalene—if Magdalenes interested you; today he was just a depressingly ordinary two-time loser.

I was sure I could guess, more or less, what had happened yesterday evening. Having been far too confidential with Augustus, Paul had had a violent revulsion. (Hadn't he told me himself that he hated people who knew too much about him?) So he had rushed out to the nearest bar, gotten blind drunk, lost all his money playing poker in the back room, and ended by smashing up his car.

And if it was really true—and I supposed it was, for Paul didn't seem capable of that kind of a lie—that he was absolutely broke, then everything from now on in would have to be paid for by me. Until somehow or other I could find a not too indecent excuse to get rid of him.

Meanwhile, I was tired and hungry and low-spirited. So, when we got to Beverly Hills—hoping to cheer myself up—I invited him to lunch at an expensive restaurant. It happened to be the same one at which I'd met him that first day, with Ruthie and Ronny.

After we'd sat down, Paul said, "I suppose you want to know what happened last night." He made it sound like an accusation.

"Not if you don't want to tell me."

"You mean, you're not interested?" He looked hard at me for a moment; then, with that disconcerting clairvoyance, asked, "Or are you so sure you can guess?" He smiled his thin, sour smile. "You know something? You just might be surprised."

"Okay, go ahead—surprise me."

"Well, to begin with—I spent most of the day with Augustus—"

"Yes, I know. I—" I stopped myself. This was a stupid slip. And Paul pounced on it. "You talked to him? What did he tell you?"

"Nothing special. Just that you'd been there."

"Oh. . . . Well, anyhow, I was there till it was time for his supper. He asked me to stay and have it with him, but I wanted to get off by myself. So I drove downtown and went into a bar. . . . What are you grinning at?"

"Because I'm so surprised."

"Let me tell you something, honey. You think bars are nothing but dens of sin and a dirty joke—that's because you're a mean old limey puritan. But what you've got to learn, if you're ever going to understand anything about anything, is that there's lots of people in this world, like for example your aunt, who do all their thinking in bars and are only really their natural selves in bars—and if they do happen to get drunk while they're there, that's purely incidental and proves nothing whatever."

"I see. I beg Auntie's pardon. . . . And, purely incidentally—" the waiter had just come up to our table—"what'll you drink?"

"A double Gibson."

"Good. The same for me."

"*Well!*"

"Well what? Go on with what you were telling."

"Well, I suppose I was in that bar quite a while. Several hours. Anyhow, around midnight, these very tough Mexican kids, they were *pachucos*, came in. They were all members of a gang, only they called it a brotherhood; and they told me all about their girls and their meetings and their gang fights and everything. And then they said they'd take me to their hideout. So they piled into my car and one of them said he was going to drive. I didn't care. I *must* have been drunk, because I knew quite well he was high as a kite on tea. They wanted me to smoke some, too, but I wasn't in the mood—which was just as well, as it happened. . . . Let's see—oh, yes, we got to the hideout, and they had tequila, and we all drank it, passing the bottle around. And then another kid came in. . . . No—before that, they said they were going to make me their blood brother, and we nicked our arms with a knife. Look—" Paul pushed up his sleeve and showed me a long scratch on his forearm. It was swollen and inflamed around the edges.

"That looks nasty."

"It's probably septic," said Paul carelessly. "So then this other kid came and they talked a long time in Spanish. And then they explained to me that one of their gang brothers had been grabbed by the Vice Squad for hustling. They'd caught him with this middle-aged guy in the park, and they were about to take them to Lincoln Heights, and it'd mean reform school for the kid. But right now the Vice were cruising around the park in their car, with these two inside. They were stalling to see if anyone would come up with a bribe. Only the middle-aged guy didn't have any money on him and he was too scared to call his wife for any. . . . So then the kids all looked at *me*, and one of them said, "The Brothers always help each other." So I asked them how much it would take to fix the officers, and they asked me how much I had with me. So I showed them, and they said that would probably do it. . . . So they went off with the money, and pretty soon this kid they'd sprung came back with them. And he hugged me and thanked me and he told me he had a beautiful sister and I could have her for free any time I wanted. Or I could have him, if I'd rather. As a matter of fact, he was kind of beautiful, in that long-faced El Greco way—they all were. . . . So then we were all to go out and celebrate some place. So we started off again, with the same kid driving—or maybe it was one of the others; if it was, he was high, too—and pretty soon he skidded, trying to get around a street corner at about ninety, skidded clear across the street into a parked car, bounced off and skidded back again into a telephone pole, so we got it front and rear. I was stunned for several minutes,

I guess. I must have banged my head, though I can't find the bruise. So the next thing I know, the cops have arrived."

"What about the kids?"

"Oh, they all got away."

"Fine blood brothers!"

"You don't understand kids like that, Chris. In the same situation, they'd expect me to do the same. It's sort of an understood thing—like bailing out of planes."

"But, Paul, I just can't seem to grasp this. . . . You gave them all the money you had in the world, and—don't you realize their story was obviously lies from start to finish?"

"Probably it was. That's not the point. Look—I don't expect you to understand this—"

"Say that *once* more and I'll scream! . . . Two more Gibsons, please, waiter."

"But I really did feel like those kids' brother. As soon as I met them, I thought, these are the people I belong with. After all, I'm a hustler too. Ruthie and Ronny never forgot that—it came out when we had our fuss. And I'd been playing along with them and acting so buddy-buddy, and all the time we were on opposite sides of the fence. Giving the kids that money made me feel wonderful. I felt I'd gotten back on my own side."

"I know this is none of my business, but—I'd always imagined you were loaded. Didn't you have some kind of—of an allowance?"

"Sure. In fact, I had two of them. Only you could never rely on Ludwig-Joachim—and now the old bastard's gone off to the Argentine. And the Condesa has most of her money tied up in occupied France; she's really strapped, so I don't blame her for not sending any. I'll have to wait till the war's over."

"So you were just using up what you had left?"

"That's right."

"What were you planning to do when it was gone?"

"Live off Ruthie, I guess. Till someone else showed up."

"So that was the moment you pick to quarrel with her! You know something? If those kids knew what a lousy whore you are, they'd throw you out of the Brotherhood!"

We got back to the apartment late in the afternoon, having stopped at a market to buy some food for supper. Paul made the marketing seem fascinatingly important; he chose fruits and vegetables as carefully as if they were neckties or socks. By now, I had quite sobered up from the drinks at lunch, but my mood was still much better than before it. Paul fixed us some coffee.

"Isn't it time for your meditation?" he asked suddenly.

"Yes—I guess it is."

"Then go ahead, why don't you?"

"How about you?"

"I'll sit in, if you don't mind."

"No, of course not." But I did, rather. These sits were among the most private things I had ever done in my life. Even sitting with Augustus made me self-conscious. And Paul would be a much greater intrusion.

"Did Augustus tell you I sat with him yesterday?" He was watching my face as he asked this.

"Well, yes, he—just mentioned it. . . . How did it go?"

"I don't know. It's funny—"

"You felt there was something?"

"I don't know what I felt and what I didn't. I can't make up my mind about it. I want to try it again, though."

So we sat down, cross-legged, on the floor. I liked to sit on the floor, Hindu style, in a corner of the room. The advantage of this position was that it was an entirely unaccustomed one. You saw everything—the furniture, the ceiling, the view through the window—from a different angle; and this in itself was a constant reminder of what you were trying to do, every time you opened your eyes. I still found I couldn't resist opening them every few minutes.

This evening, there were the usual distractions: traffic on the street, a radio somewhere in the building, footsteps, voices, the ice-box motor switching itself on and off. But Paul seemed to cancel all of these; today I had nothing but an intense awareness of his presence. It was as if we were both sitting there naked—the situation had that kind of intimacy—and yet what did we actually know about each other? How extraordinary that we should be here together like this, we two who were still almost strangers, each holding, as it were, to the life thread which had guided him to this room and this moment. Does anything happen by accident? Augustus said No. Paul and I had met because we needed each other. Yes, now I suddenly saw that; I needed Paul every bit as much as he needed me. Our strength and our weakness were complementary. It would be much easier for us to go forward together than separately. Only it was up to me to take the first step.

My excitement began to mount, as the implications of this idea became plainer. How tremendous—for once in one's life —to do something quite without compulsion, to break the greed-and-fear pattern by an absolutely free act! Well—I had just realized what that act could be. So why not? Why not dare it?

The idea I had had, the plan I wanted to propose, thrilled me so much that I longed to tell Paul about it right away. I tried to meditate, but I couldn't; I could only think about Paul. Very well, then; I would bring him into the meditation. *We are together, now,* I told "this thing." *Help him, too. Help us both. Help us both to know that you are with us.* . . . I had prayed for Paul! The thought that I had done this, and could never tell him so, was deeply shocking and exciting. Because I'd done it, I felt a great wave of love go out from me to him. From now on, we were truly going to be brothers. . . . Which reminded me, I'd forgotten to buy iodine to put on that scratch the *pachucos* had given him. . . .

When next I opened my eyes and glanced down at my watch, it was time at last for us to stop. I jumped to my feet. Paul opened his eyes too and looked up at me. He seemed slightly dazed, and I had the sense that he had been quite deeply absorbed.

"Paul—I've got something I want to say to you. And please don't interrupt until I've finished, even if you think it's crazy. Because I really *mean* it. . . . Look—as you know, I've been working in the movies all this time, and I've earned quite a lot of money. Apart from what's been put aside for taxes and so forth, I have about twenty thousand dollars in the bank. Now—" by the time I had reached this point, I was actually breathless and had to pause for an instant before going on— "I want to *give* you half of it. I mean—really give it, properly, without any strings. I want you to take it and do whatever you like with it. I'd even rather not know what bank you put it in, or how you spend it. If you'll accept it, then it's simply yours, and we'll never mention this again. . . . Wait, now— there's something else. I'm asking you to stay here and live with me, for as long as you like. We could do our sits together, and help each other keep all the rules, and maybe we could study together—read some of the books Augustus talks about. . . . You mustn't think this is some kind of a chari-
210

table offer, because I really need someone to help me stay on the rails, and I guess maybe you do, too. . . . Listen—don't answer right now, if you don't want to. Think it over first. I've said all I have to say."

"I don't see there's anything for *me* to think over. I think *you* should think this over."

I was disappointed by Paul's reply. Chiefly because, in the reaction which instantly followed my proposition, I'd become aware that I wanted to push it through very quickly, before I could regret it. "I've made up *my* mind," I said stubbornly. "Do you suppose I'd have said all this if I hadn't?"

"All right, then—"

"You mean, you agree?"

"What else would you do, if you were me?"

The temperature of my enthusiasm dropped about fifty degrees. "I suppose you've had a whole lot of offers like this, in your life," I said.

"I've *never* had an offer that was without strings, as you call it."

"You mean, you think this one has strings, too?"

"I hope not, honey chile. I hope not, for your sake."

"Well—I know you've met some pretty rotten people, and I suppose I can't blame you for thinking that I'm exactly like them and that this is just an act. The only thing is, you just happen to be wrong, and I'm going to *prove* it to you. Maybe this'll cure you of your *I know I'm dirt so you must be, too* attitude; maybe it won't. I don't give a damn." I was coldly furious with him, and this provoked me to a wild, theatrical gesture. I pulled out my check book, scribbled Paul's name, ten thousand dollars, and signed it. (I must admit that I got a deathly sick pang as I did so.) "And now," I cried, thrusting the check at Paul, my voice rising to near hysteria, "Take this and get the hell out of here!"

Paul threw back his head and roared with laughter. "Jesus! No *wonder* that studio hired you! What are they going to do when you quit show business? They'll go broke! Ha, ha—I'll be damned! You'd better get this through your head, honey —your aunt isn't going *no* place. She's staying right here and fixing your supper for you. And from now on, you're going to save that money of yours, because you'll keep away from those fancy restaurants and eat some real home cooking." Paul put his arms around my neck and hugged me. Our cheeks touched. I had to start laughing too. But I still had the check in my hand.

"Here, take it," I said.

"You keep it, Chris. Tomorrow I'll put it in a bank. That is, if you still want me to."

"Take it now. Put it in your pocket."

"Just as you say."

My big act hadn't quite come off. I hadn't had the orgasm of emotion I had expected when I made my offer. But still, everything was suddenly very snug. Something almost childishly intimate had happened between us; and perhaps Paul was embarrassed by it, as I certainly was. He went abruptly into the kitchen and started preparing our supper. I followed. I felt a need somehow to sentimentalize the occasion.

"Perhaps we should call Augustus," I said.

"Why?"

"Well—to tell him."

"Tell him what?" Paul had the most convincing air of not knowing what I was talking about.

"Why, about—" I checked myself. I had been going to say, "about us," and the phrase suddenly sounded ridiculous; like getting engaged. "About what we've decided."

"Why should we tell him?"

"Well, he likes you a lot."

"Is that what he told you?" Paul sounded slightly scornful.

"Yes, he did. But didn't you feel it yourself?"

"Honey, your old Auntie has heard all kinds of purty talk from all kinds of people. Mister Parr, he talks mighty purty. But your Auntie doesn't set much store by talk. She waits to see how folks *act*. I didn't notice Mister Parr making me no offers."

I blushed with pleasure; even though I was perfectly well aware that Paul was deliberately and even cynically flattering me. I found I wasn't displeased that Paul should take this attitude to Augustus. "I thought you liked him," I said, probing a little.

"Perhaps I like him. Perhaps I don't. I haven't made up my mind."

That night as I lay in bed, a little voice said quietly, *It wasn't so dumb of you to give him that money in a lump sum. Maybe it'll be a lot cheaper that way in the long run. Now you don't have to keep giving him pocket money and paying*

212

his bills. And he won't ever be able to ask you for any more when it's gone.

I turned my head angrily on the pillow. I disowned the voice. I refused to accept any responsibility for it. What it said was tactless and ill-timed and in the poorest taste. For this was the eve of a new life—not the kind I had planned to lead in New York, but one that was going to be truly new; a life of intention, as Augustus called it. Every moment would be a deliberate creation, and therefore a marvelous adventure. . . . Well, anyhow, that was the general idea. We couldn't hope to succeed all the time. But at least we would have each other's encouragement. And, as long as we didn't stop trying, how could we fail?

Our first week together was also my last at the studio, so it was ten days or so before the whole of our routine had been worked out and could be put into practice. At the start Paul rather alarmed me by his radicalism. He was prepared to take everything Augustus had told him quite literally, with no reservations. "Are we going to be mystics or aren't we? Let's either shit or get off the pot. I still don't know what I think of all this stuff, but no one shall say I didn't give it a try. Anyhow, I don't see what *else* there is to do. This is just about the last thing I haven't tried."

We bought an extra alarm clock. The two clocks went off at six, one in my bedroom, the other in the living room. We stayed in our respective rooms for our sits; they lasted an hour now. Paul had wanted to begin two-hour sits right away, in spite of my protests; but even Augustus, when consulted, had agreed that this would be too much of a strain and might produce "dryness." I used to wonder what went on in Paul's mind during meditation; it must surely be something more profound and exciting than the jumble of nonsense that filled mine most of the time: snatches of hit songs, headlines from newspapers, puns, rhymes, unwanted names and telephone numbers—accompanied by twinges of senseless anxiety and childish resentment. Even when Paul assured me, "All I do is sit there and feel nothing at all; it's worse than straining on the pot," I was impressed. There was something tremendously impressive about Paul's quiet determination. He never complained or tried to make his struggles sound dramatic. I could hardly believe that I'd ever thought of him as a dilettante.

213

At the end of our sit we used the bathroom, got dressed and fixed breakfast. We had arranged exactly how we would do this; it was as formal as a ballet. Paul showered first, while I shaved; I made the coffee and set the table, while Paul cooked. Until breakfast was ready, we didn't exchange a word. This was an idea we had got from Augustus, who had told us about the Benedictine practice of silence during certain hours of the day. Far from being an austerity, it soon became an amusing game. It was fun utterly ignoring each other in the bathroom and the kitchen; even when our eyes met in the bathroom mirror, we managed to keep straight faces. Also, by the time we were allowed to say "good morning," we were thoroughly awake, had shaken off any earlier grumpiness, and were eager for conversation.

After breakfast, we washed up. Then came what we called "lessons," which we read aloud to each other from some book Augustus had recommended. Paul now had to experience the nausea with which I was already familiar. I remember one book in particular, the autobiography of an ex-public enemy who had been instantaneously converted to his present state of mind—he was now a lay preacher—while in solitary confinement for trying to strangle a fellow-convict. One didn't doubt the genuineness of the author's experience; but, oh dear, who had taught him to write that honey-dripping jargon of the meek saved lamb? "How she *dare!*" Paul would exclaim.

At twelve we began our midday sit. At one fifteen we ate a light lunch. In the afternoon we would sometimes drive up into the hills and go for a walk—the beach was too dangerously sexy—sometimes visit Augustus, sometimes do chores for his friend Ian Banbury, the Baptist minister (about whom, more in a moment). The chores were always physical and we did them chiefly for exercise, though, as Augustus put it, "Even we contemplatives need to practice a certain amount of karma yoga." We would stack portable chairs and transport them to some church hall for a lecture, or make up bundles of clothes to be taken to the Quaker center for the Okie camps in the San Joaquin Valley. While we were in the car, the one who wasn't driving would read aloud to the other. This was supposed to distract our minds and eyes from attractive pedestrians; actually, it had the opposite effect; our glances became furtively compulsive and we had several near collisions. Also, the reading made us carsick.

The evening sit was from six to seven; and then came supper, the most looked-forward-to meal of the day and the one on which Paul lavished all his art. He had insisted that we should be vegetarians—I had pleaded vainly for fish—and now I had to admit I was satisfied; Paul could do miracles with vegetables, eggs, and cheese. We ate late and in a leisurely mood, since there was no urge to go out again. Paul had banned movies as distractions.

This was certainly one of the happiest periods of my life. The longer I lived with Paul, the more I became aware of a kind of geisha quality in him; he really understood how to give pleasure, to make daily life more decorative and to create enjoyment of small occasions. He rearranged our whole apartment, filled it with flowers, dyed the curtains, scribbled and daubed silly, charming drawings and pinned them on the walls in place of the French Impressionist reproductions, repainted the kitchen in bright Russian Ballet colors. Our two-man monastery took on a sophisticated nursery atmosphere—an atmosphere which is perhaps most vividly recaptured by my memory of Paul saying, *"Et maintenant, c'est l'heure du cocktail,"* as he poured our midmorning glasses of milk.

Our friendship was of the sort which naturally evolves its own private jargon; ours was made up chiefly of misapplications of Augustus's favorite phrases. If we were late for a date with Augustus—who was particular about punctuality—Paul might exclaim, "Boy, we'd better get over there with appalling instantaneity!" Hunting for the can opener in the kitchen, I would tell him, "I'm so near to this thing which is so far from me."

Paul used to talk nostalgically about the old days in Europe, and I loved listening to him. "Your Auntie's name was famous from one end of the Ritz Bar to the other," he would say: and he never tired of describing historic parties at which he had been a guest, including the ball in London during the short, scandalous period when Ludwig-Joachim had taken a house there, to which Paul had gone dressed as a nun wearing roller skates. He had skated through the streets, been chased by the police and had only narrowly escaped. He told me about beauty treatments he had tried in a spirit of experimentation—in one of them, your whole body was peeled so that you emerged, very sore at first, with a perfect new skin like a baby's; but he had drawn the line at a course of X-rays which was said to kill the growth of your beard, or give you

215

skin cancer, or do both. We discovered quite a number of mutual friends, including Maria Constantinescu, who had introduced him to hashish. Paul couldn't tell me where Geoffrey was now; however, he vaguely recollected hearing that Ambrose had taken off some years ago for an island in the Indian Ocean. (Thank goodness if he had! For it looked as if the Nazis would soon invade Greece.)

Augustus, needless to say, was greatly excited about our ménage—it was, so to speak, his first experimental farm—but I doubt if he realized how much we were enjoying ourselves. For Augustus—bless his histrionic old heart!—had cast Paul in the role of spiritual mutant, eggshell-breaking chick, and therefore took it for granted that Paul was in the midst of the most agonizing soul struggles which must be making life grim for both of us. "My word!" Augustus would exclaim when Paul had gone out of the room and we were alone together, "What a tough!" He had certainly told Ian Banbury and Dave Wheelwright something of Paul's lurid past; I was sure of that, from the way they looked at Paul. Paul himself noticed it at once. "God, Chris—they're like a bunch of old maids around a converted whore!"

"Don't you be so superior," I told him. "Us non-whores have to get our kicks somehow, don't we?"

Ian Banbury was a lean, sunburned man with thin fair hair and a gaunt, deeply lined, boyish face. He was vague and gentle in his manner; quite fearless when it came to protecting minority groups from public opinion or the police; given to dry, Early American jokes which he made so quietly that you could seldom hear them. He talked about Jesus Christ with a lack of reticence which made me squirm, although, thanks to Augustus, I could now at least have respect for his faith. And it was easy enough to like, and even rather love, Ian as a human being; he was what Augustus called "a true innocent." "You and I, Christopher, we're like people who've been crippled. We can't hope to use our own limbs again; the best we shall ever achieve in this life, if we're lucky, is a fairly good technique with artificial legs and hands. At best, it'll always be jerky, mechanical. But Ian's different. He's still got the natural, free use of his limbs. The world hasn't succeeded in crippling *him*."

Dave Wheelwright was even more admirable but much less lovable; he was a bit of a spiritual prima donna. He wasn't quite fat, but he had the plumpness of the good pig in the

216

nursery story. While Dave was in the trenches in 1917 he had had some kind of a vision of Christ. As the result of this, he had gone to his commanding officer and told him he refused to kill. I felt sorry for that officer. He was in a terrible spot; it was his duty to court-martial Dave, who would then almost certainly be shot as a deserter. I could picture him, nearly in tears, pleading with Dave to save Dave's life, and Dave being very stern with him for making such a base suggestion. Dave had finally relented, however, and agreed to a compromise; henceforward, he was to go over the top with his company and take part in the attacks, but with his rifle slung over his shoulder unloaded. Dave had not only done this, he had jumped down into the enemy trenches and shaken hands with German soldiers. The Germans must have been terrified; no doubt they thought Dave was about to overwhelm them with some form of judo—as indeed he was!

Everything Dave had done since then had been aggressively nonviolent. He had dealt nonviolently with bootleggers, holdup men, teen-age gang leaders, browbeating them into giving up their guns and knives and surrendering to the police—who, in their turn, had had to suffer a good deal of Dave's spiritual blackmail. Dave had married a cheerful, untidy-haired little girl named Naomi, a lot younger than he was, and the couple had created around them an atmosphere of intentional, high-minded poverty which made you ashamed of accepting even a glass of water in their house. They had raised their four children without the slightest relaxation of their principles, which had meant nonstop conflict with the school boards.

It was a lawyer friend of Dave's who appeared for Paul, free, at his drunk driving trial. This trial seemed almost an anachronism now. But, after all, the authorities could hardly be expected to realize that they were dealing with an entirely different person from the one they had arrested—a spiritual mutant who was a nonviolent, nonsmoking, celibate, vegetarian teetotaler. Augustus encouraged us with a lecture on karma. He was inclined to think it a sign of grace that the bad consequences of Paul's actions were catching up with him so fast, and thus being wiped out.

"What shall I *wear?*" Paul wailed. We hesitated a long time between a sweater and blue jeans and a dark formal suit with a tactful tie. If Paul wore the sweater and jeans, he'd be putting himself on the level of all the underprivileged who can't afford to dress well and are therefore treated with prejudice, as likely criminals, right from the start of their trial. Wouldn't this be the honorable thing to do? If he wore the suit, he would make a good impression on the court as a solid citizen. Wouldn't this be cowardly and vile? No, I argued—minding him what Augustus had taught us; that you must never provoke anyone to commit an injustice against you. To wear the sweater and jeans would be lacking in charity to the judge. So we decided for the suit.

When Paul stood up there all alone, slim, elegant, perfectly in control of himself and looking uncannily young, and said "Guilty" in a small, clear voice, it was, as I told him later, the greatest thing since Joan of Arc. The judge seemed to think so, too. Paul merely got fined and put on parole.

When it was all over, we had to have lunch with Ian Banbury and his wife, Ellen; and they fairly fell over themselves in their eagerness to show Paul that they didn't regard him as a member of the criminal classes. I feared this was trying him a bit too far, and when we got back to the apartment I tried to relieve his feelings for him by attacking them. "What ghastly bores they are!" I exclaimed.

"You know something, honey? While we were at lunch I kept thinking about those rich old hags in Cannes I used to play bridge with, and all those queens in Estoril. They were every bit as bad, in their own way. Maybe worse. Let's face it, nearly all people are bores, of one kind or another. At least the Banburys are a kind I'm not used to. And that makes them rather fascinating."

Paul's radicalism showed itself again when we faced his next problem: what was he going to do about military service? He had already registered for the draft as a combatant. Now Augustus and I took it for granted that he would get himself reclassified as a conscientious objector and in due course be sent to work in one of the forestry camps in the area, this being the officially permitted form of service for pacifists. But Paul wouldn't agree. "It's different for you, Chris. You were a pacifist before this whole thing started. If we get in this war and they raise the age limit, you go to a camp; that's okay. But the only way I can prove I'm on the level is to wait till I get my draft notice and then refuse to go."

"But then they'll send you to prison."

"Of course they will. And that's where I belong."

It took Augustus, Ian and me nearly a week to convince

Paul that his stand wasn't necessary. (Dave Wheelwright didn't take part in the argument; I'm sure he thought Paul ought to get himself sent to prison.) The more reasons we produced, the more adroitly Paul countered them until the argument turned into a sort of coy flirtation and I began to suspect that he simply enjoyed teasing us. Anyhow, in the end, he gave way.

But that didn't settle the matter. Paul's draft board, like most of the boards on the West Coast, included some really malevolent old men who wanted to put the entire younger generation into uniform, just because they *were* young. They called Paul a draft-dodger and sneered at his objections to military service. He probably wouldn't have been given his classification at all if Ian hadn't sent a letter to the board answering for his sincerity. Ian was well-known locally as a pacifist; and his word was respected even by a lot of people who disapproved of his views. When Paul came back from his final hearing, I could tell by his manner that he had been badly humiliated; but he didn't say much about this or seem resentful, even. "They acted pretty much the way I'd expected them to," was his only comment. In such situations, he really *was* tough.

One day Paul told me that he had got his sexual potency back. He had first realized this during a sit; and now he became the victim of the most rampant fantasies and dreams. I was certainly bothered by these myself, but Paul's temptations always sounded much more thrilling than mine. At length he came into the bedroom in the middle of the night, woke me up and told me, "I think I'm going crazy. If I don't talk to you, I'm liable to rush down the street and jump on the first thing that comes along, man, woman or animal." So we decided to buy an extra bed and put it next to mine. From then on it was understood that either of us could wake the other at any hour and talk until he "felt better."

And so I came to hear in great detail about Paul's love life. Sometimes he made me laugh a lot—as when, for instance, he described how an American woman in Switzerland with a nine-year-old daughter had told him she was nervous about leaving the child alone with him. (I could just imagine how Paul must have cross-examined and bullied her to make her confess this!) Whereupon he had given her a scathing lecture on the hypocrisy of self-styled broad-minded mothers who think sexual freedom is fine for everyone except their own children. He had gone on like this until the woman was in tears and had, as he put it, "practically begged me to help myself to her loathsome moppet. And would you believe it, Chris, the very next day, that kid came up on the roof while I was sunbathing and seduced *me!*"

But more often he described sexual acts which got me so excited that I could hardly bear to listen. Mostly they were acts done in haste or great danger of interruption, this being Paul's idea of a supreme thrill—acts on trains, in taxis, on planes, naked in the snow while out skiing, in evening clothes during a ball at an embassy, in gangs, in crowds, in orgies. . . . Then I would start to reminisce in my turn, doing my best to get him as excited as I was and not always sticking to the truth. That almost prehistoric afternoon at the bed-sitting room of Waldemar's *Braut* got elaborated into something like a scene from the Marquis de Sade. (Yet even as I did this, I felt guilty because I was perverting one of the most truly innocent experiences of my life; I felt like a dirty old man.)

And so we lay, side by side in our beds, only a few feet apart, playing this unwholesome but nearly irresistible game, which I was seldom strong-minded enough to stop. It was usually Paul who would sooner or later exclaim, "Jesus Christ, who are we trying to fool! I don't know about you but I'm getting up and taking a cold shower."

The sex talk made a bond between us, however, which began to exclude Augustus. I quite admit that I was a party to this. Not that I felt any less affection for Augustus than before, but I was mean enough to want Paul all to myself. So when Paul said once, "Thank God, honey, I can talk to you —none of the others would understand," I agreed with him that Augustus was, after all, an elderly man, and Ian and Dave weren't even attempting celibacy, so how could they possibly imagine what we were going through? They just did not have our temptations. And then Paul, taking his cue from this, began loyally flattering me. And how about money and success and being famous, he added: what did the others know about any of that? "You're the only one who's really given up *everything*, Chris." I blushed and silently agreed with him.

One morning when Paul was out, I was surprised to get a call from the Railway Express office; they had a picture to deliver to Paul. There was probably some mistake, I said. When Paul, who had been to the dentist, returned, I told him about it.

"Oh, sure—that's my Picasso," he said casually. "They've certainly taken their time getting it here, I must say. It was stored in New York. I sent for it soon after I moved in with you. It'll brighten the place up a bit."

Later that day the picture arrived. It was enormous—at least for our apartment—over six feet long and about four feet wide; a tall narrow painting of a giant girl seated at a high-legged table. The girl had a violet face, two noses, hands like the wings of birds and a crown of pale poisonous-looking flowers.

"Good God!" I exclaimed. "It really *is* a Picasso!"

"Well, *of course* it is, honey chile! Did you think your old aunt would tote a reproduction around? This is my last and only souvenir of Europe. I never told you about it, because I wanted to surprise you. The Condesa gave it to me just before I left. It used to hang in her bedroom and I always liked to wake up with it in the morning. . . . You know, maybe we should hang it in *our* bedroom. There's no sense in letting the *hoi polloi* see it—they wouldn't understand."

I knew exactly what he meant. The Picasso would disturb and even shock Ian and Dave. They would find it subversively frivolous, altogether out of place in our professed plainness. (I was sure Dave suspected us of frivolity, anyhow.) As for Augustus, he would no doubt have to be shown the picture sooner or later; but I could just see his faintly ironical smile when we did so. We were both aware already that he was making disadvantageous comparisons between our respective standards of living. Although he so obviously relished Paul's cooking, he had subtly rebuked us by saying that of course it was "much too rich for my poor old stomach." This remark had been followed by one of Augustus's almost sadistically revolting descriptions of the workings of the pylorus and that sewer, the gut.

Going to supper with Augustus was a dramatic experience; you felt like a hungry tramp who has broken into a house to steal food. For the kitchen, being part of the no man's land between the domains of Augustus and the old ladies, could only be entered at certain hours and with extreme precautions against noise. At eight thirty, by which time the ladies had presumably retired for the night ("more probably sneaked off downtown to a burlesque show," said Paul) Augustus would glance at his watch and announce in a stage whisper, "Themselves must be away by now!" and we would all tiptoe down the passage.

This kitchen, if you could believe Augustus, had more taboos and forbidden places than the most superstition-ridden Pacific island. He showed you the shelf which was sacred to the ladies' health bread and imported English marmalade, and the dish in the icebox containing their butter, which must never be touched, even if you were starving. There was a chair you mustn't sit on, and a variety of knives, forks, spoons and plates you mustn't use. It was unthinkable to dare to drink from the bottle of Arrowhead water; you would probably be hexed with elephantiasis or tertiary yaws. No doubt the ladies *were* somewhat house-proud and possessive, but Augustus made them seem like guardian demons. When I referred to them as The Good-Humored Ladies, he smiled in a way which showed he had long since thought up the joke himself and had indeed been gently willing me into making it.

Chattering away in a voice just above a whisper, Augustus would keep urging you to eat "something solid," as he called it—eggs or canned soup. He himself supped messily on scraps. His part of the icebox was full of stale oddments—bits of old cake, dried-up sandwiches, hard cheese, rotten fruits, most of them leftovers from picnics with the Banburys and the Wheelwrights. "I'm a scavenger by nature," he would tell you. If, as often happened, he'd been brought a home-baked pie or a pat of home-churned butter by Ellen Banbury, who was always trying to feed him up, he would take a positively malicious pleasure in giving it to his guests.

Paul made a point of accepting such challenges or character tests. Without even a polite show of hesitation, he would blandly take and gobble up the best food that Augustus had to offer. "I utterly refuse," he told me, "to play Miss Parr's humbler-than-thou game." And soon he went on to criticize the studied shabbiness of Augustus's clothes. I disagreed with him. It wasn't spiritual pretentiousness which made Augustus dress like this, I argued, but an instinct to make fun of his environment. In London, the home of the Bond Street tailor, he had been exaggeratedly elegant. Here in Los Angeles, the home of casual men's wear, he had naturally exaggerated in the opposite direction. But I couldn't convince Paul. And on one occasion when Augustus received us in a crudely patched shirt and a pair of jeans with the cuffs cut off and their edges left ragged, Paul remarked, in his slowest drawl, "Let's face it, Augustus, that Robinson Crusoe thing isn't really *you*." Augustus laughed, but I think he was slightly hurt; and he got back at Paul thereafter by ostentatiously changing into a better jacket as soon as we arrived at the house.

Several times we went along on what Paul called the "church picnics," which were usually held at the top of one of the local canyons. The Banburys and the Wheelwrights organized them chiefly to hear Augustus talk; the eating was incidental and somewhat apologetic, because it interrupted him. "A little more of that, please," Ian would say, as if asking for a second helping, when in fact he wanted Augustus to elaborate one of the points in his discourse. From time to time there would be group silences, during which we—or some of us—brooded over what had been said. I still have a snapshot I took which shows three of us doing this: Dave has his face buried in his hands and looks seasick, Ian is frowning as if suffering from stomach cramps, and a Quaker doctor from Pasadena named Pat Chance is staring desperately into the distance, like a castaway searching for a sail.

Unfortunately, I have no pictures of Alanna and Dee-Ann Swendson. They were sisters, and the only really young people in our group. But they weren't included merely because their mother belonged to Ian's congregation and was a disciple of Augustus. It was Augustus himself who had asked their mother to bring them to our meetings, hinting excitingly that he saw in them "something—it's only a possibility, mind you—and one does hesitate, in such cases, even to suggest—this type, perhaps the rarest and most mysterious of all—it's paralleled, of course, by the great child geniuses of Art—Mozart's already composing at the age of five—but one has to admit that very, very occasionally, one of them *does* emerge—spiritual genius, there's no other word for it—men like St. Bonaventura and Shivananda, apparently—who do seem to have come to this thing already in pre-adolescence, with almost no struggle *at all*."

I don't think even Mrs. Swendson's maternal prejudice can have accepted this kind of talk at its face value. Augustus was romanticizing, as he so often did; but this time you couldn't blame him. There was a magic sweetness about both of the girls; they were Scandinavian blondes, with marvelous pale honey-gold skin. Alanna was more beautiful and more feminine; she was nearly fourteen. Dee-Ann was twelve, and still largely a child, or a young animal. Her face as she sat cross-legged on the ground listening to Augustus somehow made me think of a young reindeer far away out on the tundra, motionless, but alert and listening under the northern lights. . . . *Dee-Ann!* How could anyone have called a young magic reindeer by that hideous name?

On one of our picnics, when Augustus had been saying with even more than his usual persuasiveness that life is only given meaning by the search for "this thing," Alanna suddenly exclaimed, with a touching, almost indignant astonishment, "But, if that's true—why do we ever bother about anything else?" The question left us all silent. Only Augustus breathed an "Ah—!" as if to indicate that the spiritual jackpot had at last been hit.

Later, as we were driving home together, Paul muttered, "Jesus, that kid makes me hot!"

"Alanna? Honestly, Paul, you can't *really* like them that young?"

"Hell, no—I mean Dee-Ann. The way she sits with her legs apart, when she knows I'm watching. She knows damn well she's got me hot for her, the little bitch. . . . You don't believe me, do you?"

"Well—I think you like imagining things like that."

"You want to bet?"

"Of course, I know—I mean, I've read—some kids are precocious. But Dee-Ann—why, that's impossible! I mean, she's so sold on Augustus, and trying to do something about this thing."

"*Really*, Chris—and you *dare* call yourself a novelist! Don't you realize it's just *because* she's like that that she's so sexy? What else do you think 'this thing' is about?"

"But you never tire of telling me that Augustus and the rest of them can't cut the mustard. Make up your mind, bud!"

"But don't you see, that's exactly why they'll never make the grade? Dee-Ann maybe will some day."

"Well, good for her if she does. . . . But now you listen to me—if I catch you fooling around with that girl, you break our compact, and the whole thing's off, do you hear? I'm not going to stand for any more of this rocking the boat. I'm having quite enough trouble keeping my end up, as it is."

Paul grinned. "You'll just have to watch over me, honey

chile." And he began dreamily singing, "Someone to *watch* over me—"

"You utter bitch! Do you know what you're doing? You're slowly but surely maneuvering me into the position of being a jealous husband."

Paul just went on grinning and didn't answer. Of course, he knew perfectly well what he was doing. He must have done the same thing to all his lovers—male or female, it would make no difference; in this respect, I felt sure, he had always contrived to get himself into the feminine role. And he could play it with me because we were tied together, too, not by sex, but by that money I'd given him. God, what ivy-binding insidious stuff it is! I had said—and honestly from my heart meant—that it had no conditions attached to it. But it had. It always has. . . . Already, out of the corner of my eye, I was watching to see how Paul was going to spend *my* ten thousand dollars. I had even been shocked at his extravagance in having the Picasso shipped out here. And only the other day he had had some shoes made for him. . . . I watched this and felt guilty because I watched.

The producer of one of the films I'd worked on had been a man named Lester Letz. He and his wife were the only movie poeple who had kept in touch with me since I'd left the studio; and this was chiefly because Mrs. Letz read Augustus's books and went to hear him whenever he gave a lecture. She had kept calling me and asking me to dinner, and I had made excuses until she had tightened the screw by saying she knew I must be a vegetarian, like Mr. Parr, and that she'd decided to become one, too. She promised me we'd have a hundred per cent vegetarian meal together. So I was forced to accept.

When I arrived at the Letz home, it was the usual Hollywood trick; there was a dinner party of twenty people. And one of them was Ronny. He was as much surprised to see me as I was to see him, but he was also delighted; this, I sensed, was a welcome opportunity for him to be aggressive.

As I sat at table with my milk and vegetables, amidst the wine-bibbers and meat-eaters, I was aware of his mocking eyes upon me throughout the meal. After it was over, he cornered me.

"Imagine meeting *you* here, Christopher! So you *do* go out unchaperoned, sometimes!"

"You, too, I see. . . . Where's Ruthie?"

"Back East. The house is sold. . . . Well, my dear, you'll be interested to hear that I'm being drafted very shortly."

"That's too bad."

"It is indeed too bad. I'm certainly not in an heroic mood. If I could get out of it any way, I would. But I'm afraid I can't. Unless, of course, you and your friends will give me an alibi."

"How do you mean, an alibi?"

"An alibi—there's no other word for it, is there? Like the one you arranged for Paul."

"Nobody *arranged* anything for Paul."

"Indeed? Well, let me put it this way—I understand one can only become a legally recognized conscientious objector on the grounds of religious training or belief. I must say I never saw the slightest sign of either in *him*."

"You mean, you think Paul is lying?"

"I never said any such thing! I merely happen to know Paul."

"And you don't admit that people can change?"

"I think they can change if they become aware of their problems—for instance, after they've been to a good analyst. But first they have to clear things up—and that's exactly the opposite, if you don't mind my saying so, of what your yogis and swamis do."

"To you, that's mystery-mongering, I suppose."

"My dear, I *refuse* to have words put into my mouth! All I'm venturing to suggest is that in the case of your friend Paul, there has been, how shall I put it, a certain amount of hiding one's head in the sand."

"Let me tell you something, Ronny—Paul wanted to refuse to go in the army and let them send him to prison. He wasn't going to use any alibi, as you call it."

"You say he *wanted* to be sent to prison? Then why isn't he going?"

"I—some of us persuaded him not to."

"And he gracefully yielded?"

"He'll be sent to a forestry camp, you know. That's fairly tough."

"Nevertheless, my dear, I'm afraid a time may very well come when I and my buddies will be envying him quite a lot, and perhaps not very charitably. Even prison may begin to seem more attractive. And I dare say it would have suited

226

Paul better than most of us. I understand you can get dope there easily, once you know the ropes."

"You really don't like Paul one little bit, do you?"

"My dear Christopher, you couldn't be more wrong! Please don't imagine Ruthie or I are still holding that little unpleasantness against him. On the contrary—I think he's a fascinating creature and the most fun, as long as he's in his own world. . . . If you'll allow me to say so, you must accept *some* of the responsibility for having taken him out of it and put him into this Oriental thing, which is all wrong for him —it really is. You see, Paul has never had any proper education; all he knows is what he's picked up from the kind of chi-chi crowd he ran around with in Europe. And for him to play this intellectual game—well, frankly, it's way above his head."

"Why do you call it an intellectual game, Ronny?" Right at the start of this conversation, I had firmly resolved to keep my temper. "It's certainly not a matter of accepting a lot of complicated dogmas and theories. In fact, it's about the least intellectual thing there is."

"My dear, I know I should never have started a discussion like this, especially with someone like you! I was bound to make a fool of myself. And, you see, I really meant the opposite of what I said, didn't I? What I meant was that this kind of thing appeals to intellectuals precisely because it's an escape from the intellect—and that's what they all long for. They long to get back—"

"Into the womb? You know, Ronny, I feel as if I knew everything you're going to say before you say it."

"That must be most amusing for you. No doubt you and Paul will have a hearty laugh about it together. Only one day you'll have to admit I was right. Paul won't keep this up, you know."

"You mean, you *hope* he won't. And you *want* him to fail. Shall I tell you why? Because, as long as he's doing this, you feel insecure. You had him nicely taped, as a drunken, doping sex maniac. Now you're badly worried."

"Why ever should I be worried?"

"Because you're afraid your whole world might crack apart if this kind of thing is possible. You're afraid that your precious psychoanalysis might be discredited. You're even afraid that you might have to do something like Paul's doing yourself. And you dread that, because religion's such a bore
227

and so madly ungay."

"*Well!* You certainly seem to know me better than I know myself, don't you? It couldn't be, could it, that you're confusing me with one of your characters? The danger with you people of imagination is that you're apt to *use* it too much."

"But, Ronny, if you expect Paul to come apart at the seams, why not the rest of us? Why not me? I suppose you think I shall carry through on my imagination—be able to fool my self, in other words? Is that what you mean?"

"Christopher, I absolutely refuse to accept any of these suggestions about what I'm supposed to be saying! I merely venture to predict that Paul isn't going to keep up this life you've planned for him."

"You're ready to bet on that?"

"Any amount you like."

I looked at Ronny in fury, which changed, after a moment, into a kind of superstitious dismay as I realized that he had absolute faith in what he'd said. He was quite, quite certain.

"Oh, well," I said weakly, "in ten years, we'll know which of us was right, shan't we?"

"You're too generous, my dear Christopher. I'm sure *one* will be more than sufficient."

When I got home from the Letz party, I didn't even tell Paul that Ronny had been there.

Dave Wheelwright had a brother, Ford, and Ford had just inherited from some deceased relative a small property with a few cabins on it, down by the Salton Sea, the big salt lake in the desert southeast of Palm Springs. The place was called Eureka Beach. This name had been given it by a group of retired businessmen from the Middle West who had come there planning to settle and found a co-operative community in the early twenties. The community had failed, because the businessmen and their families hadn't liked each other well enough to go on co-operating and sharing the daily chores in a region which heats up to 120 degrees in summer and is subject to water shortage, sand storms and flash floods out of the hills. No doubt their enthusiasm for nature had been largely theoretical, right from the start, or they would never have picked on such a spot.

Ford Wheelwright didn't quite know what to do with Eureka Beach. Maybe he would sell it later, if the value of real

228

estate in that area ever went up. (It did go up, sky high, during the fifties; and now the cabins have been replaced by air-conditioned bungalows, and there is a bar and a club house and a fishing pier, and people water ski on the lake. But Ford got no part of the profits from this; he didn't hold on long enough.) At that time, Ford and his wife and a few friends were camping out there. Dave and Naomi visited them and returned wildly enthusiastic—no doubt because the life was even more uncomfortable than in their own house.

It was Dave who persuaded Augustus that we should all spend a week or ten days at Eureka and make a "retreat," with a fixed timetable of meditation periods and group discussions. Ian Banbury took to the idea at once—I think he wanted to get away from his devoted, bossy parishioners—and so did Ellen, because she enjoyed the logistics of feeding people under difficulties. (The nearest store was over ten miles away, the deliveries of butane gas were few and far between, the well was unreliable and the only available firewood, mesquite twigs and driftwood from the lake.) Paul and I were unenthusiastic; we didn't want to leave our snug home. "It's all very well for Augustus," Paul said. "He'll have a ball turning stones into bread and being tempted in the wilderness. Well, anyhow, thank God we don't have to stay there forty days and forty nights!" Privately, I feared that someone else beside Augustus was going to get tempted; Paul didn't know yet what I'd just heard—that Mrs. Swendson was coming, with Alanna and Dee-Ann.

At length, all the necessary arrangements had been made. We left Los Angeles in a caravan of cars for Eureka, on a morning of the third week in May. (It was the day the Nazis invaded Crete.) The cars were packed full of bedding, provisions, pots and pans, tools; we were bringing everything with us we could conceivably need. It seemed funny to be making this drive of nearly two hundred miles, with enough equipment to stock a shop, simply in order to pray!

During the middle of the day, the light along the shore was unbearable without sunglasses, for the wide, shallow lake threw a blinding glitter. The water was so salt that you could float on it without any effort, but, except at night, it was unrefreshing; when you came out of it, the sun started to pickle you at once. The cabins stood a little back from the beach, among wispy gray-limbed smoke trees. Sand storms had scoured the paint from their walls, leaving the wood gray and dry as bone. A rocky trail straggled up from the cabins to the highway. And beyond the highway you could see the railroad and its telegraph poles—gray and hot and iron-dry and very much a part of the desert—as it crossed the hill slopes tufted with mesquite and creosote bushes; thousands and thousands of them, but not enough to hide the underlying baldness of the gray, gritty sand. Back of the slopes were mountains. These were faint gray phantoms in the livid midday blaze, marvelous mineral rainbows at sunset, and at night, just great black useless piles of volcanic rubbish.

One of our cabins had been built as a mess hall and was much larger than the others, but it got so hot during the daytime that you could scarcely breathe in it. So Ford and Dave made a shelter by spanning tarpaulins over a wide-open space between the smoke trees, and here we had our noon meditations, our midday meal and most of our group discussions. We got up at five and went to bed at nine, and there was a siesta in the hottest part of the afternoon.

There were fifteen of us altogether: Augustus, Paul and I, the Banburys, the Dave Wheelwrights, Pat Chance the doctor, the Ford Wheelwrights and two of their women friends (a school-teacher from Laguna Beach and a faith healer from San Diego), Mrs. Swendson, Alanna and Dee-Ann.

Here are some extracts from a notebook which I kept at Eureka. The notebook-keeping was part of a discipline I had set for myself during our "retreat."

Thursday. Beginning of full schedule. Yesterday we were still getting organized.

First watch: Disturbed by new surroundings. *Who are all these people?* Your fellow-researchers; therefore your natural allies and friends. *What am I doing here?* Living as you ought to have lived every day of your life. . . . Tried Augustus's technique of picturing members of our group as they would appear under X-rays, living skeletons without personality traits; thus aversion can be overcome. Found this hardest with Dave, easiest with Fran Wheelwright.

Aversion caused by Pat's mannerisms when reading Fénelon's letters to us at breakfast—nothing but hurt vanity, this. Why wasn't *I* asked to read?

Second watch: Acute nervous tension, because of dusty

oven-hot breeze and tarpaulins flapping. This is a farce: how can we meditate in this hell-hole?

Discussion on nonviolence. Talked too much, failed badly in courtesy to Grace Birnbaum just because she uses words that irritate me, like "meaningful." Augustus on compassion: original sin of animals, living fossils, survival of small and adaptable, *Tao Tê Ching*, be like water.

Third watch: Much better. Strong sense of interchange with Paul, sitting next me.

Friday. First watch: Still bothered by my sex dream last night about B. Found myself repeating Yeats's "Even from that delight memory treasures so—" Maudlin self-pity. Shed a few tears.

Discussion on vegetarianism. Reverence for other life forms. Meat not necessary, anyhow. Soya and peanuts for protein. Grind own grain in a hand mill. Bulk very important.

Second watch: Restlessness and jitters, excusing themselves as anxiety about invasion of Crete. Sneaked off to the store after lunch. They only had yesterday's paper. News terrible. Black gloom. Buried the paper by roadside on way back. We have voted to ban them and radio while here.

Third watch: Best so far. Thank God I'm here doing this. Everything else, *for me,* an evasion.

Saturday. First watch: Sleepy, dull. Dachine Dickinson's talk on healing: "Free the struggling Christ within us." Very important not to sneer. Try to translate what she means into my language. Augustus admirable at this.

Second watch: Happy because I'd been nice to Dachine, who was hurt by Pat's skepticism. But some disguised cowardice later; refused to ride horseback on pretext it was too hot. Also, boasting to Fran, Ford and Naomi about my German. Said I used to speak it *perfectly;* insinuated I somehow *gave it up* for the sake of the spiritual life.

Third watch: Suddenly saw how one should live this life. If you're learning Chinese, then you must talk nothing but Chinese, even if you know only a few words. The terrible temptation to relapse into "English."

Selfishness about dish washing. First I do more than my share. Then I object, because they haven't noticed this. But what right had I to do more? What right have I to behave better than the others? It's nothing but aggression against somebody or other. Apologized later to Mrs. Swendson.

Sunday. Got up before dawn and walked along beach. A sudden impulse to kneel down and pray. Terrific furtive melodramatic excitement. Then Ian and Ellen came along, saw me doing it. Realized then that I'd subconsciously wanted this, and planned it! They take that walk every morning. Utter humiliation and self-disgust ruined first watch.

Ratlike preoccupation with my comfort; avoided the broken chair. So Grace had to take it. Selfishness about lending my car to Pat; offered it too late, when I knew he'd arranged to take Ian's.

Discussion; the active and the contemplative life. All agreed they are complementary. But some friction between Augustus and Dave. A. believes that most social workers are bogged down in desire for results; quotes Bhagavad-Gita on symbolic action. D. hints that exclusive contemplation is selfish, especially during war crisis. Found myself backing D. *Motive for this?*

Second watch: Sex, sex, sex. "If you want to find God, look for him at the place where you lost him." Eckhart.

Augustus: "God *isn't* the Ancient of Days—that unfortunate Old Testament phrase! It's *we* who are the miserable, seedy ancients of days. He alone is young—with that appalling instantaneity . . ."

And so on and so forth. . . . The most significant thing about this notebook is that Alanna and Dee-Ann are only mentioned in it once. They were around, all the time, and though they weren't expected to keep to the full schedule, because they were so young, they helped a lot with the cooking and chores and were most useful and sweet.

There was a good reason for my ignoring them, however. I didn't want to admit to myself that I knew what was happening between Dee-Ann and Paul.

I don't suppose that most of the group noticed anything, because he didn't spend much time actually alone with Dee-Ann. They were together chiefly in the afternoons, when it was too hot for most of us to want to go out. Ford had told Paul of a ranch back in the foothills where you could rent horses. But when Paul went riding, it would be with both the girls, and one of the ranch hands would go along too. Then they would swim in the lake as the day cooled off, but others of us would usually be there.

Toward the end of Sunday afternoon, our fifth day at Eureka, Mrs. Swendson, the girls, Paul and I went swimming. Alanna and her mother returned ahead of us to their cabin to dress. I told them I would take another dip; then I said I'd changed my mind, and left Paul and Dee-Ann on the beach. As I took off my trunks and dried myself in the cabin Paul and I shared, I heard footsteps outside. Our cabin was a little apart from the others; if you stood close against its southern wall, you couldn't be seen from any of them. The footsteps came up to this wall. There was no talk—only quick breathing, giggling, and then the slap of a hand on bare flesh. I moved the window blind a little and looked out. There were Paul and Dee-Ann, in their swimming suits, laughing and sparring. But for Paul this wasn't a game. His eyes were watchful, like a cat watching a bird, and there was a hard, pursed look about his mouth.

After a few moments, Paul glanced up toward the window —how keenly he was on his guard!—and saw me. At once he broke off the mock fight, slapped Dee-Ann on the bottom in a casual grown-up way, and came straight into the cabin, slamming the door behind him.

"Jesus," he exclaimed, sitting down quickly on his bed, "that god-damned kid! Do you know what she did just now? She groped me!"

"Oh, crap!"

"She does it all the time. . . . I'm telling you, Chris, if somebody doesn't get her out of here right away, there'll be trouble. I just can't stand much more of it. . . . Yesterday I was with her in their cabin, alone. Matter of fact, she called to me to come in. She was making the beds. Then she started fooling around, and we wrestled and I threw her on the bed, and there I was, right on top of her. I'll never know how I stopped myself doing anything to her, but I did. I made a ter- rific effort and rolled right back off that bed, and stood up. So what does she do? Looks at me in that bitch-innocent way of hers and says, 'What's the matter—don't you like wres- tling? *I* do!' She was watching me all the time, of course, to see how far she could go. 'But Mother wouldn't like it,' she said, 'if she saw us.' She wanted me to admit I knew what she meant, but I just said, looking straight at her, 'If your mother wouldn't like it, we ought not to do it, ought we?' And what do you think that deceitful little bitch answered? 'We could go some place where no one could see us,' she said, 'like way, way along the beach. Then we could do it properly.' 'What

233

do you mean by properly?' I said. And she said, 'We could rub ourselves with oil, all over.' Then she kind of giggled and said, 'Do you know what Alanna said about you once? She said you were beautiful.' So I asked her, 'What about you —do *you* think I'm beautiful?' She only laughed and said, 'Boys aren't beautiful, silly!' And then she told me, 'But Alanna doesn't like you any more, now.' 'Oh,' I said, 'Is that so? Did she tell you why?' And Dee-Ann said, 'She says I mustn't be alone with you. She says you might hurt me— without meaning to, of course.' So I asked her, 'You mean, I might hurt you if we wrestled—the way you want to?' And she laughed again and said, 'Of course not! Alanna's silly. Why should that hurt me? It's only a game. And I know you'd be careful with me, because you're a boy, and you're big and strong—' And then, Chris, you'll never in a million years guess what she said next, and this is *literally* true—she said, 'Besides, I wouldn't mind if you *did* hurt me, just a little bit. I wouldn't even mind if you made my nose bleed.' I ask you! What am I to do? If things go on like this, I'm sorry, I refuse to take any responsibility whatsoever."

I laughed. I still pretended not to believe what Paul was telling me. Yet I knew that, however much he might be exaggerating, the situation was as he said, and highly dangerous. What I still absolutely refused to admit to myself was that *I was willing all this to happen.*

When I reread that notebook, with its soul searchings and scruples, and then remember how I was actually behaving, I have to marvel. Part of me, the majority, *had* come to Eureka with serious intentions; to use this retreat to tighten up my self-discipline. Yet, even while I was honestly trying to do this, the other part was acting like an old voyeur! That afternoon I had deliberately left Paul and Dee-Ann together on the beach. And not only did I listen to Paul's talk about her without even trying to bring him to his senses, I actually covered up for him! Once I lied to Augustus—telling him that Paul and I were going out in the car—when I was lending it to Paul to take Dee-Ann for a ride. Of course, I never told Paul I'd done this.

Had I gone raving mad? What did I think would happen to *me*, if Paul came to grief? I was relying on him more and more for my own support. And I had defied Ronny, and the whole world of the cynics, by staking my faith on Paul. Any failure of his would be my failure.

No, it wasn't madness. It wasn't voyeurism, either. It wasn't even mere delight in making mischief. This was an attempted *putsch*. Part of me—the minority, certainly, but desperate and quite ruthless—wanted to precipitate a scandal in which everything—the entire life I had been leading—would come to an end. The minority neither knew nor cared exactly what the long-term results of its counterrevolution would be. It simply hoped to find some advantage and opportunity for itself among the ruins.

At the far end of the lake there was a fascinatingly ugly little area of miniature craters, only a few feet high but active, known as the Mud Pots. Continually they spat bubbles of hot, gray mud, with smelly volcanic farts of sulphur and steam. I had been wanting to visit them. So had Dachine Dickinson and Grace Birnbaum.

We went there on the morning of our last full day at Eureka Beach, in Dachine's car. Paul had refused to come with us; he had been to see the Pots a few days before this, on horseback, with the girls. "And frankly, honey," he told me, "they stink!"

Dachine drove like a true faith healer, demonstrating her absolute disbelief in the reality of Evil. I was sorry I hadn't insisted on taking them in my own car. Fortunately, there was very little traffic. And, anyhow, it was fun being with them. Dachine was good company when she wasn't being intense and talking her vocational jargon; and Grace had a wild laugh and something crazy and witchlike beneath her official mask of schoolmistress. After we had looked at the Pots, we moved out of reach of their smell and ate some sandwiches. Both women seemed quite different outside the group, gay and relaxed, and glad secretly that our retreat was over. We were tacitly agreed to stay away from Eureka as long as was decently possible. No meditation or discussions were scheduled today, and the place was in confusion because of the packing which had to be done before we left tomorrow.

When Ford Wheelwright's car appeared, with Ford driving it and Augustus beside him, I knew at once that something was wrong. Ford wasn't the sort to go pleasure riding when there was work to be done at home; and Augustus, who had wanted to come with us, had regretted that he had too many letters to write. Also, Ford had a brisk crisis manner as he jumped out of the car saying, "Will you drive Augustus back, Chris? He wants to talk to you. I'll follow you in a little while, with the girls." I glanced questioningly at Augustus, but he seemed lost in contemplation of one of the Mud Pots. At length he murmured, "Yes—" softly and thoughtfully, as though agreeing with some remark it had just spat out. The engine of Ford's car was still running; I got in beside Augustus and we drove off. As we did so, I saw Ford put his hands on Dachine's and Grace's elbows and steer them away from the road, as if for privacy; there wasn't a living soul within miles.

"Augustus—what *has* happened?"

"I always think, Christopher, that when two people know each other very well, as we do, and the one has something of an exceedingly unpleasant nature to tell the other, it's best to go straight to the heart of the matter. . . . Nevertheless, I must prepare you for a bad shock. . . . Alanna went to her parents, about an hour ago, and told them she had seen Paul with Dee-Ann, through the window of your cabin, in an act of sex."

"My God!" Several thoughts followed each other in a flash through my mind. That I must try to seem convincingly surprised. That Paul must have gone crazy to have picked such a dangerous place. That, since he obviously *hadn't* gone crazy, he must have wanted to get caught. But that if he had wanted to get caught—well, *why?*

"How many people know?" I asked, for the sake of saying something.

"I'm afraid everybody. Except, for the moment, Dachine and Grace; and Ford and I agreed it will be better to tell them the bare facts and appeal to their discretion. Mr. Swendson, the girls' father—you knew, didn't you, that he came down here this morning to drive home with his family? —*he* hasn't, I'm sorry to say, been *at all* discreet. Of course, one must make allowances for his natural feelings. Still, I do wish he hadn't been present when it happened. . . . However, against that misfortune, we must set the truly providential mercy that there was a doctor within instant call."

"You don't mean that Dee-Ann was actually—?"

"No. That we have been spared. Pat Chance examined her immediately and thoroughly. He was able to assure us that there had been no penetration." (From just the faintest momentary gleam in Augustus's eyes, I knew that, despite his

236

genuine concern, he was rather enjoying all this excitement; well, so was I.) "The curious thing is that the child seems quite unmoved by the whole experience. Of course, nothing has been said to her directly about it; Paul's name hasn't even been mentioned. Pat Chance cautioned us very strongly on that point; there's always the danger of creating a trauma. . . . It's Alanna who seems to have been so terribly upset by what she saw. She was literally hysterical. Pat urged Mrs. Swendson to take both girls back to Los Angeles in her car at once. They've already left. Mr. Swendson, unfortunately, insisted on staying. He's determined to confront Paul."

"Confront? You mean, he hasn't *spoken* to Paul yet?"

"Nobody has."

"But, Augustus—in that case—how can we be sure? This whole thing could be some mistake. He could be absolutely innocent."

"Thank you, Christopher. One's always grateful for being reminded that no man is to be judged guilty until he's so proven. . . . And of course it's possible that our friend *may* return. He may not have just blindly panicked and run away, as one can't help fearing. . . . Which reminds me—are those sleeping pills still in his possession?"

"Great God, Augustus—what *are* you talking about?"

"Forgive me, Christopher. I'm afraid, under the stress of these circumstances, one hasn't presented a very coherent report. . . . You see, when Alanna told her parents, they naturally went straight to your cabin. They found it empty. Of course, in view of Alanna's hysterical condition, it was impossible to know exactly how much time had elapsed between the two events. . . . And then they saw Dee-Ann walking alone by the lake, and apparently, as I say, altogether her usual self. Mr. Swendson then went to look for Paul and was told by Naomi that she'd seen him drive off along the highway, only a few minutes previously, very fast—"

"Drive—" Now, suddenly, it hit me. "You mean, in—" I changed "my" just in time to—"our car?"

"Yes. I'm afraid one has to put that item on the negative side of the account. It does rather begin to look like the all-too-familiar pattern of desperation."

"I see. . . . Yes, it does." I was thinking how truly maddening Paul was, and even calculating if I could afford a new car. Could I get any money back from the insurance? Only by reporting the theft, and that was out of the question.

"What made us venture to fetch you back so abruptly," said Augustus, "was that we may need your help in reasoning with Mr. Swendson. When I left, he was still under very great strain. He even talks of having Paul followed and brought back by the police."

By this time we had almost arrived; Ford's car was old but would still do eighty. As we turned off the highway and bounced down the trail in the usual cloud of dust, I was startled and relieved to see my car parked beside the others.

"Paul's back!" I exclaimed.

"Thank God for that!" Augustus murmured gravely.

Ian Banbury came out of his cabin to meet us; he must have been watching for our return. "It's good to see you," he said, warmly but without urgency; it was as if we had been away for months. He smiled his prairie-squint smile and squeezed our hands hard and affectionately. He didn't seem in the least bit rattled.

"Where's Paul?" I asked.

"Over in your cabin. Don't worry—he's all right." (That Ian should have taken it so simply for granted that I should be worried about Paul, and that Paul was someone still worth being worried about, touched me even at that moment, and much more when I remembered it later.) "He got back here right after you and Ford left, Augustus. Swendson saw him coming. Rushed at him, shouting and yelling. Wanted to beat him up. We stopped him, of course. Dave did most of it. I'm glad he was there. At times like that, you feel so inadequate."

"And what did Paul do?"

"He was very good. Very quiet. Stood his ground like a man. I don't think I'd have had the courage, the humility to do that. No excuses. Nothing."

"You mean—he admitted the whole thing?"

"Oh yes. Didn't attempt to deny it. My, I admired him for that!"

And how, right now, I admired Ian! I suppose Paul's act must have seemed unthinkable to him; dirty, bestial, utterly outside nature. This must be costing him a terrific effort of charity. It was all very well for Augustus, that religious Bohemian, to be broadminded. Ian had a wife, children of his own, a church, a congregation; he lived in the cruel limelight of goodness. Well—*good for him!*

"Does Mr. Swendson still want to call the police?"

238

"Oh, no. He'll be all right now. Dave's tremendous—talked him out of it. They're in there together now." Ian nodded toward the cabin the Swendsons had occupied. "Swendson's still upset, of course. That's natural. Wants a scapegoat. Probably blames it on religion—indirectly. He's never been a member of my congregation. His wife and he have had words about it." Ian suddenly grinned and looked quite boyish. I could have hugged him.

"Well, now," said Augustus, clearing his throat slightly, "to proceed to the next point on our agenda—I take it that we're agreed that Paul had better leave without delay? We don't want to subject Mr. Swendson to any further strain."

"We'll leave just as soon as we're packed," I said.

Ian smiled at me warmly. "My, that's good of you, Christopher!" He made "good" sound like a cardinal virtue, not a courtesy.

On my way to our cabin I passed Naomi and Fran, who were folding blankets, and Ellen, who was putting cups and plates into a carton. It was obvious that they all knew exactly what was going on. They were helping things along in their womanly way by doing these chores, while their men struggled with the spiritual packing up. They greeted me just a shade too cheerfully.

In the cabin Paul was also packing. He barely reacted to my entrance. "Honey chile," he drawled sourly, "I'm afraid you're going to have to drive me to Indio. That's the nearest I can get a train or a bus from."

"But, Paul, I'm driving you to Los Angeles! Don't you *want* to come with me?"

"I didn't think you'd want to take me."

"Oh, what crap! Don't be that way! Don't you know what side I'm on?"

"I don't know about *sides*. I thought there was only one. Do I have a side, too?"

"You've got a home—with me, remember?"

"I saw you in a big huddle with Augustus and Ian just now."

"So what if I was? Augustus isn't against you. He understands. He does, really."

"What does he understand? Oh—you mean he used to screw little girls himself when he was young?"

"Paul! Now you're just being terribly unreasonable. Let me tell you something else: Ian said he *admired* you—the way

239

you didn't deny anything."

"Why should he admire that?"

"Well, I mean—a lot of people would have been scared. I hear Mr. Swendson wanted to beat you up—if Dave hadn't stopped him."

"Miss Wheelwright was just having herself a ball—doing her big corny nonviolent act. It was lucky for Swendson he *didn't* hit me, that fat slob. The minute he started waving his arms around and yelling, "People like you belong in the gas chamber!" I made up my mind what I'd do. I was going to fasten my teeth in his nuts. They'd have had to kill me before I'd let go."

This didn't seem the right time to go on with the discussion. So I helped Paul pack in silence. We got out to the car without meeting anyone. No doubt they had retired discreetly into the cabins. But as we were driving up the trail, a black blob appeared within the highway mirage, went through several distortions, and turned into Dachine's car. We had to squeeze past each other at the intersection. Dachine and Grace waved and laughed wildly, at Paul just as much as at me. Ford looked embarrassed. Maybe he had explained things so very tactfully that they hadn't understood what he was talking about.

As we drove, I kept glancing at Paul. I was dying to ask questions, but didn't know how to begin; and Paul, knowing this, wasn't about to help me. At last, I blurted out: "Just exactly—how did all this happen?"

"One day, Dee-Ann and I were out at the store. You know, the man who runs it collects rocks, bits of quartz and stuff, and he'll sell them. Dee-Ann was crazy about a lump of what they call fool's gold; so today, I suddenly decided to dash over there and buy it for her, as a goodbye present. Here it is—" Paul reached under the seat and handed me a heavy object wrapped in a piece of newspaper. "I hope you didn't mind me taking your car?"

I put the fool's gold on the seat beside me, unopened. "Paul —that wasn't what I meant—and you know it! I meant—how exactly did this happen with you and Dee-Ann—and Alanna?"

Paul glanced at me with his thin, provoking smile. "They didn't tell you that?"

"They said it was in our cabin. And Alanna looked in through the window."

"Then why are you asking *me?*"

"Well—I still don't know how it all started."

"Why should you want to know? Does it get you all hot?"

"Of course, if you'd rather not talk about it—"

"I didn't say I don't want to talk about it. But why should you want to know? What difference does it make to you? After all, you made your mind up, right away, without knowing—"

"Made my mind up? Damn you—don't be so bloody mysterious! Either tell me how it happened, or don't!"

"It didn't."

"*Didn't?* You mean, it didn't happen—*at all?*"

"You don't believe that, naturally."

"But, Paul, *of course* I believe you! You wouldn't lie to me."

"How do you know?"

"I just know you wouldn't."

"You say you *know*—but it didn't take you any time at all to make up your mind I'd done it. Without asking me, even. You just take the word of people like Augustus and Ian."

"Now, look here, Paul—you've got to admit—you *might* have done it. You've admitted that much, before now. With Dee-Ann being such a little teaser—"

"Sure, I might have done it. You might have done it. Augustus might have done it. Ian might have done it. Anyone might have done it. But I didn't do it."

"What's the matter with Alanna, then? Has she gone mad?"

"Really, honey, you've got to learn not to be so melodramatic! You don't need to go mad to do a thing like that. Of course, I don't know exactly how it happened, but I can guess pretty well. . . . She's always been jealous of Dee-Ann with me. My guess is, one day she went to her mother and said something about us—and her mother told her not to be silly. So that put her on a spot. She had to prove she was right, and get back at us—so she makes up this tale. And now she's told it, she'll have to stick to it. So she'll know she's a liar, and most likely she'll be scared pissless of going to hell. I hope so."

"But, Paul, wait a minute—why did you tell them you'd done it?"

"I did not tell them. I just didn't deny it. And why the hell should I? They all believed I did it from the word go. They were just hearing what they'd been expecting to hear all along. They always loathed my guts."

241

"That simply is not true!"

"Okay—I don't care if it is or it isn't. People like that have been my natural enemies since I was ten years old. I ought never to have had anything to do with them. I never would have, if I hadn't listened to *you*. Now my name's mud with them, and that's the way I want it."

"Look, for Christ's sake, let's at least be frank. It's *me* you're really blaming, isn't it? All right, there's only one thing for me to do. Since, as you say, I didn't believe in you, I'm going to Augustus and all the rest of them—including the Swendsons—and tell them the truth."

"Chris, if you *dare* do that—" Paul was really angry now— "you're lower than any of them! You're the dirtiest little hypocritical creeping Judas of the whole bunch!"

For once I had outmaneuvered him. I laughed with delight. "You really think I *would* do a thing like that, without your letting me? That proves you don't trust me any more than I trusted you! So we're quits! So why don't we both relax? Say—we'll be getting into Indio in another ten minutes. Let's find a bar and have a couple of drinks. What do you say?"

Paul didn't relent immediately, but I knew the signs. Everything would be all right now. We found a bar and drank for several hours, until it was evening and the place was crowded with local ranch hands. Then we started back to Los Angeles. Maybe it was the good Karma earned during the Eureka Beach retreat which saved me from wrecking the car, or at least getting jailed for drunk driving. When we finally staggered up the stairs and into the apartment, there was a notice from Paul's draft board ordering him to report to the C.P.S. forestry camp in a couple of weeks.

We spent the days that followed in buying what Paul called "my trousseau"—the stiff blue denims, sweatshirts, thick socks and clumsy boots he would need as work clothes at the camp. The certainty of a long separation had made us gentle and considerate with each other. Paul's aggression had disappeared altogether, for the time being; he never even mentioned the Swendsons. By common consent, we had given up most of our rules, though we still meditated, morning and evening. But after the evening meditation we drank real cocktails and ate suppers, either at home or in restaurants, which included meat and fish. "I just haven't the heart to be a vegetarian, right now," Paul said. "Besides, who knows what those mean old pacifists are going to make me eat? Human flesh, most likely." The day before he left, he suddenly decided to have his hair cropped bristle-short. "After all, as long as your poor old Auntie's going to take the veil, why shouldn't she look like it?"

Next morning I drove him sadly out to a small town among the orange groves, far to the east of the city. Here it had been arranged that May Griffith, the wife of the camp director, was to meet Paul in the camp truck and take him back with her into the mountains. As we drove, Paul began all over again to talk about his old life. "If Babs and the Condesa could see me now!" he exclaimed dolefully.

I was trying hard to cheer him up. "Tell me—what really made you do all that in the first place—go to Europe—get involved with all those people? Was it really *fun?*"

"Honey, never ask an American questions like that. Americans *have* to go to Europe—just to be quite sure that all the stuff that's talked about it is shit."

"And is it?"

"Oh yes, of course—but it's no use just saying that. You have to try it yourself."

"Good—and now you've got to think the same thing about this camp. Your Condesa and the rest of them would never *dare* come to a place like this. And they wouldn't be allowed in, if they did. I'll bet this place is harder to gate-crash than the most exclusive party you ever went to! And the boys up there—they couldn't imagine in a million years what those parties were like. The amazing thing about you—what'll make you absolutely unique—is that you'll have seen both!"

Paul brightened a little at this. For a few moments I had succeeded in making the immediate future seem glamorous. But then we reached our rendezvous, a warehouse by the railroad depot, where they stored the oranges, lemons and grapefruit from the surrounding groves. An acrid, haunting citrus smell hung in the air. It was very hot. "Look," I said, "that must be her, parked over by the wall. They said it was a blue pickup truck, didn't they?"

"Auntie's last pickup," Paul murmured.

May Griffith was a cheerful young woman. She greeted Paul with the disconcertingly *instant* friendship of the Friends. Then she excused herself for a moment; she had to ask at the railroad office about a parcel.

"They've told her," Paul said, his face darkening. "She

243

knows about Eureka. Did you see that nonaversion smile she gave me?"

"Nonsense! You're just imagining it."

"*I* don't give a damn. If that's the way they want it, that's the way I'll play it."

After this remark, I braced myself for some kind of demonstration. And sure enough—when May had returned and they were ready to leave—"*Au revoir, mon amour,*" Paul exclaimed, taking me in his arms and kissing me passionately on the lips, "*tu sais que je t'adore!*" I kissed him right back, lest I should seem to put myself on the side of the enemy.

May Griffith laughed heartily at this. Was she terribly stupid or astoundingly sophisticated? Anyhow, Paul appeared to feel that honor was satisfied. He grinned at her as he climbed into the truck, and I could see that he was starting to use his charm on her as they drove away.

During the time between our leaving Eureka and Paul's going to the camp, I had avoided seeing Augustus altogether. I couldn't have borne being together with him and Paul as long as he didn't know Paul was innocent in the Swendson affair. Paul would have been on the watch for the least hint of condemnation. And we had no right to put Augustus to such a test, even if he passed it. I had begged Paul to release me from my promise, but he wouldn't. "You can tell him one day," Paul said. "I'll tell you when you can tell him. There's something so shaming about having your name cleared. Let's leave it dirty for a while."

As soon as Paul had left, I called Augustus and we started meeting again. But our relationship wasn't quite what it had been before; there was a new reason for constraint between us. Shortly before the Eureka retreat, Dave Wheelwright had asked me if I'd be willing to work at a Friends Service Committee hostel in Pennsylvania, and I had said yes. The hostel was for refugees from Nazi Europe; they were being housed there until they could get jobs and support themselves in the United States. Many of the refugees didn't know enough English to do this at present. So the Friends needed some German-speaking helpers who were used to teaching.

For the past few weeks, I'd been encouraging Dave to get me some such work to do. (That was the significance of the rather disingenuous query, "*Motive for this?*" in my Eureka notebook.) I'd backed him at Eureka in his defense of the active life because I now wanted some action. I'd known Paul would be leaving soon, and I didn't propose to go on living according to the Parr rules when I was alone again. That would be too depressing after our happy life together.

Besides, if I joined the "actives," I would be able to write a new contract with myself. As long as I worked hard and did all my duties faithfully at the hostel, I'd allow myself every sort of freedom on my evenings off. Philadelphia would be only a short train ride away. Already I knew a couple of addresses there.

Augustus never criticized or even discussed my decision. I dare say he knew quite well what was behind it, and made allowances. He came down to the Union Depot to see me off and embraced me with an obviously heartfelt, "God bless you, dearest Christopher!" Then I heard him murmuring to himself, "I *think* you'll be all right. Yes—"

And then the train took me away from him, toward another kind of life, a kind which even The Others could understand and approve of. Many people would admire me in my new occupation, calling it "unselfish" and "useful" and "public-spirited." As for Augustus, he was going back to his old ladies and his stale cookies and the hut at the top of the garden. But I knew just enough now to realize that, quite possibly, he and a few hundreds of equally unfashionable individuals—scattered about the country and mostly unknown to each other—were in some utterly mysterious indirect manner keeping us spiritually alive through this wartime; renewing a hormone without which our community would wither and die, no matter if the Nazis lost or won. Maybe these were indeed the only people in America whose jobs could *really* be called essential. . . . It was awe-inspiring to think this. I told myself that I mustn't ever forget it in the midst of the activity ahead. But the thought didn't make me feel guilty. Nor did it spoil my enjoyment of the steak I was eating in the dining car, with lager beer.

When I had been working at the hostel about three months, I got this letter from Augustus:

EVER DEAR CHRISTOPHER,
I feel moved to write to you in the hope of being the first to communicate what I think you would prefer to hear from a mutual friend rather than from a stranger—or, indeed, from

the public press. Perhaps you even know of it already, from your newspapers in the East? It concerns our friend, Paul.

(Horrors, I thought, what can he have done now?)

We have just had a very bad brush fire in the mountains— one of the worst, I'm told, in recent years—and the boys of Paul's camp were called out among others to fight it. One's apt to fail to realize just how desperately dangerous these things are. If there's a wind, the flames can travel faster than a horse can gallop, and of course they may change direction at any moment. That is what happened on this particular occasion; and two of Paul's fellow fire-fighters had been cut off in one of those very steep, narrow canyons which can become, literally and terribly, fire traps. The poor frantic boys were trying to climb up the hillside, and of course the flames were gaining on them. It was quite hopeless. Paul himself was up on the ridge above them, out of danger, and with an easy way of retreat behind him. He sees the boys can't escape in time, and that they're in a state of blind and deaf panic, incapable of listening to or obeying the directions that are being shouted at them. So he deliberately runs downhill to meet them; and he leads them by his example to do what the Forest Rangers had been telling them over and over again to do in such an emergency. If you're trapped, you must wrap your head in a jacket or some thick piece of clothing, take a deep breath, and then turn round and run straight through the fire. *It's your only chance. If the fire isn't advancing in depth, and if you can avoid breathing in smoke or, worse still, flame, you've the chance of getting through with only superficial burns. Paul made the boys do this, and all three lives were saved.*

At this point, the idea that one must run *through* a fire instead of *away from* it led Augustus into a whole sequence of philosophical generalizations with special reference to the instructions given by the lama to the newly disembodied soul in the Tibetan Book of the Dead. These formed the main part of his letter. On a separate sheet of paper, I found the following postscript:

It's a symptom, perhaps, of one's preoccupation with a scale of values other than that of the majority, that I find I have neglected to tell you another piece of news which many might think even worthier of mention. It seems that, shortly

*after Paul's heroic act became known—and this cannot have
been coincidence—that unfortunate adolescent, Alanna
Swendson, confessed that the story she had told of the happenings at Eureka had been fictitious from beginning to end!
(The prognosis for her adult mental life is, I fear, most dubi-
ous.) This of course amounts to a complete rehabilitation of
our friend, and I need not tell you that it seems of the utmost
moment to our dear Ian and to the others. You, dearest Christopher, have already shown us that there is something higher
than the mere question of faith in one's friend. If I may say so,
it has moved and heartened me very much to see how, in you,
this mysterious thing—the greatest of the three, as we are
told on unquestionable authority—has risen superior to both
faith and hope."*

I sat down to write to Paul at once. But after various attempts to be serious, which I tore up because I couldn't strike
the right note, I merely sent a post card: "So proud of my
dear old Auntie."

To this I got a reply, also by post card: "You should know
by this time, honey, that there's *nothing* your aunt won't do
for publicity. As for that little bitch, I wanted to sue her parents for criminal libel, but the lawyer, who's a horse's ass,
says I haven't got a case because I admitted it! Screw them all.
Am deathly bored here. Why don't you write properly?
Kisses."

I had to grin as I pictured the pained gulp with which the
pacifists would have to swallow Paul's non-nonviolent vin-
dictiveness, just when their mouths were full of his praises.
That's my Auntie, I said to myself, and I wrote him a long
letter making fun of the hostel and our local Quakers and
their doings—not a sincere letter, because I really liked and
admired the Quakers very much and had begun identifying
myself with them, even to *thee*-ing, in a way which Paul
would have denounced as treason to his standards. That was
the worst of having any dealings with Paul. You were always
ending up as Judas. . . . And he didn't answer my letter anyway.

Not long after this, I also had a short note from Ronny. He
described the horrors of the army camp on Long Island,
amidst dwarf pine trees and icy wind-driven sea fog. "The
only thing I've got out of it is that I know I shall never have

to use sleeping pills again. I can sleep *anywhere*—with people singing or snoring, and the lights on, and the radio blasting. All the same, *thank God* I shall be out of this hell in a short while now."

Poor Ronny! He wrote that only a couple of weeks before Peal Harbor.

Next spring they raised the draft age into the forties. I duly registered as a conscientious objector, came before a Pennsylvania draft board and got my classification. This was no great ordeal in this Quaker neighborhood, where they were used to pacifists. But I asked to be allowed to do my service in California, because I wanted to be in camp with Paul. I wrote him about this, and got no reply.

Meanwhile, our refugees were beginning to find jobs as their English improved and the wartime shortage of civilian labor increased. At length the hostel emptied and we closed down. I came back to California in the early fall of 1942.

But this time the war was changing the appearance of Los Angeles. Hollywood Boulevard was crowded with servicemen wandering in and out of the newly opened pinball joints and the roaring bars. It was like a fun fair, but hideously sad. In the months that followed, the hotels became filled to bursting, with boys sleeping even in the lobbies, on chairs and on the floor. Others dozed in the movie theaters and the bus terminals. If you wanted to throw a party, you shouted to a bunch of them on a street corner and they piled into your car, obedient as zombies. They would drink anything you gave them, until the bottles were empty. I think many of them were scarcely aware of their surroundings; they were so numb with homesickness. This town must have seemed a kind of limbo, bounded by the Pacific and the dull dread of what was waiting for them, out there among its islands.

As soon as I could, I went up to the camp. When I phoned Paul to arrange this, his voice sounded displeased, as if I'd disturbed him in the midst of some important occupation. He even turned down the day I suggested, saying curtly that it wouldn't be convenient. Then he added, "Why don't I come down to town and meet you there?"

"But I want to see the camp."

"Whatever for? There isn't anything to see."

248

"But, Paul, I wrote you, remember? I've *got* to come there before long. I'll be getting my draft call any time now. I want to see what it's like."

"Oh, very well." I heard his faint sigh of resignation.

The road into the mountains was really rough. The day was blazing hot and the bushes and trees looked tinder-dry, ready to burst into flames. The camp was a forbidding place; long, drab barrack huts set above the ground on concrete supports.

I found Paul in the kitchen, supervising the work of half a dozen helpers. He looked lean and sunburned and healthy, but a sulkiness came over his face as he saw me. "Hullo, honey," he said without enthusiasm. "You're early. Lunch won't be for half an hour yet." As if to show me he was too busy to talk, he at once detailed one of the boys to take me around. There certainly *wasn't* much to see. The barrack beds were littered with castoff clothes; and the fact that this was so much untidier than a military camp only made it seem grimmer. My spirits sank at the thought of living in this kind of proximity without boundaries; you could never get disentangled from your neighbors. The boy took me to see the tanker trucks they used at the fires if there was a road nearby, and explained how you dug cold patches or started backfires if there wasn't. Then he went on to talk about the soon-expected rainy season, when they would be reading the rain gauges and measuring runoff. And then there were the reforestation projects. . . . He was earnest and technical, about nineteen, a Seventh Day Adventist, and he called me "sir." None of the draftees in my age group had joined them yet; and, after all, I *could* just have been his father.

At lunch in the mess hall, Paul became much more gracious, though not particularly to me. I could see how he fascinated and dominated the boys—all except for, perhaps, a few of the slightly older and stuffier ones; these I noticed were watching him with reserve. But most of them were sweet-natured simple kids, straight from the farm and the church, who had never seen anything like Paul before in their lives. And then there was a plump, bespectacled Negro named Wilson whom Paul treated with a special kind of sadistic protectiveness, frequently addressing him as "Nigger," at which Wilson chuckled fatly and called Paul "White Boy."

Paul had acquired a dog of his own—the only private pet in camp—which he had named Gigi. She was a mongrel bitch, daughter of a wild chow from the hills and an Airedale belonging to a ranger who had since been transferred to the camp at Las Madres. Paul made a huge fuss over Gigi. "I'm having a platinum collar made for her," he told me with that familiar hint of aggressiveness.

"If you come here, you're crazy," he said, when at last we were alone together and I was about to leave. "Las Madres is much better run, and the food's better, and they don't have nearly the same fire hazard. And the Forest Service Superintendent here is a real bastard. Jesus, I'd like to strangle him! We all would. He keeps telling us, 'If I see anyone turning yellow, I'll get him thrown out of this camp. If you won't fight fires, you can fight the Nazis.' He's got no authority, actually, except when we're on the project; but Clem Griffith lets him get away with it—that gutless asslicker.

"Still and all," Paul added, with evident relish, "that's your worry, honey, not mine. I never have to go out on fires any more. They've found something wrong with my heart. That's why I'm running the kitchen. I could get my medical discharge any time."

"Then you don't want to? You like it here?"

"Sure, I like it here." Paul's tone implied: But *you* won't. You couldn't take it.

As I was getting into my car, Clem Griffith, the camp director, walked over to us. He had heard I was in camp, and would be coming up here shortly, and he wanted to say that he and May were very happy about it, etc., etc. Paul listened to this sourly. When Clem had gone, he slipped in a parting word of discouragement. "This place is just hopping with rattlers. We kill them by the dozen. All this nonviolent crap— that's only propaganda for the outside. Here we kill everything we can catch up with. The Quakes are the meanest. You ought to see them beat those poor little rattlers to death."

As I drove down the hill, I asked myself if I *could* take the camp. Yes, I thought so. I could get along with the boys, all right. And the fires—well, I needn't think about them yet; the rainy season was coming. But Paul himself? That was another question.

However, when we next met a couple of weeks later in town, the atmosphere was much better between us. Paul had Gigi with him, and we went shopping together in Beverly Hills. He was in a lively but somewhat hysterical and com-

250

pulsive mood. And he spent money wildly—on a waterproof wrist watch, a de luxe sleeping bag, binoculars, a fur-lined jacket, a compass in a leather case. "You know," he said, "I'm more than halfway through your money already?"

"Only *that?*" I tried hard not to sound disapproving. "Why that's a miracle!"

"These aren't all for *me*, you know. As a matter of fact, only the jacket is. The rest are for friends of mine. A lot of them spend the evenings leafing through old store catalogues. When you're shut up in a place like camp, you can literally fall in love with something in a catalogue and go absolutely nuts. You've just *got* to have it. . . . So I tell the kid I'll price it for him in town, and then I simply buy it and bring it back with me. At first he says he'll pay me so much a month and he honestly means to. But most of them don't have a cent, anyway. And then his birthday'll come around, or it'll be Christmas or Easter or something, and I make him accept it as a gift—Paul paused and looked at me. Then he said, with a quite unaggressive and almost shy smile, "I know what you're thinking, Chris. It's true. I *am* bribing them."

I realized that this confession was also an apology and an explanation of his behavior to me up at the camp. He had simply been jealous. He wanted to keep the place all to himself. He was afraid I'd come there and usurp his position.

This was a compliment, really, and I felt very touched. I decided, then and there, to apply for a transfer to Las Madres. If Paul seemed genuinely disappointed when he found out about this, I could always pretend it was a slip-up on the part of the draft board, and probably get myself transferred back again.

Later, we went to one of the big hotels for cocktails. This hotel, like many others, was a U.S.O. center, and servicemen were allowed in to use its pool at certain hours. They were splashing and diving all over it now. There was one very drunk sailor boy from Alabama who believed hazily that he had a date with a starlet named Ellen—or was it Helen? He wasn't sure. So he asked every girl he met, "Hey, beautiful, what's your name?" A thin-faced brunette, reclining on a bamboo chaise longue in front of a cabana, regarded him with bewildered distaste. Paul decided she must be a Scott Fitzgerald character who had passed out at a wild party during the twenties and slept beside this pool for fifteen years.

Now she'd just woken up and thought this was all a horrible dream.

"Dinner's on me," I suddenly announced, feeling generous after our drinks. "We'll have it here in the hotel. With champagne."

"Why, that's just grand, honey chile! You don't mind if I invite Wilson, do you? He's in town today, too. I know a number I can reach him at. And it'll give him such a thrill, eating at a place like this."

"That's fine with me. . . . But, Paul—will they let him in?"

"If they won't we'll make the biggest stink since I was thrown out of the Savoy. Still—maybe we'd better meet him at the entrance."

Actually, there was no hint of trouble. If the hotel people had indeed any racial prejudices, they were far too worried about the safety of their furnishings to remember them; the drunk servicemen claimed all their anxiety. Wilson arrived dressed with quiet elegance, and was relaxed and charming.

But his presence made Paul aggressive again. He began by excluding me from the conversation, as he insisted on discussing leaves he had spent with Wilson in the Negro section of Los Angeles. He referred to singers, band leaders and bars they both knew, very much as he must have dropped names belonging to European café society. And there was a girl named Sandy from Trinidad, with whom he claimed to be having a mad affair. This was the first I had heard of her, but maybe he really was.

Then, when we were at dinner, he declared that the people at the next table were looking at us in a hostile manner. "They're thinking: What's that fat buck nigger doing with those sweet little white boys."

But Wilson only grinned. "Man, will you do me a big favor and leave those ofays be? I don't know what they're thinking and, confidentially, I don't care. This evening, I aim to enjoy myself."

Before that year was over, I knew definitely that I wouldn't be sent to camp, after all. They had lowered the draft age again. I felt relieved, but rather frustrated. Then I started writing a new novel. I found I could work much better away from the atmosphere of wartime Los Angeles; and a friend of Augustus's invited me to stay as often as I liked at his house, which was down the coast to the south. Augustus sometimes visited there, too. Thus it happened that I didn't see anything of Paul for several months.

Then, in the early summer, I got a letter from Pat Chance, asking me if I would come to his home on a certain date and, as he put it, share my thinking with him and a few others. The letter was phrased rather evasively, but it was clear enough that our thinking was to be about Paul. Evidently, Paul was causing trouble at the camp and they would be glad to be rid of him. But—this I read mostly between the lines—Paul refused to respond to hints; his attitude was that if they wanted him out they must take the responsibility of throwing him out. And, since Paul had been so widely publicized as a hero—largely through their own efforts, to make propaganda for the pacifist cause—they were most unwilling to have any kind of a scandal.

All of this I could well understand. And yet I went to the meeting in a hostile, pro-Paul mood. Beside Pat Chance, there was Clem Griffith and four of his stuffiest C.O.'s; big-shouldered, tanned boys with dead serious, handsome faces. An overpowering atmosphere of humorless good will prevailed.

Clem Griffith began by affirming that "everybody" liked Paul, but that his influence was "unsettling." He had been making the fellows restless and dissatisfied—no doubt by talking about glamorous sex in distant capitals, though Clem didn't say this. He had been bringing in hard liquor—but Clem had to admit that others had done it, too. There was a suspicion that he and some of his friends had had marijuana in their possession. "But there's no proof," one of the C.O. boys interrupted, in his desperate eagerness to be fair, "that is—no one ever actually saw them—er—*partake*."

Then Clem, obviously embarrassed because he felt the accusation wasn't as silly as he tried to make it sound, told us that Paul had been "trying to get the fellows to protest against what he calls my sexual monopoly." He laughed nervously, appealing to me. "Because I'm the only one who has his wife up there."

The C.O.'s smiled dutifully, but with a certain constraint, I thought. Picking the most likely-looking one, I asked, "Are *you* married?" The boy said, "Yes." Then he added apologetically, "My wife has to look after her mother as well as our

253

kids. Otherwise, she'd come and live here—I mean, down in the Valley—like the others do."

"We see each other weekends," another boy put in. But his Bible-bred truthfulness compelled him to correct himself, "that is, about twice a month, on the average." My little pin-prick had gone home. Everybody, including Clem, felt its point.

Pat Chance (whom, now that I was no longer playing according to my Eureka rules, I could dislike from the bottom of my heart) said with a bitchy smile, "It seems a bit strange that Paul should be the one to have this particular concern. One would hardly expect *him* to feel so strongly about *wives*."

"What makes you say that?" I asked, wide-eyed with innocence, as I considered how I could hit back at him.

"Well—in view of his general behavior. With Wilson Jacks, for instance."

"Behavior? Oh, you mean his calling Wilson a nigger?"

"It's much—" one of the C.O.'s began, then hastily checked himself, blushing.

"Much *worse?*" I prompted him.

"When he says *that,* I guess we all understand he doesn't mean it—well, in the usual way. . . . But—the other things—"

"Things worse than *nigger?*" I asked, with just the faintest suggestion of reproof.

The C.O. turned scarlet: "Like—Darling . . . and . . . Lover Boy."

I began to laugh. For a moment, my laughter was genuine. Then it turned into something else: an expression of sheer open hate. I was laughing as Paul himself might have laughed. Indeed, I felt almost literally possessed by Paul's aggression. The C.O.'s watched me with a kind of terror.

"I'm sorry," I gasped, at length. "I keep trying—but I just *can't*—see them in bed together!"

This created a near panic, as I'd intended it should. "But no one's accusing them of *that!*" Clem cried, as though I'd threatened to sue them all.

Pat Chance was the only one who kept his head. He now smiled indulgently, as if to say that this was all good clean fun, but quite beside the point. Then he cleared his throat and announced in his official doctor-tone that, after all, Paul *had* a heart murmur—nothing the least serious, but technically enough to exempt him from service. Pat told us that he, personally, was going to put pressure on the authorities to give

Paul another medical examination, after which he'd inevitably be reclassified 4-F and discharged.

No doubt this was what they had previously decided amongst themselves. Maybe, indeed, they'd only held this meeting in the hope that I'd offer to persuade Paul to leave camp right away and let them get his discharge for him afterwards. They had failed in this, but, still, I had walked into their trap and was now compromised. I was a witness to their decision, even if a hostile one. And if Paul found out that I'd been present here at all, he would never forgive me.

"And we *do* all like him a lot," Clem reassured me nervously, as we dispersed.

Just as I had expected, Paul sat tight at the camp and let the machinery of the draft law grind out his 4-F as slowly as it chose. He wasn't about to make things any easier for Pat and Clem. But the discharge came through at last. I drove up to the camp to fetch him.

Paul had accumulated piles of baggage, and there was Gigi, huge and shaggy and sloppy-tongued, to make the car seem even fuller. The boys crowded around Paul, obviously dismayed to see him go. He accepted their loyalty languidly, like a monarch who is fond of his subjects but finds them rather exhausting. Clem and May had the good taste to stay in the background.

Throughout the leave-taking, I had been conscious that Paul was excluding me. And as we drove away, he turned and began playing with Gigi.

"You're *my* darling, aren't you?" he said to her. "Aren't you the only one I love? Aren't you my only girl?" But Gigi tactlessly licked my ear. She was a truly adorable dog.

"Gigi's going to be trained," Paul told me. "She's going to learn to tell her friends from her enemies. They all made such a fuss over her, up at the camp, she was fooled; she thought everything was lovey-dovey. She's got to realize we live in a world where dog eats dog. That's what your Quakes wouldn't tell her."

"They're not *my* Quakes!"

"I'm through with professional good people," Paul said, ignoring my protest. "They always let you down."

To change the subject I got on to another, about which I'd been worrying. I didn't really want to have Paul live with me again—not as he and the circumstances were at present.

But I felt bound to make the gesture.

"You're coming back to my place, aren't you?"

"I'd better stay at a hotel."

"Why on earth should you?"

"Because you don't want me. You're just being polite."

"I am not!"

"Well, just as you like," said Paul indifferently. "Only I may as well warn you, I'm hot. I've got nearly fifty marijuana cigarettes in that suitcase."

"All the more reason you shouldn't stay at a hotel," I said nervously. "Paul—you mean you *were* actually smoking it?"

"Only now and then, when I was in the mood. Or things got too tiresome."

"But you never told me!"

"There's a lot of things I never told you, honey. Didn't want to put you on a spot with your *friends*."

"Bitch!" I exclaimed. "Forgive me, Gigi—not you!" Paul laughed, and after this he was quite pleasant during the rest of our ride into town.

However, when we got to my apartment, he ostentatiously lit one of his marijuana cigarettes, and I knew I was in for some more bullying. He offered me one. I refused, and he said, "I don't see how you can call yourself a writer when you're so scared of experience." Then he studied my face in silence for a while, with a detached, scientific air.

"Still meditating?" he asked.

"Sure."

"Regularly?"

"Well—more or less."

"Still a vegetarian?"

"Hell, no!"

"How about sex?"

"When I feel like it."

"What does Augustus say to that?"

"He isn't my nursemaid."

"You mean, he disapproves?"

"We don't quite see eye to eye about it. But he understands."

"He'd better. He can't afford to lose you, that's why. You're a mutual admiration club. . . . What are you doing nowadays?"

"Writing a novel. And I may get another job at the studio soon."

"I see. So you've simply gone back to Position A?"

"No."

"What do you mean, No?"

"There's a big difference?"

"What's this big difference?"

"Well—I still believe exactly what I used to. Only now I don't feel I have to be so puritanical about it. It doesn't seem to me to be so much a matter of keeping rules any more. Of course, I admit there have to be *some* rules. But the rules aren't what's really important. What's really important is—" I paused, because, just as in our conversation of nearly three years ago, I'd suddenly found there was a word I couldn't say to Paul. Only this time the word was "love."

But he never even noticed my hesitation. "*Really*, honey!" he interrupted. "Spare me these rationalizations, *please!* All I can say is, you'd better start making up your mind before it's too late. Either be a proper monk, or a dirty old man."

"Which are you going to be?"

Paul smiled complacently. "I'm different. I know what I *really* want now. I discovered that up at camp."

"And what is it?"

"I don't want any more of this autohypnotism and professional goodness. I'm sick of trying to imagine I feel things. I just want to *know*."

"To know what?"

"What I'm all about. I've decided to be an analyst."

"A *psychoanalyst?* Paul, you can't be serious!"

"And why not, may I ask?"

"Well, I just don't *see* you. I mean, most of them are such self-satisfied asses."

"And don't you think your Auntie could be a lot better than most of them, especially with all her experience?"

"Yes—yes, I guess you could. . . . Only—won't it take you an awful long time? You left high school without graduating, didn't you tell me once?"

"What do you think I was doing at camp? I took correspondence courses and got my high school diploma. With very good grades, too."

"Paul! How *marvelous!* Why didn't you tell me you were doing it?"

"I didn't tell a soul, except Wilson. Because none of you would have believed I could do it."

"*I* would have."

257

"No, you wouldn't, Chris. You only believed I could do things *your* way."

This was true enough to sting me a little, but I tried not to show it. "So now you'll be starting pre-med?"

"In the fall."

"At U.C.L.A.?"

"Are you kidding? I've had enough of this town to last me the rest of my life. I'm going to school in New York. One of the boys at camp has an uncle who'll give me a part-time job in his bookshop. Another knows an apartment where I can live rent-free, if I put in a few hours a week as a janitor. Everything's arranged. I'll be leaving in a day or two. Just as soon as Gigi and I can get our train reservations."

"Paul," I said, and I meant it, "you're the most amazing person I know!"

My astonishment seemed to appease him; after this he stopped being aggressive. Later on in the day he surprised me by suggesting we should go and visit Augustus. Augustus was surprised too, I could tell, when I phoned him to arrange this, and also delighted. It was characteristic of him never to complain of neglect or unkind treatment; but I knew he had minded that Paul had never been to see him or even written to him during the past two years.

And when we got to the house, Paul seemed to make a tremendous effort to win Augustus back to him. He was charming, eagerly interested, subtly flattering, tactful; he even referred quite respectfully to God. And Augustus was certainly charmed and won over. He started talking to Paul as though he were already a practicing psychologist. "I should so very much like to have your opinion on this—don't you feel that Jung is making a very grave mistake in regarding his archetypes as static?"

"Miss Parr is still the biggest saint in show business," Paul said, as we were on our way home. But he said it with real affection.

I didn't get an opportunity to hear Augustus's opinion of Paul until a few days later, after Paul and Gigi had already left for New York. "That will of his!" Augustus exclaimed. "My word! It could move mountains, undoubtedly. Indeed, there's something about it which is positively *epileptic*. These terrific *spasms* of energy."

Augustus was in the full cry of his enthusiasm for Paul again, and he appeared to take it for granted that Paul would go through with his studies to complete success. I wasn't so sure. Perhaps it depended on how much opposition Paul would run into in New York. For I had just realized one fact about his motivations: he could only do things—even altogether constructive things like getting a medical degree—*against* someone else. There always had to be an enemy, whose role it was to lack faith in Paul and be proved wrong. And Paul's latest enemy wasn't the Quakers, or Augustus, or the people he had known in Europe, or Ruthie or Ronny; it was me.

Well, if that was the only way Paul could function, I didn't really mind. Probably everyone Paul got to know had to take his or her turn at being enemy sooner or later.

In March 1944, Ronny landed with his outfit on one of the Marshall Islands. It had been recaptured a week or two earlier and was thought to be now more or less cleared of enemy troops. However, on Ronny's second day, when he was peaceably cycling along a road, a Japanese sniper shot him in the ankle. "Such a *vindictive* thing to do," said Ronny, telling me about this several months later as we sat at lunch in Beverly Hills. "Even at the time, I thought to myself, *really*—what's he trying to prove?" Nevertheless, the sniper had done Ronny an unintentional favor. He was sent straight back to the States and given what he described as a dream job, making documentary films for the Army on Long Island and living at Government expense at a comfortable hotel in New York. Now he had come out to Hollywood in the line of duty, to discuss one of the documentary projects with a famous film director. And how he was enjoying every minute of his new life! He really looked quite handsome in his captain's uniform, complete with the Purple Heart.

"So now you're a hero, Ronny!"

"Now one's a hero—yes! Isn't that too extraordinary, my dear! It makes one wonder if there *are* such things. Not that I don't adore it—I should be most ungrateful if I didn't, considering all the sex it gets me. And a slight limp makes one feel Byronic and insanely attractive."

Ronny had plenty to tell me about Paul. "Of course, he was always difficult. One had to accept that. But, I must say, he really is getting a little *too* much. He now disapproves of absolutely everything; loathes the Allies, the Nazis, the neutrals, the pacifists, the Jews, the Negroes, the Christians, the

Atheists, the homosexuals, the heterosexuals—have I left out anybody? I mean, it just becomes *too* monotonous. . . . It couldn't matter less what anyone says in *our* circles, because none of us dream of taking the war seriously, any more—but Paul goes into bars and meets innocent little G.I.'s and gobs right off the farm—and when he tells them things like that Hitler is the only person in the world who isn't hopelessly corrupt, or that our bombing Tokyo was the greatest atrocity in history—well, they simply don't understand. . . . He's been beaten up several times, already."

"And what about his studying? Do you mean he's given that up?"

"Oh *no*, my dear—that's the one thing he clings to! In fact, he's doing quite brilliantly, or so he tells us. And he can be most snooty and grand if he's got an examination coming up and one calls and suggests an evening on the town. Just as if nobody worked but himself. . . . No, I'm certain now that he'll go through with it and become an analyst. God help his patients! I must say, one was quite wrong about him, wasn't one?"

In September 1945, I got a post card redirected to me from my old address in London. A blue-gray card, marked *Prisoner of War Post Card, Postkarte fuer Kriegsgefangene*. Either by coincidence or design, it had been written on my birthday, August 26.

"Dear Mr. Isherwood, you'll be astonished to hear from somebody whom you think will be already dead. I had to become a soldier in Germany and was caught at the Rhein River. Who knows what my life will look like after I get discharged. Greetings. Waldemar."

(It was only later that I understood why Waldemar had addressed me as "Mr. Isherwood"; it was one of the sweetest and silliest things he ever did. He had felt that, as a member of the enemy, he mustn't compromise me by showing that he knew me well!)

I wrote back, of course, and from then on we exchanged occasional letters. Soon Waldemar began writing from an address in the Russian sector of Berlin. He had left the P.O.W. camp and rejoined Ulrike, the girl he had married just after the war broke out. Before Waldemar had been sent off to the front they had had a son, whom they had named Christoph.

In his letters Waldemar kept urging me to visit them. I dreaded the idea. I dreaded seeing those ruins. I dreaded meeting Waldemar and feeling emotionally blackmailed by his plight. So I wrote cowardly excuses and evasions, and never told him that I paid two visits to England, in 1947 and 1948. But still I knew that I would have to go to Germany and face it all before long.

Meanwhile, in the summer of 1946, I had heard for the first and last time from Paul in New York:

DARLING CHRIS,

This is to let you know that I'm leaving here and going to Europe, perhaps for a long while. I met a man at a party who will buy my Picasso for nine thousand, five hundred dollars, so at least I'll have some mad money for my comeback! Your clever Auntie arranged the sale all by herself, between cocktails. Not one cent will those mean old dealers get! Incidentally, it's just as well that the Picasso is sold now, while there's still some of it left. Since I got it out of storage and had it up here in the apartment, so many people's greasy heads smeared against it at parties, while they were sitting under it on the couch, that the paint started to rub off. But the man who bought it doesn't seem to have noticed this.

So you see I am giving up medical school, for the present, at any rate. I am doing this because I have realized that I'll never be a good psychologist until I've understood certain things for myself. I don't mean just by getting myself analyzed; I mean by living through them again. I can't explain this any more clearly because I don't have the gift of expressing myself and it would sound utterly bogus and pretentious if I tried. But I want you to know that there is a reason for all of this. Other people will say I quit school because I couldn't take it any more. Let them say what they like. You are the only person I have to talk to about it, because you are my sweet baby and you always stood by me. When are you coming to Europe? I hope soon. God bless.

When I had first read this letter, it had intrigued and rather impressed me. But then, in the course of the next six months, I heard that Paul had been seen at Cannes and in Switzerland and in Portugal, doing all the usual things with the usual people; and I began to lose faith in this mysterious-sounding *reason* of his. It began to seem like the invention of a guilty conscience. I was disappointed. My dramatic instinct demanded a more drastic exit and change of occupation. This return to his old haunts wasn't worthy of him; it lacked style. It even to some extent discredited everything he'd done since I'd known him. For now I felt that this life in Europe had been, after all, his real life, into which he had naturally subsided as soon as he got the chance. He had merely used us to sit out the war with, that was all.

I had no right to blame Paul for this, however; and I honestly did not. No doubt we'd run into each other, sooner or later; and when we did, I'd be delighted to see him and eager to laugh at the stories he would tell.

On February 10, 1952, our plane skimmed alarmingly low over the Berlin rooftops and landed on the Tempelhofer Feld amidst a snowstorm, just as night was closing in. It was too dark to see much bomb damage as I drove through the streets to my hotel on the Kurfuerstendamm, and when I arrived there, everything was advertisements and neon lights. The original building had had a new steel and glass front grafted on to its broken face. It seemed much too brightly lit and altogether overemphatic. There were businessmen with flesh-roll necks and gross cigars, and women deep in make-up and heavy with jewelry, and page boys darting back and forth like nervous fish; and it seemed to me as if they were all muttering autosuggestively to themselves, "Nothing has happened—nothing has happened—this is where nothing whatever has happened!" You felt they had almost succeeded in creating a world without a past.

But their world could only exist at night and by electric light. By daylight it ceased to convince you. You became too strongly aware of the surrounding bomb-desert which was the real Berlin, the city where everything *had* happened. Thousands of people were living here, in houses and house fragments and huts and mere holes. They scuttled around the desert, with their Berliner purposefulness and gallows-humor, keeping life going, gradually clearing the rubble away, planning parks and planting trees. I walked across the snowy plain of the Tiergarten—a smashed statue here, a newly planted sapling there; the Brandenburger Tor, with its red flag flapping against the blue winter sky; and on the horizon, the great ribs of a gutted railway station, like the skeleton of a whale. In the morning light it was all as raw and frank as the voice of history which tells you not to fool yourself; this can happen to any city, to anyone, to you.

I got back to the hotel to find Waldemar waiting for me in the lobby, with his family. In a crowd I might not have recognized him. He looked very well, very big and broad and hearty, and his voice had deepened. I could see nothing in his face now of the sullen half-tamed animal; he seemed placid and complacently middleaged. He reminded me a little of Hans Schmidt. Ulrike, his wife, was tiny and eager and neat. Their Christoph was a pale, lanky boy of eleven, taciturn and probably intelligent; he would never look like a Gothic angel.

I took them to a restaurant, where we ate Wiener Schnitzels, and Ulrike enthused over the superiority of the food and the shops in the West Zone. This enthusiasm, I felt, was meant largely as a compliment to me, as an American. Waldemar kept assuring me that they loved Americans, hated Russians, weren't Communists. He explained in a tone of apology that they had had their present apartment already before the war. Was it their fault that the occupation had divided up the city so that they now found themselves living in the Russian sector? Of course, they would far rather be over on "our" side. But they couldn't afford to leave everything behind them and make a new start in the West, at least not right now. It was so natural that Waldemar should feel he had to talk to me like this. And yet I was embarrassed for both of us.

Already they were telling Christoph to call me Uncle Christoph. Waldemar made a parade of our intimacy, referring again and again to "the old days." And this saddened as well as embarrassed me, because it was he and I, not the days, that were old now. What was Ulrike thinking? She certainly didn't seem jealous of the past. "She's a good girl. She doesn't ask a lot of questions," Waldemar told me when we were alone together in the restaurant washroom.

Next day I went to have lunch with them at their apartment. We rode out to it on a train of the overhead railway, crossing the Alexanderplatz into the through-the-lookingglass world of giant red banners with slogans, monster portraits of Lenin and Stalin, which the Russians called "The Democratic Sector." Waldemar sat protectively on one side of me, Ulrike on the other. They talked German across me and I nodded and laughed to show I understood, but I didn't speak, because of my foreign accent. In broad daylight, on the crowded train, this precaution seemed slightly ridiculous—and yet, there were plenty of police around and many passengers with inquisitive, bluntly staring eyes. And I had no permit to enter the East Zone.

When we got to the apartment, it was much cozier and more comfortable than I'd expected, and I began to feel more at ease with them. They told me about the first bad years after the war, when they had often had literally nothing to eat. Waldemar had gone out into the country and stolen beets from the fields. Ulrike had kept herself going on cups of hot water. They laughed as they told me this. They didn't seem at all sorry for themselves.

Waldemar now had a comparatively good job as an auto mechanic; he had learned how to do this work in the army. He was saving all the money he could. "It was I that taught him to save," said Ulrike. "When I met him he was so extravagant, you wouldn't believe! I cured him of smoking and drinking, and gambling, too. Gambling was the hardest! One evening he stayed out playing cards—and after that I wouldn't cook his supper for three days. That cured him!"

I glanced at Waldemar, thinking he might resent her telling me this. But he was grinning complacently. Evidently the two of them had worked out a code of domestic rules to their mutual satisfaction. When it was time to bring the food in from the kitchen and I rose and offered to help, Waldemar said, "No, let her do it. She's a woman." And Ulrike agreed, "Yes, that's a woman's duty. The man must bring in the money. The woman must have his food ready for him, and she must keep the house clean. No—just keeping it clean isn't enough; it must sparkle!"

While we were eating Waldemar said to Christoph, "Listen —you know that your Uncle Christoph is an American. If the neighbors knew he'd been here to see us, there might be talk. They'd say we were plotting something. We could get into bad trouble. You mustn't tell a soul, do you hear?" Then, turning to me, Waldemar explained, apologetically again, that Christoph was going to a Communist school; because, after all, here in the East Zone, where else could you go?

We all looked at Christoph as he gravely shook his head. Was he terribly insulted, even to have been cautioned? Perhaps he was. Perhaps he would hold it against Waldemar later. Certainly, he *wasn't* going to tell on us; even I could see that. All the majesty and power of Marx and the Party and the Russian Army and his schoolteachers didn't count for anything with this boy. Why? Because he loved his parents? Because he was a Berliner first and everything else second? Because he was sick of every kind of indoctrination already, and was about to grow up into a man who just didn't give one damn? Probably a bit of all three.

Then Waldemar brought the conversation around to America. How high were the skyscrapers? How deep was the Grand Canyon? How big was this, how fast did that go, how many dollars did that cost? He exclaimed at each of my answers with exaggerated delight and amazement, and he kept glancing at Ulrike and Christoph, prompting them to be amazed, too. But Ulrike cared far more that I had praised her stew and eaten two helpings of it. Christoph was interested, no doubt; but not amazed, not delighted. Yes—he was truly a Berliner. He and his kind would rebuild this city and make it the way they wanted it, if ever the foreigners left them in peace.

Alas, I knew only too well why Waldemar kept harping on America! He wanted me to sponsor their emigration. He never came right out with this. But just before we said goodby, he started hinting strongly: "You know, Christoph, you're no longer the youngest. It's not good for you to live all by yourself out there in California. You need a family around you. Someone to cook your meals and keep you company in the evenings, so you won't waste your money running around the town. Someone to look after you when you get sick—"

"I don't know," I muttered. "I'd have to think it over. My plans are so uncertain. We'll see. We'll write to each other." It wasn't that I grudged the money. But I utterly refused to have a family. I was determined not to be anybody's uncle. And yet, I felt guilty because I refused.

That night—which was my last—my guilt made me get drunk and go looking for a bar I remembered from the pre-Hitler days. Astonishingly enough, it was still there; the one solitary building lighted and upstanding in a dark street of ruins and dirty snow. And inside, the dancers, the waiters in leather shorts, the naughty-eyed singing pianist and the accordian players beneath the Japanese lanterns and the artificial cherry blossom were like the celebrants of an immemorially

ancient rite, an old religion which has survived all its perse-
cutions and is asserting itself once again during a breakdown
of the orthodoxy.

And then I heard behind me a "Hay-yee!" and I turned,
and there sat Ruthie and Ronny. Neither of them looked a
day older. They were both delighted to see me. "Christ,"
Ronny exclaimed, "isn't it all *too much!* What'll you drink?"

Presently I asked them about Paul. Ronny made a little
grimace. "Oh, yes—one sees him—if one's in the mood. The
Phantom of the Opera."

"How do you mean?"

"That's what he looks like. And he only goes out at night.
. . . He's living in Paris, all by himself. His grand friends
seem to have dropped him. And no wonder. He's so vague
and dazed most of the time. He's a crashing bore to be with."

"Always drunk?"

"Oh, dear, no! If *that* were all! Doped to the eyes."

"My God—"

"That was always the worst of Paul. He never could do
anything by halves—as *you* should know, my dear. . . . I
mean, the rest of us—one *has* taken these things from time
to time, naturally. But he seems to have no self-control whatsoever."

"I'm going back through Paris. Have you got his address?"

"I'll give it to you if you're sure you really want it. But
don't say I didn't warn you. He'll probably sit in dead silence
for an hour, and then suddenly tell you to get the hell out.
. . . Anyhow, Ruthie and I won't *dream* of letting you
leave Berlin yet. You know, we take your novels around with
us like a Baedeker? But you'll have to show us most of the
sacred spots, because they just aren't *there* any more!"

I found the address Ronny had given me. It was in the Rue
du Bac. I climbed a flight of stairs—not alarmingly squalid—
and tapped on a door.

"Who is it?" said Paul's voice, quite unchanged.

"It's Chris."

"Chris who?"

"*The* Chris," I said, pushing the door open.

The room was very lofty. It had raised panels on three of
the walls only; this must once have been a big drawing room,
now cut in half and converted. The thick velvet window curtains were drawn together, though this was early in the after-

noon. Paul was sitting propped up by pillows in a huge Empire bed, which was littered with books and magazines. He was corpse-white, and his face looked as though it had the firmness of hard wax and was semitransparent. There was an air about him of being somehow preserved and, at the same time, purified; his skin seemed to be absolutely without blemish. Indeed, he was marvelously, uncannily beautiful. He wore a heavy skiing sweater over pajamas. Gigi lay on the bed at his feet.

"I thought you must have decided not to see me any more," he said.

"Why should I do that?"

"Didn't they tell you I was a dope addict?" Paul spoke very distinctly, looking straight ahead of him.

"Sure, I knew that." I tried to sound blasé. "What do you take? Morphia? Cocaine? Heroin?"

"Really, Christopher—if you knew anything whatsoever about drugs, you'd know I couldn't have lasted this long on any of those without cracking up completely. I'm on the safest, sanest thing there is—much, much better than smoking tobacco or ruining your liver with alcohol—good old opium."

"Is that your pipe?" I asked, pointing toward a great clutter of objects on the table beside the bed.

"It's not much use having a pipe if you can't afford to smoke it," said Paul reprovingly. "I hear you've been working in the movies a lot lately, so perhaps you can give me some money? Or is that against your principles?"

"I'm not sure," I said, grinning to hide my annoyance at his tone; "I'll have to think it over, later."

"Not *much* later, I hope. Because when I can't buy fresh opium, I have to make a tea from the dross—that's what's left over in the pipe—and it gives me the most awful stomach cramps." Paul was silent a moment, then he asked abruptly, "What time is it?"

"Two fifteen."

"I lose all count of time here. Now that it's winter, it's pretty dark, anyway. And I lie here most of the day—reading, dozing. Sometimes I don't eat anything, except maybe a plate of cereal."

"Don't you see people?"

"Sometimes I do, sometimes I don't. I don't really care. Gigi's all the company I want, aren't you, my love?" He patted Gigi, who wagged her tail vigorously. "Gigi's mutat-

267

ing. The other day I caught her meditating. She's going to be our first dog-saint."

"Does she stay here all day too?"

"Most of the time. Now and then the concierge takes her for a run. And she comes out with me at night. . . . Really, Christopher, if you're going to start on the cruelty to animals thing, you'd better just leave."

"I didn't mean that at all—"

"Look, honey—don't be mad at me." Paul turned to me as he said this, and his tone was suddenly almost humble. "I'm feeling rather awful right now. . . . Couldn't we meet somewhere this evening? Wherever you want to go for dinner. I shan't eat anything, I don't suppose—unless it's a little caviar. Why not let's say The Ritz?"

The Paul who appeared that evening had a sinister, sepulchral elegance; Dorian Gray arisen from the tomb. He wore a perfectly tailored black suit with a black hat and a neatly rolled umbrella. Gigi was at his heels.

Paul ate only caviar, as he had predicted, but also drank several cocktails. I reminded him that he had spoken against alcohol that afternoon. "I know, darling," he answered, with a touch of impatience, "but I find I just cannot talk unless I drink. Opium makes me not want to talk. Alcohol brings my mind down to the level of other people."

"What a bore for you!"

"No offense, honey. But now, let's not be vague—have you made up your mind yet about your moral principles?"

"What principles?" I asked, just to tease him as a small punishment for his thick-skinned behavior.

"Whether they'll let you give me money, when it's to buy dope. . . . I've got to know *now*, because the man I get it from will be at a place near here for the next hour, and no longer. So excuse your old aunt for fussing."

"All right, damn you! How much do you want?"

"As much as you can possibly afford, honey chile. And remember, you probably won't be seeing me again for a long while."

I gave him thirty thousand francs—the amount I'd decided on after a long battle between pro- and anti-Paul reactions when I had cashed my travelers checks that afternoon. Paul took the money with what seemed a deliberately expressionless face, as though he were determined not to let me see if it was more or less than he'd hoped for.

"You want to meet this man?" he asked. "He's kind of fascinating."

"Do we have to go this moment? I've just ordered."

"I might have known. Of course you don't want to get involved, do you? Always so scared."

"Get out of here!"

"I'll be right back, honey chile."

And he was, too. He returned, with a small parcel in his hand, before I had finished my entree.

"Tell me, Paul," I said when we had settled down again, "just exactly what was it that made you drop medical school and come over here?"

He yawned wearily. "Oh honey, that's all far too long ago for *just exactlys!*"

"You said something in your letter about living through things again."

"Did I? Well, yes—I wanted to come back and see how I felt about everything. I mean—I wanted to see if I was *really* changed by any of what happened to me in California—meeting Augustus, and meditating, and all of that. I didn't know any other way to find out."

"And *had* you changed?"

"Oh yes—I'd changed." Again Paul seemed weary of the subject.

"So did that answer your questions?"

"Questions? Oh, no. Because by the time I knew I'd changed, I was starting to get in *much deeper*—"

"How do you mean, deeper?"

"What's the use, honey? You wouldn't understand."

"Why wouldn't I? You mean it's got something to do with smoking opium? Look, Paul, why don't I try it? Let me try a pipe while I'm here. I know you think I'm scared of those things. Well, perhaps I am, a little. But now's the time to try—"

At this, Paul threw back his head and roared with laughter. "Oh, darling Chrissikins! If you only knew how funny you are! So you want to try it? *Once! One pipe!* Or a dozen pipes, for that matter! You're exactly like a tourist who thinks he can take in the whole of Rome in one day. You know, you know, you really *are* a tourist, to your bones. I bet you're always sending post cards with "Down here on a visit" on them. That's the story of your life. . . . I'll tell you what'd happen if you smoked one pipe: nothing! Nothing would happen! It's absolutely no use, fooling around with this, unless you really want to know what's *inside* of it, what it's all *about*. And to do that, you have to let yourself get hooked. Deliberately. Not fighting it. Not being scared. Not setting any time limits."

"But sooner or later, you'll have to take a cure, won't you?"

"Oh, sure—I'll take a cure," said Paul carelessly, "when I've found out all I want to know."

"And you can't describe what that is?"

"Honey, I'm suddenly most awfully tired. Do you mind if I go home now, right away?"

"Well, of course not, but—shall I see you tomorrow evening?"

"I'm afraid not. No."

"How about the day after?"

"Look, honey chile," said Paul with weary patience, as if I had been pestering him for a date, "I'm going to be keeping pretty much to myself for maybe the next three weeks. I most likely won't go out at all."

"You mean, until you've smoked up all your stuff?"

"You don't understand," Paul told me, in a prim, chill tone of reproof. "I don't want to be disturbed more than's absolutely necessary."

"Well, in that case, I'm afraid I won't see you any more—not this trip. Because I'm only staying here three days longer. Then I'll be flying back to the States."

Paul made no comment. We walked out to the hotel entrance in silence, and I saw him and Gigi into a taxi. They weren't going in my direction.

"Well—good-by, then," I said. I bent forward and kissed Paul's wax-white cheek.

"Good-by, sweetie," he said. But he didn't kiss me back; didn't turn his head or even look at me. I felt as if he had already retreated a long way, into a vast, vague distance.

"Good-by, Gigi," I said. "Take care of him, won't you?" Gigi wagged her tail. I shut the door, and the taxi drove them away.

That was the last I ever saw of Paul. In the spring of the next year, 1953, he died.

Ronny wrote me in answer to a cable I sent him when I heard the news:

Yes—I saw Paul in Paris, very shortly before it happened. In the first place, I must tell you something which I think is enormously to his credit. Last year he took a cure and it was completely successful. The doctor at the clinic where he went—the Condesa paid for it, which I thought was pretty angelic of her, considering the way Paul had treated her—this doctor told us that while Paul was getting disintoxicated, he suffered the tortures of the damned, *but his will power was extraordinary, and he was determined to get through it in the minimum of time. Of course we shall never know if he mightn't have gone back on dope later, but there was absolutely no sign that he wanted to, up to the day of his death.*

The last time I saw him was on the Tuesday, the week before. He seemed quite his usual self—that's to say, very argumentative. There were some young intellectuals there when I arrived. They were arguing with each other about the impossibility of life after death. Luckily for me, I didn't join in! Because Paul, who had been listening to them without making any remark, suddenly said, with the most intense disdain, "You little fools!" *My dear, you ought to have heard him! It was positively shattering. And he said it with such an air of* authority; *it was as if he actually* knew *something. So, of course, after this there was a most painful silence. Very soon the boys made excuses and left. And then Paul and I laughed a lot. You know, those last months after the cure, he became very much more like he used to be, in the old days in Europe. You never knew him then. That's too bad. I never in my life met anyone who was so much* fun *to be with, and really* mad. *I don't want to hurt your feelings, Christopher, especially now—but I must say, and Ruthie agrees with me, that that was the* real *Paul, the one we both loved. Being serious just did not suit him, let's face it. He had a* genius *for enjoying himself, and perhaps if he'd devoted his life to that, he'd be alive today.*

He was found dead in the john. It happened in the middle of a party he was giving. The people who were there all agree that he seemed very happy and couldn't have been more fun; and he wasn't even drunk. He just stepped out of the room without anybody particularly noticing it. Only it just so happened that someone else wanted to get into the john a few

271

minutes later in a hurry, and banged on the door, and that's how he was found. They say his face showed no pain, and they're sure it was instantaneous. Apparently he had had a bad heart for some time, but he either didn't know that or ignored it; also lately he'd had a bad attack of flu.

We're only gradually beginning to realize how terribly we miss him. One can never go to a party without feeling it. There was nobody like him; and yet very few people really appreciated him. You and Ruthie and I were the only close *friends he ever had.*